DARK
LIGHTNING

DARK LIGHTNING

JOHN VARLEY

ACE BOOKS, NEW YORK

THE BERKLEY PUBLISHING GROUP
Published by the Penguin Group
Penguin Group (USA) LLC
375 Hudson Street, New York, New York 10014

USA • Canada • UK • Ireland • Australia • New Zealand • India • South Africa • China

penguin.com

A Penguin Random House Company

This book is an original publication of The Berkley Publishing Group.

Ace Books are published by The Berkley Publishing Group.
ACE and the "A" design are trademarks of Penguin Group (USA) LLC.

Library of Congress Cataloging-in-Publication Data

Varley, John, 1947 August 9–
Dark lightning / John Varley.
pages cm. — (A thunder and lightning novel)
ISBN 978-0-425-27407-1 (hardback)
1. Science fiction.   I. Title.
PS3572.A724D36   2014
813'.54—dc23
2014009515

FIRST EDITION: August 2014

PRINTED IN THE UNITED STATES OF AMERICA

10 9 8 7 6 5 4 3 2 1

Cover illustration by Fred Gambino.
Interior text design by Laura K. Corless.

To Spider and Jeanne Robinson

PROLOGUE

Cassie and Polly:

"Stop the ship!"

When Papa comes out of a black bubble it's always a party. Mama is always there, and us twins, many of the Strickland-Garcia-Redmonds, and anywhere from half a dozen to forty of the Broussard clan. It's a little stressful for him. You'd think that after all this time he'd be used to it, but then you don't know our father.

The bubble will vanish, and there he'll be, a short man built like a fireplug, white hair and beard, interrupted in the middle of a Hail Mary. He'll stop, look around to be sure he's not surrounded by green slime monsters from Betelgeuse this time, and when he sees all those familiar faces, his own craggy features will split into a huge grin and his Santa Claus eyes will twinkle, and he'll shout, *"Laissez les bons temps rouler!"* And then the good times *will* roll, *cher*.

This time was different. He looked around, he started to smile, and suddenly his eyes grew wide. There was a momentary pause as a look of horror slowly spread across his face, and he shouted:

"Stop the ship!"

Well, that's easy to say, a little harder to do.

The ship he was talking about was the *Rolling Thunder*, our home. And there was a slight problem about stopping her.

She weighs just short of two billion tons. That's not even counting our own 123 pounds times two.

And she was traveling at just about .77c, last time we checked.

That's 143,220 miles per second, or 515 million miles per hour, fast enough to get from Old Sun—a medium-sized G-type star that warms the planet where humans evolved, or so we are told—to Mars—where our mother was born—in about sixteen minutes.

Trust us, at that speed and with that mass, you don't just grab for the brake handle.

If anyone else had said it, everyone would have written it off as insanity, temporary or permanent.

But Papa is Jubal Broussard, and when Jubal talks, people listen.

CHAPTER 1

Polly:

I was lining up a sure shot on the nine ball, not thirty meters away, when a Hillbilly came soaring up beneath me and tore off part of my starboard wing.

Next thing I knew I was on my back, looking up at her big ass in its tight scarlet-and-mustard-striped jumper, and her smirking face looking back over her shoulder.

I recognized her at once. It was Cheryl Chang, girl gorilla. She was so hefty you just had to wonder at first how she could get her flycycle in the air. Then you saw those huge hams and thick arms and bull neck and it became clear: brute power trumped her outsize mass. There was no finesse in her cycling. I don't think she had scored a pocket all season, but that wasn't her job. She was the intimidator, the one you had to always look out for, because she was somehow able to spring out of nowhere and make you sorry you were in the air. She and I had tangled before, but never so badly.

Skypool is a full-contact sport, and I'm not a crybaby, but it was a flagrant foul and I shouted some words that would have blistered her butt if words could do physical damage, and looked around for a zebra. Naturally, all three refs were on other sides of the field, one near the up pocket and two arguing over some fine point of the last score at the east pocket. Cheryl would have checked their positions before she hit me.

And there I was, hanging out pretty much alone, within scoring distance of the bottom pocket.

But it didn't take long for me to realize that a missed penalty was the least of my problems. I was going to have a hard time staying in the game at all.

BLINKLINK: *SKYPOOL*: A game played in zero gee, invented in the starship *Rolling Thunder*, late twenty-first century. Eight players on each side compete on skycycles to carom free-floating inflatable balls, the size of volleyballs, colored and numbered 1 through 15. Six "pockets" are located at points on a virtual sphere: East, West, North, South, Up, and Down. The playing sphere is one hundred yards in diameter. Players strike any ball with a fist and must carom that ball off a target ball to score points into a pocket. All games are night games, as the playing fields must be located very near the internal sun, where spin gravity is near zero. As a proper playing field requires quite a large area of open space in near zero gee, there is no record of the game's being played anywhere but in large, hollow asteroids.

There I was, on my back, the broken part of the wing fluttering in my face. The ointment we rub onto them before a game to make them supple also makes them shimmer in rainbow colors like oil on water.

BLINKLINK: *SKYCYCLE*: A human-powered flying machine. Skycycles are extremely light, made of composite materials like buckytubes and monofilm. A high-end cycle will weigh no more than four or five pounds. They collapse to become no larger than an umbrella.

Human-powered flight is barely possible in a one-gee field, as on Old Earth, and easier in lower gravity, such as Old Mars. Much greater agility and endurance is possible in near zero gee.

A skycycle rider stretches out in the prone position and uses her legs to power an aft-mounted prop with up to twelve gear settings. Directional control is obtained by altering the shape and attitude of two sets of wings, two near the handlebars and two located near the waist of the rider.

> Skypool players must use caution to remain in the low-gravity areas of the interior playing space, as dipping lower in the atmosphere can result in uncontrollable speed and lack of directional control.
> An emergency parachute is worn while skycycling.

I pulled my left-center wing in a bit, then the right, and turned the left-front one to twist myself around. I got to where I was facedown—the nearest ground was under me, and the sun was at my back—and shifted gears to get more power from the propeller blade behind me. I knew I'd lose some lift, so I hoped to gain some speed in a power dive before pulling out and swooping back into the game.

In no time I was heading out of the playing field in a down attitude, that is, aiming for the interior surface of the ship. That didn't alarm me; during a game you can be facing any direction at all, and you have to stray quite a distance from the arena before the air gives you enough spin to make increasing "gravity" a problem.

What I didn't like much was that it got a lot darker as I passed pretty close to one of the stadium lights, then behind it.

The lights are station-keepers, like the pocket rings. There are twenty of them, at the points of a twenty-sided polygon, an icosahedron, all oriented so that they point to the center of the playing field. When you move out of the field, it gets dark quickly.

But I wasn't worried. I'd played a game with a damaged wing before. You just have to adjust your angle of attack. I was a lot more worried about getting back into the game.

This was the semifinal of the girls senior tournament between us, the Bayouville Gators, in black-and-gold tights, and the Hilltown Hillbillies, in crimson and mustard. The winner would go on to play the winner of the other semi, happening at the same time just a little north of us. It had been a hard-fought game. There were still four balls in the playing field. We were behind, but it could still go either way, depending on strategy in setting up high-value caroms. We couldn't afford even one mistake.

Maybe I pulled up a little too hard in my eagerness to get back into play, but I didn't realize how much damage that bitch Cheryl had caused.

Next thing I knew my arm was beating uselessly at the air while the damaged wing was twisting me like a corkscrew. I was powering down like a grouse hit by a shotgun blast.

I shifted gears into reverse, a gear you almost never use in flight. I mean, hummingbirds can do it, but when's the last time you saw an eagle flying backwards? I weigh a lot more than an eagle. I pedaled for all I was worth, hoping to slow down enough that I could assess the situation and not have to pop the chute. Popping the chute is a rookie move, a desperate move. It will get you ridiculed mercilessly for months to come, maybe forever. I felt the air start to blow, hard, over my back as the prop behind me began to churn the air.

Next step in the disaster: The remnants of my broken wing got caught in the draft and blew over me. Suddenly, I was blind, couldn't see a thing. I stopped pedaling and tried to remove the wing from in front of my face.

It wasn't happening. Some of the support wires had got tangled in the harness behind me. No matter how hard I tugged, they wouldn't come free.

I knew that getting back in the game was now impossible. It was going to be all I could do to land safely.

But I didn't really start to worry about that until the mainframe popped.

A flycycle is always going to be a compromise between sturdiness and lightness. The best ones look more like a sketch for a machine than the machine itself. Deployed, the wings are up to fifteen feet long, depending on the rider, and the frame is seven feet long.

The struts that make up the frame and the "bones" of the wings and prop are made of three nested nanotubes, no thicker than a pencil lead and hollow inside. These things are very, very strong for their weight, but they don't have a lot of give in them. Human muscles, and in particular the strong muscles of the legs, can strain them badly. Under enough stress, they will fracture.

That's what happened to me. It was like snapping your spine. The aft was no longer connected to the front. My feet were still strapped to the pedals, but pushing on them no longer turned the prop, it just shoved it farther away from me.

I arched my back, still trying to get the wing out of my eyes, and the severed end of the frame jabbed me in the butt.

And stayed there. It was in about four inches in the fatty layer and the gluteus, almost hitting my tailbone.

"Oh, *fiddlesticks*!" I shouted. It hurt like heck, like sitting on a long spike.

I reached around and grabbed it, tried to pull it out. But there is a problem with nanotubes. Once their molecular structure is disrupted in one place, they start to come apart. This one snapped in my hand, leaving a big piece of it still inside me.

In a few moments, the whole structure of the flycycle was disintegrating all around me. It was like being wrapped up in a dozen clotheslines hung with laundry.

I finally managed to swat the wings away from my face, and I didn't like what I saw. I was moving down at a considerable speed now. The wind was coming from one side as the ship's spinning atmosphere began to accelerate me even more. The ground was coming up rapidly. It was definitely time to pop the chute, humiliation or not. So I reached over my shoulder to pull the ripcord.

Which was gone.

Finally, I began to really worry.

Cassie:

I'm not sure what alerted me to the fact that my sister was in trouble.

I was all the way across the field, lining up a shot that would have brought us to within a couple of points of the hated Hillbillies, when I must have seen something out of the corner of my eye. A smear of ketchup-and-mustard uniform uglying up the dark sky. A *big* smear, big enough that it almost had to be Cheryl Chang, coming out of a tight turn and heading back toward the center of the playing sphere. Too far away to see the expression on her face very well, but something about the easy way she was pedaling . . . well, I just didn't like it.

All this in my peripheral vision, you understand, but to be a good skypool player you have to develop the ability to see in pretty much all 180 degrees of your visual field. Someone can come from any direction.

So I turned my attention toward her, and there was the merest flicker of something black and gold moving out of the lighted playing area.

Polly is my identical twin sister. We are mirror-image twins, she's left-handed and I'm right-handed. We are hard to tell apart. But I claim no mystical connection with her. There's no telepathy or other psychic connection, other than both of us knowing each other well enough we can often predict what the other will do. But these little cues just didn't feel right. *Spacegirl,* I told myself, *she needs your help.*

So I did something either of us would find extremely hard. I let the five ball go its own way, banked sharply, and headed toward Chang, who was powering up from the direction of the surface of my home, the starship *Rolling Thunder.*

BLINKLINK: *ROLLING THUNDER*: The starship Rolling Thunder is a privately owned asteroid belonging to Travis Broussard and his cousin Jubal Broussard. The Broussards had the interior hollowed out by compression-bubble (also known as "squeezer bubble") technology. Topsoil and plants were imported, an ecology was established.

The asteroid was an irregular "potato-shaped" carbonaceous chondrite with nickel-iron and water ice mixed in. Its exterior dimensions are eight miles by approximately four and a half miles. The interior of the ship is a cylinder six miles long and two miles in diameter. It has an interior surface of fifty square miles, but some of that is in the spherically curved ends, where the spin gravity decreases with distance from the interior surface. The flat surface is thirty-seven and a half square miles. This is around thirty-two thousand acres, though some of them are vertical. Its interior volume is almost nineteen cubic miles. The atmosphere inside is Earth-normal. The interior is divided into fifteen townships.

The ship has a population of twenty thousand, with an additional large number of colonists suspended in time stasis (also known as "black bubbles.")

The asteroid was accelerated to a speed of .609 revolutions per minute, or 98.54 seconds per revolution. This produces a spin gravity of two-thirds gee on the interior surface, trailing off to zero gee at the axis of rotation.

The interior is illuminated by a long, cylindrical tube, fifty feet in diameter and over six miles long, which uses compression-bubble technology to produce light and heat.

Just in case, I corkscrewed around in the air, picking out every Gator. Sure enough, there were only six in the lighted playing sphere, and none of them was a mirror image of me. So I changed gears and hauled ass, straight down.

Chang passed about ten yards to my right, heading up. She sneered at me, and I gave her the finger.

"Later, bitch!" I shouted.

"Yeah? You and what army?"

I didn't have time for that. We would even the score. We always do.

Once out of the light, I had the problem of finding my falling sister. My dear old home, *Rolling Thunder*, is a cylinder two miles wide. I was right at the centerline, very close to the sun. But when the sun goes off in the evening, it gets *dark*. No stars, no moon, not even little Deimos and Phobos, like back on Old Mars, Mama's home.

There are no big cities, naturally. There aren't enough people awake to make a city. What we have is a series of small villages, with fifteen of them slightly larger: the township seats. There are streetlights, and it was early enough that house lights would still be on, but I was looking down no matter where I looked, right at the roofs. Add in that my eyes were still a bit dazzled by the stadium lights, and it became a pretty problem to locate a black-and-gold sister against the dark interior.

I had been more than half expecting Polly to come limping back into the sphere, her crippled cycle barely able to make headway. But as the seconds ticked off, I began to realize that wasn't going to happen.

We don't carry radio locators, or emergency flashers, or anything like that. Come on, it's just a game of skypool! But maybe we ought to rethink that. I couldn't see a damn thing.

I kept my attention on my locator system in one window in the corner of my eye. When it's switched on it can pinpoint where I am, in the air or on the surface, to within a few inches. But it can't tell me where anyone else is unless they switch theirs on. Privacy issues, care of Uncle Travis. I wondered if Polly had thought of that. No blip appeared in my window.

"Polly!" I shouted. "Can you hear me? If you can hear me, turn on your goddam positioning!"

No answer. I was gaining speed, to the point that it was getting dangerous. The wings were shuddering a bit. Skycycles are built for maneuverability and short bursts of speed. More important, they are built for flying in zero gee, and I was feeling the insistent claw of gravity tightening around me as I descended.

There was a momentary flash of gold that might have been her, twenty degrees to my right and what I estimated was about a quarter mile below me. That was way too far below me. She must have been falling like a rock, no wings at all.

Then I saw a cluster of pinlights that I knew must have come from the edges of the emergency chute. But instead of being a nice, even circle, they were twisting around each other like a cluster of drunken fireflies. That had to mean the chute was opened but not deployed.

I swung in that direction and started pedaling hard.

Polly:

I groped around behind me. The chute handle should have been attached just over my left shoulder, where I could easily reach it in an emergency, but there was a slight chance I could deploy it accidentally. I could feel a torn patch in my jumper where it had been ripped away by something—not ripped in a way that would have deployed it, unfortunately, but just pulled free.

I twisted around as far as I was able and could just see the little yellow handle twisting in the breeze.

Not just a breeze by then, actually, more of a strong wind.

I was spinning now at a pretty good rate. I kept twisting back and forth into every position I could manage, trying to reach the handle. It was like trying to scratch that spot on your back, a few inches square, where your hand just will *not* reach.

Luckily, this spot was not stationary, but moving as the wind increased, twirling in a circle that brought it almost within my reach every few seconds. I timed it, determined to wrench my shoulder out of its socket if that's what it took. I lunged, hearing the tendons crack . . . and I caught it.

With a great feeling of relief, I yanked on the handle. The bright orange sheet unfurled, the tiny pinlights on the edges began to blink. The radio would be sending out a distress signal.

And the chute snarled in the wreckage of my flycycle.

Well, there really wasn't much else that could go wrong now. I was going to hit the ground. The only question was would I land on my feet, my ass, or my head.

The head seemed like the best idea, since it didn't seem good for much else.

I have always maintained that if you manage to kill yourself on a flycycle, it's because you did something wrong. No excuses. I didn't doubt that when they unwrapped the wreckage from my lifeless body, they would find a weak spot on the frame that I hadn't noticed—but should have—when I put it on. After all, how often do flycycle frames come apart in the air? I couldn't recall the last time it had happened.

Right then, though, it seemed to me that the only mistake I had made was allowing that gosh-darn Cheryl Chang to sneak up behind me.

Okay, girl, get a grip. A fall from almost a mile wasn't necessarily fatal, not in *Rolling Thunder*. I couldn't recall at the moment just what terminal velocity was, theoretically, but it's not as high as it would have been on Mars or Earth. Of course, hitting the ground at sixty or even fifty miles per hour is no joke.

Also on the bright side, the wind resistance of my remaining wing elements and the flapping remnants of my chute should slow me down some, sort of like a bird hit with a shotgun doesn't quite drop like a stone, it flutters some. I'd better start seeing what I could do to make sure I *didn't* land on my head. Because though my head may be hard, my neck was the weak point. I didn't want to break it.

Trouble was, I just didn't have that much control over my attitude. I was hoping to get oriented feet downward, figuring I could deal with broken ankles and legs a lot better than a broken spine or skull. Yet every time I thought I had it, the wind would catch another part of me and twist me around again.

During one of those rotations I thought I saw something I didn't dare hope for. I thought I saw another flycycle, nose down, and a flash of gold. But I didn't see how that was possible.

The ground was very near now. I made one more effort to get my feet under me, and for a while I had it. Then I felt myself starting to drift again.

That was when a hand grabbed the back of my jumpsuit and I jerked like a fish on a line, or really more like a felon at the end of a hangman's noose. All the air went out of me and my neck popped. The ground was still rushing up, but it was slowing. I heard the hummingbird whir of a flycycle rotor. Then the hand slipped, and I was falling again.

"Shit," somebody said. I knew that voice.

"Cassie!" I shouted. *"Help me!"*

"What do you think I'm trying to do, you idiot?"

I was as helpless as a baby bird falling from the nest; even more helpless since I didn't even have little wings to flutter.

Now I was falling facedown. It was dark down there, I couldn't see much, but I knew it had to be less than a hundred meters.

Cassie's hand grabbed me again, this time by the ankle. All the blood flowed to my head, and my hair came loose from its bun—somewhere in there I had lost my helmet, and I didn't even remember it. All I saw was long blonde locks streaming in front of me.

My cycle-shoe came off in Cassie's hand. I don't know how she did it, but she managed to grab my bare foot. I felt my ankle pop, and I howled.

Suddenly, there it was. The ground. I squealed and put my hands out in front of me. That was probably a bad idea, but *you* try to keep your hands at your side when the ugly, muddy ground is coming up at you.

It was muddy, all right, and smelly, too. I hit face-first, then Cassie landed on top of me, driving me into the ground and huffing all the air out of my lungs. Which was no fun, as my face was buried in muck and I couldn't inhale.

I heard the snapping sounds of Cassie getting out of her rig as I finally managed to lift my head up. It was pretty dark, but the farmer on whose grounds we landed had a few lights up on poles. It was enough so I could see my sister sitting up, taking her helmet off, ass deep in mud. She looked at me, pointed her finger, and howled.

"Oh, lord, I wish I had a camera! If you could see yourself . . ."

She was unable to finish, convulsed with laughter. And she was still pointing.

"Look . . . oh, my, Polly, just look behind you!"

I did. There was a huge, pale shape, not a foot away from me. For a moment I couldn't identify it, then it moved forward and nudged me with its snout. It was a pig. We had landed in a pigsty. And that meant that the stuff I had landed face first in was not just mud, it was full of . . .

The big porker nudged me again, and snorted.

"I think he's in love," Cassie said. And howled again.

At last she got up and held her hand out to me. I yanked, intending to bring her down in the muck with me, but she knows that trick and was ready for it. What I wasn't ready for was the grinding pain in my forearm.

"I think I broke my arm," I said, and passed out.

CHAPTER 2

Cassie:

My sister is *such* a drama queen.

After I pulled her into a sitting position and slapped her around a little until she woke from her *swoon*, she howled loud enough to frighten the pigs and wake the farmer and his family. He shined a bright light on us.

"Is she hurt badly?" he asked.

"Not as bad as it sounds," I assured him.

"Call an ambulance, darn you!" That, of course, was Polly. It was unusually nasty language for her, too.

"Where does it hurt, sis?"

"My arm, and my behind!"

"Sure you can tell one from the other?"

I got her to her feet by pulling the other arm. Sure enough, there was a piece of her flycycle frame sticking out of her butt. I touched it, and she howled again.

"Hold on, let's get a look at this."

"I'll call the ambulance," the farmer said.

"Wait a minute," I told him. Then I turned to Polly. "How badly do you want to be hazed tomorrow at school?" I asked her. "Right now, you might just get a little respect, since that crash was the most spectacular I've ever seen. How did you manage to totally destroy a flycycle? I didn't think that was possible." And I hadn't. Those suckers are *strong*.

"It wasn't my fault," she whined. "It was that Cheryl Chang! She—"

"Hold on, let me expose the wound." I got two fingers into the hole in her jumper and pulled. It ripped open, exposing most of her butt. It's a great butt, perfectly formed, drives the boys wild. I should know, because it's exactly like my own.

One thing you can never do if you have an identical twin is say bad things about her looks.

Unless she's covered in pigshit, of course.

"Good thing you landed facedown," I told her. "Both times. When you hit, and when you fainted. I wouldn't want to get any of that nasty . . . mud in the wound."

"It's more than just mud, and you know it."

"I know. I'm trying not to think about it too much."

Without warning her—she just would have pissed and moaned and worried—I yanked on the strut, and it came free. She was so surprised and shocked, she didn't even cry out at once.

"Darn you! Is it bleeding?"

"Hardly at all. It's just fat, not much blood in there."

"My ass is not fat."

"Did I say that? Not *too* fat, but everybody's ass has fat in it. Still want that ambulance? Or can we walk out of here?"

She sighed in her best put-upon way. She knew as well as I that if medical help came there, somebody would have a camera, and pictures of us covered in poop would be all over the news tomorrow.

I'd look stupid, too, but I'm not the one who had it all over her face.

I started laughing again, couldn't help myself. And I'd be able to torment her with this night for *years*. But not at once. This one was worth saving for a really golden moment. I'd let her relax, let her guard down, wait until she thought I'd forgotten about it. I could hardly wait.

In fact, about the only downside for the night is that we lost the sky-pool match to those stinking Hillbillies. With Polly and me both out of the game, our team didn't stand a chance.

The farmer—a nice man named Mr. Nguyen—hosed us down. We tossed the ruined jumpers in the trash. Mr. and Mrs. Nguyen didn't have anything to offer us to wear, being about five feet tall on tiptoes and their children ages four and seven. So she loaned us some nice blankets. They were both too polite to laugh out loud, but I saw them turn away from time to time, obviously stifling a chuckle. Their kids just stared wide-eyed at us. I suspected Farmer Nguyen and wife were considering hiring the matched set of tall, skinny blondes as scarecrows when we came back with the blankets.

It was still about an hour till sun-on. We trudged along the little dirt farm road, Polly favoring her left leg and cradling her right arm, which she was sure was broken.

"What's the big deal?" I asked her. "You're left-handed. You'll still be able to masturbate after the boys kiss you good night at the door."

She didn't bother to answer that.

We soon reached the stone-paved circumferential road—a C-road because it goes round and round the inside of the ship—and saw the streetcar just a little ways up the curve to counterspinward. It was there in less than a minute, sensed our presence, and stopped with a merry clang of its bell.

When Uncle Travis built his space ark and started stocking it with plants and animals and all the other stuff we'd need for a long journey to the stars, he first used prefabricated buildings and other cheap, undistinguished things. The result, he once told me, was something like an Antarctic station, something like a cheesy housing development, something like a refugee camp. He hated it. So he stopped doing that and began shopping for buildings. He brought a lot of them intact from the Earth and a few from Mars. Others were torn down and reassembled when they got here. The main thing he was looking for was that they be architecturally "tasty," as he put it. His tastes leaned toward art deco, Victorian, and Japanese, with a smattering of other cultures. There would be no Bauhaus in *Rolling Thunder*, he decreed. I blinked up Bauhaus, and I have to say I'm with him. Ugly stuff; about all you could say was that it was functional.

Later, when the Earth was in a really bad way from the Europan invaders, prices went down drastically on all sorts of things. He looted museums around the world. Uncle Travis was very, very rich, and he was a hell of a shopper. By the time we launched, he was broke.

One of the things he liked was old railroads and streetcars. There were to be no private cars in *Rolling Thunder*, other than farming machinery, and after looking at tubes from the first part of this century, I could see why. Insanity! Millions of cars stuck on the road, not moving.

So we have streets in the ship, good paved ones, on which you will see only pedestrians, riders on horses or wagons pulled by them, various human-powered contraptions on one to six wheels, trains, and streetcars. The streetcars are antiques refurbished and converted to battery power and automatic operation, and you never know for sure what you're going to get.

This time it was two San Francisco cable cars hooked together. They were green and gold, and a small brass plaque announced they were from the 1920s. Over 170 years old, and looking like they'd just rolled out of the factory.

I like cable cars, they're so cute.

"All aboard," the cable car said, and we climbed in. We usually ride on the outside footboard, hanging on to the bar, leaving the cabin for the old folks, but the night was chilly and our blankets didn't give us a lot of pro tection, so we went into the cabin. The seats were padded leather, with wicker backs. There was patterned carpet on the floor, and crystal bud vases with fresh flowers. There was no one else in either car. I took a seat and Polly remained standing as the *Thunderville Trolley* rang its bell again and took off.

Here's another effect you don't get on a planet. Since we were headed to spinward, and traveling at a speed faster than walking pace, we got heavier. Though it was a long way from being unpleasantly heavy, like it is in the gym down below, you could feel it, like when an elevator starts going up. But as soon as an elevator reaches its top speed, the feeling of weight goes away.

Not on the trains. As long as they move—and their top speed is about fifty miles per hour—you stay heavy. That's because you're adding your speed to the speed of the spinning ship. Your angular momentum becomes greater.

If you're going to counterspinward, of course, the effect is reversed. You get lighter the faster you go. If you go fast enough—230 miles per hour, a pretty good clip, and much faster than our trains go—you become weightless. The train, too. It could float right off the tracks.

Polly was standing with one foot barely touching the floor, favoring her injured gluteus muscle. Her forearm and wrist were swelling up, and she was sweating, in spite of the cool night air. Maybe I had underestimated her hurt.

"All kidding aside, sis," I said, "how bad is it?"

"The puncture, not so bad, but I'm real worried about infection. The arm . . . well, it hurts real bad. I can't make a fist. I'd flip you the bird, but it hurts too much."

"Don't let that stop you, Lefty."

So she used her other middle finger. She even chuckled a little. Polly and I are highly competitive, often at loggerheads; sometimes we even come to blows. We love getting each other's goat, but anyone who knows us knows we love each other in our own way. They know that messing with me is the same thing as messing with her, and vice versa. You come at one of us, and two of us are going to come back at you. One of us will hit 'em high, and the other will hit 'em low. Count on it.

"Maybe you better sit down."

She gave her head half a shake, then thought better of it, and sat. I put my arm around her.

"We'll be there soon."

"I'm amazed I survived." She paused a moment, then glanced at me. "I guess I'd better thank you for saving my life."

"Aw, shucks, ma'am. Just doin' my job."

She punched me on the shoulder. We both knew it was unlikely her life had been in danger, but a more serious injury had been possible.

Replaying it all in my mind, there on the cable car, I slowly became aware of a pain in my hand. I looked down at it.

"Shit!" I cried. "I tore a fingernail."

For some reason, Aunt Elizabeth decided to treat Polly's broken arm before she even looked at my painful finger.

"Get it fixed at the beauty parlor," she suggested. "Or go see a vet."

So I shut up. I had been kidding, of course, but though Aunt Liz has a decent sense of humor, it doesn't extend into medicine.

Aunt Elizabeth Strickland-Garcia is really our great-aunt, the older sister of our maternal grandfather, Ramon Garcia-Strickland. She's an M.D., a nanosurgeon, mostly, though she's also good at putting iodine on a scraped knee, which she did many times for both of us. She lost her right hand during the First Earth War. Her suit got punctured while she was trying to reach what she hoped were survivors of a bombing, and before she could be pulled out, the hand froze solid.

The hand might have been saved, but it would never have been as skilled as it had been. Her career in surgery would have been over. So she elected to have it replaced with a prosthetic, which was just as good or even better. She's had half a dozen new ones over the years. With the current one, she can read the date on a Mandela dollar, with a touch so gentle she can put a smile on Nelson's face.

She lives with her spouse, Dorothy, in Bedford Falls, in a small Victorian with a large yard where she breeds roses that win the blue ribbon at the township fair every year, and usually the All-Thunder Fair as well.

I presume she sleeps, but I couldn't vouch for it personally. Polly and I have never managed to wake her up, no matter how early or late we show up at her door with a new owie to treat.

She opened the door at thirty minutes till sun-on, sighed, and beckoned us in.

Dorothy, dressed in a nightgown and buttering some toast, smiled at us as we were led through the kitchen to Aunt Elizabeth's small surgery overlooking the rose garden. Her office never smells medical; it's always full of fresh-cut roses in every color of the spectrum, including a few that are blacker than Dorothy's face.

"I'm not even going to ask how you bumbling puppies got banged up yet again," she said. "Polly, let's see that arm."

She probed it gently, then got out her MRI. It was rolled up in a little box, four inches wide and long enough to wrap around a whole body. She only used a small part of it to take a look into Polly's forearm. All three of us leaned closer to look at the 3-D color image. We could easily see the crack in the ulna.

"Okay, no big deal," Aunt Elizabeth said.

"No big—"

"Hush, child."

"Don't be a crybaby," I said.

"You hush, too, or I'll spank you both. I'll just immobilize it and start an internal bonding agent." It took two minutes to spray on a cast from wrist to elbow and suspend the busted flipper from a sling.

"You should be good as new in forty-eight hours. Okay, turn around, drop that blanket, and bend over."

Polly did, just as Dorothy entered the room with a tray of tea, jam, and toast.

"Woo-woo!" she warbled. Polly looked over her shoulder and blushed.

"This wound is filthy. Where did it happen?"

"Uh . . . sort of in a pigsty," I admitted.

"Well, that explains the smell."

I guess I'd been smelling it long enough that it wasn't registering anymore.

"Can I go take a shower?" I asked.

"I'd recommend dunking them in a big jar of mouthwash," Dorothy said.

"I'd prefer formaldehyde. Hold them under for ten minutes, then screw on the lid. Future generations will thank me."

Aunt Elizabeth was looking at me from under her eyelids in that way she has of making you feel about five years old, and you've disappointed her once again.

She's in her mid-seventies, and has never been inside a black bubble, so that's both her real age and her virtual age. Her hair is snow-white and she has some wrinkles in the corners of her eyes, but like they say, seventy is the new forty. Gene therapy has extended human life expectancy quite a bit since my great-grandparents made the first trip to Mars. Regenerative techniques have done wonders for skin, too, and put a lot of plastic surgeons out of work. My aunt is a handsome woman with rather sharp features and a no-nonsense attitude. For most of her life she has been so dedicated to medicine that no one was even sure she was gay until she was in her fifties.

"I have done many odd things in my career," she was saying as she prepared to disinfect the wound, "but digging pig manure out of somebody's ass is a new one for me."

Then she couldn't help herself, she burst out laughing. Dorothy joined in. I tried to stop myself—honest I did, I already knew I was going to get enough grief from Polly—but in the end, I couldn't help myself, either.

"It's not funny," Polly fumed. Which was so untrue, with her bent over naked with her hands on her knees, that we all got started again.

"The Sherlock Holmes part of me has already deduced that this was a flycycle accident," Elizabeth said when we had control of ourselves again. "Don't bother asking; I never reveal my methods. Someday, I'll have you tell me how you two somehow always manage to avoid the manicured golf courses of life and land in the pigsties instead. Right now, it's too much information."

"The pigsty was probably a lot softer," I pointed out, spreading some strawberry jam on a piece of toast and taking a big bite.

"Yes, but how many pigs died of heart failure? Hang on, this is going to hurt."

Polly howled as Aunt Elizabeth squirted a jet of disinfectant into the wound. She kept it going for a while, until nothing that looked like manure was coming out.

"All done here," she said, slapping Polly's ass. She sighed.

"All right," she went on. "Here, swallow these for now, and while you're cleaning up I'll send out for a nano. Dorothy, can you find a few dresses for them in my bedroom? Will your shoes fit them?"

"If their feet were any bigger, they could walk on water."

"Oh, we can already do that," I said.

"We're still working on the raising-the-dead bit," Polly said. She held up her good hand, and I gave her the high five. Dorothy sighed and turned away. She knows better than to mess with us when we gang up.

"But there's no need to go to the trouble, Aunt Elizabeth," I said, stepping right into it. "We can just walk home. Myself, I could do with a snooze."

She gave me that under-the-eyebrow look again.

"Apparently your tiny brains can only hold on to one thought at a time. You seem to have forgotten what day it is."

There was a short pause, and Polly slapped the side of her head.

"*Cassie!* This morning is—"

"*Ohmigawd!* Papa's coming out of the bubble! What time is it?"

We only had ten minutes, it turned out.

We both crammed in the shower and scrubbed as hard as we could, jumped out, and put on the clothes Dorothy had found for us. The dresses would be the height of fashion if calico flour sacks ever came back in style. Aunt Elizabeth knows about as much about clothes as I know about surgery.

Dorothy had also found some flip-flops that would do. I slipped into my pair. Was that pig manure under my toenails? Too late to worry.

Back downstairs, the custom nano-dose had arrived by pneumatic mail. Polly swallowed the little metal pill that would release about a million ultratiny machines that would go to her busted arm and start pasting the bone back together.

We both had to take an antibiotic.

"What time is it?" In all the excitement, I had never turned my net connection back on. Can't have it on during a game, too many opportunities to cheat if you're plugged in. I blinked the clock on and groaned. There was no way we'd make it on time.

"Mom's going to kill us," I said. "How about a suicide pact instead? You want to go first?"

"I'd rather watch you and make sure you do it right."

"Don't worry about it," Dorothy said. "As soon as I saw you two standing at the door, I knew it was trouble. Come on, let's go."

She herded us all outside, and sitting at the curb was an ambulance.

———————

Aunt Elizabeth was not one for breaking rules, but Dorothy had no such qualms. She's a doctor, too, a psychiatrist.

Emergency services are just about the only powered flying vehicles in the ship. After all, nothing is more than a little over six miles from anything else, and the trains run every five minutes, twenty-four/seven. Why fly?

The only good excuse is when time is critical. Our uncle Travis, the Supreme Exalted Admiral of *Rolling Thunder*, has a personal flyer, and our elected officials can use one from time to time, but mostly they don't, as it doesn't sit well with the voters. This would be my first trip in a powered flying machine, if you don't count the powered flycycles I've used a few times when officiating at a skypool game.

I found I didn't like it much.

It was a boxy contraption, roomy enough for all of us inside though the walls were packed with medical gear.

Outside, it had no wings, just four humming fans in nacelles that twisted and turned for vertical takeoff and landing, then were in constant movement to adjust to the ship's quirky atmosphere. There was a big windshield up front, and Polly and I sat facing it.

You wouldn't think that a girl who loved nothing better than flying a mile over the ground would suffer from a fear of heights, and I don't think that was exactly what it was, but the ground was going by underneath us too damn fast. I had never traveled that fast in the air, and probably not on the ground, either, for that matter. We just never speed in *Rolling Thunder* . . . if you don't count the fact that we're moving at .77c relative to Old Sun.

The computer that flew the ambulance had one prime command, and that was to get from Point A to Point B in the fastest possible time. You couldn't ask it to slow down.

Luckily, the trip was only about a minute and a half. Otherwise I might have had to look around for an airsickness bag, and Polly would have never let me forget it. She seemed to be doing just fine.

We landed at our home, the Broussard Mansion, on the edge of the small town of Bayouville. The ambulance set down on Seven Acre Pond, which we own but share with the town, and turned itself into a hovercraft, then gently bumped us up against our dock. It was so sweetly done, I doubt if it even disturbed the turtles. We all piled out and hurried down the dock, past Papa's pirogue and our canoe and the rowboat suspended in the little boathouse. Waiting for us at the far end was our mother, Podkayne, with her arms crossed and an angry look on her face. But she looked concerned when she spotted the cast on Polly's arm.

"Can't you limp a little more?" I whispered.

"That hasn't worked with her since we were six."

"What have you done to yourself this time?" Mom asked.

"Whatever happened to 'Are you all right, my darling daughter?'"

"Don't you get smart with me, Pollyanna Broussard."

"She fell off her flycycle," Aunt Elizabeth said. "Don't worry, it was a minor fracture. I'm more worried about the possibility of infection from—"

Before she could say pigshit—or feces, more likely—I jumped in.

"We're not actually *late*, Mom. It's still . . ." I glanced at my clock. ". . . a few seconds to sun-on."

On cue, the tube down the center of the ship began to glow. It takes about a minute for it to reach high noon, but already it was bright enough to turn off the pole lights strung on the dock.

"And what's the deal with the ambulance?" Mom wanted to know.

"Don't fret about it, Poddy," our aunt said. "We were delayed a little while I treated her. And we did make it on time."

With a rising hum, the ambulance lifted off and threw itself into the sky. Mom didn't look happy, but she turned and went back into the house. No hugs today, at least not until Papa came out of his bubble.

When I say "Broussard Mansion," I'm being ironic. That's what we call it, that's the address you'd write down if you were sending us a package, but it's nothing like a mansion, not in size and especially not in looks. But as with many things in the ship, appearances can be deceiving.

From the outside it looks like a run-down bait shack. Or at least that's what I'm told, since I've never seen a real one. The back end—which is the front end, to me, because I seldom use the front door—is on pilings over the water. The house has a steep tin roof with a lot of "rust spots," is clad in pine siding weathered a lovely gray, and has a screen door on a spring. Most times when Polly and I hit it on the way outside to play, we'd hear Mom shout "Don't let the door slam!" and one of us would do a quick reverse and make a diving catch.

The long dock widens to become our covered back porch. Papa says in Louisiana it would be screened in if the owner could afford it. We don't need that because we don't have skeeters in *Rolling Thunder.*

The porch has a big picnic table where we eat most of our meals, and is usually cluttered with fishing poles, nets, tackle, crawdad traps, and coolers. There is a live bait well full of minnows and a box for night crawlers, an ice machine, and a drink dispenser where you lift the lid and see the various kinds of soda in glass bottles hanging by their necks. It says RC Cola on the side. I usually choose the Grapette, Polly prefers Orange Crush, and Papa goes for Hires root beer. Mom likes Vernor's ginger ale, a "Yankee drink," according to Papa. We all like Dr Pepper.

They're all zero calorie, by the way. I think some of those brands are no longer made back at Old Sun. Our beverage factory can whip up anything you like.

So, what I'm saying, from the outside the house looks like it's about one big gator bite from falling into Seven Acre Pond. That's all illusion, all for fun, done to keep everything in the ship from looking like everything else. The house is actually sturdy enough to weather hurricanes if we were dumb enough to have them.

The house is roomy enough. It's all on one level, three bedrooms, one for Mama and Papa and one each for us twins. The parental units were not the sort to make twins dress identically, and they both thought that one's own private room was important.

There's a quite large family room with a raftered ceiling and room to seat several dozen on couches and around tables and window seats. There's a big kitchen, Papa Jubal's realm since Mama Podkayne doesn't know which end of a wooden spoon to grab and which to stir with. She can somehow manage to make our smart toaster burn the bread, something the manufacturer claims is impossible. We learned to make our own breakfasts on the first day of school, when we were five.

That's it for the house. Then there's the boathouse, and a separate building with a guest bedroom, a study/lab/machine shop for Papa to do his work concerning picking apart the structure of the universe, and a music room for Mom. There's a storage shed that looks as ramshackle as the other buildings, and isn't. There's a three-room Victorian playhouse that Polly and I can barely squeeze into anymore, and a two-story tree house in our huge Spanish moss–draped live oak, both of them built by Papa and the envy of all our friends when we were young.

And that's about it for the grounds of Chez Broussard.

The main room of the Broussard Mansion was jam-packed when we entered. I figured that was a good thing. It would keep Mom's mind off her kids. Wood smoke drifted in from the open windows, from dozens of chickens and racks of ribs out on the grill, being tended to by our grand-père Jim, who at the age of ninety-four clock time (eighty-four body time) still runs the best Martian restaurant in *Rolling Thunder*. He was responsible for the heaping bowls of jambalaya, dirty rice, andouille sausage, hush puppies, okra, and boiled crawdads on the tables all around. There were also a few platters of a real delicacy: jumbo peeled shrimp. It's something that appears on our table only at Thanksgiving, and on very few other tables in the ship.

We farm all sorts of fish, but almost all of it is freshwater. We make some fairly good imitations of shrimp and crab, and we raise oysters, but we just don't have the room to cultivate ocean fish or crustaceans. Neither

Papa nor Uncle Travis wanted to face life without ever tasting shrimp or crab or redfish again, so they laid in what they called a hundred-year supply. It's rationed out carefully, and it's a good thing, because me and my sister could probably have run through the century's worth of shrimp in a few months, and would weigh half a ton together.

There was a small bandstand in a corner with a four-piece band—squeeze box, two fiddles, and a girl who played everything from triangle to washboard—thumping out a zydeco beat.

It was a real *fais do-do*.

The only jarring note was at the far end of the room. It was a black hole in space, about six feet in diameter. When I say black hole, that's exactly what I mean. It was as if somebody had used four-dimensional scissors to cut a circle in our reality, and filled it in with . . . nothing. No reflection, no sense of depth, nothing. I knew that if I touched it, my hand would feel it, but even if I put my nose right up to it, I would see nothing but total blackness. It reflected not a single photon of light.

I once asked Papa where all those photons went. He said they curved round and round 'bout a trillion time, *cher*, and then they done took off for some other universe somewheres. It's a universe he spends a lot of his time in, when he's thinking, and I know I'll never be able to follow him in a thousand years. And that's fine with me.

It was a black bubble, and Papa was inside it, not a nanosecond older than when he went in.

Those things give me the creeps. I know they're perfectly safe; Papa has been in and out of them more times than I am years old, but Polly and I never have. I don't know how sis feels about them, but I have always wished that at these parties they'd hide the damn thing behind a curtain until it's time to uncork Papa Jubal and *laissez les bons temps rouler*. ("Let the good times roll," if you're Cajun French–challenged.)

I tried to keep my back to it as I did my best to play cohostess, greeting an endless stream of friends and relatives.

You'd think all the Broussard-Garcia-Strickland-Redmond clan was there, including third cousins, grandnephews, and assorted trailer trash, but it wasn't even close. Great-grand-père Manny and Great-grand-mère

Kelly were absent, both of them in a black bubble for five years now. Other family members, including some who had free passes to stay out all the time by virtue of being closely enough related to Captain Travis, had elected to hibernate, too.

The fact was that Earth-born and Mars-born people often found life inside *Rolling Thunder* to be, well, *dull.*

We're definitely small-town in here. Our pleasures are bucolic, pastoral, not well suited to city folk who like to party on Saturday night. Oh, we party well enough, and there are dances and theater and music—mostly amateur—but some of it must look about as exciting as a barn dance or a quilting bee to the older folks.

Well, I have to say I'm a bit in sympathy with them. All us Thunder-born are quite aware of what life on Earth looked like—before the disaster—and what Mars still looks like. And the bright lights and fashions and huge concerts and stuff look like a lot of fun. But what's the point of mooning over what you just can't have? I get along okay with what we've got.

———————

It wasn't long until Mama Podkayne called us all to order.

We long ago decided not to make a big ceremony about turning off the bubble. Papa's emergence was always the occasion for a party, but being the center of attention makes him uncomfortable. So we just all gather and somebody throws the switch; we pick Papa up from where he has fallen—you never know how the person inside is going to be oriented, which is why we have a soft pad under the bubble—and give him a short round of applause. Then somebody hands him a beer, and we carry on as normal.

Mom got everyone reasonably quiet, then gestured to me. It's always me or Polly who presses the button. I thought it had been me last time, but what the hell. I knew this was no time to question Mom's decision.

The percussion girl did a roll on a snare drum, and I pressed the button.

The bubble vanished without even a pop, and my father tumbled out and landed on his side. He was mumbling a Hail Mary, which is how he always goes into the bubbles. He was wearing a look of anxiety, which is his normal expression when he goes in, and therefore when he comes out.

But then he looked around and sat up with a big smile on his face . . .

. . . which lasted about three seconds. Then he looked horrified.

"Stop the ship!" he shouted.

Which, seeing as how we were traveling at 77 percent of the speed of light, I guess you could call a party-killer.

CHAPTER 3

Polly:

"Mom, what's wrong with Papa?" I asked.

"Just stay calm, Polly," she said. She was tugging Papa, looking a little dazed, toward their bedroom. Mom is six-foot-four, and Papa is just about exactly a foot shorter than that, though he's wide enough to almost fill the hallway. Not fat wide, but muscular. The expression is "built like a fireplug."

"You and Cass get back there and take care of our guests," she added. "I'll see to your father. Come on, don't stand there gawking. Get a move on, *cher.*"

She pulled Papa through the bedroom door and closed it behind them. I looked over at my sister, standing there holding a leg of fried chicken.

"What's going on, Cassie? Did he say stop the ship?"

"That's what I heard."

"But how? What do we do?"

She shrugged and took a bite of the chicken.

"I guess we turn the ship around and start slowing down. You want to take care of that while I see to our guests?"

Sometimes she drives me crazy. Her response to most emergencies is *"Whatever."* Unless it requires immediate action, she'll wait to see what happens. She's just not a worrier. For some reason, it seems to work out that I do the worrying for both of us.

She looked at me, sighed, and took me by the shoulders. She turned me around and shoved me back in the direction of the family room.

"You heard Mom. Papa would be mortified to think there were guests in our house who weren't being seen to. Now, you go put on a good show, and I'll change out of this potato sack."

So I stumbled forward, and I hope I managed to paste a smile on my face before I got back to the living room.

There was a muted murmur of conversation that paused for a moment when I entered, but quickly resumed. I hurried toward the band and made a rolling gesture with my hand. They got the message and started into another number.

I surveyed the crowd. Many of these people I only saw once or twice a year, when Papa came out of the bubble. They were mostly family, by blood or marriage, with a few good outsider friends.

There was Great-grandpa and Great-grandma Redmond, Jim and Audrey, ages ninety-four and ninety-three by the calendar, and almost the same by their body clocks. After a couple of years in a black bubble, they had elected to live in real time, even if it meant dying before we got where we were going. Some people feel that way. They feel that time is passing them by even though not much happens in the ship, most years.

Bottom line, my great-grandparents Redmond simply didn't like the time jumps. They were content to do what they had always done on Mars, which is to run the best restaurant in town.

I chatted with them for a while, looked around for my other great-grandparents, Manny and Kelly, then remembered they were currently in time stasis. They tended to pop in and out at irregular intervals, taking to black-bubbling like born skippers. That's what we call people who elect to skip over real time like stones on water. Skippers.

The result was that, although Great-grandfather Manny and Great-grandmother Kelly were almost the same age as my Redmond great-grandparents, by the calendar, they were only eighty by their body clocks, having spent a total of about seventeen years in black bubbles since the ship set out for the stars.

The next people I saw were two of my favorites, my uncle Mike and aunt Marlee. If you think my tall mom and short papa are a mismatched set, you should see Mike and Marlee.

Uncle Mike was found by a roadside somewhere in Africa as an infant, during one of the many conflicts on that continent. Possibly his parents had been killed; there was a lot of that going around. He was adopted by Granddaddy Ramon Strickland-Garcia and Grandma Evangeline Redmond when he was two, taken to Mars, and raised by them and his older sister, our mother, Podkayne, who was eight years older than him at the time. He's very dark-skinned, and four feet three inches tall. He's an achondroplastic dwarf. He doesn't like the euphemism "little person," reasoning that a child is a little person, but they grow up. "I won't grow up," he says, and he's okay with it. Mom says he was the best baby doll a little girl ever had. They're very close.

He's married to Marlee, who is only a little shorter than me, and even paler.

And maybe I shouldn't add, but will, that our family is easy about nudity. We enjoy nothing more than a skinny-dip in the pond, and I can tell you that the short arms and short legs are the only thing short about him, if you get my drift. Some of my girlfriends have been bug-eyed, and very interested.

I hugged Marlee and Mike, talked with them for a while, then looked around to see if they had brought their son, Patrick.

They had. He was standing by the band with a few others, clapping his hands and doing a little dance step.

My heart did a somersault, as usual.

If Cassie and I were ever to kill each other, it would probably be over Patrick. When we were younger we used to share our toys. We share all our clothes, we share flycycles, we share homework—she does my math, I do her literature—but we've never shared boyfriends. Oh, once I pretended to be her and broke up with her boyfriend. It would have been hard for her, and it wasn't for me, since I didn't like the creep anyway. And once she pretended to be me, chatted up a guy I was interested in, setting the hook firmly, then handing him off to me to reel in because she's better at flirting than I am. Other than that, if we ever go on a double date, it's always clear who is with whom. We've never traded.

Patrick was the first time we were both smitten with the same boy at the same time. But the cold hard fact was that he seemed able to resist our previously irresistible charms. We didn't know how to account for it.

"Gay," Cassie said one evening after she had given it her best shot, practically rolling over on her back with her paws in the air and her tongue hanging out. But we both knew it was sour grapes. Great-grandpa Jim once told me that he remembered a time when a lot of people hid their homosexuality, and that *before* his time, almost everybody was "in the closet," as he put it. I don't know what closet that was, but it doesn't sound like fun. And in school we learned that before that, it was actually *illegal* most places.

The things you learn in history class, huh?

But who would hide it now? Who cares? So I have to admit that at first Cassie's snide remark gave me a little hope—a guy being unavailable was a lot easier to handle than the idea that he just wasn't interested in *you*. And it was true that he didn't seem to date, girls or boys. He was a bit of a loner, though not antisocial.

What does he look like? Think Michelangelo's *David*, only light brown instead of marble white. His skin was a lovely bronze—half Aunt Marlee and half Uncle Mike, I guess—and his golden hair fell in finger curls down almost to his shoulders. His eyes were amber, almost yellow-gold in the right light.

My knees wobbled just to feel the breeze from him as he walked by.

Hope springs eternal. I made my way toward the bandstand to take another stab at chatting him up.

He was engrossed in the music and didn't seem to notice me. So I cleared my throat and put my hand on his arm.

"Hello, Patrick."

He looked around and gave me a neutral smile and nod.

"Hi. Which one are you?"

Before I could answer, something happened. I can't say a hush fell over the room, but there was a change in the atmosphere, some new vibe it was hard to put my finger on. I saw heads turning, maybe that was it. My own head turned, and I saw Cassie enter the room.

I love my sister, I really do. Except when I want to kill her.

She had been out of my sight for maybe ten minutes, and in that time had managed to transform herself. Her hair was clean and done up in a flip. She wore a black off-the-left-shoulder toga that would have looked right at home in the Roman streets, if they wore Paris designer clothes in the streets of Rome, made of a shiny silk that flowed around her like water. Black sandals on her feet. One strand of Mom's pearls around her neck, two big pearls hanging from her earlobes, and a pearl-and-gold bracelet.

There were three things that really steamed me about it. One, that was the outfit *I* had intended to wear *myself*, as soon as she was finished dressing. Two, we didn't have another dress like that, so I couldn't match her and join her—both twins being dressed like that having four times the impact of just one, as we had discovered a long time ago. And three, I couldn't even cry foul because we *do* share all our clothes, and our rule has always been first-come, first dressed to kill.

So there I was, outfitted like a ragamuffin from a Charles Dickens novel, hair looking like a haystack, probably still smelling of pig poop. I figured I might as well kill myself. There was nothing left to live for.

I looked back to Patrick, and he was smiling. A nice, big smile, much warmer than anything I'd ever gotten from him.

I decided to table the suicide motion for the time being and turned to the next item on the agenda, which would be murder. Sororicide, to be specific. Not a word you see every day.

Cassie made her way across the room, stalling conversations left and right, somehow managing to look spontaneous, at ease, unaware of the stir she was causing, with the bearing of a princess and just the right amount of concern—one tiny wrinkle in her brow—over Papa's worrisome announcement. Whereas I knew that every step and gesture was as carefully calculated as the kata of an aikido master.

She paused here and there for a word or two with someone, greeted

Mike and Marlee, and obviously turned the conversation to their son. When informed that he was present and near the bandstand, she looked surprised—as if she hadn't seen him on the screen in her room while sharpening her claws and putting on her war paint—looked over at him, and waved. The crowd parted as she made her way over. The whole band was watching, and somehow the fiddle player managed to break a string.

Cassie held her hand out. Not vertically, as though to shake, but—I swear this is true—limp at the wrist and about at chest level, drawing his eyes down to the cleavage she was showing, which was a lot. Or as much as we had, anyway; we're slightly shortchanged in the bosom department.

He hesitated a moment, then gave her a wry smile, took her hand, and kissed it.

My world fell apart. Murder first, *then* suicide. Definitely.

I made my exit unnoticed, which was not difficult at all, and slunk (slinked? slank?) back to my room. I wanted to slam the door, but Cassie would hear it, and I wouldn't give her the satisfaction.

I wrapped a plastic bag around my cast and hopped in the shower. I scrubbed savagely at every inch of my skin. My arm hurt, and my ass hurt, but I didn't care. I washed my hair four times, rinsed four times. I still felt that I smelled like pig poop.

When I finally felt reasonably clean, I poked lackadaisically through our closet—*our* closet! That was going to have to stop!—for something to wear. There was nothing there. Oh, sure, there were a few hundred outfits. Cassie and I had never stinted when it came to spending our allowances on clothes. There were no designer labels from Paris or Beverly Hills or Rio or Moscow like there were on Earth, though there were a lot of copies of Earth and Mars fashions.

For the last few years, since we lost contact with Old Sun, the boutiques where we do our shopping had been forced to design their own stuff, which I guess was a good thing. Now we only had to keep up with girls from around the curve instead of imitating Old Sun fashions.

I turned my mind back to the closet. It opens into both our rooms. There was a lot of stuff neither of us had worn for two years or more and that was ready to be boxed up and sent to the secondhand shops or the recycler. There was even more we had grown out of and just hadn't bothered to take off the rack. You know how closets get.

What it came down to was I realized I was looking for the *next best thing.* Cassie was wearing the number one outfit. I was looking for number two. And when you do that, you're licked before you even begin, right?

I put on something. I don't even recall now what it was, and if you knew me, you'd realize how really depressed I was. I *always* remember what I wore to any kind of party, that's just the way I am. I like clothes, okay?

I dragged myself to the bedroom door and slouched through it, and stumbled toward the party. I thought my heart couldn't sink any lower, but as soon as I came into the room I saw my sister and Patrick. They were dancing. She looked radiant. I looked for a hole in the floor I could sink through, all the way into the black, absolute zero emptiness of interstellar space. Let me be flung into the starry void on an eternal trajectory of misery. It's my party, and I'll cry if I want to.

Cassie says I overdramatize, but I don't think so.

Well, if life was indeed to go on, I'd just have to gather up the remains of my broken heart, somehow stitch them together, and join the party with a brave face. I was getting ready to do that when I heard the parental bedroom door creak open. Mama Podkayne came out, wearing the scowl I knew well, and that usually meant I was in big trouble. I would have been running for the poles—which is what we do instead of heading for the hills—except I was pretty sure it wasn't aimed at me. And I was right.

"Polly, go in and sit with your father," she growled. "He's upset."

"Sure, Mom, but—"

"Do as I say."

She shouldered past me and down the short hallway, and stood facing the crowd. I lingered, and heard her shout. Mama Podkayne was and is a singer. When she wants to be heard, she can shatter not only glass, but steel.

She wanted to be heard.

The crowd quieted instantly, and so did the band.

"Friends and neighbors, I hate like hell to be so rude, but as you probably guessed, something has come up. I'm afraid I'll have to ask y'all to leave. My husband is very upset about something. I don't know what it is, but he's made me understand that something must be done about it.

"Now, it would be a shame to let all this fine food go to waste, so I want you all to find a bucket somewhere and fill it up and take it all home with you. I want to see nothing but empty plates when I come back. Okay?"

"I'll take care of it, Podkayne," said Great-grandpa Jim.

"Thanks, and thanks for cooking it all. Mike, Marlee, could y'all come back here with me, please? Granddaddy Ramon, Granny Evangeline, Aunt Elizabeth and Dorothy, could y'all come, too?"

I finally spotted Cassie, on the far edge of the crowd. She had maneuvered Patrick up against the wall and was standing very close to him.

They were eye to eye. Invading his personal space.

He didn't seem uneasy about it. She was talking, one hand casually draped over his shoulder. He nodded, put in a word or two here and there, and began to move toward the front door. Cassie dug her claw into him and gave him the big eyes, the parted lips, the slightly cocked head. Every ounce of her body language was saying "Kiss me, you gorgeous man!"

Still smiling, he patted her on the shoulder and deftly stepped around her. She almost lost her balance and fell over, she was so intent on staying near him. He joined a few other relatives around our own age, and they made their way to the door and out. Cassie had her back to me. She was rigid as a fencepost.

Maybe there *is* a god.

"Cassandra!" Mom shouted. "Here, now, this minute."

Cassie jumped a foot and came quickly toward us. I knew I should be heading back to see to Papa like she told me to, but I know that tone of voice and wouldn't have missed it for a brand-new Fuji flycycle.

Mom looked her up and down and hissed at her.

"Cassandra Ann, what the heck were you thinking?"

Cassie tried an innocent look, but Mom's shoulder-to-ankle gaze was about to burn the toga off her and scorch the skin beneath. So Cassie went to the fallback position: Civil rights.

"I'm a grown-up now, Mother. Don't forget that."

"And you're still living in my home. And that dress makes you look like . . . I don't even want to say it. And Patrick is your first cousin."

Well, I was sure in the mood to see my sister catch heck, but I have to admit that was unfair. Patrick was our first cousin legally, but not genetically. His father was adopted into our family, and Marlee was no relation. Children would be no problem.

Not that I was really thinking in those terms. I just wanted to date him.

To be even more blunt: I just wanted to get into his pants.

Papa Jubal is . . . different.

Our father grew up in a large, extremely poor family on Earth, completely dominated by his father, who was a religious fanatic. Our grandfather Avery was an adherent of some beliefs so strange I can hardly understand or believe that anyone could be so stupid. But I've never known Papa to lie to me, so it must be true. This sect did things like handle venomous snakes and spiders, believing that if they had faith, God would protect them. As you might expect, they had a high mortality rate, but there always seemed to be enough new believers to fill up the little backwoods church on the bayou.

They didn't believe in birth control, thus the large family. Their child-rearing practices were sub-Neanderthal, and consisted mostly of knocking their children about for any offense. Almost everything was forbidden but prayer. No reading was permitted except the Christian Bible.

Total obedience was demanded. Papa was beaten regularly. When his father discovered that he was extremely bright, with a supergenius IQ, he was beaten even more, on the theory that a child shouldn't be smarter than his father. Being that smart was seen as an affront to God.

After one violation of the rules his father beat Papa so badly with a nail-studded pine board that it was a miracle he survived. The people who were supposed to stop things like that finally took notice, and my grandfather was tried and convicted of attempted murder. He died in prison.

Papa was brain-damaged. The verbal part of his mind took the worst injury, and he never recovered fully from that. He has a small vocabulary, learns new words only with great difficulty, can never get the hang of certain concepts of grammar and so speaks with the thick Cajun accent and dialect he grew up with, garbled and inconsistent syntax, and no understanding of the more esoteric parts of language. We always understand him well enough, but his problems with communication led him to withdraw from human society, to become a loner.

To become, in many ways, a mad scientist.

There's nothing of Dr. Frankenstein about Papa. You won't find him cackling madly over boiling beakers or sparking machines. He's not in search of a way to rule the world.

No one is really sure if Papa would have done the things he did without the brain damage. He was smart before, no question. There is a theory that after his injuries, his brain rewired itself somehow to be different from a normal human brain. Aunt Elizabeth believes that Papa is different because of the damage.

To me, it really doesn't matter. Was Einstein's brain completely different from other human brains? Is that what led him to his way of seeing the universe from an angle no one had seen before? My guess is, no. If he hadn't thought it up, someone else would have.

It's not that way with Papa. One day, in his lab in Florida, he invented something that somehow screwed with space itself. He cobbled it together out of things lying around. When he was done, he was able to create these little spheres, like Christmas tree ornaments, only so perfectly reflective that you could see them only as distortions of space. They didn't interact with anything around them. The only way to hold them was to surround them with your fingers or some sort of cage, as they had zero friction.

That was interesting enough, but there was more. A lot more.

The size of the bubbles could be adjusted. If you started with a small one, say, the size of a playing marble, and expanded it to the size of a basketball, you had a pretty good vacuum inside. Then if you turned it off, the air would rush in, and there would be a loud pop.

That's what Papa wanted to use them for. Noisemakers, like firecrackers. He figured they could make a lot of money out of them.

Papa has almost no practical sense. He just fiddles around.

Luckily, my uncle Travis was the hardheaded side of the family. He had already taken a few gadgets that Papa made, patented them, and made the two of them wealthy.

Travis asked Papa how big he could make the bubbles. Plenty big, Papa said. So imagine expanding that marble-sized bubble bigger than a house Now turn it off. One *heck* of a bang.

But the real power of the things was if you reversed that sequence. Start with a bubble the size of a house and squeeze it down to the size of a marble. That's a lot of air in there. A lot of power. Squeeze it down to the size of a proton. Now you have an undetectable bomb.

There's more. Make a bubble a mile across, and instead of air, squeeze water, or rock, or garbage, or anything at all, down to the size of a marble. Now turn it off. But it would be wise not to be on the planet where this is being done. You should be a safe distance, maybe fifty million miles or more. Because that sucker is going to crack the planet wide open.

I hadn't really been all that worried about Papa Jubal when he came out of the black bubble and hollered for the ship to stop.

But while Mama was dressing down Cassie—dressing her down for dressing up—I thought it was wise to skedaddle down the hall before she turned around and saw me. I slipped into their bedroom.

Papa was sitting on the bed with his head in his hands, and he was shaking. He looked up when I closed the door. His worried expression quickly changed to alarm.

"Oh, my sweet Polly. What happened to you, *cher*?"

Papa is the only one who can tell me and Cassie apart with just a glance. I don't know how he does it. Even Mama gets it wrong every once in a while. We quickly learned never to try any twin tricks on Papa.

"*Ce n'est rien*. It's nothing, Papa. Just a little fracture." I moved the arm up and down in the sling to show that it didn't hurt. It did hurt, a little, but I trust I didn't show it.

"Oh, *mon bébé doux*! You makin' me old before my time, whizzin' aroun' on them flyin' sticks, like Holloween witches. Come here, *cher*, come here. Come give your papa a hug. Let me kiss it an' make it well."

I decided not to tell him about my other injury.

I hurried over and was trying to sit beside him on the bed, but he embraced me and twisted around until I was sitting on his lap. Papa is very strong. It had been years since I'd sat on his lap, and I was surprised at how warm and safe it made me feel. We probably looked silly as hell, he being short and wide and me at six-foot-four, but who cares? This was my papa, and I love him to distraction.

He hugged me to his barrel chest, threatening to crack ribs. I didn't mind. He had never hurt me, never would.

"Where's your sister? Your mama?"

"They're coming, Papa."

"Good, good. We need to be all together, us."

I pulled back and looked in his eyes.

"What's the matter, Papa?"

What I saw in there was despair.

"Don't worry, *cher*, I'll work something out. I'll figger something."

But his eyes were telling a different story, and that's when I began to be scared.

CHAPTER 4

Cassie:

In my experience, heaven and hell can be only a moment apart. Since I always try to look on the bright side of life, I do my best to enjoy the heaven before hell arrives.

I was in his arms. I was dancing with him! We cut a rug, tapped our toes, kicked up our heels, shook our booties, tripped the light fandango. I could have danced all night and still have begged for more!

It didn't last that long, probably only a few minutes, but who's counting when time stands still?

He had a few inches on me, and I loved that. Mama says that she and I and my sister would not stand out as unusually tall on Mars, but the majority of the citizens of *Rolling Thunder* are from Earth, where they tend to stop growing them before they're really finished, like the Chinese and Mexicans. We were the tallest girls in our high-school class. Speaking as a tall girl, I have to say that there is something deep inside me that wants to look up to a man, even if it's just a few inches. I wonder if it's genetic, built into the double-X chromosome? Mama has obviously dealt with it, being a foot taller than Papa, and I know a few other couples where he's the runt and she's the giant, but I've noticed that, nine out of ten times, you look at boy-girl matches and you'll find that he's taller. We just tend to pair up that way.

Patrick was at first reluctant to dance close, but I soon narrowed the distance and rested my head on his shoulder. I feasted on the smell of his hair.

And that's when Mama let out her supersonic screech and brought the dream to an end. Patrick turned to face her and listened intently as she, basically, told everybody to take a hike. Before I knew it, Patrick had disengaged from my embrace.

He gave me a small smile. Wistful, I thought.

"Thanks for the dance . . . uh, Cassie."

Well, there's a bit of a comedown. He didn't quite put a question mark at the end of the sentence.

"It was my pleasure, Patrick," I said. I moved a little closer and looked deep into his eyes and parted my lips. He just shook my hand and turned away.

Shy, I guess.

Well, I got sort of reamed out by Mama Pod about the dress I was wearing. I admit it was sort of radical, but it did its job, and that was all I cared about. I was sure Patrick would come calling in a day or two.

And I swear, Mama Pod says she was young once, too, but I don't see any evidence of it. All I ever get is griping and negative vibes. It's about time she allowed me to be a woman.

I waited it out, got a few sour looks from the inferior sibling, and retired to my room to get "decently dressed." I picked a pair of low-cut tartan pedal pushers that I could barely wiggle into, and a white off-the-shoulder peasant blouse with baggy sleeves. I stepped into a pair of rhinestone-coated mules with three-inch cork heels, and topped it all off with a floppy moonshiner hat. *Trailer Trash Chic*, the girls are calling it. I don't know what trailer trash is, or a moonshiner, for that matter.

A quick glance in the mirror told me I was lookin' swell, Belle, so I headed down the hall to Mama and Papa's room.

The womb-mate was sitting on Papa's lap, with her head on his shoulder. She had to scrunch up a little to do it. Papa looked up and held out his hand to me.

"Cassandra Ann, *cher*. Come to your papa."

I did, intending to sit beside him and put my arm around his beloved shoulders, but he wasn't having any of that. He pulled me over and somehow got the two of us arranged, one on each knee.

"Okay," I said. "For Christmas I want a red wagon, and a new sprocket for my flycycle, and a dolly that laughs and cries."

He looked puzzled for a moment, and I tugged on his long, white hair. Then he roared with laughter. With Papa it's usually a roar, and I don't know anyone who can hear it and not smile. If there are people like that, I don't *want* to know them.

"I look like Santy Claus, don't I? Only my beard be not long as it used to." He looked at Polly. "And what do you want, little girl?"

"I just want my papa to be happy and not worry," she said.

Oh, gag me. That's what I wanted, too, of course, but I thought the situation called for levity. Polly doesn't do levity very well.

Papa's face fell, and he hugged us both even harder. I hoped I wouldn't have bruises in the morning. Then Mama was on one knee in front of us. She took Papa's hand and pulled gently, until she had his attention.

"No time for that right now, family," she said. "We've got to get going."

"That's right, get goin'," Papa said. He kissed us each on the forehead, then slapped our behinds. I saw Polly wince, but Papa didn't notice. We got up and followed them out the door. I caught up with Mama.

"Where are we going?" I whispered, as Polly leaned in closer to hear.

"We're off to see your uncle Travis."

Well, that was interesting. Uncle Travis usually means trouble. I was in the mood for a little trouble.

———

Travis was pretty wild in his younger days. When an emergency arose in the spacecraft he was nursing through reentry, the cabin filling with smoke to the point that he couldn't see anything, he used the pistol he wasn't supposed to be carrying to blow a hole in a side window. That sucked out all the smoke, and he was able to see enough to pilot it by the seat of his pants into a dead-stick landing on a remote smuggler's airstrip in Africa that, far from being a NASA emergency landing site, wasn't even on the maps.

The nose wheel killed a water buffalo, which he and the locals and his passengers cooked and ate while waiting for rescue. What he thought he needed a .45 for on a mission to the primitive orbital space station of those days is something I never asked him. Shooting skeet at shooting stars?

It was hushed up. NASA couldn't very well put him on trial for the weapon—or the fact that it was later determined that his blood alcohol was over the legal limit for automobile driving in most states—without Travis bringing up a lot of other ugly facts concerning irregularities committed at the request of a VIP congressman who was deadheading at taxpayer expense. They couldn't charge him with losing the spacecraft—which was never recovered, and may still be sitting there to this day—without acknowledging that if he hadn't "cowboyed up," as Mama once put it—they would have lost not only the ship but the passengers as well.

They couldn't very well ever let him pilot a ship again, either, not after flying drunk. So they promoted him, gave him a nice pension and a medal of some sort, and invited him to resign quietly.

But you can't keep a good man down on Earth. Travis and my great-grandparents built themselves a spaceship and drove it to Mars.

BLINKLINK: *RED THUNDER*: Summary: Both the first spaceship to use compression-bubble technology for spaceflight, and the first to take humans to Mars and back. The ship was piloted by Travis Broussard, and crewed by Manny Garcia, Kelly Strickland, Dak Sinclair, and Alicia Jones. The ship was assembled from old railroad tanker cars, and powered by three compression-bubble engines. This gave it the ability to accelerate constantly, and the trip was made in a few days. On the return trip, the crew located the wreckage of the failed American expedition to Mars, and rescued the crew who were still alive. Blink for complete article.

Visiting Uncle Travis isn't just a matter of walking down to the trolley stop, riding awhile, then walking up to his front door and knocking. In fact, very few people can visit him at all, and all of them are FOCT.

That stands for Family of Captain Travis. This has been the source of some tension in the ship over the years. And the acronym (which Travis didn't invent) has been the source of a lot of rather obvious humor for just about as long.

Rolling Thunder is a limited democracy. That is, anyone who is awake and of a certain age can vote on many issues that might come up. Everyday matters, those things not having to do with engineering. Mostly they have to do with the economy: acreage allotments, taxes, decisions on which crops will be planted where, how many food animals will be raised, how many slaughtered, things like that.

There are also issues concerning awake time and hibernation time that can get a bit heated. The population of the ship just *can't* grow. There is no room to expand. On launch day, we were at capacity, plus a much larger number in black-bubble hibernation, some of whom would not be allowed out of their bubbles during the duration of the voyage. Sounds harsh, and it is, but people signed on knowing the terms and decided it was better to take a chance at life on a new world than to stick around on Earth, which was being rapidly rendered uninhabitable.

Then, after a vote is taken, Captain Travis reviews it on the next Groundhog Day, which is what we call the day he pops his head out of the bubble to see what's happening in his ship. If he likes the new regulations, he does nothing. If he doesn't, he vetoes them.

That's limited democracy: The captain gets the last word. Always.

Mostly people don't seem too unhappy with that arrangement though there are always malcontents. It helps that Uncle Travis seldom messes with internal decisions unless he thinks they are really, *really* dumb. And after all, it *is* his ship. He paid for it, had it built, and anyone aboard is there because of either earning a spot by helping in the construction or being invited because of certain skills. There was a test you had to pass.

What does cause a little more resentment is the whole idea of FOCTs. I've never heard it to my face, but I know there are those who say our privileges are "all focted up," or they call us fockers.

Polly and I haven't been radically affected by being fockers. It didn't make us more popular, nor did it make us the subject of either a lot of sucking up or anger. We were reasonably popular—me more than her, I believe, because I'm more outgoing—but neither of us were BWOCs. Teachers didn't defer to us or grade us hard.

Our true glory came in our junior and senior years, when we came into our own as skypool stars. I was Most Valuable Player last year, Polly was this year.

But there's no denying there are privileges of family. Like having our own private subway stop, on a subway that most people don't even know exists.

———————

At the side of Papa's workshop is what looks like a cellar entrance, not quite flat to the ground, with two wooden doors. It's just made to look like a tornado shelter, and it's phony, like a lot of stuff in my world. I'm okay with it. We don't need a weather vane, either; all we have to do is blink the climate-control site to see which direction the wind will be blowing at any given moment, and how hard. But we *have* a weather vane, a big red metal rooster, and it looks good sitting up there on the house.

The doors are a lot stronger than they look. There's no padlock or anything, but they'll only open to the fingerprints of Papa or Mama on the handle. When you pull the doors open what you see is a long flight of concrete stairs going down into darkness. Lights come on as you walk down, and go off behind you. Soon you are traveling in a bubble of light that takes you right down to a steel door, which also opens to Mama's fingerprint.

On the other side is a dark tube, about ten feet in diameter, stretching off dimly in both directions, toward the bow and stern. North and south. A single rail runs right down the middle of the tube.

The door shut behind us and a sign on the other side of the tube lit up.

CAR COMING. ARRIVAL IN 1:35.

We stood on the little platform, not saying anything. The numbers counted down, and the car arrived, decelerating rapidly to come to a standstill right in front of us.

The car resembled the golf carts I've seen in movies from back at Old Sun, except for the lack of wheels. A squat metal body had three pairs of seats, a plexi windshield, and a flat top. It hovered a fraction of an inch above the floor, and the four-inch-high vertical mag rail fit neatly into a slot in the front. Inside, the seats were bare plastic.

Mama and Papa took their seats in the front, and the sib and I got in the second row.

"Take us to the Bridge," Mama said. We were on our way.

I had only ridden on these cars three times in my life. I don't even recall why we took the trips. The subways were just another of Uncle Travis's paranoid precautions, a place to go if things got very unsettled, politically. He has hundreds of these fallback plans, including some serious weaponry if it came to that. I don't know the half of them; none of the family do, as far as I know. That's how Travis works.

We came to a big open space, one of the warehouses. Basements, if you prefer, because they are underfoot, and they store stuff.

Rolling Thunder is like a big block of Swiss cheese. It began life as an asteroid, remember, five billion years or so ago. It had a tumultuous youth, being pulled this way and that by other planets and asteroids, trying along with its neighbors to form a real planet but robbed of that accomplishment by the huge influence of Jupiter, which stripped away the bulk of the mass in the space between itself and Mars and doomed the little planetoids to wander the vast spaces, airless, waterless, devoid of life.

It was very hot at first, and the rock and nickel and iron melted into a solid mass. During those early years, it was repeatedly bombarded with smaller rocks, so that its exterior is pockmarked with craters. That lasted maybe a billion years. Then things settled down, and the asteroid assumed its place in the stately, uneventful dance around and around the sun, in the main part of the asteroid belt, until Uncle Travis came along.

He had the interior living space excavated by means of compressing the rock into enough squeezer bubbles to power the ship out to the edge of the universe, if we cared to go there. If one blew up, they'd see it easily in the Andromeda Galaxy in 2.5 million years. So much power that, after twenty years of shoving this great big rock at one-twentieth of a gee, we have not even had to replace the first set of bubbles. We're still running with the ones installed back at Old Sun and don't anticipate needing to swap them out before we arrive at our new home.

But that big empty space, the one we all live in, is not all that's inside the ship. There are hundreds of other spaces, not nearly so huge, but still pretty big from a human perspective.

Some of them contained large machinery: pumps, fans, sewage-treatment facilities, recycling centers. These were automated wherever possible but usually contained a few human workers. We had toured many of them on school outings. It was the mechanical underbelly to the agricultural and residential uses of the living space. These places tended to be noisy, and not completely clean because of their functions.

The one we were in was a warehouse, and it gleamed as spotless as an operating room.

The ceiling was about a hundred feet above us, dotted with pale white LED lights high above. All around us were shelves reaching to the ceiling. We were traveling down the middle of the main road through the warehouse, with broad aisles stretching away from us on each side to vanishing points. It was dimly lit and spooky in there, except in the few places where people were working, where sensors turned up the illumination. We saw a few forklifts picking things off high shelves, and a couple of flat transport crawlers with plastic crates stacked high.

Some of those crates were just that: ordinary crates with stuff inside. It was all stuff that wasn't perishable. Tools, raw materials, the thousand kilograms of personal belongings that each passenger of *Rolling Thunder* was allowed to take into their new life.

But most of the crates contained black bubbles.

BLINKLINK: *STASIS BUBBLES*: Invented by Jubal Broussard during his protective sequestration on the Falkland Islands. Often called "black bubbles" because of their complete lack of reflectivity. It is thought they are related in some way to compression bubbles, and are created through some as-yet-undescribed quantum effect, but this has been impossible to confirm. Stasis bubbles cannot, strictly speaking, be said to have an "inside," topologically, but it is useful to describe them in those terms. Inside a bubble, no time passes. All chemical and physical reactions are suspended, down to the subatomic level. It is possible, in complete safety, to put living creatures inside. It is thought that whatever is enclosed in the bubble is suspended in a neighboring dimension where time exists differently than in our own universe, but this also has been impossible to prove.

Inside those bubbles could be, literally . . . anything. You name it, we probably have it. Wouldn't it be a bitch to get a dozen light-years from Old Sun and realize you'd forgotten to bring a can opener, or your asthma medication? Trust me, somewhere in the vast warehouses there are a thousand can openers and many gallons of any kind of medication known at the time we left Old Sun.

The biggest bubbles contain water. I have no idea how much, but it is a lot. We conserve every drop, but there are always small losses. The water is in hundred-foot bubbles. It's way more than we'll ever use, but since we have storage space to spare and it masses nothing at all, why not bring it? Water is one of those things, you run out of it, you're screwed. We also carry vast quantities of compressed gases.

Inside some of those bubbles are plants and animals. We have a larger collection of flora and fauna than any natural history museum on Earth, and it's not in glass cases or wooden drawers, dried or mounted on pins. It's all alive. We have snakes and lizards, insects and snails, fish and anemones, birds, spiders, turtles, and mammals from shrews to giraffes. I've seen a lot of these creatures. In school, they can be brought out of their bubbles for biology and taxonomy lessons, just as vital and not one second older than when they went into the bubble twenty years ago. Wild and domestic, we have everything.

Elephants? We have elephants. I love elephants, and I once asked Travis how many we had aboard. He said he thought it was about thirty of them. Why? Well, who knows when you might need an elephant? They are terrific if you need to move something heavy and no longer have fuel for your bulldozer. Plus, they make more elephants, unlike bulldozers. Some of the elephants are brought out on holidays, for parades and to give rides to children.

"Noah was a piker," Uncle Travis said. "He thought too small. He only brought two of everything. Genetically unsound."

It's the same with plants. From trees to toadstools, we have samples of everything Uncle Travis could get his hands on. Somewhere, there are vast bubble granaries of wheat, soybeans, rye, millet, rice, oats, barley, corn, sorghum, spelt, you name it. Who knows what will flourish on our new home, and what will wither and die?

Trees? Pines and plums and pecans, some full-grown, with wrapped root-balls, some seedlings, and lots of seeds.

But the things we brought along that matter most to me, who has only known the voyage and for whom the destination is still a faraway, seldom-thought-of promised land, are the perishables. Blackberry pies still steam-ing from the oven. We can't grow blackberries, they'd soon take over the whole biome. Calamari, still squirming and shooting jets of ink. Chocolate. Maple syrup. The shrimp we had just set out on the table at the party for Papa. Things we either can't produce inside or could make only in severely limited quantities.

"None of the ecologists I hired could *guarantee* this great big ter-rarium could be self-sustaining for a hundred years," Travis once told me and Polly when the family was sitting down to dinner with him. "Some kind of bug could mutate and kill all the plants. Poisons could accumulate in the soil or in the air. Something no one had thought of at all could spring up and screw us big-time. So I made sure that, worse came to worst, we could store a lot of the passengers and have enough food in bubbles to feed us all for a couple of centuries. Besides," he said, cracking open a huge Maine lobster claw, "I've gotten used to traveling first class."

―――――――――

We passed through two more warehouses and one wastewater-treatment plant before the car began a slow, upward climb that gradually grew steeper. I knew we were now under the North End, headed toward the pole. The higher we got, the less we weighed, until when the car eased to a stop, we were very close to the axis and didn't weigh very much.

In fact, we weighed one-twentieth of a gravity. My 140 pounds of mass had turned into just seven pounds.

We were getting no weight from the ship's spin, but there was that steady, gentle but relentless push from the ship's engines, which had been thrusting nonstop for twenty years, since before I was born. That meant that the floor, or the "local vertical" as we spacegirls say, was ninety degrees from the axis of thrust, and the bulk of the ship, including all the interior living space, was directly below us.

There was a room at the end of the train line. It had a big round window . . . in the floor. There was a brass railing running all around it, for those with vertigo, but there was an opening for those who dared. I recalled our first visit to this room, when we were about three or four. It was a good memory, of standing out there on the clear plastic and looking down. I couldn't resist. As soon as we moved carefully off the car, I headed for the window, followed closely by Cassie. We toe-walked—which is the only safe way of travel when you weigh seven pounds—touching the floor very gently, out to the center of the window.

We were slightly offset from the axis of rotation, because that's where our "sun" runs the length of the living space. Part of the window was polarized, so that the big, hot, bright tube that serves us as a sun didn't burn out our retinas.

Looking to one side, we couldn't see anything of the inside of the North Pole, because it was ninety degrees to our position. Down at the rim, inside, what we would see was a huge mural, with forced perspective that made it look like the interior of the ship was a lot longer than it actually was. The best way to see from this position was to lie down, prone, and put your face against the plastic. Polly and I did that.

The surface curved away from us gradually, until about a third of the way down, when the spin gravity was big enough to be an appreciable factor, water gushed out from big outlets spaced 120 degrees around the North Pole. These were the sources of the three rivers that meandered through the living space, then plunged back underground on the flats before the upward curve of the South Pole. There was more false perspective there, in the form of sculpted "mountains" with snow painted on their peaks. The mountains were not very deep. From up here you could see they were almost as flat as scenery scrims on a stage.

About halfway down, where the curve of the end cap had become less steep—around forty-five degrees—were the first human habitations, in the medium-grav region. It wasn't a *lot* lower grav than on the flat inner surface, but it was definitely enough that you could feel the difference. A lot of the older residents lived there.

It was also the location of Hilltown, home of the hated Hillbillies, the nastiest skypool team, boys and girls both, in the ship. Home of the Horrible Cheryl Chang, the girl who never passed up a chance for an illegal hit. I was pretty sure I could pick out the school from here, looking down on Hilltown. Too bad there was no way to open a hatch and drop something nasty on it.

Finally, the slope of the North End flattened out to the main floor of the ship. I could see the rivers gleaming silver in the light: the Mississippi, the Amazon, and the Congo. None of them were anything like their namesakes, and they would have qualified as nothing more than quiet trout streams on Earth. But from up here they were lovely, the quietly flowing, life-giving arteries of my world. They fed into small ponds like the one at our house, and each one fed into a single larger lake at a different point in its course: Lake Baikal, the deepest and most placid, Lake Michigan, and Lake Titicaca, which had the best fishing.

Looking south on the plains, you would immediately see the rings. The interior of *Rolling Thunder* is a series of terraces that run right around the circumference of the cylinder. This is necessary because of the spin gravity and the thrust gravity coming from different directions.

The spin of the ship forces everything away from the center axis at about two-thirds of a gee.

The thrust runs parallel to the axis and tends to pull everything to the south at one-twentieth of a gee.

If the interior were perfectly flat, there would be two bad results. For one thing, all the water inside would flow too fast toward the south. The rivers would become more like cascading mountain streams than the placidly wandering great rivers of Earth they are named for.

Also, we would all have to walk slightly canted toward the north to overcome the effects of the thrust gravity. Houses would have to be built with one end slightly higher than the other, or else anything you dropped on the floor would roll to the south.

"I thought of just shortening everybody's left leg a little," Uncle Travis told us with a perfectly straight face one day when we were seven. "That would work fine as long as we only walked to the east. But if we walked north or south, we'd be lopsided, and if we walked west, we'd fall over." We believed this fable for a little while, thinking with a certain horror about operations to shorten legs, until Papa told us his cousin loved to "bamboozle" people, as he put it. After that, we always took anything Uncle Travis said under advisement before we believed it.

"Girls! What the heck are you doing? This isn't a field trip."

That would be Mama. We raised ourselves from the ground and jetted over to them, stopping ourselves with our hands against the wall near a double door. I got a good look at Papa, and it was no surprise that he was looking green. Papa doesn't like low-gee, no-gee, and especially variable-gee. The trip up here had been an ordeal for him.

The elevator doors opened, and we moved in, Polly and I holding Papa's hands so he wouldn't smash into the opposite wall. We all grabbed a handrail. The doors closed, and we suddenly had about half a gee as the car accelerated upward. That went away quickly as the car reached its top speed. The shaft is about a mile and a half long.

"The ceiling will become the floor in forty-five seconds." It was an automated warning. "Please reverse your position, with your feet on the surface that is blinking green. Hold on to the handrails. The ceiling will become the floor in thirty seconds."

"Song about that," Papa said, as Polly and I turned him carefully. His forehead was covered in beads of sweat, and I could feel him trembling.

"Sorry, Papa," Polly said. "What was that?"

"Song, an old song. Can't 'member the name. 'One man's ceiling is another man's floor.'"

"Paul Simon," Mama said. "The album was *There Goes Rhymin' Simon*." Never heard of him. It didn't surprise me that Mama knew it even though it was way before her time. There's not much about music that Mama doesn't know.

The weird thing was, Papa might have heard it when it was new. Papa was eighteen at the turn of the century. How weird must *that* be, living in *Rolling Thunder*, halfway to the stars, when you can remember a time when humans hadn't even landed on Mars?

Mama was reaching into her purse. She took out a pressure injector and bit off the tip. She was gently turning him around so his feet would point the right way. I eased closer and helped her. I whispered in her ear.

"Didn't you give him his pill?" I asked.

"Two of them," she said. "I knew this was going to be bad, but it's worse than I feared. I know the signs. And it's fixing to get worse."

She pressed the end of the injector to his upper arm.

"Jubal, honey, there's gonna be a little popping sound."

"Popping?"

She flicked the button, and we all heard it. The drug was forced through his skin, almost painlessly. He didn't seem to notice it.

"Prepare for deceleration."

All of us but Papa grabbed the handrails and pressed our feet to the wall that would soon be the floor. Mama and I each held on to one of Papa's arms. Polly had edged over in front, and was holding Papa's feet to the floor. The deceleration built quickly, and for a moment we all seemed to be standing. Papa looked confused and started to move away from the wall.

"This be our floor?"

"Not yet, hon. We'll hold on to you."

"'Kay."

The car came to a halt, and we were almost weightless again.

"Let's get him turned before the door opens," Mama said. Good idea, I realized. When it opened, the room beyond would seem upside down. We gently swung him through 180 degrees. I heard the elevator door open behind us.

"Okay, Jubal," Mama said. "This is where we get off, *cher.*"

We turned him around and moved slowly out onto the bridge.

Most Thunderites (or Rollers, or Rockenrollers; there are several schools of thought on the matter) have never been to the bridge.

The things that keep *Rolling Thunder* thunderously rolling (albeit silently) are managed from different control rooms scattered around beneath the inner surface, out of sight. Atmosphere monitoring, power, water, sewage, recycling, ground ecology, crop rotation, fertilization, weather control, warehousing, the jail, some other things I don't know much about, and subsystems of all of them each have underground central stations, and some have local ones. Human factors such as policing, courts, schools, scheduling of meetings and entertainment and elections, are all located in civic buildings on the inner surface.

The bridge is concerned solely with propulsion and navigation.

The computers do all the heavy lifting—which, at this point in the trip, consists mainly of small course corrections—so there really isn't all that much to do, and for that reason and for security purposes, only a handful of trained technicians have clearance to go there regularly.

And, of course, family of the captain.

The great majority of the work is done, as elsewhere, by automated systems. The ring of six almost infinitely powerful squeezer bubbles at the stern is held in place by gigantic scaffolds that must be constantly monitored for heat, but mostly for stress.

There is just one workstation for astrogation, known as the Captain's Chair, and it is manned twenty-four/seven. Uncle Travis admitted to us, during our first visit to the bridge, that he knew it was silly, but there was just something that fundamentally bugged him about an eight-mile-long ship hurtling through space near the speed of light with no one at the stick.

So there has been someone "at the stick" continually for all my life. Shifts are six hours, or until one is formally relieved.

The ceiling of the bridge is a clear dome, inscribed with lines of declination and right ascension so that it doesn't seem invisible, so that you don't get the sense of sitting on the naked rock of *Rolling Thunder*'s bow.

Well . . . actually not.

It's a superdef screen. Far from being in the actual bow, there was still a quarter of a mile of solid rock over our heads.

You hear about "empty interstellar space," but it's not really empty. Compared to inter*planetary* space, it's pretty thin, but compared to inter-*galactic* space, it's thick as pea soup. The density varies, but the average is one molecule per cubic centimeter. That's one million molecules per cubic meter, nine hundred thousand of them hydrogen, and ninety thousand of them helium. Even considering the considerable surface area of the ship, that's not enough to slow us down. If we turned off the engines right now, the ship would continue going at the same velocity forever, for all practical purposes.

However, at .77c—143,000 miles per second and change—that stuff would impact with a hell of a lot of power. I don't understand it all, but I think that it would hit with the power of gamma rays.

The other 1 percent in that cubic meter is dust. Not the sort that forms dust bunnies under your bed, but particles of just about anything, chiefly silicates, carbon, water, and iron. I think of it as wet rocks. Some of the gas and dust can be very hot. I don't understand how that can be, since the median "temperature of interstellar space" is three degrees above absolute zero. Papa says don't worry about it, it's just a confusion of terminology. As in all things physical, I take his word for it.

Some of that dust isn't much bigger than the gas molecules, but some of it is *enormous*, relatively speaking. Up to a tenth of a micrometer. That's one ten-millionth of a meter, which is pretty damn tiny, looked at one way, but when it's arriving at three-quarters of the speed of light, even if there are only a few of the "big" ones in every cubic meter, we are moving through . . . well, I don't know the number, but it's an incredible volume of space every second. It can all add up.

However, all that is mooted by the presence of the Shield.

Captain Broussard is a belt-and-suspenders guy. The thickness of the rock at the bow would be more than enough to protect us from radiation and any damage from incoming dust. It would probably take a billion years for that dust to ablate a few inches. But out in front of us, traveling at the same speed we are, is a silver squeezer bubble, something like half a million miles across. It is held permanently at the same distance from us by one of Papa's mysterious fields. It is absolutely invulnerable to anything anyone has yet discovered. Molecules and dust grains bounce off it, leaving a wide tube of space in its wake that is, as far as we know, the most perfect vacuum that exists anywhere in the universe. That tube will eventually close up, but *Rolling Thunder* will have passed through it long before that.

So in reality, *nothing* is impacting the bow of the ship.

I once asked my uncle why we needed to have all that rock between the Bridge and the surface.

"What if the Shield fails?" he said.

In the century we have been using them, no bubble has ever failed. But that's my uncle Travis. A cautious man.

———————

I recognized the watch-stander, in her uniform. She had graduated from the Bayouville School two years ahead of me and been the captain of the Gators skypool team when Polly and I joined. She was reading something in a book.

"Hi, Lori," Polly called out. "Working hard, or hardly working?"

Lori's eyes grew wide when she saw who was visiting. Papa was not in any way in the chain of command over her, but plenty of people hold him in awe. She wasn't goofing off, she wasn't doing anything wrong at all, but I guess she *felt* guilty, up there technically in charge of the ship, reading. She reflexively and unwisely started to spring to her feet and was on a trajectory to bang her head hard on the ceiling, but snagged the arm of her chair just in time. That twisted her awkwardly. She was blushing red as she got herself planted, spine straight, eyes ahead, and saluted.

Papa was way too far gone to notice her; otherwise, he would have smiled, gone over, and shaken her hand. Papa has very little sense of his own importance, and though he is terribly shy in crowds, he always greets everyone individually as a long-lost friend.

We didn't pause long enough to talk to Lori. Mama marched us right to the only other door on the Bridge, directly across from the elevator. She pressed her thumb to a panel on the wall, then helped Jubal do the same.

The door closed behind us. I helped Mama support Papa, who was still glassy-eyed but no longer looked panicky. I wasn't sure he was aware of his surroundings.

There were a few twists and turns in the passage. There was nothing obvious, but I knew there were multiple security measures in place. If we had been intruders we would have been stopped a dozen times before we got to the inner sanctum, and killed if we showed the least sign of aggression. If there had been any unauthorized person with us—perhaps holding us hostage—we would have been hit with knockout gas and Tasers. If the intruder was wearing a pressure suit, if he had been using one of us as a human shield, the defense programs were sophisticated enough to take him out without harming us. Or so we all fondly hoped.

We came to another door and had to ID ourselves again. It opened, and we entered a dimly lit room.

There was nothing remarkable about it except for the big black bubble held in place by a delicate lattice. The room was cut in half by a barely visible sheet of very strong plastic. There was a door in the center, thick as a bank vault. I could see complicated mechanisms inside it, moving like clockwork.

"Hello. Podkayne. Jubal. Cassie. Polly." It was Travis's voice, but not Travis. "What's up?"

Papa looked up and around him at the familiar voice.

"Travis?"

"*Cher*, you need to give him the password," Mama told him.

"Password?"

"The emergency code. The one that will interrupt his sleep before it's scheduled. It's never been used, and you're the only one who knows it."

"Password . . . oh, right. Only it ain't a word, it's a verse."

"A passverse?" I asked.

He glanced at me and gave me a small smile.

"Yeah, a passverse." He cleared his throat, and stood like a student reciting a lesson. Then he waited.

"Go ahead, Jubal honey. Say it."

"Okay. 'When in danger, when in doubt, run in circles, scream and shout.'"

And Uncle Travis appeared.

CHAPTER 5

Polly:

The first five seconds are always the same with Travis. The bubble goes away and there he is, a foot off the ground. The bubble has been positioned so that it is impossible to get behind it. He's facing the bulletproof and blast-resistant barrier, in a crouch, his hand on the gun in the holster at his side.

That's the thing about going into a black bubble. Time is suspended. When you come out, anything could have happened. Aliens could have captured the ship and enslaved us all. We could have been hit by the shock wave of a supernova.

"Maybe my ex-wife invented faster-than-light travel and is standing there with a court order for back alimony payments," he once said to us. Joke. Ha-ha. But he has many, many enemies back at Old Sun, and if they *did* catch up with him with powerful new technology, it could be gruesome.

And don't tell me that's ridiculous. When we get really close to small c, the speed of light, that old clock will be turning like mad back at Old Sun, while it crawls for us. Who knows what will be discovered in the next hundred years?

He drifts down to the floor, his eyes scanning the people on the other side of the barrier. This time, like always when I have been there, he relaxed visibly when he saw only friends and family. Then he glanced at the clock on the wall behind us . . .

And this time the script changed. The last thing he does, always, going into the bubble, is remind himself what that clock should be reading when he comes out. Every time before this, he had been exactly on schedule. Routine, all systems go, five by five, AOK, *tous sont bien.*

Not today. He did a double take worthy of a comedian. It was almost a year before Groundhog Day, but Captain Travis was definitely seeing his shadow. He hurried over to the door and opened it.

"Jubal! What's the haps, my friend?"

He put his hands on his cousin's shoulders and tried to look into his eyes. But Papa was completely out of it, unable to do anything but stare down at his shoes and, probably, wish they would attach themselves more firmly to the floor. Mama came close to him.

"Travis, as you can see, Jubal is very upset about something. We felt we had no choice but to wake you up early."

Uncle Travis held out an arm, and she moved near him. He pulled her closer and kissed her on the cheek.

"What is it, old buddy? Can you talk to me?"

All Papa managed was to shake his head. He mumbled something.

"It's the low grav," I said. Travis glanced at me, then down at my arm in the sling. He frowned, but didn't say anything to me.

"You want to get out of here, *cher*? Then let's blow."

He and Mama started steering Papa toward the exit. Travis held out his free arm to me, and I moved to him.

"Hey there, Chip. Come over here, Dale. How'd you bust the wing?"

That's what he calls us sometimes. Last time I was Chip and Cassie was Dale. We decided a long time ago that it's because he usually can't tell which one of us is which, so instead of getting it wrong, he uses those names interchangeably. It's a reference to some cartoon squirrels—or is it chipmunks? We don't have wild rodents, but I've seen them at the zoo. Chip is the clever, rational one (that would be me, I think most people would agree) and Dale is the harebrain (Cassie, obviously).

"It's nothing," I said. Travis cocked his head, nodded, and kissed me on the cheek. He used to kiss us on the foreheads, but we got too tall.

"Up to no good, as usual, I assume. Hey, Chip, come over here. Why aren't you looking out for your sister?"

Chip, indeed. *Dale* came over and pecked him on the cheek.

"She takes too much looking out for. I'll tell you about it one of these days." She winked at me. I had no doubt she'd fill him in on all the dirty details.

Papa perked up when he felt gravity again—well, what we use for gravity, which feels the same—and was almost back to normal when we entered the house.

Where Cassie and I were promptly told to go out and play in the sandbox with our other little friends and their toys.

I really hadn't expected that.

"Mama," Cassie groused, "why did you take us all the way up to the Bridge if you weren't going to tell us what's going on? I mean, it's—"

She caught my look, and shut up. As I said, we really don't communicate telepathically, and we don't really have a private, secret language like some twins apparently do, but we're adept at reading each other's signals. Tiny movements of her eyes or hands that others don't even notice speak volumes to me, and it works just as well the other way. We are both happy to undercut the other when there's some advantage to be gained, but when it comes to someone screwing around with both of us, it's "You and me against the world, sis." That includes unreasonable parents.

So we watched them steal off to Mama and Papa's bedroom, like spies or something, and didn't protest anymore. As soon as the door closed we looked at each other and high-fived. We took off to our own rooms.

We changed into grungy T-shirts and jeans. It was going to be dirty work.

Even here in *Rolling Thunder*, where we mostly get along with each other—except in sports—there are those who would like to learn Papa's "secrets." So many people are convinced that, if only they could listen to him in an unguarded moment, *they* could have the secret of unlimited power, too. Travis tried to keep those types out when he was approving the passenger list for the voyage, just as he automatically eliminated everyone he deemed a religious fanatic, but you can only go so far in determining what someone's inner thoughts are. There are conspiracy theories anywhere you go, and the idea that Travis and Papa are keeping the squeezer technology a secret for their own personal gain, and that it's something you could write out in a textbook and anyone, or at least any scientist, could understand, is a tempting one.

One reason it's tempting is that it is *partially* true.

When Travis and Great-grandfather Manny and Great-grandmother Kelly returned from the first trip to Mars, it was clear to the whole world that they had a new source of power, cheap, easy to use, and virtually limitless. Like most great blessings, it came with a curse, and this one was even worse than atomic power. A squeezer bubble could be made into a bomb that would dwarf any nuclear weapon ever built. It was imperative that it not be allowed to fall into the wrong hands . . . but what were the wrong hands? If Travis gave the technology to the Americans, how would the Chinese and the Indians and the Russians and the Germans react? Not well, he knew.

So he kept it to himself. He and Papa became enormously rich, but no bubble was ever used for destruction. No bubble bomb was ever exploded.

The true horror of bubble power arrived from where we were now, from interstellar space.

BLINKLINK: *DEATH STAR*: 1) A fictional space station in the movie *Star Wars* (1977). 2) A starship launched in the early twenty-first century, shortly after the invention of compression bubbles. It was one of many starships of that period, built to take advantage of unlimited thrust. During what was called the Great Stellar Diaspora, many countries and organizations built ships of various sizes and boosted into interstellar space. For unknown reasons, only one of these ships ever returned to the Sol system. It had apparently accelerated to near the speed of light, decelerated, then accelerated again with the intent of colliding with North America. It arrived slightly off course, hitting in the Atlantic Ocean and generating a huge tsunami. It inflicted tremendous damage on the American East Coast, the Caribbean, northern South America, and western Africa. Millions were killed. It was never determined with certainty who was responsible, or what their goals were. To this day, no one has been able to explain how the Death Star alone, among hundreds of other ships, was the only one to return to its point of origin.

The horrible thing is that this big secret, this key to unlimited power that so many people covet, is something that Papa would gladly give away. But he hasn't been able to. Travis always assumed that someone else would discover the secret someday. That's just how it works in science. There are no "secrets," just things you don't know the answer to yet.

But this thing turned out to be remarkably elusive. Almost a century later, no one but Papa knows how to make either sort of bubble, and Papa hasn't been able to show anyone how to do it. It seems to be a trick of the mind, and so far, Papa has the only mind that can do it.

Our house has great security, though you wouldn't know it to look at it. We're protected from any kind of listening from outside. Any audio or video or cyber bug would be sniffed out and stomped on in about a millisecond and, in most cases, tracked back to the source, and somebody would go to jail. These defenses are tested regularly with any new spying technology, and so far have never failed.

In addition, we are physically protected. The windows are not bulletproof—nothing is, against a big enough bullet—but they will stop most stuff. The walls are weathered wood on the outside, but behind that is armor plating.

We are also the only home in the ship that has guns inside it. It pained Travis to go that route, as he is a firm believer in firearms. The ship carries an arsenal worthy of a third-world dictatorship, but most of it is stored away in bubbles until we get to New Sun. There is a range where people can learn to shoot, but you have to surrender the guns after your session. It works pretty well. In twenty years, we've had only two murders.

There are guns in our home. We all know how to use them.

So what I'm saying is that if you want to attack us or spy on us, good luck with that. You're going to lose, and maybe die.

But Travis didn't plan for one thing: an attack from within. Cassie and I cracked the house security when we were eight.

We got the idea from an old movie about the U.S. Navy. The water Navy, guys riding around in battleships and destroyers in the First Nuclear War. These guys would be talking into little bell-shaped things, and voices would come out of them. We asked Papa what kind of electronics they used, and he said none. He said sound could travel a long way through a pipe.

So one day when Mama was out, we went into their bedroom and planted our spy device. The ceiling in there is knotty pine, actual wood. There is a hanging light fixture that looks like a wagon wheel with kerosene lamps on the rim, something Papa remembered fondly from a house he used to live in. We climbed up there and punched a knot out of the ceiling.

Then Cassie climbed up to the attic access door in the utility room and tried listening through the knot. When she came down, I told her the ceiling creaked when she was up there. Just as well, we figured. There wasn't much we could see down there because the light was in the way, and anyway, we didn't want to watch them. We just wanted to listen in. Never can tell when you might overhear something important, something you need to know.

So we rigged a length of flexible hose to run the length of the house to a little listening station near the attic access hatch. We attached a wire to the knot and ran it through some pulleys, then worked and polished the knot so it would lift out when we pulled, and fall back into place when we let it go.

So the first time we used it, what did we hear? You guessed it, Mama and Papa making love. We hustled our nosy little asses out of there and didn't go back for weeks.

But eventually we listened more. It was only moderately useful to us. We learned of a few plans here and there, but what we mostly heard was routine stuff. That and, over and over again, how much they loved us, how worried they sometimes were about us, how angry they sometimes got with us, and *still* loved us . . .

We tapered off to almost no spying at all. It was embarrassing, made me feel small, and I dreaded to think what it would be like if we were discovered. I don't think I'd been up there since we were fourteen.

But this was different. We didn't even have to discuss it. We hurried to the utility room and Cassie made a stirrup with her hands for me since I had the busted arm. I easily one-armed myself up into the attic; then she jumped, and I caught her arm and helped haul her up.

"Jeez," she whispered. "Dust."

There was a tiny light. I switched it on. The dust was thick, coating every surface. Cassie sat on the floor and picked up one of the earpieces and moved it toward her mouth.

"Don't blow the dust off!" I hissed. "We don't dare sneeze. Let's get as little of the dust in the air as we can."

She nodded, and we both cleaned off the earpieces—cups that fit over our ears, attached to lengths of plastic tubing we had salvaged from one of Aunt Elizabeth's old stethoscopes—and wiped them off on our shirttails. Then we sat together and put the things to our ears.

I switched on my recorder. What follows is an edited transcript of what we heard, minus all the irrelevancies. There was ten minutes of small talk, calming Papa down enough so he could think and speak. Then the interesting stuff begins:

JUBAL: *Travis, we gotta stop the ship.*

TRAVIS: *Okay,* cher, *Podkayne told me that already. I guess you know that is not going to be easy.*

JUBAL: *But we all gonna die, us, if we don't stop acceleratin'.*

TRAVIS: *Okay, my friend. But first, you have to try to make me understand what the problem is. Can you do that?*

JUBAL: *I don't know. It's one of those complicated things.*

PODKAYNE: *Meaning it's some science thing we won't understand.*

JUBAL: *I don't mean . . . I mean . . . it's not a stupid thing, it's . . .*

PODKAYNE: *Don't worry about that, honey. I know I'm not stupid, and I know that Travis isn't stupid, and I also know that neither of us are able to understand a lot of the things that you do easily.*

TRAVIS: *Remember Einstein and his thought experiments? You don't have to be able to do the math to understand them. Can you think of something like that?*

JUBAL: *I dunno, Travis. I guess I can try.*

[Long silence]

PODKAYNE: *Maybe we can narrow it down. Want to try that?*

TRAVIS: *Is it something to do with the ship? Is . . . is there something catastrophic about to happen to the ship itself?*

JUBAL: *No, nothing like that.*

TRAVIS: *The engines, maybe? They've been blasting for twenty years. Can something go wrong with them if we keep blasting?*

JUBAL: *No, the engines, they be fine.*

TRAVIS: *We're going mighty fast.*

JUBAL: *Seventy-seven percent of the speed of light. I don't think nobody has ever gone that fast, me.*

TRAVIS: *Sure they have. All those ships that went out, years ago . . .*

PODKAYNE: *And only one of them came back, Travis.*

JUBAL: *That's what it's about. Why no one come back.*

[Short silence]

TRAVIS: *I'm not sure I understand.*

JUBAL: *I looked it up. It was 553. Some of 'em no more than a dozen passengers, no bigger than a big shrimp boat, accelerating at two gees so's they could get where they goin' in a hurry.*

PODKAYNE: *Most of them were a lot bigger than that.*

TRAVIS: *But none of them were nearly as big as* Rolling Thunder. *Does that have something to do with it?*

JUBAL: *My head, it be hurtin'.*

PODKAYNE: *You want to take a break? Get something to eat?*

JUBAL: *I couldn't eat,* cher.

PODKAYNE: *So . . . it isn't the size of the ship. What else is different?*

JUBAL: *That ain't it. Most of 'em were fair-size. And pretty much all of 'em was acceleratin' at one gee.*

TRAVIS: *What does that have to do with anything?*

JUBAL: *Means they all got to three-quarters of the speed of light a lot quicker'n we done. We the slowest ship ever gone out.*

TRAVIS: *Lowest acceleration, sure. Go on.*

JUBAL: *So after not very long, they got up to 90 percent. 'Bout 170,000 miles per second. And I'm thinkin' that's where they started to get into trouble.*

TRAVIS: *Trouble with what?*

JUBAL: *With the ether.*

[Long silence]

TRAVIS: *Help me here. I thought the idea of ether was disproved a long time ago. Wasn't it the Michelson-Morley experiment?*

JUBAL: *Not that ether. The other one.*

PODKAYNE: *Guys, help me out here. You're the scientists, I'm just a washed-up pop star.*

TRAVIS: *I'm not a scientist, I'm a washed-up astronaut.*

PODKAYNE: *I'll bet you didn't flunk Quantum Physics 101.*

TRAVIS: *Back before Einstein, when they were just figuring out how light worked, and a lot of other things, they thought that space was filled with something they called ether. It was something that was supposed to serve as a medium to conduct light waves. Like water conducts waves, and air conducts sound waves. It made sense to think that light couldn't travel through space without some medium to conduct it, though we had never detected it. You want to know how they proved there was no ether?*

PODKAYNE: *Don't patronize me, Travis. I've heard of ether, I just needed my memory refreshed. What they proved is, it doesn't exist, right?*

JUBAL: *That's right. Poddy, Travis, don't fight.*

TRAVIS: *Sorry, Jubal. Yeah, Pod, they proved it didn't exist. But it wouldn't be the first time a basic law of physics got overturned. And Jubal would be the guy to do it. Is that the deal, Jubal?*

JUBAL: *No, no. Well, not that way, no. I just picked that name up, me, because ain't nobody using it.*

TRAVIS: *So you dusted it off and plugged it in somewhere else.*

JUBAL: *Dusted it . . .* [laughs] *Dusted it off! That's funny, that is.*

PODKAYNE: *Go on, hon.*

JUBAL: *Okay. It be something* like *ether. It's everywhere, only we can't detect it. It be thinner in some places and thicker in others. Like the dust between the stars. We've knew it be there for a while, we can see some of the things it do, only nobody can put they finger on it.*

TRAVIS: *Make it sit up and do tricks in the lab.*

JUBAL: *It ain't never been in no lab.*

PODKAYNE: *Listen, honey, you said that people have known about this stuff, this new ether, for a long time. Right?*

JUBAL: *Yeah.*

PODKAYNE: *So like the British used to say, what is it when it's at home? What did they call it before?*

JUBAL: *Oh, my, that where I should have started off, ain't it?*

PODKAYNE: *That's okay. So what do they call it?*

JUBAL: *They call it dark energy.*

[Long silence]

TRAVIS: *So you're saying you know something about—*

PODKAYNE: *Hang on a minute, Travis.*

[Sounds of a wooden chair being set on the floor. A short pause, and then . . . *BLAAAAAT!!!!*]

We snatched the pieces from our ears. That *hurt!*

"What the hell was that?" Cassie whispered.

"Spacegirl," I said, "I think that was the sound of our lives crashing and burning. Let's get the heck out of here."

We scrambled to the hatch and opened it. I looked down . . . straight into the eyes of Mama. She stood there with her arms crossed in a posture no child could ever fail to understand. *You're in a world of hurt, kid.*

"Rats in the attic, Travis."

"Rats? We never let . . . Oh, no. Rugrats?"

"You might as well come down headfirst," Mama said. "Then I can call an ambulance instead of kill you."

Don't worry, it was an empty threat. Neither Mama nor Papa has ever laid a hand on us.

"I can't believe I forgot about their little spy outpost," Mama was saying as we came down. "I guess it was the stress of the day. Plus, they haven't been up there listening in for years."

I saw Cassie's jaw drop. Mine probably did, too.

"Yeah, your dumb old mama ain't as dumb as you thought," she said, glaring at us. "I picked up on your spying probably three days after you set it up. I put a simple little switch under your station. When somebody was up there, your weight closed it and lit up a pinlight on the wall."

"But why didn't you . . ."

"Tear it out?" She laughed. "You kids don't know much about spying. When you discover a mole, or a bug, it's much better to leave them in place. That way you can control the information. You girls learned exactly what I wanted you to learn. Nothing more."

"Girls," Travis said, sternly, "I'm ashamed of you." But one corner of his mouth turned up the least little bit, and his eyes were twinkling. Mama looked at him suspiciously but sighed and returned her attention to us.

"I know I should have taken it out after you stopped using it. But I was . . . What's the word? Nostalgic? I thought in my old age I might go up there and root through the old furniture and keepsakes, and get a laugh out of your antics. I never expected you to be perfect, Cassie Ann and Polly Sue. God knows I wasn't. The thing is, if you're going to spy, you shouldn't *get caught.*"

All I was seeing was everybody's feet. I felt about two inches tall. I heard my sister speak.

"Does . . . does Papa . . ."

"Papa knows nothing. You know Papa loves you more than anything in the universe. And you know he doesn't notice a lot of things. He thinks different from us, and he couldn't imagine that you would betray him. If he understood that you had . . . well, we all know how much it would hurt him."

My face felt hot enough to melt.

"Ease up a little, Podkayne," Travis said.

I looked up, and he was holding his palms out as if expecting a blow from Mama. Say what you want about Mama Podkayne—and I've said plenty over the years—there is no mama bear in the forest who would fight more fiercely for her daughters. And that includes unwanted parenting advice. Travis had always steered clear of it, in her presence, though he would sometimes give us a wink or sneak us a treat when we were banished to our room.

I was expecting more fireworks, but this time she just sighed.

"Maybe you're right. I couldn't take the chance, though. When I needed to talk to him about things these little monsters shouldn't hear, I took him to the music room." She glared at us again. "Which I checked very carefully for bugs."

Another heavy sigh. We were such a trial for her, I admit it.

"Okay, here's what's going to happen. You've already learned more than I wanted you to know. There's not much point in keeping you from hearing the rest of it, whatever it is. And it might be very bad, you understand that?"

"Yes, ma'am," I said.

"I guess it's time I started treating you as adults. Trying to, anyway, though it would help me out if you would every once in a while *behave* like adults. Got it?"

"Got it," Cassie whispered, and I nodded, unable to speak.

"Okay. Let's go see your father." She started off, then turned around quickly and glared at us once again. "Go clean up. You're filthy." Then she grinned, slowly. "And when we're through here, you've brought it to my attention that the attic hasn't been cleaned up since shortly after you were born. While you're up there dismantling your spy equipment, later, I want you to make it sparkle. I'll be inspecting it with white gloves."

She turned away too fast to hear our a cappella groans.

Papa has his little laboratory out back, Mama has her music room.

Their bedroom is at the back of the house, up against a low hill. Like everything else in the interior, the hill is fake. It conceals the lower level, which is reached by a door in their bedroom that leads to eight steps going down and a soundproof door at the bottom. Beyond the door is Mama's recording studio and the bulk of her collection of musical instruments.

She started it when she got rich. I doubt she has an example of *every* kind of instrument there is, but she has a lot. There's everything from harmonicas (about fifty of them) and ocarinas, all eight kinds of saxophone (soprillo, sopranino, soprano, alto, tenor, baritone, bass, and contrabass, as we learned one day), violins, violas, a cello and a stand-up bass, hundreds of percussion instruments, and two Steinway concert grand pianos. She can at least make a creditable sound on almost all of them. She's best on keyboards, which she has been taking lessons on since before we were born.

A small part of her collection, what she likes the best, became the bedroom theme when she was decorating. Her prizes are either in display cases or mounted on the walls. It's pretty to look at; musical instruments have their own strict logic but are also works of art in themselves. There is an electric guitar once used by somebody in a band called the Beatles, an accordion—"squeezebox" to Papa—that was Clifton Chenier's, and a lot of other historical axes.

What Mama had done was grab Dizzy Gillespie's bent trumpet off the wall, stand on a chair, put the bell up to the knothole in the ceiling, and nearly pop our eardrums. I could have wished she had used Mozart's harpsichord instead. My ears were ringing for hours.

—————————

After a quick cleanup, we joined them in the bedroom.

"Jubal, you want to take up where you left off?"

Well, Papa did *want* to do that, but his language skills are never quite up to just telling a story in a meaningful sequence. That brilliant brain that understands quantum physics like I understand the sprockets on a flycycle just leaps from one thing to another without much logical sense behind it. Maybe that's what makes his mind able to make those leaps in mathematical and scientific logic that no one else can follow. All the remaining language logic circuits in his brain are already tied up in other stuff.

So there is not much point in my trying to set it all down as he told it. It took two hours to get it all in a form the other four of us could follow, if not completely understand. A summary will work much better.

This is what Papa told us:

—————————

The universe, *cher*, it be a strange place . . .

We figure that the observable universe is about 93 billion light-years across. It's 13.5 billion years old. There are hundreds of billions of galaxies, maybe even a trillion, though that's a tough number to pin down, and it refers only to the "observable universe," which is that part of the universe we can theoretically interact with. There are probably parts—maybe even the majority of it—that we can never interact with, even if we were traveling at the speed of light, because the universe can expand *faster* than the speed of light. As we head for the edge of it, I guess, the edge gets farther and farther away. If it *has* an edge, which it probably doesn't.

All this, according to Papa. I'll take his word for it.

So, say a trillion galaxies. Our Milky Way has about four hundred billion stars in it. Most of the others do, too, or even more. That comes to about one hundred sextillion stars. Some are much, much bigger than Old Sun, some are much smaller. Say Old Sun is about average in mass—I have no idea if it is, but just say. It masses about two octillion tons.

Two octillion tons (2 times 10^{27}) times one hundred sextillion stars

(10^{23}) equals two hundred quindecillion tons (2 times 10^{50}), the mass of all the stars in the observable universe. You can throw in all the planets, asteroids, comets, and such and not affect the final total much; it's like tossing a few pennies in a bucket of hundred-dollar coins. (There's also a hell of a lot of neutrinos, but let's not even go there. I don't like neutrinos; their very existence offends me.) I like to write out numbers like that, because it gives me a better sense of just how huge they are. Two hundred quindecillion looks like this:

200,000,000,000,000,000,000,000,000,000,000,000,000,000,
000,000

That's the mass of all the stars there are, and it seems like so much. It sounds pretty crowded, too, but it's not. You could travel almost eternally through it at the speed of light and your chances of hitting a star would be virtually zero. Galaxies collide with each other all the time, vast conglomerations of a hundred billion stars, but the stars are so small, relatively, and so spread out with such immense distances between them that collisions of stars are very rare.

And stars are not even the bulk of it. If you add in the free hydrogen and helium *between* the stars and galaxies, you would have to multiply that huge number by four.

And *that's* far from the end of it. That is the *visible* universe. We see stars by the light they give off, and clouds of gas by the effects they have on the starlight passing through them. Matter, all of it matter. Matter generates gravity.

However, that visible matter is only a small portion of what's *really* there. From the way galaxies behave and from the way light is distorted when there's nothing obvious there to distort it, and from other clues, cosmologists have deduced that there's a lot more matter out there than the stuff we can see. In fact, there's *five times* as much.

But we're *still* not done.

I'm not going to deal with the current prevailing theory of how it all began, the Big Bang theory. I always saw it as an explosion, with everything rushing away from a center point, like you see in films of an explosion. Papa says this is only partly true, but it can be a useful way to visualize it. But the logic breaks down quickly. From where we are, in the Milky Way galaxy, everything but our very close neighboring galaxies seems to be rushing away from us. The more distant it is, the faster it is rushing away. What, was it something we said? Do we smell bad?

Since no matter which direction you look, everything is moving *away* from us, you'd think that meant we just happen to be the center of the universe. That would be a nice thing to think, wouldn't it? Like before telescopes and such things, people thought the Earth was the center of the universe, and Old Sun and all the stars and planets revolved around it. Made them sort of special, and don't we all want that?

But it ain't so. Papa says that no matter where we were in the universe, everything would seem to be rushing away from us. That's because since the universe is expanding, space *itself* is expanding. Papa used a balloon to show us how that made sense. You draw dots on the surface of a balloon, and say those are galaxies. Now blow the balloon up. All of the dots move away from all the other dots, because the balloon is stretching. That's a two-dimensional model of what's happening in three dimensions. The balloon's surface is two-dimensional, but it's curved.

So, the universe is expanding. But gravity—including all that dark matter—should be tending to slow it down. Eventually, it would stop expanding and start to collapse back on itself, like the rocks thrown in the air by an explosion on a planet eventually stop rising and fall back to the ground.

Except about a hundred years ago they found out that's not what's happening. Everybody expected that the rate of expansion would be slowing down, so that it would eventually stop and start contracting. Another possibility was that the rate of expansion would stay steady. The third, and what most scientists thought was the least likely to be true, was that the rate of expansion could be *increasing*.

And that's exactly what they found. In some unimaginable future, the universe will stretch so thin that the light from one galaxy would be unable to reach any other galaxy. Eventually, all the stars would burn out, and the universe would consist of the dead cinders of stars, black holes, and uncountable googolplexes of cubic light-years of cold, empty space.

So have fun while you can, because the future is bleak. If you live forever, that is.

But this discovery raised more questions than it answered.

To have all those galaxies rushing away from each other faster and faster, there needs to be something pushing them away from each other, and pushing pretty hard. Remember, their own gravity is pulling them *toward* each other, and it's helped along by the gravitational attraction of all that dark matter—four times the amount of visible matter, and thus four times as strong.

This other stuff, this dark energy, or *dark lightning*, as Papa prefers to call it, has to overcome all that, and then some.

How it does it wasn't solvable at the time since we didn't have the foggiest notion of what it was or where it was hiding. We could only infer it *was* there because something had to be there to keep pushing everything apart faster and faster. But it was possible to estimate how *much* of it there was if we could estimate just how fast the rate of expansion was increasing. Then we could calculate just how much energy it would take to move all those quindecillions of tons of dark and light matter at that rate.

Turns out it's a lot.

Since matter and energy are convertible, one into another, by the old Einstein equation of $E=mc^2$, they were then able to get a better picture of the stuff the universe is really made of. Turns out all that dark lightning is the most common stuff in the universe, way more of it than dark or visible matter combined. Almost three times as much.

So here's how it adds up:

Dark lightning: 70 percent of the universe.

Dark matter: 25 percent of the universe.

The stuff we can see: 5 percent of the universe.

Of that 5 percent, 4 percent is free hydrogen and helium, leaving 1 percent for everything else.

Of the "everything else," that 1 percent, about 60 percent is stars, which are mostly hot hydrogen and helium, 35 percent is those gosh-darn neutrinos, and 5 percent is left over for the "heavy" elements: the cores of stars ready to go supernova, the cores of gas-giant planets like Jupiter and Saturn, rocky planets like Earth and Mars, asteroids, *Rolling Thunder*, you and your family, me and my sister and our family, and my little blue budgie, Chip.

In the hundred years since its discovery, Papa said some progress has been made on finding out what and where the dark lightning is. But almost all of it is on paper, or rather in huge computer models.

Cosmologists and astronomers and physicists and mathematicians and people who are combinations of those disciplines—because there's a lot of overlap—love to sit around and think about it all. The astronomers bring in new data as their telescopes get better and better. The physicists smash atoms together in larger and larger and more powerful machines. The biggest one, when the ship left, was around the equator of Ceres. They get more data about how the basic stuff of the universe is put together by breaking it apart and seeing what comes out. Then the cosmologists and mathematicians get to work on all that data and try to come up with a theory that accounts for it all, including dark matter and dark lightning.

That's what we have when it comes to dark lightning. Theories. About twenty of them, according to Papa.

Theories come in varying degrees of reliability.

The "theory" of gravitation is proven to everyone's satisfaction, in that we all agree that gravity is an inherent property of all matter. Our understanding of just *how* it does what it does is still far from complete—there are four or five theories about *that*—but the fact that gravity is a property of matter *in all cases* is a done deal.

The theory of relativity is proven out to twenty decimal places.

The theory of evolution is proven, both historically and experimentally, to a similar degree.

The Big Bang theory is just that: a theory that fits the known facts better than any other theory. Not proven, but robust, as the scientists say.

It's certainly incomplete and may never be completed, but it's useful, and large parts of it *have* been proven.

All the theoretical models of dark matter and dark lightning simply cannot stand in such company. If gravitational theory is a ten on a scale of one to ten, the best model for dark lightning would only rate a point zero one. There simply isn't enough data to back any of them up, to "prove" them. Dark lightning remains almost as elusive as it was in the twentieth century.

Except that now Papa thinks he has figured out some things about it. And it's not good news.

CHAPTER 6

———

Cassie:

So that's the background of what Papa was trying to tell us. A universe that is mostly made up of stuff we simply can't see and can only detect through indirect means.

But all that was learned in observatories traveling at very sedate speeds, in orbit around Old Sun. For telescopes on Earth or the moon, that speed is 18 miles per second. For Mars, it's about 15 miles/sec. For a telescope near Neptune, the orbital speed is only 3.3 miles/sec. The very most distant telescopes, way out in the Kuiper Belt, are hardly moving at all, relative to Old Sun.

There's also the motion of the galaxy itself, which is spinning at the dizzying rate of one revolution every two hundred million years. The whole solar system is moving at about 170 miles per second. The whole Milky Way galaxy is moving relative to the center of mass of our local group of galaxies—the only ones that aren't moving away from us like we're a plague carrier—at 25 miles/sec.

It would be possible to add up all those velocities and come up with a number for Old Sun's speed through the universe, but there's really no point. Whatever it is, it is trivial compared to *Rolling Thunder*'s speed relative to Old Sun and to our destination.

Old Sun stirs up what is called a "bow shock" wave. It is where the solar wind becomes too weak to overcome the star's passage through the interstellar medium. That's an important concept.

The solar system's movement as the galaxy rotates means little, as everything around it is moving at pretty much the same speed, including the interstellar medium, so its relative velocity is low.

Think of a boat plowing upstream on a raging river whose water is moving at forty miles per hour. The boat is also moving at forty miles per hour. Another boat with its engines off is being moved along by that same river. The first boat is going forty miles per hour *relative to the water.* Relative to the shore, it is motionless. The second boat is moving at forty miles per hour *relative to the shore.* The second ship is motionless, relative to the water.

The first ship encounters a great deal of resistance, the second ship encounters none. That second ship is Old Sun, moving with the rotation of the galaxy. Got it?

Rolling Thunder is like that first ship, plowing through the water at great speed, but here the analogy fails. We are rushing through the interstellar medium of thin atoms of hydrogen and miniscule bits of dust, but the ship is so massive that it's barely possible to register the tiny bit of resistance we're encountering. It's all soaked up and deflected by the million-mile bubble way out in front of us, so we're traveling through the most perfect vacuum ever encountered by humans. But we *are* plowing through it, at a speed of 143,000 miles per second. That's faster than any humans have ever traveled . . . and lived to tell about it.

Though that very much remains to be seen.

We haven't lived to tell about it yet.

There's the matter of those hundreds and hundreds of other ships that set out for the stars around midcentury. Only one of them ever returned, to devastating effect on all the countries of the North Atlantic. Whoever was aboard never had a word to say about their experiences at near-light speed; they were moving at near-light speed when they returned, almost fast enough to catch up with any radio signal they were sending out. It was a matter of "Here we com—*BANG!*"

What they actually managed to say was "Death to—*BANG!*" It was their second miscalculation, after their slightly faulty aim, so that their suicide ship only hit the Earth a glancing blow instead of impacting North America. Granddaddy Ramon says that anyone alive at that time could easily fill in the blank, as it was a phrase very popular for the first forty years of the twenty-first century: *Death to America.*

He also said most people had a pretty good idea of who the mass murderers were, too. At the time all the ships were leaving, much of the trouble on Earth was being stirred up by radical Muslims who wanted to return all the societies of the world to a point around the seventh century. It was a culture rich in people willing to commit suicide if it would hurt the "infidels." They would strap explosives to their bodies or drive dynamite-laden vehicles into crowds of people and blow themselves up. Hard to believe, but true. Even children did this. History can be appalling, can't it?

The impact with the Earth had all the hallmarks of radical Muslim terrorism. Right at the turn of the century, a group of them flew airliners full of people into skyscrapers full of people.

They got over it. The second part of the century was pretty much free of that kind of barbarism. The Muslims aboard *Rolling Thunder* are good, peaceful people. Not that there's a lot of them, not fervent believers, anyway, though there are plenty of people with Islamic backgrounds. It ain't discrimination, Travis says, at least not against Muslims. Strong, intolerant religious feelings of *any* kind were a deal breaker if you wanted to board *Rolling Thunder.* We have our religious people aboard—about 35 percent believe in a Supreme Being of some sort, according to the polls—and we have our churches and synagogues and mosques, and I've visited one of each on field trips, but if you believe in crap like discrimination against females or the infallibility of the Pope or don't believe in evolution or gay rights, Travis didn't want you aboard. So conservative Catholics, ultraorthodox Jews, and hard-shell evangelical Christians were just as unwelcome as wild-eyed Muslims.

Sorry, got off the subject there for a minute. Organized religion puzzles me. I've found the services interesting, for the ritual, but pretty boring overall. My version of spirituality is my own, thank you very much, not to be trotted out in public.

So we were discussing the one ship that returned from an interstellar voyage, out of hundreds that set out, and the near certainty that it was piloted by religious fanatics unafraid to die, or to kill millions of infidels—and even other Muslims, as they had done many times in the past—because as martyrs they were guaranteed a place in the afterlife with ninety-seven virgin sluts, or some horseshit like that.

Why did they survive when, so far as we can tell, no one else did?

That's where the discussion began, in the Common Council Chamber.

Government is small in *Rolling Thunder*, in accordance with Travis's libertarian leanings. Anything that can be done efficiently and competitively by private enterprise is left to take care of itself according to good old capitalist/socialist principles. But Travis is not a fanatic about it. He believes in democracy . . . up to a point. He *is* Captain Broussard, after all, and his word is the final one.

Each of the fifteen townships has an elected mayor and council, and each of them elects a representative to the Common Council, which elects a governor.

The CC meets in the Council Building, one of the nicest and largest structures in the ship, with what is probably the grandest interior. Travis didn't want to spend a lot of time or money on new architecture, so he got the builders to dig out old plans of other buildings that he knew were serviceable and use those. The Council Building is an exact copy of the General Assembly Building of the United Nations, in New York.

That's gone now, of course, torn down many years ago. When it existed, it sort of crouched at the feet of a much taller building, the Secretariat. The Council Building is made of white stone, long and narrow, and the roof swoops gradually, higher at one end than the other. One end has a lot of glass in it, and inside is a spacious, very-high-ceilinged lobby with four boomerang-shaped balconies overlooking it.

Behind that is the meeting chamber. It's round and tapers upward to a domed ceiling. There's a raised area backed by a gold wall that leans outward, bearing the seal of the good ship *Rolling Thunder*. That is flanked by two curved wooden walls that also lean. The rest of the room is filled with comfortable seating for a bit over a thousand people.

Polly and I were the only ones sitting in the audience. The lighting out there was from dim, overhead bulbs that created a restful ambience. We were trying to be as quiet and unobtrusive as church mice. We were there on sufferance.

Mama had been against it. But Travis had pointed out that if she barred us from the meeting, we might do damage to the building, drilling holes in it in our attempts to spy on them. Mama sighed one of her long-suffering sighs and relented.

The council platform was brighter. There was a long table up there, seven chairs on each side of a larger chair for the governor. There was a row of seats behind them, for aides and such. All those chairs were vacant, as were almost all the council chairs. Of the Common Council, only Governor Wang and two others were present. (In *Rolling Thunder*, not even the post of governor is full-time. Alice Wang taught Earth History at our school, and Polly and I had both been in her class. She had been a good teacher.)

The governor wasn't sitting in her chair but standing to one side of the platform. Two people were in other seats at the table, and some others were either standing, pacing back and forth, or sitting with one haunch on the tabletop. Papa was one of those sitting in a chair, looking miserable. Travis was one of those pacing, and the only one talking at the moment, trying to explain what Papa had just told us all. Mama was standing behind Papa, massaging his shoulders.

Travis had gotten all the preliminaries out of the way quickly. With this group, he didn't need to explain dark matter or dark lightning, except maybe to Governor Wang. The other people present were all friends of Papa and constituted Travis's informal science advisory group.

"I didn't know a lot of what I'm going to tell you," Travis was saying. "Some of you may, but I'd better outline it briefly.

"At the time the rogue ship hit the Earth, a little over fifty years ago, we were not able to determine all that much about it. We knew its exact course coming in; all we had to do was draw a line from the hot plasma trail it left behind after being vaporized by the collision. But quite a few ships had gone out in that direction.

"People kept working on it, in astronomical records and back on the Earth, using improved equipment, both observational and computational. Little by little they teased out some more information. This is what Jubal learned a few years ago, before communications with Earth and Mars were shut down. Back on Mars, they are now 99 percent sure that the rogue ship was the *Mejd Allah*, which I'm told translates as the *Glory of Allah*. It was built by some Saudi billionaires with radical connections."

Uncle Travis is a good storyteller. He had everyone's undivided attention as he paced back and forth across the dais, never looking at anybody. Polly and I were transfixed. She had grabbed my hand and was squeezing it a bit, and I don't think she even knew she was doing it.

"Remember, there was a positively mad scramble to build ships and head out for the stars not long after Manny and Kelly and Dak and Alicia and I got back from Mars in the *Red Thunder*. Then it tapered off, and the next big thing was going to be the *return* of the first ship from the stars.

"Never happened. No one came back.

"After a while, fewer and fewer ships were leaving. It was enough to give you pause, all those ships leaving, some of them now long overdue. What was happening to them? Until somebody figured that out, only crazy people were likely to board a starship."

One of the council of mayors spoke up.

"This is all fascinating," he said, "but I'm sure most of us have a pretty good understanding of the era of the diaspora. Where are you going with this, Captain?"

It was George Bull, the mayor of Freedonia Township. He was one of only three mayors present, plus Governor Wang. Naturally, it would be a politician to interrupt the flow of the story. He was built like his name, with a barrel body and cannonball-bald head, but the face pasted on the front of the head was more of a bullfrog's, with big wet lips and goggling eyes.

"Just ordering my thoughts, Mayor Bull," Travis said. "If you'll bear with me a few more minutes, we'll get to the reason I invited you all here."

It had been more of an order, I knew, but Travis was being polite.

"I'd like to hear it all, Mayor Bull," said one of the other mayors, Oringo Ngoro, the mayor of Sweet Apple township. "I'm not up on my solar history, I admit it."

We had visited Mayor Ngoro's orchards and picked apples, of which he had about fifty varieties, all of them tasty. He was around forty in body age, and probably the same in calendar years. He had been the chief ecologist from the outset, which would have made him about twenty when we started, so he must have been extremely bright to hold such a position at such a young age. Which meant he had probably never had to go into a black bubble. He was too valuable.

"Let's resume, then," Travis said, a little testily, I thought.

"Until recently, most people thought the rogue ship had gone out with the first wave. It was about twenty years from the beginning of the first wave of exploration until the arrival of the killer ship. Plenty of time for at least fifty ships that went out in that direction to get there and come back.

"So. The *Mejd Allah*. The billionaires who funded it said they were subscribing to a theory—I don't know who proposed it—that the problem was that these other ships were spending too much time in interstellar space. They theorized that there was something out there, something that wasn't in planetary systems, that was killing the crews. They thought it was akin to the situation even in the solar system, where if you spend too much time in a badly shielded spaceship, the dose of radiation you get will sicken you and eventually kill you. They didn't know what it was, it was just some hypothetical 'something,' but the key to surviving it was to minimize your time between the stars. Maybe they believed this theory, maybe they didn't. Whatever, it gave them a good excuse to do what they planned to do, anyway, which was boost at a higher gee than anyone ever had before.

"Just about the one thing that all starships had in common, other than being powered by the squeezer drive, was that they boosted at one gee. A few of the larger ones boosted lower than that, but otherwise, why not one gee? It'll get you nudging the speed of light pretty quick, and for the middle part of your trip, your clocks have slowed down, so saving time wasn't really a factor. No matter how far you were going, the middle part of your trip, still boosting all the time, was going to be relatively short, to the crew, though centuries might go by back on Earth.

"But to these guys, speed *was* a factor. That's what they claimed, anyway, that they intended to spend as little time as possible between the stars, vulnerable to whatever mysterious thing was destroying starships. So they intended to boost at two gees."

He paused for a moment to let that sink in.

"Certainly it could be done, several years in twice the gravity you're used to. But imagine the backaches, the fallen arches, the sagging flesh, the sore muscles and aching joints. Even a minor fall could cause a lot of injury. Imagine having your twin brother sitting on your shoulders all day, sleeping on top of you every night."

My twin sister and I glanced at each other. She made a face.

"The thought is a frightful one," came a voice. There was a momentary ripple of laughter, because the speaker was Max Karpinski, who was reputed to be and almost certainly was the fattest man in *Rolling Thunder*. He was a friend of the family, especially of Papa, and had spent a lot of time in our house when we were growing up. He always remembered our birthday, and was always there with presents, always something sweeter than we should really be eating, according to Mama, but since it was only once a year, and because she liked Max, she let it slide. He was okay with his corpulence (when you're around Max you learn words like corpulence) and frequently made jokes about it. I would say he's around sixty real years, masses in the neighborhood of four hundred one-gee pounds, and, after Papa, is the smartest man in the ship. He's the Chief Relativist. If anyone could frolic with Papa through the quantum leaps of bubble theory, Max was the one. Though the idea of Max's leaping made me smile.

Travis grinned at him, and even Papa looked up briefly from his gloom.

"We don't know who they chose, Max," he went on, "but I'll bet three of them could fit in your pant leg. Skinny would definitely be best. And these guys were martyrs; they probably liked suffering. What they said was, the main purpose of the trip was that the first men to return from the stars should be true believers in Islam. When they got there, for instance, if they found a planet, and if it had intelligent beings on it, they intended to tell them about the Prophet and the One True Faith. And, I don't know, maybe kill them all if they didn't convert.

"They took off with little fanfare, but you know how carefully and thoroughly we monitor solar space, looking for the signature of squeezer drives. And how long we keep the records, which I guess will be forever, or until the Earth is destroyed. Researchers were able to go back and see the trace on old records, heading smack-dab for Centauri, at a backbreaking two gees. We've known that about them for some time.

"Everyone had always assumed they had intended to boost at two gees out to the midpoint, when they'd be damn close to the speed of light, then turn around and proceed at two gees deceleration for the same period until they got there. However, there are now some new techniques for analyzing some of that old data. It's pretty amazing stuff, and I don't know how they do it, but they can learn things from those old records, and one thing they were finally able to see was that, yes, the *Mejd Allah* did accelerate at the rate of two gees . . . for about a week. Then somebody turned on the afterburners, so to speak, and the rate moved up to four gees."

Travis paused again. Polly and I knew some of this, from sitting in on Papa talking about what had come to him while he was in the bubble. Which, by the way, is pretty mysterious, because time doesn't pass in the bubble. Not even a trillionth of a trillionth of a picosecond. It takes much, much longer than that for a synapse to fire in the human brain, so how did Papa get an idea while no time was passing?

I had asked about that, and Mama said they knew it was possible for something to happen during that no-time, and that she would tell us about it one day soon, and for now why don't you just shut up? I did.

"Two gees I can believe. Three, I guess it *might* be done, but I don't think there would be much left of you when you got there. Four . . . I can't see it."

"I'd weigh almost a ton," Max put in.

"Well, we don't really have to wonder about it because the last we could detect them, they had upped the ante to ten gees. No one could survive that for more than a few minutes. There's just no way, short of a black bubble, and no one has ever had that technology but us."

"So, you're saying there was no one aboard?" That was George Bull.

"There might have been, at first. Men willing to die, to commit suicide before the gravity crushed them painfully. Testing out the ship, making sure it was reliable at high gees, is the theory we're working with. *If* there were men aboard, I feel sure they must have sucked the gas pipe, or hung themselves, or whatever a martyr does to off himself when there are no innocent women and children to take along with him.

"Personally, I think there were men aboard. According to the gossip we heard before we fell out of contact, I'm in the minority. Most people back home feel that it was an automated ship from the start.

"It doesn't really matter, since it was certainly an automated ship by the time it arrived back home and kissed the Atlantic Ocean long enough to kill twenty million people. The last thing the people back home learned about the ship came from using those new techniques to analyze data from observatories out beyond Pluto. And it's the most startling of all.

"Back shortly after the impact, the exhaust trail of the incoming *Mejd Allah* was too faint to detect from the distances we're talking about. It was moving as close to the speed of light as anything we've ever seen. And apparently it reached that speed rather quickly, as we now think it was accelerating at the rate of fifty to one hundred gees."

"Fifty . . ." Max Karpinski had stood so quickly that he knocked his chair over.

"That's right, Max. Somewhere in there. They wanted to squeeze out every ounce of relativistic mass they could. It's impossible to figure out how long they accelerated away from the sun at ten gees or more, or how long it took them to slow down. Too many variables. They might have accelerated at fifty gees on the way out, too, or kept it at a steady ten gees. They might not have been standing on the accelerator, so to speak, at a full fifty gees all the way in.

"It doesn't really matter. We know they were dead by that time—if they were even aboard. We know the ship must have been automatically guided, probably from shortly before they stepped it up to four gees, on the way outward. And I think we can assume that fifty to one hundred gees must have put a tremendous strain on such a large spaceship. Even before the squeezer drive, back in the 1970s, we made a missile, the Sprint, that accelerated at one hundred gees, but it was only twenty feet long and four feet wide, and it only boosted for five seconds. The *Mejd Allah* was much bigger than that, at least three hundred feet long. I wouldn't want to try to engineer a spaceship that size that could stand up to a hundred gees over a sustained period. With those kind of stresses, something was bound to go wrong eventually."

"Maybe that's why it missed," Governor Wang suggested. "Well, almost missed."

"Almost was bad enough, but yeah, if it had hit dead on, it would have been much worse. And I agree with you. However long it was boosting, something snapped, something failed under all that weight."

Travis stopped and sighed deeply.

"But I got sidetracked a little there. Sorry about that. The main thing we can take away from all this new information is that it seems clear now that *no one living* aboard that evil ship ever got anywhere *near* the speed of light. They were all dead long before the ship got up and over .9c. Which means that we have *no* evidence that *anyone* has *ever* traveled at a speed higher than .9c and lived to tell about it. Or come back to tell about it, anyway.

"Did their ships blow up for some reason? The *Mejd Allah* didn't, worse luck. Were they captured by space aliens? Jubal thinks he may have the answer, and it's not a good one for us. It's so bad, in fact, that he wants us to turn around, stop the ship, and go back."

This pause went on a lot longer. Max collapsed back into his chair and contemplated his enormous gut. Mayor Ngoro got up and started pacing. Rachel Walters, a mathematician and one of Travis's brain trust, was looking skeptical, while the other mayors wore looks that ranged between baffled and frightened.

"Naturally, such an extreme step will have to be discussed, debated, eventually told to everyone, But for now, I'd like to keep it in this little group until we learn a little more. Can we agree to that?"

He got nods from most of them. A few still looked like they would need a lot of convincing. Well, hell, so would I, not that I thought my opinion amounted to much compared to Papa's.

"All right. Now I'll try to explain the problem, as best I can.

"What it boils down to is, Jubal thinks it's not possible for living beings to travel beyond a certain speed. Not and remain living beings, anyway. He thinks all those other ships are still speeding away from us, with a cargo of corpses."

CHAPTER 7

———————

Polly:

After the meeting was adjourned, the family returned to the house. You would never have known there had been a big, messy party there earlier in the day. There was not even a dirty dish. Mama took Papa into their room, putting her finger to her lips and looking sternly at us, signaling that she needed peace and quiet to try to settle Papa down. I nodded, and we went out the screen door and onto the dock.

There at the end of the meeting, when he was doing his best to explain his crazy theory, he had been seized by a panic attack so strong that Aunt Elizabeth had to be called to give him a sedative. So no one knew all the details of what had scared him so badly, though before he freaked out, he had managed to give everyone a general idea.

Me and the clone were at a loss as to what to do with ourselves. For once, motormouth Cassie didn't have anything to say. I didn't, either. We strolled to the end of the dock, and I sat down and patted the water gently. A couple of the huge, gold-and-white carp that live in the pond came swimming over. Some of the biggest ones are older than I am. I lifted the lid of the bucket we keep out there and took out a handful of fish pellets. I tossed a few pellets in to get their attention. Then I lowered my hand into the water with some pellets and let them swim up and eat them out of my hand. I looked out over the pond, up and around the curve. Trees, buildings, the straight rows of farmed fields, rivers, small lakes.

Home.

It was horrible to think that this lovely, peaceful place could soon become a giant coffin, hurtling out toward the edges of the universe with no one alive to see it.

What was time like then, relativistically speaking? Didn't Einstein speak of time in terms of the observer? What if there was no observer? Is it like the tree falling in the forest with no one to hear it? Is that cat in the box in the famous quantum thought experiment alive, or dead, or both at the same time? And what does that feel like to the cat? Is the cat allowed an opinion?

"Hard to think of all this being dead," my twin said.

"Papa says it wouldn't necessarily affect the plants. At first."

"I don't think he knows for sure."

"Neither do I."

We were quiet for a moment, and I got to my feet.

"The way he said it, the animals would die first."

"The brain first, he said. He thinks it's more vulnerable to this stuff."

"This dark lightning."

"Whatever. So, with us and all the animals dead, what happens in here? The plants grow wild. It continues to rain on schedule. The sun goes on and off every day. The pumps keep working, so the rivers keep flowing, bow to stern. I wonder how long it would all keep working."

"Travis built it pretty well," I said. "But it all needs maintenance. A few decades, maybe, before it starts to all fall apart?"

"I guess so. The pumps would silt up and stop. I guess all the water would pool in the stern. The rain would stop, the plants would die."

"Then one day," I said, "the sun would fail. Blow up, or just stop coming on. It gives me the creeps to think of this great big empty space, totally dark, totally dead, rushing out to the stars."

Cassie shivered, then shook her head.

"Screw it. I don't need to think about that yet. That's still in the future. How about we go for a run, get it off our minds?"

That's Cassie for you. If it ain't on the horizon, it ain't worth worrying about. Sometimes it drives me crazy, and other times I envy it. What would it be like, not to be a worrier? Oh, hell. Why not?

"Where's my running shoes?"

We got into our running shorts and halters—bright orange for me, yellow for Cassie—and running shoes, tied our hair back with scrunchies, and did a few stretches. We walked down to the road.

"The usual route?" Cassie asked.

"Sure, why not?"

When we were in training we did at least one circuit a day. *Rolling Thunder* provides some of the longer circular running tracks ever built, only they wouldn't look circular to a planet person because they go more or less straight ahead until you get back to where you started.

It's six and a quarter miles around the cylinder. When Travis was instructing the architects who laid out the interior, he told them not to use a perfect grid. He wanted hills here and there, and said the roads should go around them. The roads meandered, crossing small streams and the three rivers at angles. It made a pleasing pattern when you looked up the curve, a colorful quilt but not a strict geometric one.

Our route quickly took us into the village of Freedonia, capital of our home township of Freedonia. That may be a little confusing to people who aren't from here.

The awake population of *Rolling Thunder* is around twenty thousand. It's pretty evenly distributed through the townships, which gives each one about 1,350 souls. That's a density of around 540 per square mile or, as Travis once put it to me, about the density of Delaware before the tsunami.

It doesn't feel crowded. The capital of each township is always the town with the largest concentration of people, though none of them would qualify as much of a town back on Earth, or even much of a village. Travis compares the population centers to old English villages, and from the pictures I've seen, he's right. Not that they all look English, but they all are rural villages with only a few medium-sized buildings. There are apartment houses, but about half the population has living quarters underground, or else it *would* start to look crowded.

We've always had it easy, not having to live underground, I know that. And I don't feel particularly guilty about it. We chose our parents well, as Cassie likes to say.

South of Freedonia is the township of Mayberry, and north is Dogpatch. Since he was building and paying for the whole thing, Travis got to name anything he chose to name, and he decided on famous fictional places that he liked. From time to time—from residents of places like Dogpatch and Frostbite Falls—there is a movement to change the names, and Travis never opposes them, but the names seem to be entrenched by now, with a majority of residents proud of them.

Freedonia Township is a cluster of buildings with five streets paved with cobblestones. Mama says the theme of the buildings is Medieval Balkan, whatever that means. Many of the roofs are steep and thatched with (fireproof) straw. A stream runs through town, and there's a real stone-grinding mill powered by a waterwheel under some towering chestnuts.

There's a market, a cheese shop, a bicycle shop (called a blacksmith, and she does shoe horses), a few dozen other small businesses. *All* businesses on the interior are small. We have no big corporations here.

The second and, occasionally, third floors above the ground-level businesses are all apartments.

There's an old stone multidenominational church, brought in from somewhere in the Balkans and reassembled, a town hall, a constable's office, and the three-room schoolhouse we went to for twelve years, with a gym and athletic fields. There is a little theater which puts on shows twice or three times a year. Cassie and I played Blanche Dubois, alternating nights, last summer, to pretty good reviews.

There was the normal amount of traffic as we jogged into town. Lots of people on foot, a few on cycles of one sort or another—we have a *big* variety of foot-powered vehicles—and three horses tied to rails in front of the market. Some of the trees had turned to fall colors—I don't know how the ecologists manage that since we don't really have an "autumn" here, but they do—and there were red and gold leaves blowing around in the gentle breeze. The smell of fresh bread and cinnamon rolls was coming from the bakery beside the mill, and I heard music coming from some of the upstairs windows. One of them was playing an old load from our mother, who was a very big deal in the music business back on Mars. I smiled when I heard it. It was one she used to sing to us to get us to go to sleep.

Naturally, we knew almost all the people in town, and acknowledged those we saw with a hand wave. People know not to bother us when we're on what they call the "hamster wheel," our run around the circumference.

In no time at all we were back into the countryside. The fields around us were mostly planted in grains destined for the mill. Wheat, barley, oats, rye, buckwheat, millet. Again, there is no particular season for harvesting in our ship. The ecologists get three or four crops every "year" out of most of the land. And what we were seeing was only a part of what was actually grown in the ship. Down below in huge, low-ceilinged rooms with harsh lighting, the bulk of our daily diet was grown hydroponically, and much of the livestock was raised. But many people felt it wasn't the same and were willing to pay a premium for "surface-raised" food.

Before long we were in Grover's Mill Township, though you wouldn't know it if you hadn't seen the carved stone announcing that fact. Off to the right was Maycomb, and to our left was Castle Rock.

"Ready to pick up the pace a little?" Cassie asked me.

"Go for it." I was being thrown off my stride by the sling around my arm but was slowly adjusting to it. It didn't hurt too much, but I wondered if it might be a problem around mile four or five.

"How's your ass?"

"Prettier than your face."

She snorted and pulled ahead of me slightly. The truth was that the wound in my butt was throbbing a little. I sure didn't want to give up before we'd completed the revolution, but I was already resigned to the fact that I was going to lose in the last quarter mile, which we always turned into a sprint race. I thought I could tough it out to the finish line, but I didn't have all that much in reserve.

I got a short reprieve when the weather alarm sounded in my head. I blinked on the heads-up display and saw that a rain shower was scheduled to start in two minutes. Grover's Mill was 1920s art deco. Curved corners on stucco buildings, pastel colors, and lots of little architectural flourishes I've always liked. Travis says the buildings are patterned on old hotels in Miami Beach, where he used to spend a lot of time. In fact, one of them, the Breakwater, used to *be* a hotel in Miami Beach. It had been dismantled and moved to Las Vegas, and so escaped the destruction of the Big Wave, and was later bought by Travis and moved here. It's lovely, bright white with blue and yellow trim.

The town was arranged around a square with a bandstand, a fair amount of grass, and a lot of palm trees of various sorts. We took shelter in the bandstand and watched parents rounding up their children from the playground. Some of them joined us on the bandstand, and others found refuge under picnic shelters.

The sky opened up and gave us a real downpour.

You can *just* see the clear plastic rain pipes that interlace the sky in the interior, but you have to know what to look for and where to look. They are a few thousand feet up, suspended from a wire lattice.

It would have probably made more sense to have all the crop water delivered by ground-level irrigation, either sprinklers or drip lines, but Travis said, as a Florida boy, he'd miss the daily tropical rains. So his engineers figured out this system, and I'm glad they did. The rain washes everything clean.

As it was, the rain came down in sheets for almost five minutes. Cassie jogged in place, while I rested my uninjured butt cheek on the wood railing of the bandstand. I watched the rain pelting off the brightly colored playground equipment. In the center of it was a twenty-foot-high sculpture on three springy legs. At the top was a silly, cartoonish "Invader from Mars." Every twenty minutes or so it would bounce around and shoot out rays of light, and bellow "Surrender, Earthlings!" There were other signs of alien invasion around town, which was named after a fictional place where Martians landed in a story by H. G. Wells, back in the early twentieth century, and were quickly up to no good. Or so I'm told.

I was hurting by the time we got to Lake Wobegon Township.

The arm was okay, but the wound in the butt was throbbing with every step I took. I wondered if it was bleeding. But sis and I are so competitive, and have trained so much together, that neither of us liked to admit that we had any quit in us.

Off to my left I could see Grand Fenwick, home of a lot of dairy cows and producer of the best cheese in the ship. We crossed a bridge over Brink Creek. I could see it meandering along among smooth stones, cascading over a few little waterfalls. Not far away to my right, the capital city of Tottering Township was situated on the waterway. Crossing that Brink Creek Bridge was always a welcome sight on these hamster runs because it meant we were less than a mile from the finish line.

With our huge old live oak in sight, we passed the flat rock that had WELCOME TO FREEDONIA chiseled into it, under cartoon images of Groucho, Chico, and Harpo Marx. We have watched a couple of their films and I'm afraid I don't understand a lot of the jokes, and I think most of the music is pretty awful, though I did laugh a lot at the scene where they were stuffing people into the small cabin of an ocean liner. It was the signal that we had only a quarter mile to go, and it's where we always forced ourselves into a sprint to the tree, and home.

Cassie started out in a sprint, and I labored to keep up with her, but it was no use, the pain was too great. After about a hundred yards of watching her ponytail bounce at an increasing distance in front of me, I gave in. I limped to the side of the road.

Ahead of me, Cassie looked back and slowed to a walk, then turned around and came back to me.

"Don't start," I gasped.

"I wasn't going to say anything," she said, leaning over with her hands on her knees, breathing hard. "I'll tell you the truth, spacegirl, I was beginning to worry that you were going to outlast me, busted butt and all."

I had to laugh.

"I don't know what's wrong with me," she added, standing up straight. "You think we're just too worried about Papa?"

"I don't know, Cass. A lot has happened today. I can hardly believe that last night we played a skypool match."

As if on signal, the sun dimmed quickly and shut off. Streetlights came on, including one just over our heads.

"Come on, Poll, turn around and let me take another look at your ass."

"You can kiss it while you're down there." But I turned. She squatted and lifted the hem of my shorts. She clucked her tongue.

"Shit, babe, you're bleeding."

"How bad is it?"

"Well, it hasn't reached your sock."

Cassie pulled off her halter and ran it up the back of my leg. She showed it to me, and it wasn't too bad, though I never like seeing my own blood.

She lifted the back of the leg of my shorts and poked around a little.

"What's it look like?"

"*Big* bruise. Covers most of your cheek. The dressing is coming off. We need to change it. This might not have been the best idea we ever had. I'm amazed you got this far, dude."

She stood up and came around by my side. She pulled my uninjured arm over her shoulder and took a lot of my weight.

We hobbled on home.

At the end of the dock we stripped off and took our customary plunge into the warm waters of the pond. Well, Cassie plunged and I lowered myself carefully, not wanting to get the cast on my arm wet. I hung on to the dock as I dunked, paddled around a bit, then waded ashore with Cassie. We squeezed the water out of each other's hair and hurried to the big live oak.

Our tree house is a wonderful sight to behold. "Swiss Family Robinson," Papa Jubal said when he finished building it. It's two stories high, with a terrace on each level. Living room below, bedroom above, tiny kitchen off to one side. When we were young it was a play kitchen, suitable for baking mud pies, but later we put in a hot plate, a microwave, and a small cooler. A long set of stairs leads to a crow's nest so high up that it sways in a gentle breeze.

Access is by rope ladder. We climbed it, and Cassie pulled it up behind her. We had never put up a sign saying NO BOYS ALLOWED, but that was the idea. In fact, we had never invited anyone but a few of our best girlfriends up there. Once it was finished, Papa never came up unless he was invited or was adding something on, and Mama Podkayne only did a monthly safety inspection when we were very young. She hadn't done that in years. The tree house was our refuge, our own private place.

It was cozy inside. A little too cozy, in fact. Papa had built it without realizing his daughters would top out at over six feet. These days we brushed our heads if we stood up straight.

With typical *Rolling Thunder* artfulness, Papa had built it on the outside to look like the "dilapidated" bait house we lived in, with wood weathered gray and looking slightly out of kilter, and a rusty tin roof that sagged in the middle. The windows all looked like they had been salvaged from other buildings, none of them matching.

Inside was a different story. It was all fine woods that glowed warmly yellowish in the light from what looked like hurricane lamps. There were nice carpets on the floor. The walls were lined with shelves and cabinets that held dolls and dollhouses, popguns and bows and arrows, train sets, and lots and lots of books. The kitchen was a ship's galley. The back deck looked like the prow of a sailing ship, with a mast, ropes leading up to cross sprits, and a bowsprit pointing out over the pond. Under that was a painted figurehead that looked a lot like Mama Podkayne, and on the deck were two small cannons that made enough smoke and noise to drive Mama crazy some days.

Inside again, a spiral stairway led up to the bunkroom. Oh, yes, we'd had it good growing up.

We grabbed towels and dried off, and Cassie went upstairs and threw down some fresh clothes, shorts and tops. I was nosing around the kitchen. There wasn't much in the freezer but a frozen pizza. I sniffed it dubiously.

"How old do you think this is?"

"No more than two years," Cassie said. "Let's eat it."

It was tough as leather, but we wolfed it down and chased it with cans of cold Dr Pepper. We dumped the dishes into the pneumatic trash bin, where they would be whisked away to the central washing facility, sterilized, and shipped off to who-knows-where. We once tried marking a couple of them to see if we ever got the same ones back, and got a nasty mail back from Housekeeping telling us we'd ruined the dishes. Another thing we got, of course, was a lecture from Mama.

Cassie treated and redressed my wounded behind *almost* painlessly. By then we were both yawning, so we climbed the stairs to the bedroom, the most girly place in the tree house. There were tons of stuffed animals, lots of lacy trimmings, two vanities where we had played with makeup and dress-up. There were closets and dressers for our clothes.

"I've had it," Cassie said.

"Long day," I agreed.

"Long, strange day." She paused for a moment. "What do you think's going to happen?"

"I think we're going to keep accelerating for a while. Papa finally agreed that he doesn't think we're right on the edge of whatever critical speed it is that will kill us all."

"Yeah, but he isn't sure."

"Of course not. He has to do more experiments, he said. Anyway, you don't just stop the ship overnight. If we have to turn around, it's going to be a nightmare. So many things to do."

"Yeah, well, we would have had to do all that eventually, even with our original flight plan. But still . . . I don't want to go back, Polly."

"Neither do I."

Last we heard, the Earth was still trying to cope with the alien invasion from Europa, and not doing well at it. Mars was better, but still overwhelmed by refugees, even with 95 percent of them in black-bubble suspension. It was a horror story we had grown up listening to, and it had made a deep impression on our young minds. *Rolling Thunder* was fleeing a catastrophe, there was no other way to put it. Old Sun was a scary place to me and my sister.

———————

We put on our jammies and crawled into bed.

From the time we were old enough, which was about six, we spent two or three nights every week in the tree house.

Cassie pulled a thin sheet over herself, fluffed up her pillow, and closed her eyes. In thirty seconds, I could hear her soft snore.

It drove me crazy, how she could get to sleep so fast. Somehow, she can just turn off the worry machine inside her head, the same machine that can keep me sleepless for hours before a skypool match or a big date.

About an hour later, I fell asleep, too.

———————

When I woke, I was alone. Another thing about Cassie: She's an early riser, and I'm not. She's bright-eyed in the morning, and I'm not. She'd go so far as to say I'm grumpy. I climbed out of bed and went down the stairs to the main room. Cassie was out there, sitting on the deck with her legs hanging over the side. The clock said the sun had been on for about half an hour. There was a steaming mug of coffee beside her, and I could smell a pot in the kitchen, so I went in there and poured my own mug. It is cylindrical and rather tall, has my name on it, and a map of the interior of the ship glazed on the side. A crude map, I admit it; we all made and fired our own mugs as a class project when we were ten.

I eased down beside Cassie, wincing when my butt touched the deck.

"You need a pillow?" she snickered. "Maybe I can find you one of those inflatable things like a donut, for old folks with sore rectums."

Things were back to normal.

"I need you to put a plug in your piehole, or I'll see if this mug will fit into *your* rectum, sideways."

Content to have gotten the day started with mutual insults, we sipped the coffee and looked out over the pond. There were a few dozen ducks swimming out there, dabbling for the algae that grows in the shallows: mallards, wood ducks looking like they had been hand-painted, some redheads and mergansers. Travis was a sucker for the prettier species of most animals and plants. There were a couple of the live-oak branches that hung out over the water. If we walked out on those branches, we could count on the ducks assembling under us and making a lot of noise about it. Right now, they were mostly quiet, and so was the rest of the world.

"You ever wish we had been born and grown up on Mars?" Cassie asked.

"Not really. Why?"

"Oh, I don't wish that. But I do sort of wish I could have seen it. Or Earth, for that matter. I'd like to know what it's like to be on the outside of a planet instead of the inside."

"You can go outside if you want. As long as you hold on tight."

"Sure, go out there, see the stars, it's great. But I'd like to see a starry night from Mars, or the Earth."

"Not many starry nights on Earth," I said. The invasion of the giant crystal beings from Europa before we were born had left Earth's weather so violent and erratic that it was dangerous to even go outside most of the time.

"Why are you always so negative? I'm just freewheelin' here. And with what's happening, there's a chance we may be going back."

She was right about that.

"Just what would you like to see on Earth, other than the stars, which you can see right here?"

"Sunrise," she said. "Sunset. They look so beautiful."

Again she was on the money. I had to admit that I had sort of thought from time to time that it would be nice for the sun to come up in the west and sink slowly in the east. Or was it the other way?

"The moon," I said, suddenly. "I wonder what that looks like in the sky? How big do you think it would be?"

"There's some way to simulate it," she said, "but I can't recall what it is. Is it holding your arm out straight and looking at your thumbnail?" She suited her action to the words, and we both looked at her thumbnail. Somehow, I'd always thought the moon seen from the Earth would be bigger than that.

"Or two moons on Mars," she went on. "A lot smaller but moving a lot faster."

"Jupiter from Europa," I said. "*That* must be something to see." Mama Podkayne had spent some time on Europa, and in fact had been there when the Europan crystals began their once-in-sixty-million-year voyage of destruction to the Earth.

"I'll just stay on Earth and Mars in this dream if you don't mind," Cassie said. "If we end up back there, I'd like to see mountains and glaciers. And the sea, of course, I have a hard time imaging the sea."

She wasn't the only one. It just seems so outrageous, all that water in the Pacific Ocean. And all the creatures in it, most of which we couldn't bring along because we had no environment where they could thrive.

"Deep-sea diving," I suggested.

"Riding around in hot cars." We'd seen all this stuff in movies from Old Sun. Lots of it looked like fun. "With boys."

"Well, of course, with boys. Only I'd want it to be my car, and I'd want to drive."

"Hell, yes."

"But there'd be no skypool."

"Shit, you're right." She shook her head. "Well, screw it then."

We both laughed.

"I'd always hoped to see those things, or things a lot like them, when we get to New Sun."

"Yeah, New Earth might have its own spectacular stuff," Cassie agreed.

"Well"—I sighed—"let's hope so. If we have to turn around, we'll be eighty years old by the time we get back, unless we go into a bubble."

"There you go again, Little Miss Bummer. We're not going to turn around. Papa Jubal will think of something."

As if her words had summoned him, Papa Jubal came out the back door of the house. He was carrying a metal box with a handle on the top and steam coming out of some holes on the side.

"Hi, my darlings," he called out. "I thought y'all might like some breakfuss."

CHAPTER 8

Cassie:

I lowered a rope and Papa attached the box to it and I reeled it up.

"Avast below!" I called out, and Papa stood to the side as I kicked the rope ladder over the side of the terrace. Polly carried the box to the table inside as Papa clambered up. I held out a hand to help him, but he didn't need it. He gave me a big hug, and I felt good in his powerful arms.

Papa spends a lot of time in his boat when he's visiting us, either sitting there with a fishing pole or, more often, rowing endless laps around the pond. His big hands are tough as leather, and he once described his arms as "Like Popeye the sailor man!"

He says it helps him think, and it also helps him deal with stress. I wouldn't have been surprised that morning to see him out rowing, as I doubt he'd ever been as stressed as he was yesterday.

But another thing he does to deal with it is cooking, and he's good at it. Much better than Mama. The difference is that he loves it, and she doesn't. When Papa is in the bubble, half of our meals are delivered from restaurants all over the interior, or even from the commissary, where we take potluck of whatever's on the steam tables that day. One more reason to be happy to see our father, as if we needed another.

When Papa makes breakfast he doesn't stint on it. He's a firm believer that the day should be started with food that "sticks to the ribs." You will not find yogurt and fruit or a slice of dry toast on our breakfast table (though you will find plenty of fruit in the other two meals). You will find heaps of crisp bacon, andouille sausage, and eggs scrambled with peppers, garlic, onions, tomatoes, Tabasco, and cheese.

That's what we filled our plates with that morning of the second day of Papa's return from the bubble.

Not much was said as we scarfed it all down, but we exchanged a lot of looks and smiles. It was good to get Papa off with just the two of us, no Mama or Uncle Travis to take up his time. I intended to do everything I could to ease his transition into this new part of his life, where once again something he thought of looked like it was going to revolutionize the world. Or our little world, anyway.

So after breakfast we stuffed the dishes into the pneumo and dressed in grubbies: khaki shorts with lots of pockets, tie-dyed tees, deck shoes, and old baseball caps—Miami Mariners for me, Orlando Disneys for sis— and hopped into our flat-bottomed boat, the *Bayou Queen*, and rowed out into the pond for a day of fishing.

And that's what we did for the first two hours. Fish. We opened bottles of cold soda and sat there with hooks dangling in the water. Papa had never been into all that fancy casting stuff. "Too much like work, *cher*." As usual, I had to put the minnows on the hooks for pukin' Polly, who couldn't stomach it. I'll admit I don't exactly *enjoy* hurting the little buggers, but I sort of figure it's a minnow's destiny to be bait. I'm sure a minnow would disagree.

Our fishing is mostly catch and release. We hook into bass and catfish, with the occasional perch. There are lakes for pike and walleye, but we don't frequent them.

For us, there's a Goldilocks fish. Not too small, not too big. We're easy graders when it comes to the little ones, tossing anything back that wouldn't fill a frying pan. Same goes for the honking big cats and bass, fish that might have been alive for the whole trip of *Rolling Thunder*. We call them old-timers, and treat them with respect.

Well, I don't suppose it's really respectful to put a painful hook into their lips and jerk them roughly out of their element, but I have to figure it's better than the pan.

My feeling about fishing is that if it's too icky for you, then be a vegetarian. More power to you.

After two hours and with three big cats on the string, Papa broke out the oyster po'boys and we dug in. These were smoked oysters, not from Papa's precious reserve of bubble-fresh raw ones, but they were good. Papa makes the sandwiches wet, with lots of mayo, cayenne, and remoulade, hot enough to turn your face red. You need a bib if you care about your clothes, and afterward you need a good hand-washing in the pond.

We really had enough fish for the night's meal, but none of us were eager to head for shore, so we baited hooks and dropped them. But after that, it was a lucky day for anything we caught. A minute to admire and take a picture of a big one, and then back to Davy Jones's locker with a horror story to tell your friends.

"Can I talk to y'all about something?"

It startled me. Sure we'd talked a little in the last hours, but it was about ordinary stuff, all the things Papa wanted to hear about after a spell in the bubble. What we'd learned in school, where we'd gone, what we'd done, how old friends were doing, any new friends. We were careful talking about boyfriends and dates because Papa worried about that. He wanted to hear play-by-plays of all our skypool games though he had never attended one because he was too afraid for us. Naturally, he was horrified at Polly's fall and injury, though we were both careful to minimize it, laugh it off.

But his tone of voice was quite different just then. Just like we know when Mama's about to give us a blistering, we know when Papa is worried about something.

"Anything, Papa," Polly said.

"Y'all know it's hard for me, 'cause I can never talk right."

"We can always figure it out, *cher.*"

He smiled at us, and nodded.

"That true. I don't know how y'all do it, untying my tongue and all. But I'm gonna do my best, me, to tell you something I don't even rightly understand myself."

Well, *that* was going to be a challenge.

"I'm all ears, Papa," I said.

"Well, y'all know that when somebody's in a black bubble, ain't no time passes. No time at all."

"That's what you always told us," Polly said.

"An' it be true. In one way. But not true in another."

"Is it some sort of quantum thing, Papa?" I asked.

"No, honey, it's different. What I know for sure is that *something* going on in wherever it is we go when we go in a bubble."

"And where is that?" I asked him.

"That, I still don't know for sure, *cher*. I'm working on it. But it seem like it a multidimensional space that ain't really like our space, and ain't really like our time. I don't figure it may actually be in our universe at all."

"But you can go there and not be hurt?" Polly said. "I mean, you come out the same as you went in, right? As least, as far as I can tell you do."

"Far's I can tell, me, too."

"So, Papa, the one thing different is that you . . . you had some sort of *idea*. Something must have changed in your *mind*, because you were feeling fine when you went in the bubble and you weren't fine when you came out."

"*Exackly*, sweetness. And it done happened before, too."

"When was that, Papa?" Polly wanted to know.

Papa frowned and bit his lip.

"It was back when your mama was in the bubble her ownself. You know about that, don't you?"

Oh, yes, we knew.

———————

Mama was under the Europan ice, in a black bubble, when the giant crystal beings began their migration to Earth. No one knows why they did it, but it seems they had been doing it almost since the beginning of the solar system, causing huge numbers of extinctions. Every sixty million years or so, they erupted from Europa and went to Earth. It seems likely they killed the dinosaurs, among other creatures.

During the ten years Mama was under the ice, Papa was also in a black bubble. He spent much of his time there. Otherwise, he would probably be dead by now, or alive at the age of 112. As it is, his internal clock is reading fifty-seven. Papa didn't find life on Mars very satisfying. He longed for his familiar surroundings in Florida or Louisiana. The big habitat Travis constructed for him on Mars felt like just that: a habitat, like in a zoo. No one was staring at him or throwing him peanuts, but that's how he felt.

He couldn't go back to Earth; he was too famous, too much a target for those who were convinced they could pry the secret of the bubbles out of his poor, abused brain.

So he and Mama were in their own separate bubbles at the same time. No big deal, right? After all, at any given time there were many thousands of people inside black bubbles, in suspended time for one reason or another. At that time it was mostly people with fatal diseases hoping for a cure sometime in the future. Now, it's millions of refugees from Earth in vast, underground, Martian vaults, and no one really knows when they will be taken out.

If they will *ever* be taken out. There's no room for them on Mars, and Earth is less habitable every day.

On top of that, Papa and Mama were separated by somewhere between a billion and half a billion kilometers from each other, depending on where Mars was in its orbit.

But apparently distance didn't matter when you were in a bubble. At that time, Mama and Papa had never met. But when Travis brought Papa out of the bubble to see if he could do anything about the Europan invasion, the first thing he asked for was Podkayne.

Well, he'd heard her name and for some reason was asking for her, right?

Nope. Mama wasn't even born when Papa went into the bubble.

Somehow, in a way Papa said he still doesn't completely understand, he made contact with Mama while no time was passing. He did something, or she did something, or *something* did something to *them* . . . in other words, something *happened* in a place that isn't even really a place, a place where nothing *can* happen, by definition.

"So that's now I met my sweet Poddy, my darlings. The fallin' in love part, that come later."

Papa had told us the whole story many times. Neither of us minded. We liked all his stories, and this was one of our favorites. It was like when we were children and he or Mama would read us a story from our little library of paper books, like *Alice's Adventures in Wonderland* or *If I Ran the Zoo*, only better, because these stories were true. Well, most of them were, though Papa later admitted he had made some of them up.

"I been puzzlin' on it for a long time, me, and I figure it may be the one thing I need to . . . the one thing that will . . ." He trailed off.

"Is it that key to everything you've talked about, Papa?" Polly asked.

"That's it. The thing that locks everything together, you know?"

I did know, in general terms. People have been working on it since at least Einstein, the "Theory of Everything" that would tie together all the fundamental forces of nature, of the strings that might be at the heart of quarks, of gravitation and electricity and matter and energy, quantum mechanics and relativity, dark matter, and dark energy. In science class we learned that Archimedes might have been the first one to set out on that path, but Einstein was the first one who had enough useful information and enough tools to make a good start on the problem. Others have advanced it over the years, including Papa, but the final equation remains elusive.

"So it done happened once," he went on. "Something happened to me and your mama while we was suspended. And now it done happened again. When I come out of that thing, it just hit me all at once. I knew something I didn't know before. I seen how another part of the puzzle fitted together. But it wasn't like I figured anything out. It was . . . it was just *there*. Like someone done pulled the handle on a adding machine and the tape come up, and it said we was in big trouble."

I didn't know what he meant by the handle on an adding machine, so I had to blink it. I got a picture in the corner of my eye of a boxy contraption with a lot of buttons on the front, like the cash registers I'd seen in old movies. A hand pulled the crank on the side, and some metal bars came up and printed a number on a strip of paper. Pretty ingenious, how they managed to work around the lack of electronics in the ancient days. It was for people who didn't know how to use an abacus, I guess.

"See, the thing about this dark lightning stuff . . . you know I told y'all about the different dimensions that might be out there. The three regular ones, and time, then other space dimensions? I've figured for quite a while that the dark lightning is hidin' in one of those other universes, which normally we can't get to at all. It's other stuff over there, I don't know what to call it, so I guess callin' it what we call what it does . . . I mean, we call it dark matter and dark energy, but that's only its shadow, the shadow of this other stuff. I'm gettin' tongue-tied again."

He stopped. Neither of us said anything. In a normal conversation, both of us were good at offering gentle suggestions that usually got him over a verbal roadblock, but this? How do you help him when he's talking about the shadows of some stuff that ain't matter and ain't energy, and is hiding in the eighty-seventh dimension? I glanced at Polly, who gave me a tiny shrug that meant "It's way beyond me, too, spacegirl."

"But this stuff," he finally went on, "they's so much of it that it reaches over into our universe some whichaway, and it show itself as a different kind of energy and a different kind of gravity. We ain't got nothing can detect it except by lookin' at far-off galaxies and stuff like that. But it's there, and it's all around us, all the time, yes indeed. It's passing through us right now, lots of it."

"So what's so bad about it?" I asked.

"Most of the time, ain't nothing bad about it at all. Only when you get goin' fast enough, it's a different story. Here's the deal. Way back, they done proved that there ain't no ether. Space ain't water or air, and we don't need a medium to carry light waves, which ain't really waves, anyway. And that still holds up. But this new stuff, this dark lightnin' . . .

"This stuff just be there, all over the place. It look like it's thicker in some places than in others, but it's there. It leakin' over from some other universe, and it be the most important stuff *in* our universe. I don't think there could *be* any regular space without it. I think it may be what creates space its *own*self."

"But what *is* space?" I asked.

"If I knew that, I'd really know somethin', *cher*. I been nibblin' at the edges of this idea most of my life, me, and I done come up with some things. Just little tricks you can do even though you don't really understand it all, but if you have a sort of hint where these other dimensions might be hiding."

"Little . . . tricks?" I said.

"Yessum, ways to twist parts of our universe into the other universe, or little bits of the other ones into this one."

It dawned on me that he was talking about squeezer bubbles, which supplied virtually all the power to all the humans back at Old Sun and, of course, here in *Rolling Thunder*, too.

I glanced at the twin, and she silently bugged her eyes and dropped her jaw. She had gotten it, too.

I put it out of my mind for now. We still hadn't reached the important stuff, the things I was sure Papa had brought us out on the boat to talk about.

"So, back to this medium, Papa . . ."

"Okay, right." He paused, gathering his thoughts. He noticed for the first time that something was tugging on his line, though I had seen it several minutes before. I hadn't wanted to interrupt his thoughts. He reeled it in, meeting little resistance, and came up with a sheepish-looking koi with a distinctive gold patch between his eyes.

"Well, hello, Boudreaux," he greeted the fish. Not all our koi have names, but many of the biggest and most distinctive of them do, most of them named by Papa. All our koi are Cajuns, oddly enough. "Wouldn't be a good day of fishin' if we didn't catch you once or twice."

"Dumb old fish," Polly said, reaching over with the wire cutters to snip the barb off the hook. Old Boudreaux hung there in the water for a moment, possibly waiting for some fish pellets, then swam slowly away.

"Don't be too hard on him, *cher*. He older than you are, and he do pretty good for not having a brain much bigger than a BB."

"I don't know, Papa," she said. "If koi tasted as good as bass, he'd have been fried up a long time ago."

"Well, then it was plumb smart of him and the other koi to taste so bad, wasn't it?"

"Can't argue with that, Papa," I said. He noticed that Polly and I had taken in our lines—we'd both done it fifteen minutes before, but he'd been in his other universe, where the dark lightning dwelled. He put his pole down into the rack beside ours and shipped the oars. He started rowing us slowly back toward the dock.

"Need any help, Papa?" Polly said. "I'd be glad to row us, but I've got this broken arm. I'm sure Cassie would be glad to help."

Papa doesn't like the classic raised-middle-finger gesture, but he doesn't mind the good old fist and forearm jerk, so I laid one on her. Papa laughed.

"No, girls, this help me keep my thoughts in order."

"The medium, Papa," I prompted him.

"Right, the medium. Well, water be a medium. A pretty thick one. See how it fights me when I stroke an oar through it? I gotta push a lot of water out the way with these here paddles to move the boat in the other direction. And when I stop rowin', the boat stops pretty quick. How come?"

"Friction," I said.

"Friction," he agreed. "But we movin' through another medium, and that be the air. Only it don't fight us so hard, right? If I be rowin' real hard, we can feel it. If a breeze come up, we can feel that. But it ain't nothing like the thickness of the water.

"Now, you girls never been on the bayou, so you don't know just how hard a wind can blow. But b'lieve me, my darlin's, it can blow mighty hard in a hurricane. I done lived through three of 'em, name of Earl, Katrina, and Peggy. Earl and Peggy weren't much, but Katrina, she a real nasty one. Hundred and fifty miles per hour, she blew, and washed out the levees and a bunch a people got killed. Y'all got no 'sperience of bad weather, y'all probably can't imagine it."

"Probably not," I agreed. Just thinking about it gave me chills. Weather like that was the new normal back on Earth.

"Well, girls, air can be even worst than that. When an old-time spaceship like Apollo or the Space Shuttle or the VentureStar come back into the at-mosphere, that ol' friction like to burned 'em up. *Did* burn up a couple of 'em. Nothin' but air, and pretty thin air, at that. Even on Mars you can't hit the air goin' real fast and not burn up, less you got somethin' to radiate that friction heat away.

"So now we got this new medium, this . . . what I'm callin' dark light-nin' ether. It be thin . . . oh, my, real thin, not much thicker'n the space between the stars, and we don't even have no instruments that can 'tect that we be passin' through it. But it be there . . . and I'm workin' on some-thin' to find me some."

"So . . . what's the problem, Papa?"

"I wonder why things get old, why they wear out. Life be a delicate thing, girls, it be a lot of real complicated chemicals, long strings of DNA, there's plenty that can screw it up. Only takes a little bit a regular radi-ation. So I wonder . . . maybe this dark lightning ether could be why we get old and stop fixin' ourselves. Why we grow awhile, then we stop growin', and get sick, and die a old age. Even when it ain't hittin' us all that hard, back on Earth.

"But out here, it be passin' through us like a real hurricane. The faster we go, the worst it will get."

I felt a chill run down my spine.

"So how fast is too fast, Papa?"

He looked up at us, not happily.

"I don't know for surely yet, me. But I figure it ain't much faster."

We bumped gently into the dock, and I hopped out and tied off the line. Papa got out, too, but Polly just sat there for a moment, looking sad. She looked up at us.

"I'm just thinking about the rabbit," she said. Right. The poor little rabbit. I had thought about him, too.

At the Council meeting, Uncle Max had wanted to know why we didn't just send out a probe with a guinea pig on it. It would forge ahead of us, and when the guinea pig died, we would know if Papa's theory was right or not.

"Already being done," Travis had said. "I've got some guys slapping something together, about ready to go. There's a rabbit aboard, and a lot of food and water, and an automatic cleaning system. But we don't want to boost it over one gee. Might kill the rabbit. So it's gonna take a while for it to pass whatever the threshold is. Jubal isn't sure, he says he needs to do more testing. And there are other variables he hasn't been able to take into account. Bottom line, if the rabbit dies, we could already be right up against whatever the speed limit is. You can't give us any better information, Jubal?"

"Not without more testing," Papa had said, sadly. Now, we all three fell silent. The rabbit would accelerate away from us, to live or to die. Either way, he wouldn't be coming back.

"I wish there was another way," Polly said. Well, I did, too, but I wasn't going to lose any sleep over it. But Polly would. She's maybe a little too sentimental.

"I thought about goin' out myself," Papa said. "Acceleratin' at one gravity, I wouldn't get space sick, like I do. Then, if I died, I'd come back and tell y'all about it."

I looked at him, waiting for the punch line. Then I realized there wasn't one. I looked at Polly, and she shrugged.

That's the thing with Papa. He is the world's champion genius when it comes to physics and math, and the world's best at love and sweetness. But his mind is childlike in other ways. He is often unable to detect a simple contradiction like that, and I'm not sure he understands death any more than a six-year-old does.

He needs looking after, he needs protecting. But that's what Polly and Mama and I are there for.

CHAPTER 9

_____

Polly:

> *Hail, hail to Bayouville, hurrah for the old gold and black!*
> *Hail, hail to Bayouville, our friendship will ye never lack!*
> *Ever faithful, ever true, as we sing our song of you!*
> *Black and gold, we're all true blue, all hail to Bayouville!*

Okay, it ain't "La Marseillaise." It ain't even "The Star-Spangled Banner." But it's the old school song. (We're not as old as Yale, not even twenty, but in our defense I'll say it's not as dumb as "The Whiffenpoof Song." What was *that* all about?) It's the anthem of the institution of which I will soon be an alumna—summa cum laude, no less! I've been singing it five mornings a week for twelve years, and as the day of graduation grows nearer, I find I now sometimes get a little thrill in my heart when we sing it. I guess that's because I won't be hearing it from now on unless I go to skypool or football games and, down the line a bit, PTA meetings. It's nice to be a part of something, to have school spirit and root for or play hard for your team. There's a lot of good memories tied up in the school, and I realize that at this point in my life, it's all I've known, and that the future is a big question mark, an unknown zone for the first time in my life, which has been so secure with my loving family and the school to give it structure.

Of course, until a week before, when Papa came out of the bubble, the biggest unknowns concerned what course of study would I take for my further education, what career did I want to pursue, did I want to move away from home (tentative answer: no, not yet), would I find a boy and fall in love with him. Little things like that.

Today the question was, would I have *time* for any of that?

They say teenagers think they are immortal, and I wouldn't have argued much about that a month ago. I didn't spend much time worrying about death. That was a long ways in the future.

But I'm not stupid. I know we all could die. Maybe growing up in a structure that is visibly limited, unlike the seeming infinite vistas of planet-surface people, we all know we are vulnerable, even us oblivious teens. It's not hard to imagine some catastrophic accident that could destroy us all.

My sister would say, why worry about something you can't do anything about? I know she's right, but I'm a worrier by nature, and now I had a lot more to worry about.

And the worry was beginning to spread.

———————

Travis has told us what schools were like when he was a boy.

They were great big buildings with hundreds, sometimes thousands of students. And those were just the elementary and high schools. The colleges and universities sometimes had tens of thousands. When he graduated from high school, they were barely using computers, which were pretty new.

It's hard for me to imagine.

Our schools are very different. There are fifteen of them, one for each township. They are all much alike, some a little larger than Bayouville, some a little smaller. They are each contained in one building. Ours has three classrooms, some have as many as five. In addition, there will be an auditorium, a gym, a pool, and extensive athletic grounds. Don't picture a one-room schoolhouse like the ones Travis showed us. The classrooms are large and free-form, with study stations that can be assembled into groupings as needed. We move from one to another as we finish work, and so do the teachers, who will typically number between ten and fifteen.

Do the math. There are fifteen townships, each with a waking population of between ten and fifteen hundred. Of those, only a few hundred will be of school age at any one time. We don't need big schools. Our graduating class will number eighteen, which is considered large.

One of the ship's regs is that, once you start school at age six, you and your family can't be put into a black bubble until you graduate, or fall so far behind academically or become such a problem of discipline that you are considered hopeless. Nobody, including Travis, thought it would be a good idea to have classmates vanishing for three or four or ten years, only to pop back into reality as young as they went in. Adults have to learn to cope with that, but not children.

Of course, when you turn eighteen, you'd better have some way of making yourself useful, or your whole family might be chronologically pickled until we arrive at New Sun. There are several effects of this rule, the most important being that it is one *hell* of an incentive for keeping your grades up. The second effect is that it encourages families to have children. You could raise them in security, then all go into a bubble upon the graduation of the youngest one.

Or not.

As that day drew near, I was feeling more guilty than I had ever been about my special status. I still didn't know what I wanted to do with my life, and ordinarily that could have been a problem for me and Cassie and Papa and Mama Podkayne. Not a *huge* problem, since going into a bubble was a common occurrence; most people in *Rolling Thunder* expected to spend some time in there. Some of them even *wanted* to. There were thousands and thousands of passengers who would arrive at New Sun that way, some of them having spent almost no time in "real" time. We'd just have to resign ourselves to missing the rest of the trip, not coming out until the journey was over.

But we were "family of the captain," and thus exempt.

What bothered me was, it seemed there was really nothing special about me, other than a talent for skypool, and there's nowhere to go with that. We have adult leagues but no professionals.

I couldn't sing, be an entertainer like Mama. I wasn't a supergenius like Papa. I had friends who were planning to go into medical training, ecology, and many other fields. I knew two girls who were already paired up, one of them married and the other one pregnant. (Seemed to me to be a little early to start a family, but to each her own, and she was ensuring the next eighteen years in real time.)

I wondered a lot about Patrick. As the son of Mike and Marlee he had a pass, just like me, but I somehow knew it wouldn't be necessary for him. He was always studying, I knew that, and it seemed certain he had a plan in mind for his future.

Why the hell didn't I have one for mine?

———————————

We don't formally segregate by age or sex at our schools—except for athletic teams at puberty because boys get bigger and stronger. Naturally six-year-olds are not taught together with seniors, but we might all be in the same room in different groups, with the teachers moving among us. There's very little difference between a second-grader and a fifth-grader, socially. Boys mix with girls a lot more easily than they seem to have done in the old movies I've seen about schools on Earth. Naturally a junior is unlikely to hang out with a first-grader, but the junior will *know* the first-grader, and probably help in teaching the little one.

We don't have summer vacations, but instead have three one-month breaks spread through the year.

We don't get off for Christmas, Yom Kippur, Ramadan, or any other religious holiday. *Rolling Thunder* is strictly nonsecular. Anyway, would you celebrate those holidays according to the calendar back at Old Sun, or our own internal calendar? They're quite a way apart now. Muslims, Christians, and Jews differ among themselves on that question.

At least the Muslims don't have a problem with facing Mecca. It's back *thataway*, many light-years. Kneel facing the South Pole, and you're fine.

There is no real reason why we start primary schooling at age six and move on to higher education at eighteen except that that was how it was in Travis's day.

Early on in the trip, an educator felt that we might be becoming a little too insular in our education, and the exchange program was instituted. Someone once said it was a bit like the customs in some Earth tribes of marrying outside of one's immediate tribe, thus ensuring genetic diversity. I don't know about that, but the effect was good, in my opinion. So for one month out of the year, each of us attends another school. I always enjoyed these sojourns. Except for the very youngest, who might sorely miss their parents, we were shipped off away from our friends, our usual social circle, and even our homes. We stayed with families in the new township, and got to know new people. I made a lot of friends that way, and among the exchange students who spent time at Bayouville. I spent time in twelve of the townships, missing only Bedrock, Bedford Falls, and Dogpatch.

Another good thing was that it separated Cassie and me for a while each year. Twins can tend to become too reliant on each other, or so we both felt. I enjoyed getting away from her, and I enjoyed reuniting. So it all worked out pretty well.

So, there's a broad overview of our education system. It will serve to give you an idea of how really small-town we all are, and there are things that all small towns have in common. One of them is that news, even secrets, travels fast.

Bayouville School is a round building with stucco sides and a conical roof that is ridged and painted to suggest straw thatch. There are lots of windows and skylights. At the top of the roof is a peaked cupola with a bell hanging inside. I had rung that bell many times myself; it's considered an honor and a treat. It was ringing now, as it did every morning at eight, as Cassie and I parked our bicycles in the rack and entered the gym.

The interior of the building is divided into five equal rooms, each taking up 72 degrees of the circumference. The three classrooms take up three-fifths of the space, with the auditorium and gym accounting for the other two pie wedges. The pool is outside, surrounded by a tall cyclone fence, and it is entered through the gym. It is Olympic-sized, but it has a deep end with a high diving board.

We're allowed to design our own schedules of study, and Cassie and I and a few of our best friends had been scheduling gym period at the first of the day for several years. When we entered the girls' locker room, I could see that most of the team were already there.

I had hardly sat down in front of my locker before Pippa Mendez sat on the bench beside me. She had brought her gym clothes, apparently intending to chew the fat while we got dressed.

"Well, if it isn't Polly-wanna-cracker," she said. "It *is* Polly right? Not Castor Oil?"

"How're they hangin', Pimpa?" I asked.

"Fabulous outfit, Pol."

"Thanks." I was wearing pumpkin gypsy trousers that billowed around the ankles, with a cornflower embroidered top that Mama had given us two years ago and neither of us had worn recently. I thought the combo worked pretty well.

"So how's your ass?"

"Prettier than your face." She tried to punch me on the arm, but I grabbed her wrist and wrestled her to the ground. She got up, laughing, and resumed her seat on the bench. I slipped out of the pants and turned around.

"See anything you like?"

"That's a bad bruise, *hermana*. But it's fading out. Wait, wait! Is that the face of Jesus I see?"

"Jesus . . ."

". . . my ass!" we both said at the same time. It had been a catchphrase for a while.

"I heard a rumor about some pigs," she said, pulling off her shoes and grabbing her gym socks. She had a pretty good image of the *Mona Lisa* on one of her great toenails. Pippa is one of those girls who are into nails. Me, I stick to one color.

Pippa is the same age as me, with lovely olive skin and lustrous, long black hair. She helped us learn Spanish for three years, to the point where we're both competent if not exactly fluent.

"Be careful what rumors you listen to," I said.

"*Es verdad*. But I heard another—"

I didn't get to hear what else she had heard, at least not then, because a loud voice interrupted us.

"Listen up, all you flyin' fools."

It was Coach Peggy, standing on a stool in the middle of the room. She was dressed, as always, in her white track suit. She needs the stool because she's just a hair over four feet tall. She can also arm-wrestle me to humiliation, probably throw me over the top of the schoolhouse, and is absolutely deadly in any number of martial arts. When the boys' coach needs to break up a fight among the testosterone-poisoned humans who were now in the other dressing room, all he had to do was threaten to sic Coach Peggy on them, and that was usually enough to stop the hassle in its tracks. We were all terrified of her on one level, and we all loved her—even the boys—on another.

"Today is group-picture day for all you skypool ladies," she went on. All coaches should have big, authoritative voices, and Coach Peggy did, though it was hard to figure out where she kept it in that tiny body. She seldom needed a bullhorn. "So before we work out, I want you all in your playing uniforms. Let's get going, then, sweethearts. Pour those lumpy bodies into that spandex, chop-chop."

I was already in my gym shorts and sports bra, and there was a problem. My uniform was in a pigsty somewhere in Duckburg. I put two fingers between my lips and whistled our *Mayday* whistle. Cassie hurried over from across the room.

"I don't have a spare uniform," I whispered to her. "Can I borrow yours?"

"No," she whispered back. When I gave her the stink eye, she smiled just a little and leaned near my ear. "But you can rent it." She kissed me on the forehead and quickly got out of kicking range, then sashayed back to her locker. She snagged a passing sixth-grader and handed her the black-and-gold jumpsuit, pointed her in my direction.

"Thanks," I told the little one. When the evil twin "rents" me something, she's not talking about money. Someday soon there would be something she wanted of me, some unpleasant task most likely. And I'd be honor-bound to do it. I'd done it to her often enough, but we're both so competitive we hate to be behind in getting-even accounts.

We assembled in the football field, at the small grandstand. The photographer was just finishing up with the boys football A-team, eleven of our finest sides of beef in lovely black silk shorts and gold tunics, only three of whom I'd kick out of bed. In fact, I'd hooked up with two of them, but they were brief affairs. Well, I figure if you don't practice, you won't be very good at it when you find Mr. Right.

Somebody had unfolded a black-and-gold flycycle and put it on a stand in the bleachers. When the photographer dismissed the kickers, he gathered us together and studied us critically.

"Young ladies, I'll be setting you up in several different groupings. If you all listen to me and do as I say, quickly, this can all be over before you know it, and with very little pain. First we'll do the A-Team, as a matter of right. Then we'll group all of you together, regardless of age and team status. Okay?"

"First of all, Ms. Click and Ms. Clack, you two are the tallest here. I'd like you as fenceposts, corralling the group. One of you to one end, the other over there."

We'd heard them all, Chip and Dale, Dum and Dee, Dumb and Dumber, even Scylla and Charybdis. We were used to it. I moved to one side and was immediately joined by Pippa and Jynx Molloy.

"Okay, that works," the photographer said, and turned his attention to placing the other team members. It seemed to me that Pippa and Jynx were almost jostling for position beside me. Jynx is part Australian aboriginal and part Chinese, at least according to her. Neither of those gene pools was prone to produce basketball players, and she came up to just above my shoulder. The shape of her eyes was Chinese, but a little something else must have crept in there somewhere, as the eyes themselves were a startling blue. She styled her hair in kinky spikes, and her skin was as black as anyone's I'd ever seen. Her face was knockout gorgeous, and her figure outstanding. She was our power forward because she didn't know how to be anything but aggressive in the playing globe.

Or anywhere else, for that matter.

"So I heard your old man is out of the black again," she said. I looked past her and saw Pippa roll her eyes. I figured they had some sort of plan to double-team me and get my attention while one of them sneaked up on my blind side. That's how Pippa would have done it, but Jynx just couldn't constrain herself.

"So how's he doing?"

"Oh, you know. Papa never likes going black. He's a little upset, but he'll get over it. He always does."

"That's not what I heard," Pippa said, abandoning all hope of subtlety. "I heard he was really upset about something."

"That's what they're saying," Jynx confirmed.

"Who's *they*?"

"You know. People talking. My mother heard it from somebody, and I overheard her talking to a friend of hers about it."

"That's how wild rumors get started, spacegirl. Don't you—"

"Ladies! Ladies!" Coach Peggy shouted. "Can we knock off the gabbing for just a minute here, and all of you face the camera and at least *pretend* that you're a team who will soon be battling for the bronze medal?"

Maybe that's why we all felt a little uninvolved. Due to our recent loss to the Hillbillies, they would be meeting the Maycomb Finches for gold and silver, while we had to be satisfied with a shot at the Castle Rock Queens for third place. Normally, I'd have been even more upset than the rest of us, because it was my mishandling of the evil Cheryl Chang that had caused the loss, but now I had other, more important things on my mind.

"All right," the photographer said, "say 'orthodonture,' and . . . Okay. Hold your positions. Now, this time, I want big smiles, *serious* smiles. There are thirty-two teeth in the human mouth, girls. There are eight of you. I want to see all 256 choppers when you smile."

"If you've still got all thirty-two," Cassie piped up from the other end, "you're not playing hard enough." That got a laugh, and the photographer took a picture. She's lost three teeth and I've lost two. That's about standard, if you're any good. I like the new ones better. They're stronger.

"Not in this bunch," Coach Peggy called out. "Four of those are wisdom teeth, and these girls don't have them. You can't have wisdom and play skypool."

That got a big cheer, and the camera snapped again.

"Okay," the coach sang out. "Enough of that smiling happy crap. I want a few with your *game faces* on. I want you to mean business. I want you to look so fierce you'd scare a junkyard dog back into the doghouse. I want you to make my hair stand on end, and all the fleas jump out and run for their lives. Let's hear you growl, Gators!"

We did the best we could, and I think the photographer was impressed. He snapped three quick ones, then called all the skypool players in, which meant just about the whole school, male and female. The A-Team boys had changed into their tights, which were even sexier than the football uniforms. You never saw so many tight butts and ripped calves.

This gathering was pretty informal, just grouping more or less by size, with the very young ones (who played 2-D kiddiepool on bicycles on the ground until they understood the rules and were ready for flycycles) out in front, and us short-timers in the back. I did my best to shake off Jynx and Pippa, but they clung to me like leeches. Cassie had figured out what was happening, and she joined me, but she had picked up a lamprey of her own, in the person of Milton Kaslov. Milton is one of the few boys in school who is taller than us, so naturally, with a stunning lack of imagination, he soon picked up the moniker of Milt the Stilt. He's about six-nine, with a big shock of unruly black curls and a honking beak of a nose. But when they were handing out chins, he really got shortchanged.

He's a pain in the ass.

It's not because he's not much to look at, honestly. I know a few boys that look worse than him, and we get along fine. He's very bright, but it's not because he's a nerd, I have no prejudices on those lines. It would be pretty silly to disrespect smart people with the father I have.

It's that he's as boring as a whole colony of termites, one of those species that I *don't* believe we brought along. If we need termites at New Sun, I guess we'll just die.

Travis once said that somebody can be like a knife, keen on one side and dull on the other, and not have a point to him at all. A person can be real smart and thick as a brick, all at the same time. One of my friends once suggested that Milt the Stilt lies somewhere on the autistic spectrum, maybe with Asperger's, which would mean he has a disability, and would make me a mean person. If he does, it would be in his academic records somewhere, and confidential, but I don't buy it. None of the teachers have ever given him any special-needs attention, he's just in the advanced academic group for all the science subjects. Plus, I read up on it, and scientists agree that you can be an Aspie and a nice guy, or an Aspie and an asshole.

That's not how they put it, but you get the point.

Talking to Milt for ten minutes made you have thoughts of suicide. We all avoided him, but he was oblivious, and would walk right up to you and start talking about the first thing that came into his head. He would actually reach out and grab you when you tried to move away, and have no idea that the reason you wanted to leave was that you were afraid your head was going to explode if you hung around one more second.

I had tried to like him, I really had, when we were all younger. When that didn't work out, I had tried to feel sorry for him, but couldn't manage that, either. Then I tried just to not dislike him and failed at that, too. Three strikes and you're out, which I think is a term from cricket, a game we don't play in *Rolling Thunder*.

Lately, it had gotten even worse. He had become fixated on us. It was clear it didn't matter to him which one succumbed to his masculine charm and rapier wit. In fact, he had hinted that he wouldn't be averse to having both of us in bed at the same time. (Which is something we discussed, once, after seeing a fairly shocking lesbian video, and quickly agreed was definitely *not* for us.) So in addition to being boring and overbearing and obnoxious in many other ways, he had now added creepy to his list of endearments. He had done everything but come up and hump my leg, and I had tried every variant of the word no I could think of, including a slap on the face. I figured the next way to say no would be a kick in those dan-gly bits that boys are so proud of.

But today he wasn't looking to get laid. He was after the same thing Jynx and Pippa wanted, which was gossip.

"They say your dad thinks the ship is going to blow up," he said. Subtle as a ball-peen hammer, our Milt.

"'They' are doing a lot of talking," Cassie said. "The way I heard it, we're about to fall into a black hole."

"No shit? Man, we better . . . Aw, you're just jerking my dick."

"There's an appetizing thought. I'd have to find it first, though."

"Come on, Cassie. Everybody knows something's going on. They say he's really upset about something. He was up in the control room. What was he doing up there?"

"I'm Polly, you jerk," Cassie said. We do that to keep people on their toes, especially people we don't like. Looked like somebody at the Council meeting had blabbed. Well, Travis hadn't exactly sworn them to secrecy. Not that he could have even if he'd wanted to.

"You were up there, too," Pippa said.

"And your father wasn't in very good shape," Jynx added.

"Good grief!" I exploded. "Why is everyone suddenly so concerned about Papa? Everybody knows he is easily upset. It's just the normal anx-iety he gets when going into the black, that's all. And is there some kind of law against his going up in the control room? The control room of the ship that *wouldn't even be here* if it weren't for his inventions?"

"Nobody's saying your dad doesn't have the right to be there," Jynx said. "It's just that he never goes there. Something else everybody knows is, he hates weightlessness."

"And I'm hearing that your uncle Travis is out, too," Pippa piped up. "Quite a bit ahead of schedule."

"How would you know what his schedule is?" Cassie wanted to know. "That's a secret, always has been."

"Not to your family," Milt said, darkly.

"What's that supposed to mean?" Cassie turned on him and gave him a shove in the chest. He backpedaled and almost fell on his butt. "Our family business is just that. Private family business and no concern of anyone else. You know the rules. We live close together in here, and we're all entitled to privacy."

"No one's saying you aren't," Jynx said, quietly.

"Yeah, then why are the three of you giving us the third degree?" A small crowd had gathered, some of them pretending to not be eavesdropping, some of them not even bothering to hide it.

"And all the rest of you!" she shouted. "Butt out, okay? There's nothing wrong with Papa, and there's nothing wrong with the ship."

"You're a poor liar, Polly," Pippa said. "Oh, excuse me, I meant Cassie."

"Come on, sis," I said, not committing myself to which of us she was, though it was obvious that Pippa knew. "Let's leave this gossip group to get along without us."

"Yeah, they seem to be doing fine without any actual facts," she said.

We turned and headed back to the school building. I glanced over my shoulder to see if anyone was following. No one was, but most of them were looking at us.

"I feel like we're making our escape, somehow," I said.

"Yeah, like any minute they'll break and start running after us."

"With torches and nooses, maybe."

"Shit, sis, let's really make our escape. I don't have any finals today. How about you?"

"Nothing important. Got an essay to write."

"Do it at home. Let's blow this joint, then."

"Suits me."

We hustled into the gym and changed back into street clothes, then outside to our bicycles. We made it down the road without being seen.

We weren't supposed to be home at that time of day, and Papa would have been disappointed in us if he'd known we were cutting class—something we almost never do, by the way—and neither of us liked lying to him, so there was the problem of where to go. Without a clear destination in mind, we found ourselves headed south into Mayberry Township, where there are a lot of fish farms, going down many levels. The ones on the surface are long, concrete tanks with water constantly bubbling, and fish in different stages of growth in each tank. It's mostly trout and salmon. Somehow, the genetics people have modified salmon so they don't need to go into a salt-water ocean to grow, and all the fish have been altered so that they grow faster and have more edible flesh. But they still look pretty much like the wild salmon and trout I've seen in pictures from Earth. Mayberry is not a really attractive place, with all the geometric lines of the tanks, but it makes you feel good with the sound of the bubbling water and all the negative ions in the air. And the sardine tanks are pretty, with silver flashes everywhere.

We were about halfway across Mayberry, still with no real destination in mind other than we knew we would soon be in Fantasyland, when we saw another cyclist in the distance, coming toward us on the hard-packed dirt road. We were just moseying along, sitting upright.

I could soon distinguish that he was male, and he was moving along at a pretty good clip, bent over the handlebars and pumping hard with his legs. When he got a little closer and looked up ahead of him, my suspicions were confirmed. It was our cousin Patrick. I felt my heartbeat accelerate, and a little flash of heat just under my belly button. That seemed a funny place for passion to manifest itself, but there it was.

When he saw us, he straightened up and stopped pumping hard. He glided up beside where we had stopped to wait for him, took off his helmet, wiped his brow with a red kerchief, and smiled at us. He was wearing skin-tight spandex in black and green stripes, short-sleeved and reaching to midthigh. It looked very good on him, outlining the definition of every muscle like an anatomy lesson. He wasn't one of those pumped-up freaks with biceps like beach balls and a neck that angled from the jawline straight to the shoulder. He was wiry, and hard-muscled. Looking at him, you just wanted to put your arms around him and feel that hardness against you, and maybe reach around and squeeze that tight butt.

"I was just going to see you girls."

The twin curse again. "You girls." A *set*. With someone like Patrick, you didn't want a sister around, and you wanted him to address you by name. But what could you do?

"I think Polly has a class she had to get to," my bitch sister said with a big smile. "But I have some free time." She survived the next five seconds, proving once more that looks *can't* kill.

"Cassie is confused," I said. "I already aced that one. It was just this morning, remember, sis?"

"Oh, yeah," she said, reluctantly, shooting me a middle finger where Patrick couldn't see it.

"So," I said. "Just a friendly visit? I'd be happy to cook lunch for you. Cass, how about you jet off to the market and get some lamb? Do you like lamb chops, Patrick?"

"I love them, and I'd be happy to take y'all up on that offer, but that's not why I came."

Notice the "y'all." *I* was the one who invited him.

"So what's the deal?" Cassie asked.

"Mom and Dad would like to see you if you don't mind. They have something they'd like to talk to you about."

Well. I glanced at the bitch, and she raised her eyebrows at me, then shrugged. A bit of a comedown that he wasn't the one who needed us, but there it was.

"Sure, Patrick. Lead the way."

CHAPTER 10

Cassie:

Rolling Thunder was by no means a finished project when we started our journey twenty years ago. Everything needed for survival had been built, tested, and was functioning perfectly when the ship left, but much of Travis's shopping spree was still in storage, including a great many buildings bought entire, dismantled, shipped, then filed away for reassembly when all the critical work was done. A lot of trees and crops had been planted, but there were large stretches with nothing but the thick layer of topsoil and big piles of rocks and gravel.

I can dimly remember some of the very early times when a lot was barren, and during our first six years, the place was crawling with bulldozers and cement mixers and trucks hauling building materials. Some of that still goes on, but it's now a much more peaceful and static place. There are no more rivers to landscape, no more ponds and lakes to be lined and fitted with pumps and filters. We have as much surface housing as the interior could comfortably accommodate and a stable population, so very few new buildings get erected.

In addition to whole buildings—Travis once said to me: "I'm a twenty-first-century William Randolph Hearst!"—he also bought *things*. All kinds of things.

Frivolous things, such as the Hope diamond as a wedding ring for Mama and Papa. We used to play with it when we were kids, and we've each worn it set in a necklace pendant to school dances. I recommend it as a way to impress your friends.

Practical things like a fleet of airplanes (impossible to fly in the ship, but probably useful at New Sun) and large oceangoing ships (again, useless in here, but probably worthwhile when we get there). He bought trains and streetcars and sawmills and textile mills and refineries and canneries, the great majority of which were stowed away under the surface.

He bought very few original artworks—"Digital copies are just as good, and besides, we'll be making our own art." He didn't buy any Egyptian mummies or Neanderthal skeletons or Ming vases or copies of the Magna Carta on parchment or Gutenberg Bibles. He bought very few cultural or anthropological or sociological artifacts at all except those that appealed to him, such as the *Spirit of St. Louis* and the *Apollo 11* capsule, a few sculptures by Rodin, and the world's largest pipe organ.

He got all this stuff at bargain-basement, fire-sale prices. Remember, the whole of Planet Earth was a fire sale after the Europan crystals arrived. And when Travis was done, both he and Papa were broke. Which didn't matter, as they had no further use for Earth or Mars money.

Of the things he bought, mine and Polly's favorite things when we were young were two merry-go-rounds, one from Central Park in New York City and one from Balboa Park in San Diego. They were set up when we were five, and we usually rode one or the other every day after school.

They became so popular, in fact, that they eventually became the core of our entertainment district, Fantasyland Township. That's where Patrick lives, still with his parents, like us, and that's where he was coming from when we met him on the road.

Like I said, the interior of *Rolling Thunder* was pretty basic when we started out. There was much to do, and most of it had to do with survival. For recreation, people mostly watched the entertainment we had brought along with us, which was virtually everything that had ever been recorded and digitized, everywhere. There was live music and some theatricals and dances in the parks—as soon as we had built them—on bandstands and small stages. But for an amusement park, the two carousels were it.

Gradually, as our leisure time increased to the relative ease we now enjoy, other amusements grew up around the carousels. At first, these were simple games of the sort Travis said you could find at county fairs on Earth. Tossing rings or balls, shooting baskets, hitting a clapper to ring a bell. Old-fashioned stuff. Step right up, ladies and gents, knock over the milk bottles and win a teddy bear! You could buy caramel corn and cotton candy and candy apples.

Soon this simple beginning was joined with some new rides, like a Ferris wheel and a Tilt-A-Whirl and a loop-the-loop and little cars you could "drive" on a track and little boats that followed a small, serpentine river. They were mostly for younger kids, which suited Polly and me fine.

But *Rolling Thunder* is chock-full of engineers, and eventually they had some time on their hands like everybody else. Somebody designed and built a roller coaster and, at age eight or nine, Polly and I thought it was the scariest, neatest thing ever. We would ride it a dozen times in a row.

It became something of a friendly competition. The townships agreed that all amusements should be confined to Fantasyland, then each township vied for building the newest, scariest ride there.

By now the place really lived up to its name. It was best to visit it at night, when the LEDs encrusting almost every surface were flashing in all the colors of the spectrum and some that seemed to be imported from another spectrum entirely. There was a roller rink and an ice rink, a fun house, spooky rides, thrill rides, splash rides, waterslides, wave pools where you could actually surf for ten or fifteen seconds.

A few of the rides were copied from some of the old Disney and Universal resorts, but most were original to the ship. Most of it was completely automated; we hadn't come to the point where we could spare much labor to operate a helter-skelter. Much of it looked horribly dangerous, but that was the idea. It was actually safe as a quiet walk in the park.

At the far end of the midway was something that had been a major source of controversy when it was first proposed. That was the Seven Dwarfs Casino.

When Travis was writing up the ship's regulations—that later were mostly confirmed by popular vote—he admits it was a hurried and sometimes slipshod affair. His guiding principle was that anything that doesn't hurt someone else should be legal, that government interference in private behavior should be minimal to nonexistent. His feeling about prostitution was that pimps, should such trash appear in the ship, should be black-bubbled until we arrived at New Sun. He didn't give much of a damn about drugs, either, as long as they didn't wreck your life. Showing up impaired for work or duty was also a black-bubbling offense.

He had nothing to say about gambling. Later, when I asked him, his comment was simple: "People will gamble. Get used to it."

So we had always had "friendly" bets in the ship, on races between people on foot or on bikes or skycycles or horses. Some people raced dogs and pigs. I even saw a turtle race once. There were people who played games for money: poker, bridge, chess, go, bocce, bowling, football, tennis, Chinese checkers, old maid, you name it.

Winnings or losses were not legally enforceable. If someone welshed, you just had to eat it and never bet with him or her again.

There were, of course, bets on skypool, and naturally we players were forbidden to bet. It wasn't a problem. If any girl on my team was ever shown to be shaving points, the rest of us would beat the shit out of her, and she would never be able to hold her head up in public again. It's never happened. We take skypool very seriously.

The rules on gambling were just like the ones for prostitution and drugs: Keep it under control, or wake up in a few decades for your trip down to our new home. Problem gamblers were defined as those whose debts threatened the livelihood of their families. We have no social-welfare programs in *Rolling Thunder* except for those who become physically disabled. We don't need them. Earn a living, or get bubbled. Slackers, deadbeats, anyone who looked like a burden to his or her neighbors or was failing to support his or her family got voted off the ship for a long, long snooze. There were plenty of people in stasis who would be happy to take your place.

But there were those who enjoyed the sort of games they remembered from Earth or Mars, where gambling had been big business as an integral part of the huge tourist trade—at least until the crystals cut severely into everyone's leisure time. My family has a long history in tourism, the hotel business, restaurants, and gambling. My great-grandparents, Manny and Kelly, opened the very first hotel on Mars, and my family ran it for many decades. There was a large casino in the hotel.

When the casino was proposed at Fantasyland it quickly became one of the more controversial issues in a body politic that is not really known for a lot of dissent. After all, it couldn't be clearer that we all have to pull together to make the voyage work, and most radicals of any stripe were weeded out when the crew and passengers were selected. But we do have differing opinions from time to time, and casino gambling was one of them. Polly and I were too young to vote—you have to be sixteen—but we knew our family was largely for it, and we followed the issue on political barometer sites like Soapbox and PublicSquare, where most decisions are made without the need of a formal referendum. This was one close enough that an actual vote was held, and it won by a narrow margin. So the casino was built and soon opened for business, and our uncle Mike got the job as manager. So for the last five years, Mike, Marlee, and Patrick had lived above the only gambling establishment for several light-years.

I like the casino even though I've only been there when visiting Uncle Mike and his family. It's all glitz and noise and the smells of beer and gin and excited human beings. The most animation is always around the dice tables, the least around the slot machines, where some people sit like zombies, pumping quarters into the one-armed bandits.

Slot machines are one of the things Travis did *not* bring along, but they are easy to make. Not the old-time ones with an actual handle and spinning drums inside, but the electronic kind with a screen. Mike insisted that they only accept and pay off in coins—actually tokens, since we don't have coinage in the ship, everything is in even-dollar amounts—so there's the constant clatter of metal hitting the tray beneath. The machines are brightly colored and full of flash and sound effects, highly animated. They look like fun, but the attraction wears off pretty quickly, I found.

Polly and I each played here a couple of times and found that table games and slot machines don't do anything for us. I started with fifty dollars, turned that into eighty at a slot machine, turned that into twenty at roulette, made it back to forty at blackjack, then lost it all playing craps, a game I never really fully understood. Polly actually came away with a profit but was no more excited by it than I was about my loss.

We both understood that our results would always be much like that . . . with a small difference. Mike operates what may be the only casino in history where the house doesn't take a cut. So, theoretically, if we played frequently at such games we could expect to break even, barring a run of good or bad luck.

Poker was a different story, of course, because you played against individuals, and skill was a big factor.

That was part of the compromise that allowed the casino initiative to squeak by. Anybody can win big or lose big on any particular day, but over time it will even out . . . *if* the house doesn't take a cut.

One more difference between *Rolling Thunder* and Las Vegas or Monte Carlo casinos is that Mike won't take your marker. No credit is extended. In fact, at a certain point he will stop taking your bets. That amount is determined by how much you have to lose, something you have to disclose before you're allowed to gamble. Your daily wagering allowance is determined by your savings and your income. When you reach that point, you are sent home, to try another day.

These measures have largely subdued the opposition to Uncle Mike's enterprise. He makes his money serving food and beverages, and it's enough for a good living. He's a respected member of the Fantasyland community, not seen as a predator on the helpless any more than a bartender is. And in *Rolling Thunder*, we do *not* blame the server of alcohol for the idiotic behavior of the drunk. Travis, a former drunk, was adamant about that.

Patrick had called ahead so Uncle Mike was down on the casino floor to meet us, dressed in his working clothes of a tuxedo and mirror-shined shoes. We took turns bending down to kiss him, and he led us through the clanging, scintillating, roaring, flashing, chattering explosion of light and sound. I paused to put a dollar in a slot machine, as I always did when visiting, and the machine seemed to have a nervous breakdown, clattering and whooping and flashing lights in my eyes, doing everything but sending up flares, and five-dollar tokens began clattering into the tray.

I saw on the screen that I had won a hundred dollars. That had never happened to me before!

"Congratulations," Uncle Mike said, with a big smile on his face. "Should we all stick around until you lose it back?"

"In your dreams, Uncle Mike. This will buy a couple of new outfits I've had my eye on for a long time."

"Let's see if I can win a replacement for my broken flycycle," Polly said, putting a coin in the slot next to my winning machine. She pulled the handle, and we watched the video reels spin.

"Thanks for the buck, sucker," the machine said, and chuckled. Polly didn't look surprised. My gloomy sister always expects the worst.

We entered an elevator and rose to the floor just above the pool level.

Up there was the owner's suite, a nice apartment whose chief attraction was a view down on the rooftop pool and park. The pool is huge and free-form, lined with trees and tropical shrubs, with tiki bars and other grass-roofed businesses. All very lovely and exotic, very South Pacific.

At the far end was a putting green and the first tee of the only permanent nine-hole golf course in the ship. (For three months of the year, a cornfield is converted to grass, mowed, and shaped into a full eighteen-hole course. If you want to play it, make your reservations now. It's booked up for the next two years.)

Closer to us, about ten feet below the level of Mike's balcony, was one end of the pool, full of splashing swimmers and lined by people lying on lounges.

Aunt Marlee was up there to greet us. She asked us if we wanted anything to drink, and we both asked for Dr Pepper.

If you wanted to invent an anti-Mike, a human being who was, in almost every possible way, the exact opposite of Mike, Marlee would fit the bill perfectly. Male, female. Very dark skin, skin as pale as skim milk. Eyes dark brown, eyes sky blue. Hair dark and kinky, hair long and straight and almost white. Four-foot-three, five-foot-eleven. How this Wagnerian goddess who would look perfect in a recruiting poster for the Hitler Youth and this self-described chocolate Munchkin ever hit it off is a question for the ages, but it's clear that they are crazy about each other. One of the girls in my class once whispered to me that Mike must need a ladder to . . . well, you know. I got in trouble for punching her out. When Mama Podkayne got to the bottom of what the fight was about, she called Mike to our house and had me tell the story. He had a good laugh.

"We don't do it standing up, Cassie dear," he said. "That would be silly. No, when we're in bed I think of us as a hot fudge sundae. A little bit of chocolate poured over a mountain of scrumptious vanilla ice cream."

I was still a virgin at the time, and I blushed right down to my toenails. Sex was still a scary mystery to me. Well, it's still a mystery, sort of, one I'm having fun figuring out, and that's good, but it's not scary.

"You're forgetting the chocolate-covered banana," Mama Podkayne said, and the two of them laughed until they hurt.

So I blushed some more, and apologized to the girl I hit, and she apologized to Uncle Mike, who said it wasn't necessary, and proceeded to charm . . . well, I was going to say charm the pants off her, and I'm sure she would have been willing if Mike wasn't a faithful husband. But they're good friends now, like he is with almost everyone he meets.

Mike not only makes jokes about himself, he is secure enough in who he is that he doesn't mind it when others joke.

I wish someday to be that secure and tolerant.

Marlee brought our drinks and a tray of lovely bar noshes sent up from the kitchens below. Mike told us that Marlee likes to cook and is pretty good at it, but she seldom has time. She is involved in a huge number of projects around the ship, some of them dealing with art. She is a sculptor who works in clay and porcelain and stuff like that, molding things with her hands, sometimes painting them, then baking them. Some of the objects are useful, some of them are just decorative, and some of them are frankly a little weird, but I like her stuff.

We all sat around a big bamboo table in comfortable wicker chairs, sipping our drinks and talking about this and that. Then we got down to it.

"Cassie, Polly," Uncle Mike began. "I don't know how much you've been told, or how much you've heard, but you should know that the whole ship's talking about Jubal and what he said when he came out of the bubble."

"And that would be . . ." Polly asked.

Mike sighed. "You're not betraying any confidences here. Everyone knows that he said the ship has to be stopped. This is a small town, after all. Word has gotten around."

Of course it had. It's inevitable in a wired society.

They used to have these things called telephones. They sat on your desk or kitchen table, and they rang aloud. You picked up a piece of the telephone, and you spoke into it. That was all.

By the time of my grandparents' generation everyone was wired right into their skins and were starting to be wired right into their minds. At first it was just subcutaneous phones that were implanted near the ear, but soon electrodes were being implanted subdurally, with tiny wires leading to different parts of the brain.

The same technology that allows my aunt Elizabeth to perform surgery with her prosthetic hand, or microsurgery with a waldo hand so tiny you need a microscope to see it, could be used to control just about anything. You no longer needed a keyboard or even voice to do things, all you had to do was *think* about it.

Billions of tiny tricolored pixels were burned onto your corneas, and 3-D moving pictures were displayed directly to your eye.

Sounds pretty amazing, doesn't it? And I guess it was. Granddaddy

Ramon and Granny Evangeline had implants like these, and they've told us it was pretty damn convenient and opened a whole new world of experience.

But as with so many new technologies, there were problems.

One problem was with worker productivity. There was no way to tell how much time an employee was spending in a virtual world of information or amusement while he or she was supposed to be doing a job. Offsetting that was the fact that so many jobs had been robotized, not requiring a human worker at all.

Everything that happened online was recorded *somewhere*, so vast data banks were being accumulated. Combining the Internet, which by then had incorporated medical monitoring of things like blood pressure and chemistry, heart rate, body temperature—all for your own good, and eagerly installed by most users—with a highly precise global positioning system of satellites homing in on devices buried *in your brain* . . . well, it wasn't an exaggeration to say that somewhere was the information that your daily bowel movement had been at 0821 hours, that it had taken three minutes and forty-five seconds, that the color was a healthy brown and the consistency smooth.

Most people were okay with it, just as they had been with the original Internet. Who cared if someone was keeping track of your shopping preferences? And why would you have a problem with monitoring that could detect a heart attack before it happened, or see the first signs of cancer years before you might be aware of it?

All well and good, if no one is studying you with any evil intent. But there's always someone out there wanting to take advantage of you.

But even that wasn't the main drawback. What no one had thought about was the possibility that, given that nerve impulses could be detected and translated into operating instructions for a galaxy of mechanical and cybernetic machines . . . maybe the vast net could operate the other way. Maybe instructions could flow into the operating system of the brain.

Maybe it could be used to control actions, even thoughts.

Maybe we had created a huge puppet master, and who knew what the motivations or intents of the potential string-pullers might be.

It was one thing to turn on your computer in the old days of the Internet and find that a virus had infected it and destroyed a lot of your data, or turned your machine into a secret agent, sending who-knew-what to millions of other computers. It was something else entirely to think some electronic virus had infected your mind.

––––––––––––

Opponents of what came to be called Direct Connect had a long, long list of odd and frightening instances of aberrant behavior by previously mentally healthy people. There were accusations of ballot-box stuffing in a new and ingenious way, by programming people to vote for Candidate B while thinking they had voted for Candidate A. Maybe false memories inserted into people's brains. There was a frightening increase of a previously rare condition: alien hand syndrome—sometimes called Dr. Strangelove syndrome—where parts of the body inexplicably began to function on their own, often to the detriment of the person they were attached to.

It was said that some people were suddenly falling into or out of love with others, only to gravitate to someone they had previously loathed. Natural behavior, or mind tampering?

All of it was alarming, almost all of it was impossible to prove. If you believed the worriers, there was a vast conspiracy of meddlers, known as Controllers. They might be part of the government, or the shadowy commercial and financial (and possibly fictitious) oligarchs, or just basement tinkerers. Who knew?

On the other side, the DC proponents argued that, by limiting the natural and organic expansion of the vast intermind wiring network, we might be shutting ourselves off from nothing less than the next step in human evolution. It was a concept known as "singularity." A machine-brain symbiosis, a gestalt consciousness long imagined by science-fiction writers, or even real scientists. Something very like telepathy was within our grasp. Already mind-to-mind communication had been demonstrated on a primitive level. Do you want to cripple this new being, this über-human consciousness, just because of a few paranoid fantasies, backed up by very little evidence?

I'd just as soon keep other people out of my mind, thank you very much, said the doubters.

On and on it went.

The important thing for me, and for *Rolling Thunder*, was that Travis was one of the doubters. Big-time.

One of the cardinal protocols of *Rolling Thunder* when the crew and passengers were being selected and boarded was that *There Shall Be No Neural Implants*. Yea, verily, and shout hallelujah!

(Except in special circumstances like Aunt Elizabeth's prosthetics and other situations where very fine virtual control was necessary, and even those could not be connected to a network.)

So . . . I have no way of knowing in just what way the people of Earth and Mars and the outer planets are wired in these days. Here in the ship, though, we have frozen such things at a point around the 2030s.

We have wireless person-to-person communication, but it is limited to external devices. Some are incorporated into jewelry. Bracelets, necklaces, earrings, hair barrettes. They can be in a belt buckle, or in the soles of your shoes, or sewn into or pinned to your clothing. Some people spend most of their days connected to what we call the Rollingnet, talking or messaging their friends singly or in cybergroups. Polly and I tend to leave the connection off, so the call tones aren't constantly ringing in our ears, and access the messages while we're not doing anything else. Neither of us is a net rat.

Sound is provided by a simple and tiny subcutaneous unit implanted into the mastoid process.

Three-dimensional imaging is achieved with adhesive contact lenses that you wear all the time, which can be removed with an eyedrop. The vision part won't work when you're moving. You have to stop walking, and preferably you should sit down to view real-time or recorded messages, or visual media. You can keep window apps open in your peripheral vision, and if you want to see them, all you have to do is move your eyeballs in that direction.

It's a simple system, easy to learn and use. Children usually get them at age four or five, though some get them earlier.

So that's how our social networking works. It's the core of the rumor mill that is actually faster, sometimes, than normal small-town conversations. This is what Uncle Mike was talking about when he said "everybody knows" something.

And now, back to the casino.

And another handoff to the 3-D photocopy . . .

CHAPTER 11

Polly:

Well, thanks a lot, twin. And so you leave it to me to explain how the two of us managed to remain largely ignorant of the spread of the biggest story since the launch of *Rolling Thunder.*

"We're not extremely plugged in," Cassie said. This is true. I don't even turn on the messaging bing when I'm riding my bike or running, and neither does Cassie. If we had, it would have sounded like jingle bells binging in our ears.

"It all started coming out in the last couple of hours," Patrick said in our defense. I was grateful, though not really sure why I should feel defensive about it. So we had been on our bikes and virtually unplugged while the story was spreading like wildfire, far and wide through the entire interior. Where was the crime in that?

"Maybe we could have a few minutes to catch up?" I suggested.

"It'll take a bit more than a few minutes," Marlee said. "But I think that's a good idea, don't you, darling?"

Uncle Mike nodded, and I blinked the heads-up display into activation. The contact lenses stuck to my eyes started doing their thing, and bright flashing windows appeared at various distances in my field of vision, skillfully managing not to block out the faces of anyone there. I did what I usually do when there's that much information—not that I've often had to deal with all that much—I closed my eyes. It all reorganized itself into much more logical sets of data.

The bulk of the messages had come in shortly after Cassie and I cut school, so I assumed that was when whoever it was at the meeting we had attended had started really spilling the beans, or at least when he or she had talked to someone with a big mouth.

There were forty-five messages in the Friends folder, ranging from classmates to acquaintances from most of the fifteen townships. I blinked on a few of them at random, and most of them boiled down to "What's the deal with this STOP THE SHIP stuff I'm hearing about?" One of them had the nerve to ask if Papa had gone nuts, earning himself an immediate delisting from the Friends column.

There were nine messages from Mama, Mike, and Patrick, and one from Travis. The ones from Mama just said we were to come home as soon as possible. I didn't bother with the ones from Mike and Patrick. The one from Travis asked us to please not talk about any of this to anyone until he had had a chance to get us all together, family and friends of the captain. I didn't understand why he needed to ask that until I got to the next batch, which was from strangers.

There were over two hundred of them, sorted into several categories. I didn't bother with the ones classed as "private citizens." Some of them were even hiding behind anonymous net names. Who cared? Not me, especially when I saw where some of the other messages were coming from.

We have five or six or seven major news sources—depending on who is doing the counting—sites updated in real time and employing up to six or seven actual reporters whose only job is going places and interviewing people for stories. There are even a couple dedicated to "investigative reporting," that is, looking for wrongdoing on the part of elected officials or government functionaries. It's all pretty tame compared to the scandals I've read about back at Old Sun. A little gerrymandering, a little featherbedding, a little nepotism, a little election cheating. Most of it is small enough to be dealt with by means of a fine.

Each of the townships has its own newsletter that reports on social matters, runs reviews of writing and music and shows. We all read our local rags, of course, but few would deny that it's pretty dull stuff.

The only times me and Cassie have appeared on the real newsfeeds, as opposed to the small-time newsletters and blogs, had to do with spectacular skypool plays. So it was a bit of a shock to see that every major news site had left a message for me. The messages were all very similar: *Must interview you. Call me ASAP.*

One of them even offered me a hundred dollars.

Cassie was saying, "The nerve of these people! The *New York Times* stringer is offering me five hundred dollars for an interview!"

"We all got interview requests, Cassie," Mike said, "and most of us got offers."

"What good is the *New York Times* having a stringer on board?" I wanted to know. "She can't send any stories back to Earth now."

"I understand she can, just barely," Patrick told us. "She has to send them multiple times, and it will take a lot of computer power to decipher them when they get there, twenty years from now. They'll be pretty stretched out, even if you're using the X-ray laser to send them. But that's not what she really is anymore. She *is* the *Times* in *Rolling Thunder*. Or whatever she wants to call herself."

"Doesn't impress me much," Cassie said.

"No, she's just one of many," Marlee said. "She's a passenger like all the rest of us. And like pretty much all the passengers, and crew, she's not only curious to find out what the hell's going on, she's also worried."

"Scared, even," Mike added.

"Hey, wait a minute." Cassie sounded worried. "Take a look at this one."

She forwarded it and I saw the text pop up in front of me.

"Your f*cking family and your f*cking crazy father and your f*cking dictator uncle 'Captain' have run this ship too long. Now you're putting us all in danger. Watch your step, Broussard, and your ugly sister, too."

Holy criminy! I've had nasty texts before, but they were mostly insults centering on skypool matches. I'd had nasty messages from other girls over some boy or another, some of them signed, some of them not. But I'd never had *anything* that attacked my family. I felt my face burning, and suddenly I was breathing heavy.

I wasn't frightened. I was *angry*!

"This pisses me off!" Cassie shouted. "Can we trace it?"

"I don't think so," Patrick offered. "I got a variation on it, sounds like maybe the same person. I couldn't get anywhere tracking it back."

"Travis intentionally made it almost impossible to do that when he was setting up the Rollingnet," Marlee told us. "He was protecting freedom of speech."

"Isn't this a threat?" I asked. "Isn't that an exception?"

"Or just hot air. Some idiot letting off steam."

"I think a judge would see it that way, too," Marlee agreed. "It really has to rise to the level of 'I'm going to kill you,' that specific, to invoke the threat regulation."

"Could Travis override that?" Cassie wanted to know.

"Probably. He can override almost anything, I guess."

"Which is one of the reasons this person is so angry," Patrick pointed out. Which didn't endear him to me.

Nobody said anything for a while, then Mike sighed.

"You girls know that your mother and your uncle Travis have been looking for you. I'm not going to say the family is real worried about this stuff, but let's say we're concerned. We are interested now in finding out how deep and how widespread these sorts of feelings are."

"What about Papa?" Cassie asked.

"You won't be surprised to hear that we're keeping this from him, for now. He won't be at the meeting."

"Which meeting is that?"

"Meeting of the Fockers," Patrick said. "Close family of the captain."

"I don't know who all that includes, but I gather it will be a small group," Marlee said. "We'll be there, and your mother and you two are invited."

"Would that be a command from Mama Podkayne?" Cassie asked.

"That's between you and her."

"Never mind," I said, glancing at Cassie. "We wouldn't miss it for the world."

Mike said, "Stay in touch, okay? Keep your phones on for a while."

That turned out to be more trouble than it was worth.

All the way home on our bikes, we kept getting pinged by strangers, or newspeople. We finally had to stop and set some limits on messaging, suppressing calls from everyone but a small list of family and a few friends. Even so, we got pinged every few minutes from one of those friends. I don't blame them; I'd want to know more if I were in their position. But before long we eliminated the friends on the list, too. It was getting right down to the bone, just us fockers against the world. Or so it seemed.

I didn't like the feeling.

As we approached the Broussard Estate, we could make out some people standing around in the road that came closest to our private property. There were maybe twenty or twenty-five of them, in several groups, talking to one another.

"Media?" Cassie asked.

"Would be my guess," I told her.

"Remember that movie about Michael Jackson?"

"Don't have to," I said. "Remember the one about Mama."

We had seen both biography pictures, centering around one of the biggest stars from the twentieth century and one of the biggest of the twenty-first, our dear old mom. Judging from the one they made about Mama, the one about Jackson must have been full of baloney, with only a scattering of facts. That's how *Pod People* was, and we had Mama to point out the many errors.

But the scenes I recall most vividly were what Mama referred to as a "feeding frenzy." That was when a mob of reporters were gathered someplace where Mama had to go. They apparently lost all contact with their humanity, and behaved like a bunch of rabid dogs. They shoved cameras and microphones in the faces of celebrities, blinded them with lights, shouted stupid questions, shoved and even punched others to get in position for a photo.

I remember watching those scenes of the actress playing Mama with my jaw dropping. How could civilized people behave like that?

"Because they're not civilized," Mama told us. "The reporters of the celebrity press are pigs, to a man and woman."

"Was it really that bad, in real life?" I wanted to know.

"Worse. It got to where I couldn't do normal things like go shopping, unless I made an appointment and came in the back way. I had to live in a gated community. I missed normal things."

That was about the longest rant I ever heard from her concerning her celebrity back at Old Sun. Mostly she didn't talk about it, except to say how glad she was to leave Earth *and* Mars a few light-years behind her.

"Let's not get famous," I said.

"That won't be a problem for you since there's nothing for you to be famous for unless you count bull's-eye landings in pigsties. Me, I have to be careful to hide my electric charisma all the time."

"Otherwise, you'd have to constantly beat the boys off with a stick, right?"

"Oh, I have to do that already. I'm talking about not letting the larger world get a glimpse of my true greatness."

"Please continue to do that," I said. "You've done such a good job so far, no one suspects a thing. That, or you're truly boring."

"Bitch."

"Boring bitch."

When we were younger, that could have gone on for a long time, but we're mature now, and above it.

"Dumb bitch," she whispered.

"Silly bitch," I whispered back.

We decided we didn't want to run the gauntlet of reporters milling about at our driveway. Luckily, we were old hands at sneaking in and out of the

Broussard Estate. We knew a dozen ways. The best for this situation was the pond.

We got off the road and abandoned our bikes in the stand of pine trees that grows densely on the spinward side of the shore. It was a short walk to the water, but not so easy getting in. There's only a small amount of sandy beach on our lake, and it's on the other side. The rest is "wetlands," which is sort of a swamp. There are cattails and water lilies and lotus, and some of our friends who aren't used to dirt and mud would never follow us into something like that.

But we've been doing it all our lives, so we slipped off our shoes and waded in among the reeds. I've always liked the feel of mud between my toes, and the smell of the stagnant pond water. Some find it unpleasant, but to me it's the smell of living things, of a complex ecosystem, of "nature," such as we have it in our totally controlled environment.

A bullfrog about the size of my foot protested our presence, and leaped into the water in front of me. In twenty or so yards, the water was deep enough to swim in. We eased into a quiet breaststroke, barely rippling the surface.

We reached the dock easily and pulled ourselves out, streaming water and a certain amount of green algae. Cassie's hair was a wreck, and I assumed mine was, too.

"Mama, Papa, we're home," Cassie shouted as she slammed through the screen door, leaving me to dive for it so it wouldn't slam. It was wasted effort. There was nobody home. We stuck our heads into every room, and even looked out the window and up at our tree house. No one there, either.

"Call 'em, I guess," she said.

"Showers first."

"Best idea you've had in a long time."

So we did that, and considered our closets.

"What do you think?" she said. "What do you wear to a family meeting?"

"Let's skip the formal gowns," I suggested. "Besides, you probably split a seam on that slinky number the other day."

"You mean rubbing up against Patrick?" She winked at me, the bitch.

"No, I mean you did everything but spread your legs. And I saw how enthusiastic he was, and so did everyone else."

Every once in a while you throw a barb that really hits home. She tried to keep a brave face, but I could see the hurt behind it. It didn't make me feel good. Ribbing each other mercilessly is just how we get through the day, but it is seldom intended to hurt. We have a way of dealing with it that works most of the time.

"My regrets, twin," I said, and held up my hand.

She slapped it, maybe a little harder than necessary.

"Forgotten, twin" she said.

Usually, it really is. I wasn't so sure this time. Patrick could become a real problem between us.

I picked out a mustard sleeveless knit top with a turtle neck that stretched to fit tightly, with a charcoal pair of jeans that ended midcalf, and black penny loafers. I found a black beret that went pretty well with the ensemble, and accessorized with a silver chain necklace and bracelet. Cassie went with the same sort of idea but in different colors.

We found no sign of the parents until we reached the kitchen, which is where we should have looked first. Papa doesn't own or operate a personal phone. Our low-tech solution was a blackboard in the kitchen. It saves paper, and it's fun, and Papa hardly ever leaves the property when he's out of the bubble anyway, so it's not like he's hard to find. Chalked there in Papa's childish block letters was the message:

I AM IN THE LABERTERRY

We ambled out to the backyard and down a short path that followed the lake to the other structure that made up the Broussard Estate. Like the rest of the place, it was not what it appeared to be.

There was a rusty tin roof, weathered siding, and a wide screened-in porch. The porch opened onto a landing and a short dock, where a wooden pirogue was tied up. The place does look like pictures I've seen of bait shops on a bayou. But it's just a façade, one that appeals to Papa. Inside is Papa's laberterry.

There's a screen door, but once you've opened it, you can't just walk in. The security there is just as strict as at our house, probably more so. I pressed my palm to the plate and leaned forward to look into the twin lenses. A dim red light flashed, and Papa's recorded voice called out.

"Come on in, Cassandra Ann!"

"What the . . ." Cassie looked shocked, too. We had never been misidentified by a machine before. People, sure, but this shouldn't have happened. I looked at Cassie, and she shrugged, so I did, too, and opened the door.

A grizzly bear, ten feet tall standing on his hind legs, raised his front paws and gave out with a heart-stopping roar. Well, it would have been heart-stopping to anyone who wasn't expecting it. But not for long.

"Hello, Winnie," Cassie said, and patted him on the side. A little dust and some hair puffed out from his pelt, which had seen better days. Some of the seams were coming apart where he had been sewn together, and one of his hind legs was split open so you could see the metal strut inside. He also clicked when he moved.

"You need an oil can, silly old bear," I told him.

We had named him Winnie a long time ago. He was part of Papa's oddball collection of stuff that he had brought with him from Earth, then from Mars. He had been part of an amusement park that Papa had built animated figures for, many years ago.

You had to go around Winnie to get to the stairs, which went down for three flights to end in another door with another palm plate and another set of lenses. I let Cassie operate that one, and sure enough, it greeted her as Pollyanna Sue. Then it opened and admitted us to the inner sanctum.

Don't call my papa a mad scientist, at least not in my presence. I'll rearrange your face . . . or at least hurt your feelings real bad. But "eccentric scientist"? I'd have to let you get away with that.

What we entered was not the lab of a mad scientist from old movies, with dry ice bubbling in beakers full of colored water, and electrical arcs from Jacob's ladders humming and sizzling up toward the ceiling. It was part machine shop and part museum. It was quite a large room, much bigger than the bait shop above it.

Haphazardly spotted around the room were some of Papa's toys, like an X-ray machine, an MRI, an electron microscope, a huge hydraulic press, several drill presses, and racks and racks and racks of hand tools and power tools. If someone somewhere ever invented a tool that Papa doesn't have, it probably wasn't good for anything. He has stamping machines and furnaces, and analytical machines from chemical labs and hospitals. There are bins and bins of hardware.

No one gets in the lab but Travis, Papa, and Mama, and their two little puppies. *No one.* That means no maid service except for guess who. We had been down there two weeks ago, in anticipation of Papa's arrival, and cleaned it from top to bottom. That is no small job, believe me. Mama does a white-glove inspection, and it all has to shine.

We are saved a little effort because of one cardinal rule: Don't move anything! The one thing Papa can be strict with us about is his lab. We clean only surfaces, leaving everything just where we found it. He wants all his projects to be exactly as he left them when he gets out.

We found him after a short search among things best left undescribed. Or maybe I should say things I'd be hard put to describe if someone asked me to, so don't ask, okay? The things Papa builds seem to defy logic, and often look like nothing more than a random selection of junk tossed into a garbage can with some epoxy glue squirted in, shaken up for a few minutes, then dumped out on the floor. Sometimes they emit sounds or lights or even steam, and I steer clear of them. They look like they might bite.

He was sitting at a workbench wearing some sort of magnifying glasses, peering into a box about a foot on each side.

"Stay back a minute, my girls," he said. "I'll fix this up in no time."

He went back to his work, and it really didn't take him long. He finished up and sat back with a satisfied sigh.

"That's done," he said, and turned to us grinning. "Come give your papa a hug, my darlings!"

We did that, and when we moved away he looked at us with an odd expression.

"Didn't have no trouble gettin' in, did you?"

"Papa," Cassie said, "for some reason the door . . . Did you do that?"

He laughed. "Pretty funny, huh? Even the door cain't tell y'all apart."

"Pretty funny," I agreed. Behind his back, Cassie rolled her eyes, but she assured him she thought it was pretty funny, too. It could be worse, I always figured. He might like itch powder and exploding cigars.

"What's in the box, Papa?" Cassie asked.

He got serious real quick.

"It's for something I gotta find out, me."

Cassie was looking into it, frowning. I did, too.

It was like all the things I'd ever seen Papa build. No, actually, I mean invent. He was quite skilled as a carpenter, a machinist, any manual skills at all, really. If you wanted him to build a house, he'd make a great one, and it would be just according to a normal house plan. Building our tree house, he had let his imagination loose a little, and the result was a lovely fantasy, a toy. Ask him to build a mechanical device from plans, something that already existed, he would faithfully copy it.

But when he was inventing, he went into some sort of creative trance and grabbed the first object that came to hand that would serve his purpose. That's one reason he has so much unsorted junk scattered around the lab. He always knew where each item was, could go directly to it. And then he would build something weird. And always it looked like a mess, but it always did its job.

This box was no different. There was some greenish light down near the bottom, and a couple of reddish lights elsewhere, but I couldn't see the source of either light. It was making a very faint hum, so quiet I didn't notice it at first. There was a faint smell I couldn't identify, but suspected was some sort of lubricating oil. Maybe the slightest whiff of ozone.

No telling what it was for. I just had to hope Papa could do a better job of explaining it.

"Does it have to do with the problem with the ship?" I asked.

"It do, *cher*," he said, with a frown. "This thing ought to tell me something 'bout that, if I done her right."

"So . . . when are you going to do your experiment?"

"That gonna be a little hard to do," he admitted. "I was hoping you girls might be able to he'p me with that."

"Anything you say, Papa," Cassie told him.

"You got it," I agreed.

Well, I'll abbreviate a little here, because I'm still a little pissed off.

Mama arrived while Papa was struggling to explain what he needed. Essentially, he needed someone to take the box somewhere and do something with it. The box was some sort of detector for dark lightning, or something like that. I didn't understand it completely. What Papa wanted to do was train someone to go to this place and take readings.

Sounded simple enough. Wasn't simple at all.

The procedure wasn't all that complicated. A reasonably smart chimpanzee should have been able to handle it, and Cassie and I understood it after a few run-throughs. A few lights, a few buttons, a few notes to take, since Papa hadn't had time to invent and program an automatic register for the thing.

In fact, he'd been in such a hurry, it was a wonder the thing worked at all. Several times while he was demonstrating how it worked, it just stopped. He had to open the top and fool around in there with a screwdriver. Once it gave off a shower of sparks, making me jump and causing Papa to suck on a singed finger.

It soon became clear that whoever operated the box was going to have to know how to keep it running right, and how to fix it when it didn't work. And no one needed to point out that there was only one person in the room who could do that.

Papa was really upset.

"I'm going to have to go with whoever takes this thing where it need to go," he said, in some agitation.

"Why can't you . . ." Cassie said, and stopped. I knew she had been going to ask why he couldn't go there and do it himself, and didn't bite her tongue in time. I glared at her, and she gave me an apologetic shrug.

"Because I get flusterpated, my darling," Papa said, sadly. He knew his limitations, and though he had long ago come to terms with them, it wasn't a source of pleasure to have to acknowledge them, even to himself.

Papa needed someone from his family, preferably me or Cassie or Mama or Travis, to keep his anxieties in check. He was going to have to take the device himself to do whatever it was he intended to do with it, but he was going to need a minder, a human security blanket, to keep calm enough to do what had to be done.

Mama and Papa discussed it, with helpful asides from Cassie and me that never seemed to be appreciated, at least not by Mama. Well, Mama never seems to appreciate us. (Insert put-upon sigh here.)

There were really only four possible minders, and Mama said she and Travis were not on the list because the family meeting they were holding was too important for either of them to miss.

"Well, Papa," Cassie said, "how long do you think it would take you to . . . well, to beef up that box so it isn't breaking down all the time?"

"Too long, probly. A couple a days, at least."

"That's too long?"

"I'm really worried, *cher*."

So was I, and even more when I heard that Papa seemed to think it was really an emergency that required action that fast.

"Anyways, my darlings, I'm afraid your old papa would need somebody to babysit hisself even if I do clean the box up some." He didn't look at us as he said this. I reached over and squeezed his shoulder. Cassie put her arm around his waist.

"It's okay," I said. "I'll be happy to go with you."

"Me, too," the twin piped up.

"We'll both go," I said.

"No, you won't," said the Mama unit. "I'm going to need one of you. There's a lot of things we have to cover in this family meeting. A lot of things to be decided, and if they go one way, I will need someone to run some errands."

"Then I'll stick with Papa," Cassie said quickly.

I glared at her. "I offered first." I was determined to be the one to stick with Papa because we would be going someplace I'd never been before, and in the finite—although quite large—universe of *Rolling Thunder*, you didn't get to do that every day.

Mama interrupted, a deep frown on her face. I thought she was going to read us the riot act and render a decision that had a 50 percent chance of being unfair, but that wasn't it.

"Jubal, honey, are you sure this is safe?"

Papa's frown was even deeper.

"That's a hard one to answer, *cher*. I run some numbers, me, and I figger it ain't no more dangerous than staying right where we are now." He pointed to the floor. "Course, ain't no place real safe right now, I figger."

When our destination had been announced, I had done my own estimate, and couldn't see how it was much more dangerous than standing right where I was, as Papa had said.

Anyway, safe or not, I intended to go.

"Let's arm-wrestle for it," I suggested. Believe it or not, we are not totally evenly matched. In upper-body strength, I had a slight edge.

"Flip a coin," she countered. Too random for me. So I made another suggestion, and after a moment, Cassie agreed.

"Two out of three?" she said.

"Let's do it.

So . . . one, two, *paper*! She had rock, and paper covers rock. I only needed one more to win.

One, two, *scissors*! She had rock again, and rock smashes scissors. *Damn!*

I took a deep breath. One, two, *paper*!

CHAPTER 12

Cassie:

. . . *scissors!*

Scissors cut paper. Two out of three. Hurray for me!

Someday, when we're old and gray, I'm going to give you a gift, twin. You have a tell. You know what a tell is? It's some sort of tic that lets your opponent know what's in your poker hand, or what your hand is going to do in our little game. In poker, maybe you sniff loudly when you've got something good. Maybe your eyelid twitches.

On *two*, your other hand telegraphs what you're going to choose. That's your right hand as, being left-handed, you play with your left. Two fingers will twitch when you're about to show scissors, four will twitch when it's paper, and your hand doesn't move when it's rock. I let you win the first one, but I knew what it was going to be.

I've known this about you for years. I seldom use it. You're not stupid, you would catch on soon if I won all the time. So I don't bother looking when it's small stuff, like who has to do a chore, or who gets first pick out of a box of donuts. But for the important stuff, I win.

I really do love you, spacegirl, and it sometimes hurts me to see how bad you take it when I win something that matters to you. Not enough to *lose* to you, of course; we all need an edge now and then.

You might get the impression that Polly and I are inseparable from what's gone down so far. Since that bad skypool game, we had seldom been out of each other's sight. It's not normally like that. We each have our own life.

When we *are* together, we often act as a team. We know there are circumstances where we can count on unquestioning loyalty from the other one. But we are not dependent on each other, though I believe Polly is a little more dependent than I am. It may look the opposite from her perspective.

But there was no teary good-bye that day when we split up. She just sighed and took her medicine, leaving with Mama while I got Papa together for his ordeal.

We found something to carry his gadget in. I went back to the house and packed a purse that was almost as big as a carpetbag with the things I thought we might need. One of those things was a bottle of Papa's tranquilizers. I made him take one before we set out, and by the time we got out the door, he had a slightly glassy-eyed look.

We were halfway down the driveway before I remembered the crowd of pimps lying in wait on the road. As we came into view, they all jumped like someone had stuck an electric prod up their asses. They started their patented chattering of stupid questions, holding their cameras toward us.

"Mr. Broussard, can you confirm or deny . . ."

"Sir, there's a rumor going around that . . ."

"Hey, Jubal, just a minute of your time . . ."

"What gives you the right to start a panic . . ."

Several of them were actually coming up the drive, right past the NO TRESPASSING signs. I turned Papa around and told him to go back to the house. He did, amiably enough, not even looking back over his shoulder.

"This is private property," I shouted. "Access is denied to all of y'all. I'm recording this. I will count to three, and if your asses aren't on the other side of our property line at three, you're going to be very sorry. *One!*"

I didn't have to get to three. Grumbling, they all moved back over the line. Property rights are taken very seriously in the ship's regulations. A citizen's home is his or her castle. Penalties for uninvited invasions are stiff, even if you are a "reporter."

I caught up with Papa and hurried him along.

"We're going out the back door, Papa," I said. Actually, we went around the house to the boathouse in back. I loaded our stuff into the motorboat. I sat in the back and turned it on, and powered out of our little bay and into the pond.

I know it was silly, but I kept looking up and around the curved landscape of the ship. There was no way I'd be able to spot what I was looking for, but I was pretty sure they were out there, up the curve in one direction or another.

We don't have helicopters or airplanes for the press to harass you with, but that doesn't mean we have privacy. When your world curves like a rolled-up paper tube, it means that anyone up the curve of the tube can look down on you. It's easy to set up a telescope and see right into someone's backyard.

They could see us, and could be coming after us now, from any direction. If they encountered us on the public streets, all bets were off. They could shove their cameras in our faces with impunity.

That was our disadvantage. On the plus side, it wasn't going to be easy to catch up with us. There weren't any fast cars for them to jump into. They could keep an eye on us and guide the pack of press at our driveway in the right direction, but they would be limited to bicycles or the same transportation I was planning on using, the streetcar network.

I was betting we could outrun them.

We beached the boat on the far side of the pond, not far from a road. I hurried Papa to the nearest station, and we got there just before a car arrived.

It wasn't crowded, so we got seats. Maybe a dozen people aboard. And inevitably, they recognized Papa.

No one moved, no one said anything. A couple of people even looked angry. It was a nervous fifteen minutes. People got off, people boarded, and I kept looking for the press posse.

Finally, someone spoke. It was a woman about Mama's age, and there was no hostility in her voice, just concern.

"Mr. Broussard, what's going on?"

Papa smiled at her.

"You can call me Jubal, ma'am. And I'm fixin' to find out what's goin' on, me."

There was conversational buzz then, and I could see them gearing up for a real question-and-answer session, but we were saved by the trolley.

"This is our stop, Papa," I said, getting out of my seat.

He looked around the car as he rose. "Nice travelin' with y'all. Everybody have a safe trip." I don't think he got the irony of that. All those people were very worried, not about the trolley, but about our little trip to the stars. Which, to a lot of people's way of thinking, he had just put in jeopardy.

Our destination was the town of Wayback, the capitol of Frostbite Falls province. The trolley left us in the center of town, at the intersection of June Foray Avenue and Paul Frees Street. The streets here were cobblestoned, and the buildings mostly made of red brick. In the middle of the park in the town square was a slowly rotating statue of a cartoon moose holding up a flying squirrel wearing a crash helmet. Some old television show Travis liked, which I haven't seen.

I led Papa a block south to Daws Butler Avenue, where there was a doorway with a sign over it reading IRON MAN GYM in raised gold letters. Little LED figures of a man and a woman in skimpy clothes endlessly lifted and put down barbells with huge round weights on the ends.

Inside, there was a small, unattended lobby with a few chairs and potted plants. A screen on one wall showed a montage of the facilities available at the gym, which were all no-nonsense weight machines and treadmills and stair climbers. No spa at the Iron Man, no massages, no saunas. All those things and more were available next door. Apart from that, the only thing to see was a gleaming elevator door, right in front of us.

This elevator had only top and bottom floors. It started down slowly, then accelerated smoothly.

The distance we were going?

Half a mile. Straight down.

That is, of course, actually straight *out*, away from the center. But it felt like down. And every second I was getting heavier. At the bottom I would be carrying an extra third of my body weight because at that point, the spinning of the ship would work on me at the rate of exactly one gee.

That half mile also happens to be the average thickness of the rocky shell that was left over after the asteroid was hollowed out. At a depth of a mile and a half, we would be on the outside surface of the ship.

Which would be over our heads.

Under our feet would be a floor, and beyond that nothing but interstellar space for many, many light-years. Papa was perfectly happy to feel the weight settle on him gradually, then peak as we slowed down and stopped. Myself, I was wishing for arch supports. And other supports, for that matter. The one time I worked out down at the Iron Man, I didn't like the way I looked in the mirror. Everything sagged. Face, boobs, and butt. I never went back, and neither did most of the girls I know. I find it hard to believe that human beings evolved in a one-gee gravity field; we're just not sturdy enough. I'd be a total wreck in a week.

I guess if you grew up on Earth, you just didn't know any better.

We got out of the elevator to the usual smell of sweat and testosterone, the clank of barbells, the pounding of feet on the treadmills and the running track.

The only other attraction of the gym was that it was one of the few places where people could come and see outside. There was the North Pole, of course, but that was weightless, and a lot of people didn't care for that. Some didn't much like one gee, either, but found it tolerable for a couple of hours. So there were several places to look out at the stars.

We turn every 98.5 seconds. That means the stars outside don't exactly *fly* by, but they move pretty fast. In a minute and a half, the same ones will reappear. Papa doesn't like any kind of motion like that, so we hurried out of the gym and into a safer, windowless corridor.

You could have been coming to the gym for twenty years and never have entered this corridor. It wasn't long, and at the end there was nothing but a strong door that said NO ADMITTANCE—AUTHORIZED PERSONNEL ONLY. It opened to my thumbprint.

We entered a spaceship hangar.

This was one of five hangars in the ship. The first three were up at the pole, and they were enormous. Each one held around fifty very large ships, cargo ships in near weightlessness to facilitate loading.

Then there were the two on the outside, this one and another 180 degrees around the circumference. These housed smaller craft, both manned and drones, that were used for inspections of the outer surface and the drive structures at the aft end. They were much smaller, "about the size of two city buses," according to Papa. Well, they're a lot bigger than the streetcars we use. They're roughly cylindrical, with bulges in the front and rear where the bubble engines are, and they have wheels on struts that they sit on when in the hangar. At the front end there is a wide window, and toward the rear there are stubby wings. If needed, they could enter an atmosphere, fly a bit, and land. When I asked Travis why he decided they should be able to fly, he said "Why not?" Good question. I couldn't think of a reason why not.

There are a few dozen of them, and they are painted a variety of bright, bold, shiny colors. Lined up in a row, they looked like giant Easter eggs. Well, sort of elongated Easter eggs, but still. The ships were launched by simply dropping them through a lock to the outside. That way, they already had a good velocity when they entered space.

But this wasn't our final destination.

We walked past several groups of people either doing routine maintenance of the ships or standing around not even trying to look busy. We didn't talk to anyone at all. Papa was preoccupied, turning over some arcane quantum theory in his head, maybe, and I . . . well, I wasn't sure I liked the way they were looking at us. Maybe I was paranoid. Seeing Papa out in public is unusual. Maybe they were just surprised to see him.

We walked the length of the hangar. When we reached the end, there was another door. This one was unmarked but had extra security. I felt eyes all over my back and I pressed my thumb to the plate and put my eye to the lens. There was a click, and we hurried through.

We entered Travis's private hangar.

———————————

The ship inside was a slightly larger, much plusher version of those ships we had passed on our way here. It was painted a metallic gold with black highlights—black and gold being our school colors, so I was down with that—and reminded me of nothing so much as a fat bumblebee. Bees being one of the bugs we *do* have in the ship because we need them to pollinate, and, of course, for the honey.

I got Papa up the ramp and into a seat near the middle of the gig. The interior was comfortable. There were six seats in this lounge area. Back of that was the head and two staterooms. The ship would be flying itself. A good thing, too, because I had no idea how to fly a spaceship.

I got Papa settled down and brought him a glass of iced Dr Pepper. He was busy setting his gadget up on a small table, running tests on it. At one point, a little wisp of smoke curled out of the box, and I looked a question at Papa.

"Not to worry, *cher*. It's okay. Not gonna blow up or nothing." He went back to his adjustments.

So I went forward and through a curtain in a permanent bulkhead. Beyond it was the control room.

The top half of the front end of the ship was perfectly clear. Below that was a dashboard with a few pressure points glowing, and several touch screens. Not real complicated controls. There were three comfortable, leather-covered chairs facing forward, the one in the center being slightly more substantial and obviously reserved for the captain.

"Welcome, Cassandra," said the autopilot, a feminine voice. "Podkayne alerted me that you and Jubal Broussard would be boarding. I see you have already provided a cold beverage for Jubal Broussard. Is there anything I can prepare for you? Snacks? A drink?"

"Not just now. Can you just call me Cassie?"

"As you wish, Captain Cassie."

"Captain? When did this happen?"

"When I questioned your mother as to command, which would normally devolve upon the eldest passenger if I lacked other instructions, I was informed that Jubal Broussard was in a state of emotional fragility such that taking command was precluded. Thus, you are the captain, by default."

"Okay. What do I call you? Autopilot?"

"You can call me Sheila."

"Sheila it is."

I sat down and immediately knew that I could sleep like a puppy dog in a chair like this. When I got my own home, it would have a chair like this. When I was ancient and spindly-legged and gray, I'd want to drool away the days in a chair like this.

"Your father wishes to find a point half a million miles from *Rolling Thunder*, and slow to a standstill there, relative to the ship. Correct?"

"That's about it, yeah."

"That's easy enough. Is there anything else I should know? Such as the purpose of the trip? If there are any extra dangers involved?"

Some AI programs are a lot smarter than others. I figured Sheila was about as smart as they come. It was typical of Travis that he'd want the best for his little ship, so Sheila was subtle enough in her thinking to sense that something else was going on. Or at least that she hadn't been told every part of the story. She would be completely loyal to her captain—in this case, me!—no matter what she was told to do.

"You're one smart cookie," I told her. I've never been sure if flattering an AI had any effect at all, but I figured it couldn't hurt. "This *is* an unusual mission, and I'll fill you in on all I know and try to get Papa to explain what he knows. In the meantime, why don't we get under way?"

"We're not really ready to get under way until you and your papa are strapped in. I understand the need to minimize the gee stresses on your papa, but a short period of free fall is unavoidable."

So I went back to the lounge, where Papa was still tinkering. I went down on one knee beside him.

"It's time to get going, Papa."

"Oh, lawsy, *cher*. I hate that, me."

"It'll be just for a minute. Here, I'll secure your invention here, so it doesn't float away."

He fumbled with his seat belt, and I watched to be sure he had it fastened right. Then I looked around. There had to be something . . .

Aha. In a small drawer under the seat were containers little changed since the days of the Wright Brothers, I guess. Barf bags. I looped the string on one of them behind his head.

"Just a short time, Papa." I patted his leg, which was trembling, and hurried back to the cockpit. I sat down and strapped in.

"The sooner, the better," I said.

———————

The doors in front of us moved quickly back and we rolled into the launch area. I could hear the doors closing behind us.

I heard a faint *pop* as the very thin air around us was blown out. For just a moment, the little bit of water vapor still around crystallized into very dry snow, but then it was gone.

"Launching." And just like that, I was weightless. I heard a moan from back in the cabin.

The forward port arched over my head, so I looked up and saw the rectangular opening of the launch bay rapidly shrinking away from us. It looked like a door in an infinite black wall. That would be the outer surface of the ship. But that view lasted only about five seconds, and the ship rotated quickly through 180 degrees.

Then, no more than ten seconds after we dropped away, the engines came on, fore and aft, and gently boosted us up to one gee in no more than another ten seconds.

"Are you okay back there, Papa?"

"A little green, *cher*," he called back. "Didn't have to use that bag, though." He sounded proud of that, and I smiled. I was proud of him, too. People can't help motion sickness, and I've never thought it was funny. I just thank fate that it's never affected me.

"Dim the lights, please, Sheila."

After a few moments, my pupils dilated enough to see the stars in all their harsh grandeur. And it was a sight I wouldn't soon forget.

When we go to the bridge, we see a dome of stars, a simulation of what the sky would look like if you weren't still quite a ways underground. But it's false. It is a representation of what the stars would look like if we were motionless relative to those stars. In other words, some are brighter and some are faint, none of them twinkle, a few of the brighter ones show some color other than diamondlike white, and, most important, they are more or less evenly scattered across the sky. The reasoning is that it just looks better that way, and it is an accurate projection of where we are in space.

The way it really looks is deeply disturbing. Because the universe *should not* look like that.

The ship was oriented with *Rolling Thunder*'s bow to my right, the stern to my left. We were blasting away from the big ship, but we weren't going up like the traditional rocket ship, nose up, tail down. The thrust was coming from the front and rear, balanced, and thrusting away from the deck that was now our floor. That way, instead of being pressed backwards into our seats and needing a ladder to get from the nose to the tail, we were able to get up and walk around normally.

Directly in front of me and above me, there were very few stars at all. They got more and more attenuated, more separated from each other, the more I looked to my left. It was a vast blackness, a blackness so deep it seemed to draw my eye down into the depths of infinity.

Then, as my eye moved more to the right, I began to pick up a few faint stars. The more I looked to the right, the denser they became, until when I was looking right in the direction of *Rolling Thunder*'s forward motion, the stars became like a thick soup of light. They were crowded together, the brightest ones nearest the center of the region, the others getting fainter and redder the more distant they were from that area.

Right in the center of the brightest light was a perfectly round circle of blackness. It was big, covering a large area of the star soup, but there were plenty of superbright stars all around it.

It looked like nothing so much as a monster black hole. It looked like something was pulling every star in the universe down into its devouring maw. It looked like the end of the world, the end of space and time.

What it was, was the million-mile squeezer bubble floating in front of us, protecting us from the impacts of interstellar gas and dust. Beyond that bubble would be even more stars, more crowded, more intense.

———————

I'm the one who's good at physics, but I'm not that good. The phenomenon is known as "aberration." This is a relativistic effect whereby, somehow, the light from stars that are actually *behind* you impacts your eye from such a direction that it seems like the star is *ahead* of you. For a further explanation, consult a physics text or ask my papa.

We don't do constellations in *Rolling Thunder*. They keep changing. They change at Old Sun, too, but over thousands of years. In my world, you can see some star displacement in just months.

These days, as we're traveling at .77c, soon to pass the .78c mark, the huge majority of stars are near celestial north, which is defined as the direction we're traveling. They are squeezing together tighter and tighter. Everything in that area has been significantly blue-shifted, which means that if a star is actually a red giant, it now looks like a blue giant. But some of them have shifted right out of the single octave the human eye can see. Those stars that started out blue have now been shifted into a higher wavelength, in the ultraviolet, and are no longer visible to the naked eye. But they've been replaced by stars that used to be red, and are now yellow or orange.

This sky, this squeezed version of the natural order, which was an even spread of stars in all directions, brought it home viscerally just how incredibly fast we were moving. It's one thing to call up the little speedometer app in your vision and get a number. It was something else entirely to see with my own eyes just what our speed had done to the universe around us.

From the frame of reference of Old Sun, our clocks were going slower, and the length of the ship was much shorter than when we began.

Scary thoughts, those.

———————

After staring at that narrowing universe of stars for a few minutes, I unbuckled and went out of the cockpit and into the main cabin. Papa was engrossed in his gizmo. He was so wrapped up in his work that he had forgotten to take off the barf bag, which still dangled from his chin, covering his white Santa Claus beard. I sat beside him and pulled it over his head. He didn't even notice at first, then he glanced at me.

"Thanks, *cher.* I didn't mess it up, me."

"If I may interrupt," Sheila said. "A few moments ago I detected a stomach rumbling. Maybe I could fix a meal, as we have several hours to kill. I am able to prepare most of the simpler foods."

I realized with an embarrassed shock that it had probably been my tummy that had rumbled. I hadn't really noticed it during all the preparations, but I was really hungry.

"How about a sandwich?" I asked.

"I make a pretty mean bacon cheeseburger with thin-sliced purple onions and succulent beefsteak tomato slices, accompanied by steak fries and a special dipping sauce."

I managed not to drool, but suddenly I could smell the burger.

"I like mine with some sliced jalapeño peppers melted into the cheese, if you have 'em," Papa said.

"I have 'em," she said. "Toasted buns?"

"That'd be great," I said. "Do you have any bleu cheese?"

In ten minutes, the console next to Papa's chair opened and delivered two plates almost covered with big hamburgers, a wicker basket heaped with fries, and two Dr Peppers. There were little bowls for mayo, mustard, pickle relish, and catsup. It was something like getting meals from the community kitchens, delivered by pneumo tube, only much, much nicer.

Only the best for my uncle Travis.

I was halfway through devouring the burger before I felt like talking again.

"How's it going, Papa?" I said. "Is that thing going to work?"

"Hmmm? Oh, yeah, just makin' some final adjustments."

"Maybe you could tell me how it works," I ventured.

He looked at me, sadly. "I cain't tell you that, darlin'. Some of it ain't real clear to me, even. But I can tell you what it does."

"Perhaps it would help," Sheila put in, "if I had an idea what you're looking for, as well. To better understand the purpose of this mission."

Papa thought about it for a moment.

"What it does, I hope, it measure the difference between how much dark lightnin' we're gettin' in the ship, and how much there is outside. And then if there be any difference with how much is outside the shield."

"Dark . . ." Sheila trailed off.

"Dark matter," I clarified. "Or dark energy. Or maybe both. Right, Papa?"

"Maybe two different sides of the same thing, *cher*. One of the things I'm hopin' to find out, me."

"I am familiar with both concepts, of course," Sheila said. "I didn't know that a detector had been invented."

"I didn't know m'self until a few days ago," Papa said, and laughed. "But if I'm right, this here t'ing should do the job. If I'm right."

Sheila and Papa spent the next half hour talking about dark lightning. I sat there, quiet as a mouse (however quiet that may be; we have no mice in the ship, except probably in time stasis) and listened intently at first, then with increasing dismay, and finally with a profound sense of inferiority as they tackled matters that maybe Einstein could have followed. And maybe not. I soon had a headache. I thought I could feel frown lines permanently etching themselves into my forehead.

I took a break, going back to the bridge and pulling up some music. I listened to some of Mama's greatest hits, and some from my own time, and, gradually, I felt better.

When I got back to the main cabin, they were still at it. We had been boosting for about an hour and a half. There was still another hour of boosting away, then two and a half more of decelerating. I wondered if anyone was interested in a few hands of gin rummy.

No, not really. A screen had popped up from a table and was displaying rows of equations. I settled back in my comfortable chair and considered calling up a movie or a book. This was supposed to have been an adventure, but so far it was about as exciting as watching a tennis match with no ball.

Then a call came in. I blinked receive, but didn't get a picture. Naturally, it was Polly, checking up on me.

"'Sup, sis?" I answered.

"Well," she said, with an unmistakable tone of resentment, "so far it's about as exciting as a meeting of the Alzheimer's Remembrance League. How about you?"

"Oh, not much happening," I said, "after we fought off the attack of the fleet of star destroyers and dodged our way through the kryptonite meteor swarm. Papa thinks he can repair the burned-out megatron inverter if he can only find a bobby pin."

"You should never leave home without a bobby pin, stupid."

"The truth is, other than eating a world-class burger and fries, I haven't had a damn thing to do. Papa and Sheila have been jabbering fluent Inuktitut and writing Sanskrit."

"Sheila?"

"The resident AI. A great cook, and apparently an even better mathematician."

"It couldn't be more boring than what's happening here. Mama and Travis and most of our family and friends are talking, talking, talking. And when that's done, they talk some more. I took a break to powder my nose. I guess I'd better get back . . . Uh-oh, Patrick just came out of the room, and it looks like he's looking for me. Gotta go."

Chalk one up for the evil twin. Here I was rocketing away at dizzying speed from all that was near and dear to me, on an errand I had not much faith in. There she was, ready to dig her claws into my beloved. I felt the blood rush to my face.

I would have thought that sleep would be impossible, but I was wrong. I wasn't even aware that I had fallen asleep until Sheila announced that we were fifteen minutes from our destination.

We had been decelerating for two hours and fifteen minutes. At some point, Sheila had flipped over and instead of our exhaust pointing back at the ship we were moving away from, we had been blasting away from the ship, slowing down.

It's possible to turn the ship while still thrusting evenly. Sheila could adjust her thrust so finely that no one would feel it at all. And that was the case. Papa hadn't even been aware that we had turned ship.

When I realized we were thrusting toward *Rolling Thunder*, I reflexively looked up, thinking I'd see the outside of my home. If we had been in a solar system, it would have been easy. The ship is not particularly reflective, but at half a million miles an eight-mile oblong rock would have been visible as a star as bright as a planet. Out here there was just starlight, and it wasn't nearly enough to light it up.

So I went back to the cabin and sat down across from Papa. He was still fiddling with his detector.

"Learned anything new, Papa?" I asked him.

"Oh, sure, *cher*. I'm always learnin' something new, ever minute of every day."

"So what do you know now that's new?"

"I know that the background of dark lightning is steady out to three hundred thousand miles. No change so far. In a minute, I'll know if it changes in three hundred and twenty thousand miles. See?" He pointed to a screen where there was a line on a graph. It was almost straight, with just a few small bumps above or below the line.

"What are those little variations?"

"Not important, within the samplin' error. What's really puzzlin' me, *cher*, is that it be passin' through the big bubble out front of us. It shouldn't be doing that. I got to figger out *why* it's doin' that. And how. And I got to see if all of it's gettin' through, or just some of it."

"Which is why we're out here."

"Like I said, I learn a lot more about this stuff every minute. I 'spect we'll be learnin' even more when we get out to the boundary line, out past the shadow bein' cast by the big bubble out there."

"I assume you'll be careful, Papa."

"Oh, always, *cher*. I'd never risk my sweet Cassie on anything dangerous. Me and Sheila, we done worked out a careful plan when we get out there. We'll take it a step at a time."

———————

Pretty soon I was bored out of my mind. So I checked my mail.

There were more anonymous nasty ones, more than I had expected, actually. The more reasonable ones asked me when the hell my family was going to tell everyone more about what the hell was going on. Others alleged a conspiracy. What the purpose was, I have no idea. Did they think Papa *wanted* to turn the ship around?

I got an urgent ping from the captain himself. I moved back to the cockpit to take the call. Travis popped up front and center on my corneal screen. And it wasn't a pretty sight. He was scowling at me.

"Cassie, what the hell do you think you're doing?"

I was shocked. He was blaming *me* for something?

"Just what I was told to do, Uncle Travis. Helping my father try to find a way to save all our asses."

"That's ridiculous. I don't want him out there, it's not safe."

Well, what about me? I had a momentary feeling of uncertainty, but then I remembered what Papa had said.

"You're the one who's being ridiculous. Papa told me he would never put me in danger, and I believe him."

"But he doesn't know what's out there! How can he be sure he's not putting himself in danger?" Pause. "And you, too, of course."

Of course.

He went on. "I want you to turn that ship around and come back, right now. I'll take his gizmo out there myself and get his readings for him."

I thought about that for a moment and wondered if I should go back and tell Papa what Travis wanted. But I didn't want to get him more upset, and besides, I'd had just about enough of this shit.

"No can do, Travis. You're not in charge here. Papa is."

I'd read of people "sputtering," in books, but I don't think I'd ever seen it in real life until that moment. I'd also read of people so mad that steam seemed to be coming out their ears and wondered if I'd be treated to that sight.

"It's my ship!" he sputtered.

"No question. But I'm the acting captain. Sheila?"

"Yes, Cassie?"

"Am I or am I not in charge of this ship?"

There was a long, long pause, which made the tiny hairs stand up on the back of my neck, something else I'd read about. I was just reflecting on how much thinking an AI could do in a nanosecond, and she was taking half a minute?

"You are the acting captain," she finally said.

"Sheila!" Travis shouted. "You know damn well I'm the captain."

"Not the only captain, sir. My programming, which you approved, provides, and in fact requires, that when you are not aboard, someone must be in charge. As Jubal is not competent to make the sort of decisions that might need to be made, Cassandra is the only other option. Without her aboard, I would not have been authorized to take this voyage."

"I'm exercising the emergency override," Travis said, gritting his teeth slightly, I thought.

"I'm sorry, Travis, but I have had to weigh several competing mandates in determining that Cassie must remain in control until I return to the ship. One is that, having worked with Jubal for a while now, I recognize that no one but he is able to keep his jury-rigged detector working properly for the length of time needed to take his measurements."

"He can come back and we can take a little time to make a better one. Then I can go out and get his data for him."

"I also feel that he is more competent than you to judge the urgency of the situation. And lastly, his daughter is more able to keep him steady and working toward what he wants to find out than even you would be."

"Travis," I said. "What are you so uptight about? You know Papa wouldn't risk my life. He would risk his if he thought it was important, but me, or Polly, or Mama? Never. He never would, and you know that."

He sighed and looked away from me for a moment.

"Goddam uppity AIs," he said. "When did they start refusing orders from humans? There's something not right about that."

Travis gave us another of his long-suffering sighs and capitulated.

"Okay, you two. If you're gonna gang up on me, I guess I'll have to let it go. But when you get back, Sheila, expect me to meet you with a pair of pliers and a soldering iron. You need some adjustments. Cassie, you take care of him."

"Travis, he's my *father*, okay?"

"Yeah, yeah, you're right. I've gotta go. The meeting's dragging on. I expect to see you in a few hours."

"You will see her in as long as it takes," Sheila said.

"Goddam AIs."

The rest of the trip out to the edge of the "safe" zone (we would soon see just how safe it was) was uneventful. Arriving there was not.

Papa knew that weightlessness was going to screw him up big-time. Sheila eased us to a stop at the point she had calculated was right on the edge of the safe shadow, about half a million miles from *Rolling Thunder*. There was nothing different to see with your eyes.

"Cassie, *cher*," Papa muttered, as we lost the last few pounds of apparent weight. "Cassie, come here, I need to talk to you."

"Sure, Papa." I kicked gently and floated over.

"I'm gonna be very, very sick, me," he said. I could see the effort he was putting into keeping his gorge down. Clearly, eating that hamburger had been a bad idea, but it was also true he would have been throwing up even if his stomach held nothing but bile.

"*Cher*, I might not be in my right mind," he wheezed. "I mean, I may not be able to run this machine I made."

"What can I do, Papa?"

"There be some things me and your mama didn't ever get around to tellin' y'all," he said. "I ain't got time to fill you in now, and anyways, I always knew your mama would have to do the tellin'. All I can say right now is that it takes one of us to use this here gizmo. Me, Poddy, Polly, or you. That's why I come out here. But it lookin' like I ain't gonna be no good at all. So it have to be you, my sweet Cassie."

I had no idea what he was talking about, but I tried not to let it show in my face. He didn't need any extra worry.

"Okay, Papa, just tell me what to do."

For the next couple of minutes he fought his way through the nausea and showed me a few things about the "gizmo." There wasn't much to learn. It was much simpler than many other devices I had mastered. Just a few buttons, a few dials, a touch pad, and a screen that was recording the intensity of whatever dark lightning was.

He drew a wavering line on the screen with a fingernail. There was already a line there, generated by a computer, showing the intensity so far. It was almost straight.

"If it get to this line here, I want you to come and get me, no matter how sick I be. Okay?"

"Sure, Papa."

"Now, Sheila know what to do with the ship. We goin' out to about a hundred thousand miles and stop, and you take a reading."

"Got it, Papa."

"Now, *cher*, I think I'm gonna be really sick, so I best go to the head."

He got up . . . or tried to, then seemed to discover something in his right hand. He looked at it like he'd never seen it before, then whacked his head with his other hand.

"Almost forgot the most important thing, me," he said, swallowing hard. I expected him to vomit at any moment. He handed me the item. I took it, and studied it. It was a shiny cylinder of metal. I have never seen a real cigarette, but I've seen them in movies, and if you chrome-plated one of them, it would be about that size. There was about an inch of flexible wire coming out of one end that looked like an antenna of some sort. Papa had apparently been concealing it in his big paw.

"You got to hold on to this, Cassie," he said. "It don't work at all 'less you be holdin' it. You understand?"

"I understand what you said, that's easy enough. But I don't understand why."

"I'd try to 'splain it to you, but I think I'm runnin' out of time, me. I gotta get to the bathroom, right now."

Once more he tried to stand, and since I had quietly unfastened his seat belt while he was talking, this time he rose out of his chair and banged his head on the ceiling.

I'd been ready for it because he always overreacted in zero gee. I was holding his hand, and I pulled him down and grabbed a rail with my free one and propelled us down the passageway to the door to the head, pulling him along like a big inflatable Santa Claus. I kept waiting for the eruption to hit me in the back, but it never came.

I got the door open, twisted in the air, and shoved him into the small water closet.

"Handholds right here on either side," I said. I pushed his head a little closer to the opening. It was so sparkling clean you could have used any surface in the head for surgery. It smelled a little like lemons. "Keep your head close, Papa. I'll get this done as soon as I can, and we'll head for home." I brushed the switchplate that turned on the fan. I could immediately feel the breeze passing through the room from ceiling to toilet.

"Thank you, Cassie. I think I be sick now."

I pushed out and closed the door. Instantly I heard him retching.

Poor Papa.

We accelerated out of the cone of safety.

It doesn't take long to cover a hundred thousand miles when you're boosting at one gee. When the weight came on and pressed me back into my seat, the nasty sounds from the head slowed down a bit but didn't completely stop. Then the engines cut out and we turned, and I could hear Papa moaning and barfing again. More acceleration—actually, *deceleration, but it feels just the same*—and then we were weightless again.

"The joystick, Cassie," Sheila said.

"The what?"

"That's what your father calls the little cylinder you're supposed to be holding."

"Oh great, spacegirl," I chided myself. I'd forgotten all about it. I picked it up from the clasp on the table which had prevented it from getting lost floating around the cabin. With it grasped firmly in my sweaty palm, I peered at the screen.

There had been no change. I turned a few of the knobs this way and that, as Papa had showed me. I depressed the intercom button on the console beside me.

"No change, Papa. The line wavers a bit, but just as much up as down. It's pretty much where it was when we were in the safety zone. Nowhere near the line you drew."

"No change. Huh. Okay, *cher*, on to the next station."

We traveled another hundred thousand miles. He seemed to get even sicker when we were motionless again, two hundred thousand miles from *Rolling Thunder*.

When we came to a weightless halt again I gripped the "joystick" tightly. And the line continued right across the screen.

"Nothing, Papa. No change."

"No change."

"Let's go back, Papa. There's not going to be any change."

"I concur," Sheila said.

"Okay. Let's do that."

Shortly after we started boosting again and a slightly uncomfortable—for me—one gee settled in over my body, I crept quietly to the head. I eased the door open and saw Papa with his arms around the toilet. He was sound asleep. He was snoring like a buzz saw. But he woke up and looked at me.

"No change," he said, and scratched his fingers through his beard. His eyes had taken on an intensity I hadn't seen since we boarded the ship.

"That be interesting," he said.

You bet. And when Papa says something is interesting, there's no telling what he's going to think of next.

CHAPTER 13

Polly:

As Cassie likes to tell me, there is usually a good side and a bad side to everything, and I tend to see the bad side first. Though I really hate to agree with her when she's talking about me, I have reluctantly concluded that she is right.

My first reaction when I lost the scissors-paper-rock game was to mope because she was going to be taking a trip outside the ship, having an adventure, while I was going to be stuck with the family having a meeting about this ruckus stirred up by what Papa had said. I mean, is there anything more exciting than sitting around a table with your relatives, talking about stuff most of them, including me, don't even understand?

But as the guests began to arrive I realized there was a silver lining to the cloud. Mike and Marlee came walking down the driveway and right behind them came Apollo. Excuse me, I meant Patrick.

And where was my sister? Why, about a hundred thousand miles away and receding fast.

Eat your heart out, bitch. I've got him all to myself.

I smiled at him as I held the back door open for them, but I didn't overdo it. I wasn't going to make the same mistake Cassie had made, throwing myself at him, practically dropping my knickers and waving my ass at him. What I decided to do was sneak up on him, insinuate myself into his space as if accidentally, and see what developed.

I wished I had a better idea how to do that. Not to toot my own horn, but though we may not be exactly the *most* gorgeous girls in the ship, we're attractive enough that we've seldom had to make a play for a particular guy. They usually come on to us if we just wait. Now I was wishing I'd more carefully studied the techniques of the handful of real flirts in our social circle.

"Everybody's gathering in the music room," I told them, and watched Patrick pass through the kitchen and turn right to go down the hallway. The dude looked good from every angle. Fantastic buns.

Mama Podkayne had assigned me the role of greeter and bartender, and that's what I did for the next hour as guests arrived at the back door.

Travis was already back there with Mama.

Granddaddy Ramon and Granny Evangeline came in together, followed quickly by Aunt Elizabeth and Dorothy. I offered everyone beverages and plates to fill with the snack items Mama had ordered from the commissary. Granddaddy asked for a beer, Granny wanted a glass of white wine, Aunt Liz opted for sparkling water, and Dorothy asked if we had any of that eighteen-year-old Glenlivet (now thirty-eight-year-old, since there was no point in storing hard liquor in time suspension), and I told her of course we did. Although Travis is an admitted alcoholic, for many years now he has been able to drink as long as he keeps it to one glass of Scotch per week, when he's out of the bubble. We always stock it.

I fixed the drinks, taking a sip of our ship-grown Chablis and finding it acceptable. Scotch tastes like medicine to me.

While I did that, Great-grandpa Jim and Great-granny Audrey arrived, and I poured some more of the wine for them.

There were more relatives arriving and more drinks to fix, then Patrick came into the kitchen with orders from Travis (Scotch), Mama (Dr Pepper), Marlee (gin and tonic), and Uncle Mike (Singapore sling). That last was Uncle Mike busting my balls, challenging me to see if I could make one. I had to look it up, and I had to place a quick order to the liquor store for cherry brandy and Benedictine, and they arrived within five minutes.

(Want to make one? Two parts gin, one part cherry brandy, one part pineapple juice, one part lime juice, one-half part Cointreau orange liqueur, one-half part Benedictine herbal liqueur, a little grenadine syrup, a dash of bitters. Pour into a shaker over crushed ice and do the cha-cha-cha until the shaker is frosted, strain into a tall glass, and add a stick of pineapple and a cherry. Then *you* drink the whole mess. It sounds awful to me.)

I found a little paper cocktail umbrella and set it afire, blew it out, and stuck the twisted remains into the cherry, making sure to get a little bit of the ashes on the surface of the drink. That's me busting *his* balls.

It got a little frantic there for a while. I hadn't realized there were going to be so many friends and relatives at the meeting. There were third cousins I only saw on rare occasions, like when Papa came out of his bubble.

In addition to family, most of the people who had been present at the meeting in the Common Council chamber showed up. There was Governor Wang (sparkling water), Mayor Bull (Pernod, I had to order out again), Mayor Ngoro (just plain tap water, please, how about a slice of lemon with that, okay, thank you sweetheart), Rachel Walters (white wine), and Max Karpinski (vodka and red wine, yuck). I soon picked up an assistant, my ten-year-old cousin Katy (strawberry soda). I didn't allow her near the alcohol, but she seemed to enjoy taking the tray in and distributing the drinks as I mixed them. She had a big grin after taking the drink to Uncle Mike.

Things eased up, and I managed to get down to the music room to see what was going on. Mama and Travis had been kept busy moving the pianos and harpsichords and display cases and replacing them with folding chairs from the basement. She had dragooned two cousins to help out. It was lucky that the room was large, even bigger than our huge family room, because it was almost filled up. I'd say there were sixty or more people sitting around, chattering. It seemed more like a sedate cocktail party than a critical meeting, and I saw Travis pacing impatiently in one corner, eager to get things started. I checked the snack table and saw that, while it had been attacked by the mob, it was still holding up okay. It was pretty noisy in there, between the talking and the crunching of potato chips.

I spotted Patrick across the room, talking to another cousin. I believe her name was Natalie, one of the huge Broussard clan. I assayed her critically and reluctantly decided that she had all the goods, and they were all in the right places. But I was pleased to see she didn't know how to dress. She was wearing some dreadful leather shirt with fringes that swayed back and forth as she moved.

Unfortunately, it's well-known that most boys don't give a damn how we dress. They are much more interested in getting us out of our clothes.

I looked down at myself. I hadn't had time to change into something nice, and there was a dark stain on my shirt where I'd spilled something. Should have worn an apron.

I decided to take a break. Mama has strict ideas on hostessing and feels no one should have to make their own drinks, but screw that. I wasn't a servant. Let them fend for themselves for a while.

I made a pit stop, and when I got off the pot, I had a great idea to break up the boredom and break somebody *else's* balls, namely the carbon copy. I phoned Cassie and shot the breeze with her for a bit, then dropped my bombshell.

"Uh-oh, Patrick just came out of the room, and it looks like he's looking for me. Gotta go."

And then I hung up, and turned off my phone. I had a big, silly grin on my face. That should keep her worried. Now, to make it come true.

I took a quick shower, then hit the closet.

What would be the most effective counterpoint to Natalie's pioneer-mother covered-wagon Annie Oakley duds? Well, a cocktail dress would shut her down for sure, but obviously it was the wrong setting for that. I needed something casual.

I flirted with the 1950s, not the pleated skirt, silly hat, high heels, pointy-boobs bra and girdle look, but bohemian. Beatniks, they were called, and the girls wore tight pedal pushers and loose, sloppy sweaters or sweatshirts.

Nah. *Too* casual.

But just a decade later, everything changed. Women's clothing loosened up. Hair got long and straight instead of permed and teased. Bras became less confining, or vanished altogether. Sandals replaced foot-ruining high heels. Some women wore very short skirts known as minis, some wore long, flowing ones with peasant blouses.

I went with some faded jeans and a tie-dyed top that was a beautiful riot of color. Combed my hair out, put on a headband with peace signs around it. Tied a knitted belt on to cinch in and show off my waist. Stepped into a pair of light brown soft leather moccasins. Some feathered earrings, a couple of bracelets, a gold necklace—accessorizing is critical!—and I was almost ready. I freshened my makeup and looked myself over. Go get him, girl. All of this took about twenty minutes.

I left the bedroom and went back down the hall to the music room. Inside, they still weren't down to business. Patrick was still talking to Cousin Natalie. I decided her drink refill would be rum and Coke and a lot of Tabasco sauce.

Uncle Travis was off in one corner, talking into his antique radio-telephone, something almost a hundred years old. Or the shell was, anyway, though I doubted the insides were original.

He looked pretty upset, pacing back and forth, gesturing with his free hand, all while trying to keep his voice down. I edged around the room and tried not to look snoopy as I trained an ear on him. I couldn't make out many words, but a few names came through. There was Jubal, and Sheila, the AI. But the name I heard most often was Cassie, and it was clear he wasn't happy with her.

I didn't know what to make of that. Normally, I wouldn't worry much about Sis's getting chewed out, but she was way, way out there, and Papa was with her. The sort of trouble you could get into out there was not something to be flip about.

I was trying to get closer, but he hung up.

The meeting got started, with Travis grabbing a tambourine said to have been used by Janis Joplin out of a display case and hammering the skin with his fist—which caused Mama to wince. Well, the thing was getting on to 150 years old, and that skin was delicate. But it held up, and he put it down and raised his hands over his head as the noise quieted down.

He asked everyone to take a seat, which most everyone did, with a lot of murmuring and scraping. Governor Wang and George Bull and Max Karpinski and Rachel Walters joined him, standing on each side of him. There were two other people who I didn't know, and I assumed they were either scientists or from the government. I leaned back against the wall far to one side, near the door, as befitted my role as hostess. Mama did the same on the other side of the room.

"Thank you all for coming," Travis said. "As you all know, we have a big decision to make in the coming days. Jubal Broussard is at this moment probing the edges of what we call the 'safety zone,' that area that is cleared of the very thin gas and dust of interstellar space."

That caused a lot of surprised reactions from the crowd, and not everyone looked happy to hear it.

I got a better chance to gauge the crowd now that I wasn't hustling back and forth with drinks and bowls of snacks. I saw now that there were a lot of people not of the family. I knew the names of some of them, like the minister of education and the chief engineer, and I knew others by reputation or from appearances on the news or entertainment shows. There was Fiona Kelly, the head newsreader for RTBS, and two of the prominent reporters. Some faces were familiar, but I couldn't put names to them. By their dress, I assumed some of them were businesspeople and others were community leaders of one sort or another. You really can tell a lot about the majority of people by the clothes they wear to a meeting like this.

After a quick and informal head count, I estimated that about half the room was relatives and the other half movers and shakers in the ship. For the first time, that struck me as a little odd. It's a quite different circumstance from anything that existed back at Old Sun, to live in a world that is actually *owned* by someone, that someone being my beloved uncle Travis and, by extension, his family.

In other words, by me. I actually own shares of the Rolling Thunder

Corporation. I don't know exactly how many—it's never seemed important to me—but it's not a lot compared to Mama and Papa and the other older members of the family. But if it came to a decision by the corporation, I'd have to vote those shares.

It was a sobering thought. A very important decision was going to be made soon, and I wasn't sure which was more important: the elected representatives or the corporation. Looking at the faces of the people gathered there, I saw concern, and fear. I figured the meeting might get interesting after all.

I couldn't have been more wrong.

Oh, there were differing opinions expressed, but after a half an hour it seemed to me that nothing was really getting accomplished. It was civilized, no shouting, no finger-pointing. If they wanted to keep things as they were, they found it easy to believe that Papa was wrong.

If they feared dying from this strange stuff Papa said he had discovered more than they feared the upheaval stopping the ship would cause, they trotted out all the great things he had done. If not for him, we might still have hardly made it to Mars, much less the other planets, and here we were, light-years from Old Sun, using engines invented by Papa.

But what about Jubal? said the go-ahead faction. He's always been a little bit crazy, right? Papa is crazy, no question. It's his own wonderful brand of crazy. But what if he's losing it? He has too many phobias to count, the naysayers pointed out. How can we tell this isn't just another one? He shouts "Stop the ship!" What the hell? How does he go into the bubble cool and calm and collected and come out of it *with zero time elapsed* babbling nonsense about some mysterious "dark lightning"?

And so forth.

I've found that most meetings are like that. People stake out a position at the outset and keep repeating the same arguments over and over, as if by saying them twenty times they will convince everyone to see it their way. I have also found, in everything from meetings of the Girl Guides to the solemn deliberations of the Council, that very few minds are ever changed.

But that doesn't stop them from talking.

I kept my eye on Travis, wondering what his strategy was. He kept quiet, listened politely to what everyone had to say, content to let Governor Wang chair the meeting.

I figured Travis was waiting them out, and I think a lot of other people realized that, too. And I'll bet that what they expected at the end was not a vote but a pronouncement from Captain Broussard, even if the pronouncement was simply to wait until Papa got back with his new data.

Which is what I expected. We still didn't know enough to make a decision. We were sounding each other out, trying to see how the sides would be drawn when it came to crunch time.

It was all boring as hell, even when tempers began to flare up. And to my surprise, it was all rather hot and sweaty. It must have been pushing ninety degrees in the music room. That room is carefully temperature controlled because of all the antiques in there. If it was hot in there, it was because Mama, or Travis, or both of them *wanted* it to be hot. I smiled to myself. I think they were counting on attrition from the heat.

I was about to nod off myself when Mama caught my eye and made a circular motion with her hand. I wasn't sure what she meant, then she took advantage of a short lull in the jabbering and held up her hands and let out a whistle. I wish I could do that; my whistle is pathetic.

"People, it looks like we'll be here awhile. I want to take this opportunity to freshen everybody's drinks. You can have water, coffee, soft drinks, beer, wine, cocktails. How many want coffee?"

Mama was looking at me.

Oh.

I quickly took the orders. I pushed open the door, closed it behind me, and went down the hall to the kitchen.

I had water heating in the big coffeemaker and dumped some French roast beans into the grinder. Since we couldn't grow coffee in the ship, Travis had made sure there was enough of it in stasis to last everybody even if we decided to cross the galaxy. It came out of the bubbles still hot from the roaster.

The grinder made such a racket that I didn't hear Patrick come into the kitchen until he spoke.

"My mother suggested that you might need some help," he said.

I almost jumped out of my skin, but I hoped I covered it well. He was standing a few feet away, with a friendly smile on his face.

"I should have thought of it myself, I know, but frankly, ah . . ."

"Polly," I prompted.

"Anyway, Polly, I waited so many tables in the last few years that I've got a real aversion to carrying a tray. I swore a mighty oath never to work in the service industry."

"Not following in your father's footsteps, right?"

"No way. He doesn't care. In fact, he discourages it."

"I decided not to follow in Papa's footsteps, too," I said. "So I've ruled out being a physics genius."

He looked puzzled for a second, then got the joke.

"I think I might rule that out, too. Considering I barely squeaked by in senior math."

"Same here. In fact, all the sciences are my weakest subjects. Cassie is the big brain of the pair." Hoping he wouldn't want to see a girl who was smarter than him at something. Sorry, but that masculine domination thing is still alive and well, even after more than a century of equality. I think they carry it in their testicles. They want to be taller, smarter, and stronger than the girl they are with, and I'm willing to let them think they are, poor fools.

I showed him where the coffee mugs were, and the serving trays, and he began setting it all out.

"Spoons?" he asked.

"That drawer right there."

"Sugar bowl? Cream?"

It was pleasant, mostly, working beside him. I was awfully self-conscious, almost close enough to touch him now and then, and I felt big and awkward. We were almost eye to eye. One of us probably had a half inch on the other, but I wouldn't bet on which one it was.

I got the coffee perking, then, for a moment, there wasn't anything else for me to do. A dozen mugs were lined up neatly on one tray, and the sugar bowl and cream pitcher and napkins and spoons on another. I turned around and leaned back on the counter, smelling the good coffee as it flowed through the ground beans and into the big pot.

"What we need with this is some cookies," he said.

"You think?"

"Definitely. Unless you want to order up some sinkers."

"Sinkers?"

"That's diner slang for donuts. You dunk them in your coffee."

"Papa does that. I sort of think that ruins the donut."

"I'm with you. I like my coffee black and strong."

I decided not to mention I load mine up with three sugars and three little buckets of creamer. Somehow, drinking your coffee black and strong just sounds tougher, doesn't it? Not that I wanted to sound *too* tough . . .

Truth was, I was still flustered.

"You have any cookies?"

"I don't know. We usually do unless Papa breaks his resolution in the middle of the night."

He laughed. "My dad's the same way. Let's look, okay?"

So we embarked on a quest for cookies. They would be in the pantry if we had them, so he followed me in there and we started looking on the shelves and into bins and compartments.

Our pantry was fairly large. But two people was rather intimate company. I was getting a little light-headed, bumping into him now and then as we moved about. I was nervous being that close to him; I couldn't seem to find anywhere to stand, or figure out what to do with my elbows. I had a severe attack of the klutzes, something I've had around boys before. I felt knock-kneed, fumble-fingered, cross-eyed, duck-footed. It was a miracle I didn't dump a canister of flour from the top shelf all over his head.

I could smell the pleasant masculine scent of him. I wondered if he could smell me, and if it was a good smell. I was thanking my lucky stars that I'd had time to shower and freshen my face and hair, and regretting I hadn't used just a dab of perfume. Something subtle, like Doe Bunny in Heat, or Ravish Me, You Gorgeous Hunk.

It didn't take us too long (dammit!) to determine there were no cookies in the pantry.

He shrugged. "Oh, well. They don't deserve them, anyway."

"You think not?"

He rolled his beautiful eyes. "A lot of hot air if you ask me."

"I'm so glad to hear that. I thought I was going to die of boredom for a while there."

"Don't worry. I know CPR."

"Chest compression? Mouth-to-mouth? Like that?"

"Sure. Like this." He leaned forward and kissed me on the lips.

My head didn't explode, but it was a close thing. My toes curled, my ears flapped, my eyes rolled up, and up, and all the way around like a two-window slot machine, all the muscles in my legs changed to peach jelly, and my nipples turned into cherry pits. As for the little girl in the boat, let's not even go there.

He pulled away and looked into my eyes from about four inches away. I was about to fling myself on him—I mean, literally, I saw my arms around his neck, legs wrapped around his hips—when he touched my cheek in a friendly way, smiled again, and turned and left the pantry.

Now, what was *that* all about?

The kiss hadn't been passionate, but it hadn't been brotherly, either. I wanted to put my hand on his crotch and see if I'd had any effect on him, as he'd had on me, but I'm too well brought up for that.

Keep calm, spacegirl, I kept telling myself. This could be the start of something big. Don't blow it.

Hard advice to follow, when you're floating three feet in the air.

On the other hand, I cautioned myself, it could be just a line he had used a hundred times. "I know CPR," and *smackeroo*!

On the third hand . . . what exactly was the problem if it *was* a line? Did I care if he just wanted to get in my pants? I sure wanted to get into his. But for now, it seemed, we were just going to pretend it never happened. This is, unless I threw myself at him and told him I had lived all my life for that moment, and please do it again, and would this countertop do? But somehow I sensed it wasn't the time or place.

Which just goes to show you, you should grab every opportunity that comes by. You never know when you'll get another.

So I poured hot coffee into all the cups, and he arranged everything to his satisfaction on his tray, and I started to pick mine up.

"Best way to carry it is up high," he advised me.

"How's that?"

He took the tray with the coffee and, in one smooth motion, had it up and balanced at shoulder height on the palm of his hand.

"See? This way you can raise it or lower it as you make your way through a crowd. You can see where you're going. And it leaves one hand free." He smiled, and set the tray back down. "Now you try it."

I thought of telling him there wasn't likely to be a crowd in the hallways between the kitchen and the music room, but what the hell. I was game, or wanted to look that way. So I shakily and carefully lifted the tray and had it halfway up . . . and had a vision of the whole thing falling right onto him. No, this wasn't the time or place to learn waitressing skills.

"Sorry," I said, setting it back down and lifting it by the handles. "I'd better stick to what I know."

"Suit yourself. Sure you don't want me to carry the coffee?"

"I can handle it."

He gestured gallantly with his free arm, and I passed him and went into the hallway.

The kitchen is in front of the house, close by the family/party room, and the music room is all the way in the back. The hallway was a good thirty or forty yards from front to back. It's wide enough for people to walk three or even four abreast.

He had the free hand, and he was a gentleman, so he pulled the door open and gestured me inside. I took two steps and froze.

Max Karpinski, my darling uncle Max, all four hundred pounds of him, was standing near the middle of the room with his back to me.

Standing beside him was Governor Wang, and her face looked very funny. I realized she was wearing some sort of mask. Goggles over her eyes, and a thing over her nose and mouth. She looked like a frog.

Uncle Travis was sprawled a few feet away from Max, prone, his face turned toward me. A .45 automatic was about a foot from his right hand.

Everyone else in the room that I could see was either on the floor or sitting in chairs, loose-limbed, heads lolling or thrown back. No one that I could see was moving.

I caught a whiff of something that smelled a little like peppermint, a little like ozone. Just a whiff, and for a moment I was dizzy. I exhaled hard and held my breath.

Uncle Max started to turn, ponderous as a minor planet. He had something in one hand that looked like a weapon, and a gas mask on his face.

I hurled the tray with the hot coffee at him. A little splashed on my hand, but I didn't even feel it. Max, on the other hand, felt it plenty. He howled, tried to backpedal, and fell right on his huge behind. One of the mugs hit his face and drew blood.

I slammed the door closed.

Then I was backpedaling, running into Patrick and knocking him off balance. There was a clatter as spoons and sugar and the tray came crashing to the ground.

"Hey—"

"Shut up. Patrick, try not to breathe. They've all been gassed."

"What do you mean—"

"I mean they've all been gassed. I think they're all alive . . ." I was playing the tape back in my head, and I was pretty sure I saw a couple of people breathing, and I hoped it wasn't wishful thinking.

Mama, Mike, Marlee, Travis . . .

No good thinking about something I couldn't do anything about. We had to get moving.

"That sideboard," I shouted at him. "We need to knock it over."

"What—"

"Don't ask questions, just *do it*!"

I moved to the far side of the sideboard. I think it was a sideboard. It was an antique, Georgian, I think Mama said once. It was tall and narrow, with drawers on the bottom, a shelf, and glass-fronted doors at the top. About seven feet tall. I put my shoulder to it and shoved. It moved a little.

"Help me, dammit!"

He still stood there, stunned. I screamed, and hit the thing again, and it rose up on two claw feet, teetered . . .

. . . and went over just as the door started opening. A hand came through, holding Travis's gun. The sideboard hit the door and the hand, and someone—I'm pretty sure it was Max—howled and dropped the pistol.

The glass doors opened and broke—sorry, Mama—and all the antique crockery we never used came spilling out all over the floor, shattering into a million pieces.

I pushed the door again, jamming the fingers hard enough to break them, and the same someone howled again before getting his hand back. I got the door closed and shoved the sideboard against it.

I picked up the pistol, ejected the magazine, and saw I had a full load of seventeen. A Glock, I think. Probably a hundred years old but obsessively maintained, like all of Travis's weapons.

"Cassie," someone shouted on the other side of the door. "This isn't what it seems. Come in, and I'll tell you what happened."

"No thanks, Uncle Max."

"They're alive. I had to—"

I jammed the magazine back home and aimed at the door, holding the gun the way Travis had taught us. I really wanted to fire at chest level, hoping he was still standing there. But I thought better of it. You have to be very careful with a gun, and most of the people I loved were in that room. Alive, if Max was telling the truth, and I thought he was.

"And I'm *Polly*, you fat son of a bitch!" I shouted, and aimed at the top part of the door.

I put three rounds through the upper part of the door, so they would hit the ceiling. The shots were deafening there in the hallway. Splinters flew. I heard something heavy hit the floor. No way I'd hit him; he was merely hitting the ground and trying to make himself small. Good luck with that, you quarter ton of pork.

When I turned, Patrick was standing with his palms pressed to his ears and cheeks, stunned.

"We've got to get moving," I told him. I grabbed his right hand and slapped the pistol into it. He looked down at his hand as if it were an alien thing. He'd probably never touched a firearm before. "Keep your finger away from the trigger unless you mean to use it. The safety is off."

He was holding it by the barrel. Well, maybe that was safest.

I grabbed his other hand and pulled him along the hallway to my bedroom.

I left him standing in the hallway, still looking down at the gun in his hand. Inside the bedroom, I hurried to the wall safe. I pressed my hand to the touchplate, and the door opened.

Inside was an automatic, in a pretty pink leather holster that could fasten around your waist or be adjusted for shoulder carry. It had been manufactured shortly before the ship left Old Sun, so it looked nothing like the old Glock. I quickly strapped it around my waist.

There were many things I wanted to do, but I only had time to do one thing. I clicked to the security camera in the music room. I saw Max slowly crawling across the floor, getting as far from the door as possible. He was talking on his phone, but there is no sound in those cameras. Governor Wang was cowering in a corner.

I quickly zoomed in on Mama, who had fallen over and was almost hidden behind a display case with several instruments in it. I zoomed in even closer, on her head and upper body. After a few seconds I was sure she was breathing. I felt a great weight lift from my heart. If she was alive, they were most likely all alive, and Max and Wang were not mass murderers.

So the . . . Let's call them what they were, okay? The mutineers were only two in number, and they didn't seem to be armed. Max had taken the gun from Travis. Patrick and I were both armed now. Storm the room. Move the sideboard, pull the door open, and come in blasting.

But . . . no, dammit, they were both still wearing their gas masks, and if it was me, I'd take the damn things off as soon as the gas had cleared. So going into the room probably meant we would pass out. I remembered that moment of dizziness when I'd first opened the door.

The issue was decided for me when alarm warnings started appearing on the screen, and a calm voice alerted me to an unauthorized trespass from the road. The scene switched, and I saw a group of a dozen people, all dressed in black, hurrying through the trees and up the private road. I didn't see any firearms, but some were carrying clubs, and ropes. Following them was a large panel truck.

I noticed it had begun to rain. I automatically checked my weather almanac, and sure enough, a fair-sized downpour was scheduled.

Another camera showed another group coming through the woods.

I frantically flipped through the outside cameras. The rear of the house—the dock and the boathouse and the pond—seemed empty. It looked like our only chance.

Time to go.

Patrick was still in his semistupor and had begun to wander back toward the music room. I grabbed his hand, and he pulled it away.

"I need to see if my mother and father are all right," he said, and started down the hall. I grabbed him by the back of his shirt and swung him around.

"Patrick, they're alive, I saw them breathing." A lie, but I was confident the part about their being alive was true. "But there are people in there who wish us harm. Max was going to shoot us, you understand?"

"Max? But can't we—"

"We don't have a lot of options right now, Patrick. I saw a large group of people coming up the driveway, and some are carrying weapons and ropes. There's at least one vehicle that looks like it could carry a lot of unconscious people away. We have to run."

"Run where?"

"Out the back door, for now. For later . . . I don't know. Listen, you just stay right here for a minute, okay? There's one more thing I have to do. Will you stay?"

". . . Okay."

"Good boy."

I took the old Glock from him and ran past the music room, down to the end of the hall, and opened the back door. I could see both groups coming toward the house. They were still about a hundred yards away. It was raining heavily now.

I took my shooter's stance and aimed into the dense woods, just above their heads, and shot four rounds at each group. I could see some of the rounds knock bark off trees.

A few of them hit the ground at once, but most just stood there dumbly, not quite realizing what had happened. *Gunfire?* Was that *gunfire*?

"Yes, you stupid pricks," some of them seemed to be yelling, motioning for the standees to get down and take cover.

I didn't intend to shoot anybody. I didn't really know who they were and what they were up to. My point was to let them know I *could* shoot them, and with any luck that fear would slow them down considerably. And it ought to be pretty unpleasant, lying prone on the ground, which was rapidly turning into mud.

I had seen the driver and passenger fling themselves from the truck and crawl for cover. So I aimed at the truck and shot the pistol until the slide stayed open. I could see and hear the windshield glass break, hear the rounds hitting the sides of the truck. That should give them something to think about.

Time to go, go, go.

Back in the house, I could see that Patrick was shaking, maybe going into shock, wavering between heading for the back door and the music room. There was no sign that Max had grown a pair of balls and started shoving at the door. I grabbed Patrick's hand and pulled him toward the back.

There were so many things I wished I had the time to pick up in the house, but as I thought of each one, hurrying through the family room, I rejected it, realizing it would take too much time, and I was feeling strongly that time was running out. If the house got surrounded, we'd last until the bullets in my pistol ran out. I hadn't expected to encounter guns from the opposition; Travis had controlled that too strictly. But it could be possible to make useful pistols or rifles. A bullet from a zip gun could kill you just as easily as one of my explosive rounds. And there were always bows and arrows, easy to come by, slings and spears and who knew what. People had been killing each other long before gunpowder.

Someone had planned all this out. It might not have been the greatest plan in the world—else why were Patrick and I still running around loose?—but I couldn't count on stupidity on the other side.

So. No time to lose. I pulled Patrick through the screen door in back, then down the pier to the very end. By the time we got there, we were soaked, almost as if we were in a shower stall.

"Patrick, we have to go. Now."

"Okay." He still seemed dazed, but getting him outside seemed to have awakened him a little.

"Here's the plan. The weak point in their perimeter is the pond back here. We need to swim someplace where we can get out unseen and find someplace to take cover, at least for a while."

"Okay. Where?"

"You just follow me, got it? I know this pond like Mama Podkayne knows Pod music."

We sat down on the end of the pier. I took off my shoes and shoved them under my gun belt. Patrick stuck his under his waistband. Then I lowered myself into the water. No diving, no big splash to alert the pursuit.

"Just a slow breaststroke, okay?" I told him. "Keep as low as you can, underwater as much as possible."

He nodded, and we were off.

———

So you may be asking yourself, how did she do it?

How did an eighteen-year-old girl who had never encountered anything more violent than a hair-pulling match on the playground or anything more life-threatening than a fashion disaster at the junior prom manage to make all those split-second decisions, avoid dozens of pursuers, and just generally behave like a ninja assassin in a stupid, virtual-reality video game?

Well, part of the answer *is* video games. But not ordinary video games. The rest of the answer is training, practice, and a certain innate ability. You might say I was born to be a ninja assassin, then trained up to the role.

Since we were big enough to hold a pellet gun or a .22, Cassie and I have shot on the practice range at least once a week. When Travis is out of the bubble, he trains with us. But we both soon became better shots than he is. So we are quite familiar with weapons that no one else but Cassie and I, Mama, Uncle Mike, and Marlee even have access to.

Chalk it all up to Travis. Eternally paranoid, he insisted that Cassie and I train for the worst possible scenarios. In this, he had the support of Mama, who had been in a worst possible scenario and survived, and of Granddaddy Ramon and Granny Evangeline, who had fought in the Second Martian War and also knew what danger was.

So we learned to handle weapons. And we played video games.

Not the usual kind. Those are mostly a boy thing. There are no reset buttons in real life, more's the pity. So the games we played were different.

Our video games were adapted from military, police, and real guerrilla-warfare training games. No monsters out in those simulated jungles and deserts and city streets, just a lot of real smart virtual guys and gals out to kill you before you killed them. Winning didn't depend on body count, only on staying alive.

The games could take place anywhere on Old Earth or Mars, or in a hypothetical best-guess New Earth, where the exotic made-up animals lurked, but the ones I liked best happened all over *Rolling Thunder*. They could be human-violence or physical-emergency scenarios. Floods, breakdowns, explosions, cave-ins. The most frightening ones happened in a simulated interior of our own home. Which is why I was able to react quickly. I'd already been there, done that.

Training. Practice. And a sense of where you are, and what's around you. Travis called it the ability to twist around in any situation and land on your feet. He has it, strongly, and so does Mama.

And Cassie and I have it even stronger. It's one of the things that make us such good . . . well, I'll go ahead and say it, *great* . . . skypool players. We're good at seeing things developing, patterns, multiple possible outcomes, alternatives. Split-second decisions. I imagine all athletes have it.

In case you think I'm bragging, I have independent confirmation from Mama. She didn't tell us for a long time, saying she wanted to keep us sharp, but not long ago she revealed that she was having trouble coming up with situations we couldn't handle.

"I just can't seem to kill you girls anymore," she told us.

We kept low in the water. Every minute or so, I went over on my back to take a look behind us, and for the first ten minutes I saw nothing. The gunshots had probably been a huge shock to them. They would approach the house carefully, or maybe not at all until reinforcements arrived.

The house had dwindled quite a bit when I finally saw a group of people come out on the dock. I couldn't tell if they had come around the house or through it. But they were looking all around them. One of them looked like he had a pair of binoculars.

"Patrick, we need to move closer to shore."

The closest side of the pond was lined with reeds and cattails and other growth sprouting from the water and trees that overhung it. Good cover, but also the obvious place for fugitives to hide. Anyone with any sense would be searching there first. On the other hand, the opposite shore was bare beach, and anyone coming out of the water there would be totally exposed. I headed us into the nearest shallows. Looking behind us, I could see a party of three moving along the opposite bank and a group coming along the shore in our direction.

"Patrick, *carefully* move in behind me here. Try not to stir up the silt too much. Try not to break off any of the reeds."

"Toward the shore?"

"We have to conceal ourselves, even if it means moving closer to the ones over here. We need to vanish."

He looked dubious, but he was still willing to follow my lead.

I paddled into the reeds. When I was a few yards in, I stopped. I raised my head a little, but the reeds were too tall to see over. I could hear people talking, though, which meant they were entirely too close.

I broke off one of the heftier reeds, got a three-foot length of it, and put it in my mouth. I could blow through it. Not a lot of air, but it would be enough to keep us alive for a while. I illustrated what I had in mind by holding my nose and easing myself over backward into the water and sinking until I could feel the bottom with my back. I stayed there for a few seconds, then came up.

"Could you see me?" I whispered.

"Looking straight down, yeah. But probably not from the shore."

"Let's hope they don't wade in, then. I may have to kill them."

"Kill . . ."

"Yeah, I don't know if I can, either." Needless to say, I'd never killed anyone real, never even given much thought to it. "We have to hide until they get past us. Hold the reed steady. We don't want them seeing one moving back and forth, though in this rain . . ."

Was there anything I hadn't thought of? I reviewed it and couldn't see anything I'd missed. It was a bad situation, but other than coming out of the water and shooting at them, I didn't see any other choice. I handed Patrick another reed. He looked at it.

"Polly, I don't think I can—"

"Don't think. Just do it."

"I'm . . . I'm sort of claustrophobic. I can't get enough air through this thing. I'm afraid I'll panic."

"I know you can do it, Patrick. Me and Cassie used to do this all the time, playing commando with our friends. I know it's scary, but you'll get used to it." At least I hoped so. Claustrophobic? I forgive any phobia in Papa, but am not quite so understanding about others. Except about bugs. Fearing bugs is okay.

"Here's what I'd rather do," he said. "I'll swim for the other shore. They'll see me and go after me, and you can get away."

"What? Let yourself get caught?"

"Maybe I'll get away."

"Not a chance. I will *not* have you do that, Patrick. Now get that damn thing in your mouth and *submerge*!"

He did, reluctantly. I sank back into the water, holding my nose. Things got murky as my face went under the water. Our little pond is not dirty, but it's no blue mountain tarn, either. Its purpose is fishing, and as such it is full of algae and moss.

Looking up, I saw a school of minnows and a tadpole swim over me.

Then there was a splashing sound right next to me, and a cloud of silt rose around us. I swam up and broke the surface, and saw that Patrick's head was clear out of the water and he was breathing hard.

"What's the matter?" I whispered.

"Something jumped on me. It was creepy."

"Probably just a big old bullfrog."

"Yuck. Frogs give me the creeps."

"You'll have to get over it. Patrick, there's absolutely nothing in this pond that can hurt you. I've been swimming in it all my life. But those people on the shore, *they* can hurt you."

"How do you know they aren't friends, come to help us? Jesus, Polly, you *shot* at them!"

"If they're friends, we'll find out soon enough. Right now, we have to assume they arrived when they did because they are allied with Max. Now shut up and get your head down."

He did, even more reluctantly.

I started a count, imagining them moving slowly along the shore, looking into every patch of brush and out over the lake. After what I hoped was enough time, I slowly eased my head up. The water drained from my ears. I paused for a moment, hearing nothing but the pouring rain. I checked my weather schedule and saw we still had ten minutes of rain to come. I turned over and lifted my whole head out of the water. I couldn't see a thing over the reeds, which were thick, and up to three feet high.

I reached down and got Patrick by the arm and pulled him slowly to the surface.

"I thought I—"

"Quiet."

"I thought I was going to die down there," he whispered.

"I didn't like it much myself. Now stay low, and I'll take a look around."

He nodded. I got my feet and hands under me and took it an inch at a time. When I could see the shore, I kept as still as possible while slowly turning my head from side to side. Sudden movement is the easiest thing for the human eye—any eye, come to that—to see. But if you take it slow, the brain won't really register it unless you're looking right at the motion. One of our lessons in Survival 101.

I never got higher than waist deep, just able to see over the tops of the reeds, but in both directions and straight ahead I could see no people.

"We've only got a few more minutes of rain, and it's about twenty minutes to sun-off. I'm trying to figure out what to do next."

"I don't see how we're going to get out of this."

"I don't either, but that doesn't mean we give up without a fight."

"There's too many of them, Polly."

"You don't know that. I saw a couple dozen."

"There could be hundreds of them."

"If there are, they'll probably get us." I put that thought out of my head. Mama, Travis, all my family . . . I was their only hope. Well, Cassie, too, if she ever got back from her little pleasure trip out to the ass end of nowhere.

"We need to set a destination. I'm thinking they'll be looking for us at your place. But you know it better than me. Is there any way to get in your apartment without being seen?"

He looked blank.

"Didn't you ever sneak out at night?"

"When I was younger, we didn't live there," he pointed out, without answering my question.

"We need to go to ground, get organized, make a plan. We need to get out of the open." I gestured upward where, for only a short time more, the mist and almost clouds would cloak us from observation from the other side. "If we wait until they get night-vision equipment, we're sunk. They'll track us like bugs on a plate."

"Maybe they already have night-vision."

I was getting tired of his defeatism. I guess he was still in shock. Maybe I was, a little, too, but I think it was more likely that I was putting that part off, the sitting-down-and-crying part.

I sighed and started wading toward the shore. I got on dry land and looked back. He was stepping carefully, scowling down at his feet. Then he slipped, did a banana-peel dance for a moment, and fell flat on his ass.

"Could you possibly make any more noise?" I whispered. "Wash that stuff off as best you can. We may need to look presentable."

He did that, grumbling. I hurried into a small copse of brush and trees. There was a small clearing more or less in the center. Cassie and I had pitched a tent in there from time to time. I hadn't been back there in years, and it looked much smaller than I remembered.

I was shivering though it wasn't really cold. I peeled off my clothes and squeezed each item as hard as I could. When Patrick saw what I was doing, he stripped, too, and wrung out his clothes. We dressed again, and I found I was still shaking. Not only that, I felt weak and faint. I sat down suddenly and wrapped my arms around my knees. Patrick sat beside me and looked me over.

"You want my shirt? I'm not feeling cold."

"I'm not cold, either."

"You okay?"

"I will be. Just give me a few moments, okay?"

I knew it was because this was the first moment I felt even a little bit safe since I threw the tray of coffee. The first time I could let anything out. It wouldn't do to overdo it, though. I fought hard against a crying jag.

"Oh lord, Patrick, what are we going to do?"

"I was hoping you had some ideas."

"I do, but nothing I have a lot of confidence in."

He put his arm around me, and I leaned my head on his shoulder for a moment. It felt good. And then my phone pinged.

I almost jumped out of my skin. Who could be calling me? I had set the phone to accept only emergency calls while I was swimming away from the house. The ID said it was Uncle Travis.

"Hello?"

"Have I reached Cassie?" Max said. What the hell.

"Yes." What must have happened, he went through Travis's phone list, came to Cassie first, alphabetically, and dialed. Cassie was not available at the moment, away having fun, so the call was forwarded to me.

Why did I agree to be Cassie? An important rule of survival is that any misinformation your opponent has is usually a good thing for you.

"I've had the devil of a time figuring out this antique," he went on. I could see him holding the old-fashioned phone with its tiny screen. "You'd think that with a doctorate in physics a man could deal with something children used to deal with." He chuckled.

"Say what you have to say."

He sighed. "First, everyone you saw is okay. It was knockout gas, not lethal at all. We are not killers. We don't plan to hurt anyone. In fact, we plan to release most of the people in this room in a day or two."

"Not killers," I said. "Mutineers."

"That's a very ugly word."

"For a very ugly thing, you pathetic sack of shit."

"Do we have to—"

"Yes we do. I see no reason to be cordial. I'll wait for that until I'm on the witness stand at your trial. Mutiny is a capital crime in this ship. Did you ever see that in the regs?"

"You persist in calling it mutiny. We are a committee of safety. When the captain of a ship is putting the lives of his passengers in jeopardy through his ill-considered actions, it is incumbent on ship's officers—in this case, the elected civil government—to lawfully detain him and take temporary command. That's in the regs, too."

"Tell it to the judge."

"I won't have to. Young lady, it will be you telling your tale to the judge, and very soon."

"We'll see about that. It's a big ship."

"Not that big. And we are in control of it now."

"You took over the ship violently," I tried. "That's not going to go well for you when you're arrested. But if you give up this insanity now, I would testify that you don't deserve to be put to death."

He laughed. Well, it probably deserved a laugh.

"Funny, I was about to suggest the same to you. We won't even charge you with attempted murder for firing through that door, and for attacking the people approaching the house."

"I was . . ." I stopped myself. I was so angry I was about to explode, and anger in a situation like this is an enemy.

"You had invaded my home, and those people were trespassing. I made sure I didn't hit anyone. Believe me, I could have, including parking a few rounds in your fat gut. If you'll read the regs again, you will find that in defense of her home, a citizen is entitled to do anything—anything!—to someone trespassing, invading. Up to and including killing them. I'm beginning to wish I had."

I stopped again, as I was in danger of boiling over.

"Well, I can see there is no reasoning with you. We will have you soon, and you know it. Meanwhile, I have many things to do, including moving the people we've arrested to a secure location. I may call you later and let you speak to them. For now, I must say good-bye."

And he hung up.

"What did he say?"

"Give up," I said.

I had stopped shivering. Maybe talking to Max was just what I had needed to get over my panic attack. He had managed to bring my mind back to a hard, laser-sharp focus with him at the center. I was going to get these bastards and, if it came to it, watch them hang.

"Maybe we should think about that."

"Shut up, Patrick."

He looked shocked, but he shut up. I got to my feet, checked the time. Only a few minutes until dark.

"We have to get moving. We need a place to hole up for a while and sort out our options. We need some things other than these pistols."

"I don't see how they're going to do us any good."

"Frankly, I don't think they'll be all that useful myself. We're not going to be able to shoot our way out of this. But one rule is, in a bad situation it's better to have a gun than to be unarmed."

"You said 'rule.' Where did you get this rulebook?"

"It's issued in the school of survival, where I was valedictorian. Compiled by Uncle Travis during a hard, scary life."

"Travis, huh?"

Did I detect a hint of disdain? I wasn't sure.

"Okay, here's what I figure our options are. Back behind us we know there are a lot of people. If we go spinwise or antispinwise, we're just going in a circle that takes us back here. So unless you know of a place to hide in Grover's Mill or Lake Wobegon, that leaves sternward, which is toward where you live. I think we need to go there."

"If we can get in."

"We'll see when we get there. Meanwhile . . ." Right on time the bright mist that had been surrounding us began to dim. Within a minute, it was very dark.

"Crap," Patrick said. "I can hardly see."

"That's the good news, because it means they will have trouble seeing us. More good news is that I know the land between here and Mayberry very well. I've played here all my life."

"So what's the bad news?"

"That you are being so negative and still don't seem to be thinking constructively," I almost said, but held my tongue.

"That most of the people I love are being held hostage by people who don't mean them well," I said. "But there's more good news. We are going to outsmart those people, and we are going to get the ship back."

It was too dark for me to see his expression very well, but his posture told me that he still wasn't completely with me on that one.

He sighed. "Okay, let's go."

And we set off sternward, toward the lights of Fantasyland that were just now looming through the thinning mist.

CHAPTER 14

___

Cassie:

I had dozed off in the captain's chair when Sheila woke me with a gentle alarm. I sat up, bleary for a moment.

"We back at the ship?" I asked

"Not yet. There's been a development."

"The gizmo . . ."

"Isn't functioning, as it hasn't since you stopped looking at it. It seems your father was right. It won't—"

"Papa is always right, so far as I know. About physics, anyway."

"If you say so. I've never heard of a device that needs to be observed to function, but if it is based on quantum principles, it might be possible. But as of now, the screen is blank."

"Okay. So what's the deal?"

"There has been an anomaly back at the ship. Specifically, the monitoring equipment at your house is no longer working."

"The monitoring . . ."

"The cameras I told you about, various other detectors. It's down, all of it. There is no information coming out of your house into the computer network."

I must have still been groggy, but I wasn't liking what I heard.

"What could have caused that?"

"There are routine glitches, most of them highly unlikely. But I doubt that is what happened. That is because there are other peculiar things happening, and they started at the same time."

"Tell me about it."

"There is a cyber attack of some sort being waged on the network. Files that are supposed to be accessible to only a few people have been opened, programs initiated."

"Just spit it out, will you?"

"I infer that an attempt is being made to take over the ship."

Take over the ship. You don't take over a ship. It's just not done. That would be . . .

Mutiny.

The nastiest word you can use on a ship of the seas of water or the seas of stars.

"Ohmigod, Sheila, my house . . . the meeting, my family . . ."

"Yes. I thought you should be notified."

"Can you . . . can you tell me anything else?"

"Very little at the moment. I myself am not involved in the cyber war that's taking place. I'm . . . off to one side, observing and noting. The techniques involved are quite sophisticated. Someone is in possession of information they should not have. At this point, I would not want to predict the outcome."

"Can I call anyone? Mama? Polly?"

"I can't tell you the whereabouts of anyone who was in that house. It's all being blocked. Phone service is down in the township of Freedonia."

"What can I do?" I didn't like the quaver I heard in my voice.

"Very little at the moment. I will continue to monitor the situation. And I am awaiting your orders concerning our return to the ship."

Right. Awaiting orders. Okay, time to get it together, spacegirl.

"For now, keep on course to the hangar. In the meantime, show me what sort of armaments Travis installed here."

It never occurred to me to ask *if* Travis had armed Sheila. The only question was how much was available and how lethal was it.

"External weapons consist of six small high-velocity squeezer-powered missiles, each with a half-megaton squeezer warhead. These missiles can accelerate at two hundred gees, and continue at that rate for a very long time.

"There is a three-megajoule laser, also powered by squeezer energy.

"The most lethal weapon, however, is a silver bubble generator capable of engulfing almost anything, from a small spaceship to a planet, and squeezing it down almost infinitely."

Great. All I had to do to quell the mutiny was blow up the ship, slice it up with a laser, then squeeze it to oblivion. All that should be quite helpful.

This was how Travis equipped his personal yacht. There was little point in asking how he had armed *Rolling Thunder* itself.

"Okay. Now show me to the weapons locker."

"Right this way."

Lights on the floor blinked in sequence, leading me to the back of the cabin. I passed by the head, where Papa was still sitting on the floor, snoozing, whacked out from all the exertion of throwing up for hours.

In the back, a bed was rising from its position on the deck, folding up against the wall. Under it was Travis's arsenal. If someone from a hundred, two hundred years ago looked at it she might not be at all sure these were actually real weapons, and deadlier than whatever they were using. They would probably look like toys.

The main structural difference was that there was not much metal in them. The barrels and firing chambers were made of composite materials, carbon fibers, layered buckytubes, and other high-tech materials. The barrels were tubes about as thin as a tin toy but much stronger than steel. The muzzles wouldn't look intimidating to a twentieth-century shooter, as they were all .25 caliber. But the rounds they shot were much higher velocity than old guns.

The propellant was not gunpowder but a small charge of high explosive called C-7. All the guns were automatics, and all the ammo was caseless; there was no "brass" to eject. The bullet magazines were not in the handle, as in most old automatics, but mounted in a small round cassette that snapped quickly onto the side of the weapon. It was made of clear

Lexan, or something like that, so you could see exactly how many rounds you had left. The ammo belt coiled up inside was consumed each time you fired, so you didn't have a belt hanging off to one side. The handguns were very light, and the rifles not a lot heavier. The rifles had longer barrels and took larger magazines, but otherwise they were very similar. They were battle-tested for over fifty years and hardly ever jammed. If they did, the jam could be cleared in one motion of the other hand.

They were smart guns. They would only fire when being held by a person authorized to use them. That way, if it came to it, you could toss them and not worry about someone else's picking them up and shooting you.

"Can I use these? Do you need my fingerprints, or something?"

"As captain, you are automatically an authorized user. But you were already, along with your mother and sister."

"Good enough."

I picked up a pistol, opened it, looked down the barrel. Keeping these weapons clean was not a problem, even stored for a long time, but it was my training always to examine my weapons. This one looked good. I could feel the grip adjusting to my hand until it fit like a glove.

There were four rifles and four pistols, and plenty of ammo. There was also a box of grenades and a bulky, clumsy-looking gun that fired rockets the size of beer cans with high-explosive warheads. They scared me just to look at them. My training hadn't included actually using stuff like that. Even the simulations were scary.

I put a pistol aside in a drawer and told Sheila to close the arsenal. I didn't want Papa to see it.

"How long to get back to the ship?"

"An hour to turnover, as the flight plan stands. I can get you back faster if I boost at, say, two gees, and decelerate at the same rate."

"Do you think that saving that much time is essential?"

"Not that I can see. I'm still awaiting developments, and I haven't learned much new yet. I can't tell you what might await us when we arrive."

"Okay. I'll keep thinking about it."

So there wasn't much I could do at the moment but hope Sheila could get some new information. And there was one more chore I couldn't put off.

I sighed, and went toward the head.

Papa was still asleep, in an awkward position that was not quite embracing the toilet. I watched him for a moment and felt a lump forming in my throat. God, how I loved this man. Nobody could have asked for a better father, even though he was gone a lot. We all knew why that had to be, and we treasured him all the more when he was with us.

And now I was going to have to do something a bit underhanded. No way could Papa cope with the notion that his whole family was out of communication, whereabouts and condition unknown. Hell, I was having trouble with it, myself.

I tried once more to raise Polly on the phone. Out of service. Same with Mama and Travis. Same with Mike and Marlee.

I leaned over and shook Papa's shoulder gently. He snorted. I shook him a little harder. He came awake slowly, blinking, then groaning.

"Oh, *cher*, my tummy sure do hurt."

"You did a lot of throwing up."

"Yes'um, and my throat hurt, too. But it my belly muscles feel like somebody used it for a punchin' bag."

"Papa, I've got an idea."

"I could use an idea 'bout now. Hope it don't have to do with food, though. I think I'm gonna give up food forever, me. It so nasty when you see it for the second time."

"You got that right. Papa, that's what I wanted to talk to you about. What I figure is, your work is done here, and we've still got a fair amount of weightlessness we can't avoid to get docked with the ship again."

He looked a little green just thinking about that. He got up, and I got out of his way as he walked back into the main cabin.

"Did you know there is an escape capsule on this ship?"

"Escape . . ."

"You know. It's a black bubble that can be generated inside a small capsule that's equipped with emergency beacons."

"But we don't need rescuin'."

"Your tummy does. What I'm saying is, you can pop into the bubble for a few hours, until we get settled on the ship. Then you come out, and no space sickness."

He thought it over.

"I dunno, *cher . . .*"

"Come on, Papa. You know it's the right thing to do."

"I just don't like leavin' you alone out here."

"I got Sheila, Papa."

He thought some more, then nodded.

"Okay," he said. "Let's get her done."

I followed him through the bunk room. At the very back, there was a round hatch that opened as we approached it. It was about four feet in diameter. Papa stepped over the edge with one foot, then ducked in and pulled his other leg after him. I bent and looked into the room, which was perfectly spherical. If you stuffed people in like sardines, you could probably get six people inside. Seven or eight if you got really ruthless, which you probably would if the ship was about to explode in a few minutes. It didn't matter, since you would either be coming out of it in zero time, or you'd never be coming out at all, to the heat death of the universe, amen.

The inside was lined with struts in a latitude-and-longitude pattern. When the panic button was hit, the black bubble would form just outside that framework.

I was figuring I should shut the door, when Papa stuck his head out and looked into my eyes.

"There's somethin' going on, ain't there, Cassie."

I hesitated just a second too long. But I probably couldn't have lied to Papa anyway. I could shade the truth, though.

"There's been some sort of dustup back at the ship," I said.

"How bad . . . I probly shouldn't ask, I guess."

"You don't need to worry about it."

"Is . . . is your mama okay?"

Turns out I could lie after all.

"She's fine, Papa."

"Polly? Travis?"

"She's got the situation under control, *cher*. Now get your head back inside and in just a jiffy everything will be all right. Half a jiffy, even."

He sighed, and held out his hand. I took it, and leaned down to kiss him on his cheek, and turned my cheek so he could kiss me.

"See you in a quarter of a jiffy, *cher*," he said, and pulled his head in. I could hear him muttering. "Hail Mary, full of grace . . ."

I closed the door and turned the airlock wheel. I could see part of one of his legs through the little clear window. Then it went black, an infinite flat blackness deeper than space and time itself.

Then there was little to do until we got back. Sheila kept me updated, as much as she could, but there was not much news coming in. Things seemed to be chaotic on the cyber level. And yet, apparently, most citizens weren't even aware that anything dire was going on. The sun was working, the weather was working, and the ship rolled placidly on. Meals were served, work went on.

"Some people closest to the computers and other machinery have noticed a glitch here and there," Sheila told me, "and there must be a few hundred who are very worried, both on the crew side and the side of the mutineers, but so far the news has not been broadcast."

"What about my family?"

"I've been able to observe a great many people entering your house, and they are taking people out on stretchers."

"What about inside?" I was getting the creepiest feeling. These bastards, whoever they were, invading my home. In my very room, probably, free to go through my things. I felt violated.

"Still nothing from inside. All cameras are dark."

Then nothing happened for a while. Nothing happened a bit more, then a bit more, and soon there was a string of nothing happening that stretched for over an hour. That's the worst kind of waiting. Helpless, no information coming in, good or bad.

For something to do, I kept trying to call Mama, Travis, Polly, but the calls never went through. I knew it was futile, but I kept dialing, anyway.

"I have something," Sheila said. And at the same time, I got a ring.

"Cassie?" It was a very quiet voice, a whisper.

"Polly! Polly, it's me! What's happening?"

She said something, and I couldn't make it out.

"You'll have to speak up. I can't hear you."

"Turn your volume up all the way," she whispered. I did that, and it improved the sound a little bit.

"I don't know how long I can talk," she said. "I'm worried they might be able to trace this call, so you need to just listen. Max and Governor Wang released some sort of knockout gas. I only got—"

"Max? Uncle Max Karpinski?"

"He's not our uncle now, never really was. Yes, that Max, and shut up, Cassie, I don't have much time. I . . . How is Papa? Is he okay?"

"He's fine. When I learned about this, I decided to put him in the escape bubble."

"In the . . . Okay, I guess that's a good idea."

"And Mama, Travis, Mike . . . Patrick?"

"All I know is it looked like they were breathing, and Max called me later and told me they were alive."

"Sheila told me she has seen what looked like people being carried out of our house, on stretchers. There's some sort of cyber war going on. They're trying to take control of the ship. The security programs are still fighting them, so it's not over."

"Who is . . . Oh, yeah, the AI. They're searching for us, we know that. We got out by swimming through the pond, and—"

"We?"

"Patrick and I. We were in the kitchen."

Wow.

"It was sheer luck that we got out. Listen, I think I'd better end this call. I'm amazed I got through at all, and who knows when we might be able to talk on the phone again."

I was still digesting the news about Polly and Patrick on their own. Together. And what were they doing together away from all the others? I know, it's stupid, but I'm sorry, that's just where my thoughts were going.

"We have to get together when you get back into the ship," she went on. "I'll try to meet you where Mama wrecked her flycycle."

"Where . . . Oh, yeah, you mean—"

"Don't say it. We better assume someone might be listening in."

I remembered. We were seven, and she was teaching us to ride with gyro-stabilized bikes—called "training wheels," for some reason—and she made a bad turn and crashed into the South Pole far up the slope.

"Got it. But Polly, Sheila isn't even sure if we *can* get back in."

There was a short silence on the line.

"Okay," she said, finally. "I'm sure the two of you will do your best. If you can, meet me twelve hours from now. And you take good care of Papa, you hear?"

"I kissed him for you, *cher.*"

There was a catch in her voice as she said, "Good enough. Get in here, and we'll save Mama. And all the rest."

"Will do."

The line went dead.

I went dead for a little while there, too. Things were not looking good. I wondered about Polly's ability to avoid capture, or worse. Who knew how gentle they would be if they cornered her, and she fought? I sighed deeply and shook it off as best I could.

"Sheila, is there any way they could locate us from that call?"

"It's possible. But it's moot. They know where we are, if they're even looking for us. I still don't know how the fighting is going. But they surely are able to monitor the functions of the external radar, and I've been pinged once every three seconds, as is normal."

"Can they lock us out?"

"That remains to be seen. They may not even want to. It might be easiest if they simply wait for us and take you captive when I enter the ship and you deplane."

"Can you do anything about that?"

"You saw my list of armaments. I could cause considerable slaughter. I could destroy the whole hangar."

"That seems extreme."

"I thought so. But you're the captain."

"Let's see if we can get in, first."

Returning to the ship is a lot trickier than leaving it. Going out, it was just like dropping away through a trapdoor. Coming home, Sheila had to match velocities with *Rolling Thunder*. Not linear velocity, as we were both moving in the same direction at the same speed. Rotational velocity. It meant she had to blast at steadily increasing thrust away from the ship, thus pushing us slowly toward it, and at the same time add a side thrust to keep us moving in a circle around the ship as it rotated. The net result was that the spinning ship seemed almost motionless directly over my head.

It was child's play for Sheila. She got us in position and moved us gradually closer. I could see the yellow outline of the hangar door, a big rectangle painted on the bare rock.

"Attempting to activate hangar doors."

I held my breath.

"No response. Activating emergency override. Second attempt. Third attempt. The doors are not responding," she said.

Well, shit.

CHAPTER 15

─────────

Polly:

I hung up on Cassie and peered out through the giant glass eye of Rex, the Mardi Gras King. There was nothing happening out there. Other giant figures loomed in the darkness, quiet and motionless now, but ready to burst into light and animation at the flip of a switch.

"I think it's time to get moving now," I said.

"You really think they can locate us through our phones?"

"I don't know enough about how the system works to be sure, which is why we need to relocate and see if anyone comes for us."

From what I knew of Travis, who wrote the specs for our phone system, we could probably not be tracked by our phones. At least, I was pretty sure we couldn't be pinpointed, but it was possible someone could find out what township we were in. And since we were in Fantasyland, that narrowed the possibilities; other than in the amusement park and casino, there weren't a lot of places in the township where one could hide.

─────────

The trip across Mayberry and into Fantasyland had been nervous-making. In addition to trying to keep an eye out ahead, to both sides, and especially behind us, I found myself constantly glancing upward. I knew it was futile.

But I kept getting an itchy feeling on the top of my head that made me want to hunch my shoulders and make myself small.

Most of all, I wanted to get out of the open.

There was no way to do it, though, in the endless tanks breeding fish. I'm sure there were hatches leading down somewhere, but in the dark I couldn't locate them. So we hurried, jogging for a bit, then slowing down.

It was because of Patrick. I could easily have jogged all the way. Hell, with hounds at my heels, I probably could have sprinted most of it. But Patrick wasn't in as good shape as the Broussard twins with our daily runs and bike rides. The boy was not an athlete.

In fact, I was trying to figure out just what he was, other than the prettiest boy in the ship. To be blunt, I was getting a little tired of Patrick, of his falling behind, of his lack of ideas, of his lingering inability to realistically deal with our predicament. Sure, he didn't have my crisis training, but that excuse was wearing a little thin.

But we crossed into Fantasyland and approached the flashing lights of all the rides and other attractions. The good news was that if they were standing around the perimeter, we would see them outlined against the lights. The bad news was that if they were concealed, hunkered down, we would be lit up, easier to see the closer we got.

There was no way to know if they had managed to locate and get into any of Travis's weapons caches. I was hoping they hadn't and would still be armed with nothing but edged weapons and clubs, that sort of thing.

Our first problem, once we got close enough to see that there were no obvious guards around the entrance gates, was that we looked like something that had been dredged out of a sewer.

We were waiting in the parkland that surrounded the amusement park, a pretty little place with lots of carefully selected trees, baseball diamonds, horseshoe pitches, playground equipment, and picnic tables. It was very pleasant in the daytime.

At night, like now, it was almost deserted, with lights only along the bike paths and a basketball court where diehards were always playing. And I mean, *always*. There was a ship's legend that the pickup game had been going on for twenty-two years, since before the launch. Cassie and I had played there frequently. I could hear the thump of the ball on concrete and the shouts of the players.

I knew there were security cameras all over the place, but they mostly covered the paths, which we had avoided.

"You look awful," I told Patrick.

"Right back at you," he said, with the first smile I'd seen since we left the house.

"I had to leave my bag behind," I said. "You have anything in your pockets? A comb or something?" I realized I didn't really know what boys carried with them, but I'd seen some pull out a pocket comb. I preferred a brush, and always carried a little basic makeup, but I'd be happy for anything he had.

He produced a comb from the back pocket of his jeans and handed it to me. I started the gruesome project of combing out the snags and tangles in my hair, looking him over as I did it. His pants had been white when we went into the water, and now they had an interesting pattern of black, brown, and green stains that looked a little like jungle camouflage. His shirt was a dark brown that didn't look all that bad. But there were a few actual strings of moss and algae in his blond hair. It had been too dark to see them before. I examined the comb and found strings just like his that I'd combed out of my own hair. I attacked it savagely, pausing now and then to clear the comb of crud and tangles.

"Is it getting any better?" I asked him.

"It's not debutante grade, but I think it'll do for Fantasyland."

I handed him the comb and examined my own clothes. I wished I had selected a black top to match the jeans—which looked okay, but still felt wet and clammy around the crotch—but who knew I'd be swimming?

"How are we going to get in?" he asked.

"I was hoping you'd know a way. I hope we won't raise too many eyebrows because we look like drowned rats. We might have been playing rugby or something."

"Dressed like this?"

"A pickup game. I'm not so much worried about the staff at the gate as the electronics. Do you think our credit has been flagged by the muti-neers?"

"How the hell would I know?" he said, angrily.

He was right, but sometimes it helps if you talk about it instead of just shutting down. You might pool your differing viewpoints and hope to find information you didn't realize you had.

"I guess it all depends on how well they planned this out. And what they expected. I'm hoping we're the unexpected thing. The plan seems to have been to get us all at once and announce the coup after it was already over. So maybe they don't have us flagged."

"I guess we have to hope so."

"Yeah. Well, we have to get in there."

He was watching me, silently. I sighed.

"Okay. I think we need to just walk up and try to get in."

"Really? Isn't that taking a big chance?"

"Unless you know a way over, under, or through the fence, I'd say it's our only choice. We have to get in there, to your house, and go to ground for a little bit. We need to prepare a little better."

"For what?"

"*I don't know yet! Okay?*"

He just shrugged, dispirited. "If you say so."

"Let's do it."

We approached the entrance gate, a big, arched structure meant to symbolize a rainbow, with a pot of gold sparkling at each end. Lights flashed all over it, and cheerful music poured from hidden speakers. Brass, electronic percussion, steam calliope, all meant to evoke a circus atmo-sphere. Beyond it was the long midway, winding between the carnival-type rides, leading to the center of the park and the pathways to the themed areas and the big thrill rides and other attractions.

We lingered off to one side for a while, trying to spot anyone who might be looking for us. But how does a mutineer secret agent dress? A red kerchief, an eye patch, and a parrot on his shoulder? A black suit and sunglasses, with a bulge in the breast pocket? The white robes and black belt of a ninja assassin? No, of course not; she would dress just like you or me, though probably more like you and a lot better than me at that moment.

What I was looking for was anyone keeping an eye on the people going in. It was an intermittent stream. During the time we watched, maybe fifty people paid the gate fee and went through the turnstiles. There was a ticket taker, a teenager with an after-school job. He wore the Fantasyland Park uniform that looked like the dress military jacket, pants, and shako of our high-school marching band. I knew he was bored as hell. He was a greeter, essentially, not a security guard. The other reason he was there was to deter turnstile jumpers.

Since going over the fence would set off alarms, and because Patrick didn't know any secret way in or out—somehow I felt sure that Cassie and I would have figured something in all those years, but maybe we were just sneakier than he was—there seemed no alternative to just trying to pay our way through the gate.

"Okay," I said. "Put on your game face."

"And what would that be?"

"In this case, happy, loose, out to have some fun, maybe a wee bit drunk. Not too smart."

"I can do not too smart."

"Act deeply involved with each other. In love."

He didn't say anything. Jeepers, was that going to be all that much harder than not too smart?

Well, I took hold of his left arm and leaned into him. He put his arm over my shoulders. We started walking toward the gate. In a few steps, he was forcing me into a rather wobbly line.

"Not *too* drunk," I whispered, smiling up at him adoringly.

"Sorry."

We got in line behind two other couples. The gatekeeper wasn't paying a lot of attention. I hoped no alert had been issued to be on the lookout for two muddy, bedraggled fugitives.

When it came our turn, we each stuck our right hands under the scanner and let the machine read our credit-chip implants. At once I could tell there was something wrong. The guy was frowning at his screen. The screen facing me told me nothing but the fact that my credit had been accepted, and the twenty-dollar admission fee was displayed. His was obviously displaying something else.

"Um . . . uh, I'm sorry, but you'll have to wait here a moment. It's no big deal, but—"

That's all he had a chance to say, because I shoved him, hard. He went down hard. His hat went rolling on the ground.

"Sorry," I said, and then, *"Run!"*

Once more, I had to grab Patrick to get him moving. But he must have had a surge of adrenaline this time, because within a few yards he was ahead of me. I knew I'd beat him in the long run, but in a sprint he wasn't bad. I looked back over my shoulder and saw that the guy was starting to come after us. I turned and backpedaled a few steps.

"Don't be a hero," I shouted at him. I pulled my pistol and fired it into the air. He screeched to a stop, almost leaving skidmarks on the tarmac. In another situation, it might have been comical. Then he and several people who had been in line behind us ducked for cover.

"Dammit, Polly, you can't go around shooting guns!"

"I can't let them chase us. We've got to hide."

"Where?"

"I was hoping you'd have some ideas."

We were side by side now, jogging, and that didn't seem like a great idea since people were looking at us. I'd put my gun away so no one saw that, and the sound of it could easily have been one of the sound effects from the midway games and rides.

There are few straight paths in Fantasyland. It's all arranged so you go around a curve in the road and come on some new wonder. So it took no time to leave the gate behind us.

"Time to stop running," I said, taking his arm. "We're being looked at too much. Try to look like you're having fun."

"If I have any more fun than this, it will kill me."

"Same here. Have you had any ideas where we could hide for a bit? Other than your house?"

"I guess there are places. But I don't have much experience in stuff like this. Sneaking around. Hiding out. I got the impression that you and your sister did that a lot."

I could have taken offense, but there was no point. It was true. Cassie and I didn't have anything to run away from at home, where we were loved—well, Mama was a strict disciplinarian, but never unfair. We did it for the sheer fun of sneaking around. Seeking adventure.

But the worst that ever happened to us when we got caught (which was infrequently) was being grounded for a few days. No desserts at dinner. Extra homework. That sort of thing.

"What's down there?" I asked, pointing to a side path that didn't have any of the helpful signs that were all over the place elsewhere.

"No idea. I've not really spent a lot of time here."

"Let's look."

A few steps took us around a bend, and now we saw a sign saying EMPLOYEES ONLY. Just a little beyond that was a chain-link fence threaded with multicolored vinyl strips.

"I think I know now," Patrick said. "This is where the Mardi Gras parades start and finish. There's a big warehouse back there, holding all the floats. I visited it once."

"Could we hide there?"

"Not from a search by dozens of cops. But if there are only a few . . . there are a lot of places to hide."

"Let's do it."

I jumped and grabbed the top of the fence, about eight feet up. I got my feet on the fence and vaulted myself over. I heard the chain link rattle, then a grunt as Patrick lost his grip and landed back on the ground.

"Hurry!"

"How did you do that?"

But he gave it another try, got his arms over the top, swung his leg up, and pulled himself onto the top. He hit the ground and rolled onto the gravel. He needed some parachute-jump training, no question. Cassie and I were experts, having learned to jump and land from our tree house in the backyard. He got slowly to his feet, brushing off gravel. He glared at me, and I didn't say a thing.

We were in a narrow space between the fence and a quite large warehouse made of corrugated aluminum painted in bright Fantasyland colors. It stretched a long way off behind us, just a few feet ahead of us, and was about fifty feet tall. We hurried around the corner and found ourselves looking at a big sliding gate in the chain link and a pair of big sliding doors in the warehouse. Beside that door was a small, human-sized door that said CAST MEMBERS AND DRIVERS ONLY.

I grabbed the doorknob and turned it. It was unlocked. There wasn't even a lock on the knob, nor a bolt above it. Another nice thing about *Rolling Thunder*'s very low crime rate. The place is full of unlocked doors. We hurried inside and closed the door behind us.

It was spooky. Huge shapes loomed in the darkness, with only a few distant overhead lights. These were the floats for the Mardi Gras parade, happening twice a day at noon and ten. There were enormous golden boats, towers of oversized artificial flowers, a 1959 Cadillac built at three times the scale of a real one, and vast human shapes, some up to forty feet tall. All was quiet and dark now, but in operation they would blaze with lights and music and motion. Some of them bristled with confetti cannons and had racks of beads for passengers to throw to the crowd.

I'd only seen the parade a few times. I enjoyed it when I was younger, but as I grew older, I began to see it as a bit excessive. Still, it was perennially popular and had been running every day for over ten years.

"I need to make some phone calls," I told Patrick. "You been calling anyone?"

"I've tried a couple times, but nothing has gone through."

"Same here. I still feel too vulnerable here. Maybe we should—"

"I have an idea," he said.

I followed him around one of the big floats. He ducked his head and walked under a part of it, then found a handle cleverly concealed behind what looked like a big stack of coins spilling out of a pirate treasure chest. A square hatch opened up, and I followed him inside.

It was pitch-black inside. Couldn't see the hand in front of my face. I heard Patrick groping around, and then there was a click. A few small work lights came on.

We were in an irregularly shaped space, longer than it was wide. Steel ribs followed the shape of the external shell, and other braces held it all together. We were standing on a catwalk, and Patrick got moving again.

"I got to ride on one of these when the parade was new. Had on a silly costume and threw beads to the crowd. Mortifying. All my classmates were there, laughing at me."

"Sounds like fun to me."

"It was." He grinned back over his shoulder. "I came to school the next day with more beads than anyone. That shut 'em up."

The hatch had been about midway on the float. When we were close to the front, Patrick stopped and looked around.

"Is this private enough for us?"

It felt too close to me. I'm not claustrophobic, but when you're hiding out, going to ground, you like to have at least two ways out. And it helps to be able to see outside. I told Patrick that.

"Okay . . . if I remember right . . ."

He moved to the side a little and took hold of the rungs of a steel ladder I hadn't seen. He started climbing, and it seemed the whole structure rang like a gong.

"*Ssshush!*" I shushed.

"Sorry." He planted his feet more carefully. When he was high enough, I started up after him. We reached a platform with just about enough room for both of us to sit.

"This structure telescopes up," he said. "It's the tallest in the parade, and it's too tall for this warehouse. So they roll it out, then crank it up."

I saw two round windows about two feet across. I realized I was looking out through the eyeballs of Rex, the King of Mardi Gras.

"This little door down here leads to a balcony where the guests who win the lotteries get to ride in the parade. We can get out here, if we have to, it's not too far to the ground, and there are handholds. Or back to the way we came in. Where we are now is where the driver sits, looking out through these windows."

I looked it all over again. The controls looked simple. The floor was a metal mesh, and below it I could see boxes of Mardi Gras beads, where they would be handy to people on the balcony when the full figure was extended.

"Looks good to me," I said. "We can't stay here long. The next parade is in . . . three hours. Let's make our phone calls."

———————————

Patrick had no luck at all with the phone, and I was only able to get through to Cassie for a short time. It hurt me to hear that Papa was back in a bubble, but like I said, it was probably the best place for him during a crisis. I wondered if she would be able to get back in the ship and if she would be able to meet me at the rendezvous we had set.

"I think it's time we got moving now," I said.

I heard a door opening, saw light briefly brighten the big glass eye I had been looking through. I held my finger to my lips, and Patrick nodded.

I kept very still and looked out of the eye at an angle. I spotted two people with flashlights. One was dressed in the uniform of a Fantasyland security guard, the other, a woman, in an ordinary pantsuit. They played their flashlight beams all around, up and down. I noticed a little latch on the eye window. I eased it open half an inch.

"Spooky in here," the man said.

"We need to get some lights on and search the place."

"Are you kidding? Two people? You could hide a regiment in here. It would take twenty people a few hours to look in every nook and cranny."

"We'll just have to bring in more people." It seemed the woman was the boss.

"You know we can't do that. The whole security detail is searching for those two. And I just don't get it, anyway. For turnstile jumping? That hardly ever happens, but when it does, we just wait for them to leave when the park closes."

"We have to find these people. I'll let you in on something, okay? They are armed and dangerous."

"Armed and dangerous? What does that mean?"

"It means they have guns and have shot at police officers."

There was an extended silence, then the man laughed.

"You've got to be kidding me."

"I'm not kidding at all. Now let's start looking."

"No, you misunderstand me. I'm not stupid enough to go looking for them if they might shoot at me."

"You have to. It's your job."

"I like this job, but I can live without it. You got a gun? Can you shoot back? I didn't think so, and who cares, anyway? I'm not getting in a gun battle. You can take this job and shove it up your ass. I'm outta here."

And he turned and walked back toward the door they had entered by.

The woman watched him, looking frustrated. The door slammed loudly, and she sighed. She looked around. Then she turned and, with her back to me, started talking on her phone. She was too quiet for me to hear what she was saying. She got angry for a moment, but I still couldn't hear her. Finally, she said a nasty word and cut the connection. She headed for the door, looking back over her shoulder. I heard it slam again.

"Well, we scared them away, and I didn't even have to reach for my gun." I told Patrick what I had seen, and he smiled faintly.

"Sometimes you don't even need to shoot them, I guess."

"We've got a reputation now. But, Patrick, we really have to get moving. We need clothes that don't stand out so much, and I—"

The door opened again, slamming against the wall this time, and I heard voices. A lot of voices. I looked back out through the eye. Seven or eight people had entered in a group. Boys and girls, high-school or college age, laughing and larking about.

"It's the cast members getting ready for the parade," Patrick said. "Oh lord, what if they find us here? The driver will be in sooner or later."

"Okay, okay, okay, we don't want to panic. How many people are involved, do you know?"

"At least a hundred. They're students earning a little extra income. They commute a couple of times a day, just for the one hour. Some of the dancers have to audition, but most of them just ride the floats and throw things. Confetti, beads. They come and go."

They come and go. That phrase circled around in my head for a few seconds and then came in for a landing.

"It's not a tight-knit crew."

"No, I wouldn't think so."

"Someone new wouldn't stand out too badly?"

"Probably not."

"Then this is our shot."

We headed back toward the middle of the float. I took a deep breath, looked at Patrick, who looked twice as scared as I felt. I winked at him, and dropped through the hatch.

I saw a lot of people passing in both directions. A few of them looked at us as Patrick came out, and we got a variety of knowing looks, and one whistle. It was clear everyone thought they knew what we had been doing in there. I felt myself blushing, and realized that was a good thing. When we were out from under, I grabbed Patrick, threw my arms around him, and kissed him passionately on the lips, putting a lot of body language into it. He was stiff for a moment, then got the gist and responded. And you know what? So did I. Even nervous as I was, I felt a genuine rush, a thumping in my chest.

A few people clapped. We broke the kiss and a guy patted Patrick on the back as we headed toward where most of the people were going. I realized that our disheveled condition could only contribute to the notion that we'd had some pretty wild sex up there in the head of Rex.

"Where are we going?" Patrick whispered.

"I have no idea. Follow the crowd."

We did that, and most of them were heading for some wide doors on the opposite side of the warehouse. A few were getting into the floats. The drivers, I presumed.

"Fifteen minutes to showtime, boys and girls," an older woman was shouting. I spotted her by the doors, a matronly figure with silver hair and a tad too much makeup, in my opinion. I stared at my feet as we shuffled closer with the crowd. I was hoping we could squeak on by and figure out our next step from there. No such luck.

"Hey, you two. Who the hell are you?"

"Uh, we're new," I said.

"I can see that. What have you been doing, mud wrestling? Why don't they keep me up to date on these things?" She sighed heavily, and it was plain this wasn't the first time this had happened.

"Did they give you assignments?"

"No, ma'am."

She sized us up. She didn't seem pleased at what she saw when she looked at me. Her expression changed considerably when she looked Patrick up and down. The bitch.

"I can always use another clown. You'll walk in front of the Circus float." She tore her eyes away from him and looked at me.

"Showgirl. You've got the height for it, the legs. We can do something to make the boobs look bigger. You'll walk in front of the Vegas float. Now go on with you, shoo, shoo! Twelve minutes to showtime."

Well! I never.

We entered a scene of controlled mayhem. People were rushing around all over the big room. All the walls were taken up with makeup tables, mirrors surrounded by lightbulbs, just like in the movies. The rest of the room was crammed with rack after rack of costumes. It was a whirl of color and motion and sound. I wished I could have been less frightened and able to enjoy it all. It looked like it might be fun. People were chattering with each other, helping each other out with costumes.

"Looks like clowns over there," Patrick said. "I guess I should join them. But I know nothing about clowning."

"Just watch everybody else and do what they do. That's what I'm planning to do. If I can find the showgirls in here . . ."

"Over there." He pointed over my shoulder, and sure enough, I saw a bunch of tallish girls and a lot of feathers.

"Good luck," he said, and was gone.

I shoved my way through the crowd and joined the half dozen other girls getting fitted out for the Las Vegas float.

Oh, my.

Some of them were almost done, and they were a sight to behold. Starting from the bottom, they were in four-inch spike heels, bespangled with gold glitter. After that was fishnet black stockings. Gold gloves that reached above the elbow, and a . . . I guess you'd call it a swimsuit. It had a huge cutout over the belly that was filled in with sheer nylon and sequins and made a deep V right down to the crotch.

But that was the easy stuff, and not the first thing I noticed. There were two girls who were fully outfitted and electrified. The most stunning parts of the outfits were two things. There was a fan of peacock feathers, three feet wide on each side, that attached to the small of the back. And there was a hawklike gold mask with a beak that stuck out almost a foot and covered the face from the lips up. Exploding out of the top of the mask was a crown of fiber-optic filaments that added another three feet to their height before bending back toward the ground like a water fountain. The peacock fan and the swimsuit and even the stockings were festooned with white mini-LEDs that sparkled like a snowstorm in a spotlight.

"Hey, spacegirl," someone said. "You're running late. New here?"

"Yeah. I didn't know what I was getting into, I guess."

"Here, put this shit on. Stockings first, suit second, shoes at the last possible moment." She tossed me those items and was gone.

Oh, well. The things you'll do to rescue your family from pirates.

I skinned out of my clothes. The other girls were hanging theirs on the racks. I never wanted to see these again, so I quietly dropped them on the floor and kicked them under a rack.

I got dressed—if dressed was the word—quickly. I'd worn high heels a couple of times, at fancy parties, so I wasn't entirely unfamiliar with them. But I tottered around, trying to get into the absurdly tiny, one-size-fits-all suit. I managed to stretch it out enough to feel like a sausage, then addressed the problem of the fan and headdress.

"Five minutes, whoever you are." It was my helper from before. She attached the fan to a socket in my ass. The headdress fit tightly over my head, with an almost invisible strap to hold it in place. My helper let it go, and I almost fell on my face. It was a lot heavier than the fan.

"Remember, rookie, you're about eight times wider than you normally are, and a lot taller. Don't knock off the hat. They're expensive."

I promised I wouldn't. No one ever did anything about my boobs. I felt they filled out the top adequately.

People were pouring through the doors and out into the float warehouse. I was never able to count the floats, but I estimated there were around a dozen of them. I joined the other showgirls and followed them to the Las Vegas float. Off to my left were a dozen clowns, and I realized that I had no idea which one was Patrick. They were wearing size 32EEEE shoes and fat suits and weird hats and wigs and, of course, clown makeup. He could have been any of them.

I realized he probably wouldn't recognize me, either. Most of my face was covered. We had both achieved the anonymity we had been seeking, and now what? I hoped he remembered the plan we had worked out. There was no point in parading in the full circle and ending up back at the warehouse.

The Las Vegas float was second in line, after one that was themed as a zoo. People were dressed up as all sorts of cute animals. I stayed with the other girls and we all scrunched up behind that float. All of them were fully lit up now, almost bumper to bumper. The zoo float rolled and started up some sort of jungle music. When all the girls stepped out, I stepped right along with them, looking left and right to see what they were doing.

It wasn't complicated. The whole show moved at about five miles per hour, maybe less. The showgirl step was a sort of strut, throwing hips side to side, arms held out and turning in a circular motion. I figured I was going to be okay; and then we turned the corner and the music changed to some thumping dance music, and all the girls started to shake their booties.

Booties was about all we could shake. I think I'm a pretty good dancer, but you try getting down with a fifteen-pound electric chandelier upside down on your head. Not to mention that pesky fan. One of those plumes kept getting hooked under my beak and making me sneeze. I finally pulled it out and tossed the darn feather to a girl in the crowd.

The crowd was not enormous, but most places it was four or five deep. Most of the park lights were turned off, so the only light came from the floats and our headdresses. That was going to help out later on.

So I dipped and turned and kicked. I decided I could handle this though my feet were already hurting.

Our getting-off point was about halfway through the parade route, which wound around many of the attractions. The casino was our goal, and it was on the far end of the park from the entrance we came in. I almost missed it. The path leading off the park proper and into the casino was marked by a huge, flashy arch, but it was turned off, and I was concentrating so hard on my dips and didos I was startled to see it off to my right. I moved to my left and got close to the girl over there.

"I'm feeling sick to my stomach," I told her. She glanced at me, her wide toothsome smile never wavering.

"Well, don't ruin the costume," she said. "Leave the headdress on the float. There's a restroom over there on the left."

I'd already spotted it. I hurried back to the float and hung the headdress on one of the giant slot machines that spewed gold-foil-covered chocolate coins every few minutes. Then I pushed my way through the crowd and toward the restroom.

Once away from the parade, I had to walk carefully, as it was very dark back there. I was grateful for not having the darn light show on my head, but my tail feathers kept getting snagged on the low shrubbery lining the path to the lonely lights at the restroom doors. So I yanked the fan off and tossed it aside. I kicked off the torture devices on my feet. *Much* better. I had a ten-minute wait while several more floats rolled by.

Finally, send in the clowns.

They were capering around the circus float, where more skilled performers were doing a trapeze act above a "lion tamer." This was a woman in a red cutaway coat and white riding pants and black top hat, holding a lightweight chair and sort of poking it at a full-grown male lion. I happened to know the lion. His name was Metro, and we had made his acquaintance when we were ten, at a little show at school. He was tame as a kitten, and would lick your face with his sandpaper tongue. I have a picture of me with him, somewhere. He was now halfheartedly roaring and pawing at the chair, for which he would be rewarded with lion treats after the show.

My thoughts had been wandering. I was very tired, and didn't see where I'd have a chance to rest, ever again. Then a clown separated himself from the group, came through the spectators, and hurried down the path. Halfway to me, he tripped and fell on his face. He said a dirty word.

It was easy to see why he had tripped. He was wearing cherry-red shoes long enough to go canoeing in. His costume consisted of a shirt that looked like old-fashioned pink flannel long underwear and a pair of britches like an inverted hoopskirt, held up by a pair of elastic suspenders. The pants tapered down to his ankles, so he couldn't even see his feet. When he got up, some mechanism in the suspenders caused the pants to fall down almost to his knees, then bounce back up again.

"Damn," he muttered as he came near. His shoes made a honking sound with every step. "That's not supposed to happen until I squeeze the little trigger." He looked up at me under a thundercloud brow and raised a fist. "If you laugh, I'll knock you right to the other end of the ship."

I had been practically strangling in my attempt not to laugh, and of course that set it off explosively. The tension we had been under was enormous, and I was powerless to stop its partial release in laughter. He glowered at me for a bit, then started laughing himself.

"We have to stop this," I choked out. "We're not out of the woods."

"I know," he said, looking solemn. Then he cracked up again.

"Stop it!"

"I will if you will."

We recovered a little, and he beckoned me closer.

"Look at my shoe," he said.

"I don't see anything."

"You have to bend down and get closer to see it."

I did that, and the upper opened like a clamshell. A little critter that looked like a chipmunk popped out with a tiny fire hose, swiveled to point it at me, and squirted me in the face with water. I was so startled that this time I was the one who landed on my butt. This set Patrick off again. He offered his hand to pull me up. I knew a judo move that would have thrown him into the shrubbery, but enough was enough.

"The kids love it. You want to see what's in the other shoe?"

"I'm incredibly curious, but we have to get moving. You know where we're going, so lead the way."

We started off, both of us still giggling. I was a few feet behind him when the suspenders did their thing again. I got a view of the back of the long johns, which had a drop seat that was hanging down, exposing an enormous pair of hairy, rubber butt cheeks. I had to stifle a howl of laughter and almost doubled over with the effort.

"That's enough of that," he said, and shrugged out of the suspenders. The pants dropped to the ground, and he stepped out of the shoes. He kicked it all to the side of the path, followed by the fake butt. I saw not his own bottom, but a tight pair of jockey shorts.

"Insurance, in case the butt falls off," he said. "At least that's what the head clown told me. Come on, the parade is almost past us. This path won't be private for long."

As the music faded behind us, we groped our way through one of the few relatively empty spaces in the park, a few acres of trees and grass that lay between the amusements and the casino. We could see the flashing lights ahead of us, and our progress became easier as we neared it.

It also became slower, because we had to be on the lookout in case the mutineers had staked it out.

Patrick took us around the casino to a private entrance to the living quarters above. The only people we encountered as we skirted the building were three pairs of lovers who had sought out some darkness for purposes of billing and cooing. One couple had passed quite beyond the bills and coos and into more serious business, with clothing strewn about, her legs in the air, and . . . well, this isn't porno. All I could really see were two pale shapes in the gloom. Maybe it was a judo hold. None of them took any notice of us.

There was a small, porchlike structure set into the side of the building. We hunkered down in the shadows and waited to see if there was any movement. After five minutes by my clock, I'd seen nothing.

"I say we do it," I said.

"Maybe another few minutes."

I realized he was scared again. Well, so was I. I reached behind me and drew out the pistol from the small of my back, where I had concealed it while changing clothes. He looked alarmed when he saw it.

"I won't hurt anyone unless I have to," I assured him. "But we're not playing games here, Patrick. This is for keeps."

"You're right. Okay, let's go."

I followed him, walking backwards and keeping my eyes on the many shadows around us. Nothing moved. Then came the scary part, as he stepped into the light. Patrick put his palm to the door, which opened into a small foyer. We both scrambled in and closed the door behind us. I was facing the elevator door when it opened, with my pistol in my hand. It was empty. Patrick glanced at the gun as we entered.

"Do you think that's really necessary? If someone had entered without permission, there would have been an alert on the screen."

"I'd rather have it pointed in the right direction if I need it."

"Whatever."

I didn't like his tone of voice, but I let it go. And I didn't let it stop me from aiming at the door when it opened into Patrick's home above.

It was dark, with just a few night-lights around the floor. Patrick turned to a security panel in the wall beside the elevator. He pressed a few switches, and there was a quiet tone and voice.

"High alert. Siege protocols enabled."

We had the same thing in our house and had been drilled in its use. There was a short pause, and then the AI spoke again.

"I detect a nonresident female, tentatively identified as either Cassandra or Pollyanna Broussard. Please verify."

I pressed my palm to the ID plate.

"She's here with my permission," Patrick said.

"Verified," said the AI. "Patrick, there have been attempts to hack the security systems. None have been successful thus far. Is there anything I should know that will help me evaluate potential threats?"

"It seems there is an attempt to take over the ship," Patrick said.

"Mutiny," I prompted him. "Piracy. Kidnapping."

"Yes, all those things. My mother and father have . . ." For a moment he couldn't go on. I put my arm around him and squeezed. He got himself back under control. "Mother and Father, Polly's mother, and a lot of others, including Captain Broussard."

"I'm consulting my protocols," the AI said. "I am putting the house on a war footing. I will monitor all outside activity and alert you to anything suspicious."

"Very good," he said.

"I have unlocked the weapons locker. Is there anything else you would like me to do?"

He looked at me. I shook my head. I noted that he seemed much more confident than he had been since the moment we dived into the lake. Clearly he felt more secure in his own home. Most of us would, I imagine.

"I would advise you not to linger here. I have indications that you are being searched for by park security, and possibly others."

Patrick didn't look happy to hear that. I already had known that we didn't dare linger.

"Let's get to it," I said. "Who showers first?"

First, we located flashlights in the kitchen and Uncle Mike's den. Then Patrick showed me to his mother's bedroom, where I rummaged through her closets and underwear for something to replace the ridiculous show-girl outfit. We were similar in size, me being maybe two inches taller. I peeled out of the costume as I moved quickly through the hanging outfits. She tended to fancy dresses, gowns, dress suits, but she had some stuff suitable for outdoor activities. I wanted dark clothes. I took some things into the bedroom. Silk knickers, black sweatshirt, a dark fishing vest with lots of pockets, black jeans. Shoes might be a problem. Marlee had tiny feet, and I couldn't get my size forties into them without resorting to Cinderella's sisters' solution for fitting into the glass slipper.

Back into the shower for a quick scrubbing. Shampoo was a necessity because the extreme rattiness of my hair would stand out if we mixed with people. Dirt poured out of my mop as I rinsed.

I dried as quickly as I could, put on the clothes I had laid out, and hurried from the room in my bare feet and with my hair wrapped in a towel. Patrick was still where I'd left him, at the side of one of the windows, looking out cautiously. Neither of us had felt it would be a good idea to shower at the same time, both of us out of our clothes and at our most vulnerable if anyone should force their way into the apartment.

"Your turn," I said. "Before you get in there, do you think you would have any footwear I could borrow?" He glanced at my feet. "The sturdier the better. Boots?"

"I've got something." He hurried down the hallway to his own room and his own shower, and in a moment he was back, tossing a pair of lace-up high-top black boots at me. They seemed at least in the right range. I sat down and found a pair of woolen socks in each boot.

The boots were a wee bit too long, but that was no problem. I laced them up tight. They would do nicely, and in fact were better than anything in my own closet. They would be suitable for going to war, long marches in the infantry. I wondered what Patrick wore them for.

He had told me where the armory was. I went down a hallway and made a left into a storage room. There were no windows, so I eased the door almost shut and turned on the lights. Directly in front of me a concealed door had opened. I went through it.

It was not an arsenal like Travis's, but it was respectable. There were four handguns, all modern weapons like my own pistols. There was ammo. There was a long rifle and a shotgun. I couldn't see myself skulking around with any of them. There were shoulder holsters and belt holsters. I picked one of each and strapped myself with a pistol in the small of my back, and one under my right arm, handy to my left-handed draw.

I located two dark canvas backpacks and started filling them with stuff. Extra ammunition, flashlight, a few lightsticks, a basic first-aid kit, two good knives, a multitool. What else? A card that reputedly would open most non-palmprint-enabled doors in the ship. An all-purpose lighter. There were smoke grenades and real grenades. I stuffed several into our packs.

Food? Well, maybe a little. Some energy bars and a little candy and some jerky. Water? Joggers usually carried a water bottle, so that wouldn't mark us a fugitives. I set aside two sealed bottles.

I had it all laid out on a wide shelf when Patrick came into the room, giving me a start. He was wearing jeans and boots, with a shirt in his hand. He also had some clothing draped over his other arm.

"Here," he said, handing me what turned out to be a dark brown jacket from a man's suit. "I figured that you'd be carrying a gun, and I thought this would hide it."

"Thanks." I held it up and didn't much care for it. I'd look a little like a butch pop musician. But this wasn't the time for fashion sense.

We finished dressing. I tossed the towel away and fluffed my hair half-heartedly. Call me crazy, but I somehow wasn't wild about the idea of going out to face possible death with hair like a sick dandelion. Oh, forget it, girl. No one cares what you look like in the morgue photo. We turned off the light and made our way back to the main room.

"A police vehicle is approaching from the north," the AI said.

"Oh boy," Patrick breathed. We both looked out the windows over the empty pool area. I didn't see anything odd out there, so they must have been traveling without lights.

"A second . . . and now a third vehicle is slightly behind the first one," the AI said. "I identify them as special forces units."

Without warning, the windows were flooded with unbearable light. I was blinded, and fell to the floor with shimmering blue spots swimming before my eyes.

"Polly, can you see?"

"Not much. We have to stay cool here. Your vision will come back." I hoped. So far as I knew, there were no white light weapons on the ship capable of blinding anyone. Lasers, now, that was a different story.

No sooner had I had the thought than I heard a sizzling, crackling sound, and a reddish haze penetrated my closed eyelids. I cautiously opened my eyes, and saw through the persistent dazzle a line of laser light tracing out the edges of one of the big glass windows. The laser would have gone right through the glass, but the putty or metal strips or whatever held it in place was boiling and flaming. In a moment, the big pane fell inward, intact, and hit the floor with a huge thump. It didn't break.

In the next moment, a hissing, sputtering object the size of a can of soup came arrowing through the opening and crashed against the far wall. It fell to the floor and started spewing smoke. Gas grenade! But what kind?

I'd just missed being knocked out by gas, and I couldn't believe I'd been so stupid as to not plan for it.

"Gas masks!" Patrick shouted, and I didn't need any more prompting. I glanced back at the smoke, saw it was rising toward the ceiling.

"Stay down!" I yelled, and threw myself to the floor on hands and knees. "Try not to breathe!" Now I could only pray this was the kind of gas you had to breathe and not the kind you absorbed through your skin . . .

It wasn't, or that would have been the end right there. We scrambled back toward the armory, Patrick a little ahead of me. We hurried into the room and slammed the door closed behind us. I sipped air cautiously and saw that Patrick was doing the same. I didn't feel light-headed, but would I? I'd never been gassed before.

There were gas masks on a shelf near the back. I grabbed one and yanked it over my head. The straps in back adjusted themselves to my stupid head, and the soft plastic of the mask itself fit itself snugly to my face.

"What do we do now? Try to get out through the back door?"

"I'd expect they have that covered. You mentioned something else. A last-resort escape."

"No, I don't want to use that." He said it firmly.

"We might—"

"No, there has to be another way."

I shrugged. First we needed to see what the situation was outside. We opened the door, and I led the way, with a gun in each hand. We made our way back to the living room, which was still lit up like a movie premiere in Old Hollywood. I hurried to the wall, not exposing myself, and edged one eye around the side, through a window that still had glass in it.

Or it did. The laser outlined that one, and this time it fell away instead of in. I heard it crash. Another gas grenade came flying through the empty space.

"Pollyanna Broussard and Patrick Strickland-Garcia," someone bellowed through a bullhorn. "Come to the window with your hands up and no weapons in them, and you will not be harmed. It's in your best interests to surrender peacefully."

"The heck with that," I muttered. The lens in my mask had darkened when the harsh light hit it, another nice feature.

"You will have an attorney as soon as the current state of martial law is lifted. You are guaranteed a fair and impartial trial by a jury of your peers, and you—"

That steamed me.

"There is no state of martial law!" I shouted back. "You are part of an unlawful coup, a mutiny. Everybody out there, if you can hear me, these people have—"

A regular volley, a fusillade if you will, of gas grenades came through the window, at least eight of them.

Well, the heck with that.

I aimed at the big spotlight and fired. Missed the first time. I was ashamed of myself, realized my hand was shaking. Calmed down, fired again, and heard glass shattering. Suddenly it was very dark, both out there and in the apartment. I risked a look around the edge again. People were running for cover. There were park security in their uniforms and others in black uniforms. They seemed startled to be shot at.

Behind them, not being held back by any sort of crowd control, were what looked like dozens of civilians. None of them were running or taking cover. Clearly, they had never heard real gunfire. One of them was actually clapping. I realized that most of them thought it was some sort of new show put on for their benefit. I saw what I thought might be the laser cutter they had used. Taking careful aim, I squeezed off three shots. I heard them ping into the unit. With any luck, I had screwed up the insides. Even if I hadn't, I don't think I would want to fire it up with a few holes in it. Who knows what might happen?

About that time, I heard what sounded like an explosion.

"I think they're blowing the doors to the elevator," Patrick said.

There was another explosion, a lot closer. Everything in the room rattled and swayed.

"That'll be the main doors," I said. Nobody came pouring in, so they were either worried about getting shot or hadn't managed to penetrate the armor I knew would be in the doors.

"We've only got a few seconds," I said. "We have to take the last-resort exit."

"Uh-uh, I don't think so," he said. Dammit, what was the problem?

"Don't be silly, Patrick. Now where's the door to the roof?"

"I'm not going up there. You go, I'll stay here."

"Where is the door, Patrick?"

He sighed and gave in. I followed him down a hallway to an inconspicuous door near the end. He put his palm to it, and the door opened just as I heard a louder explosion behind us. I could hear shouted voices, both demanding our surrender and talking excitedly among themselves. It sounded like a dozen or more.

There was a narrow staircase. I made sure the door was locked and barred, and started up the stairs after Patrick, who didn't seem to be in all that much of a hurry. I shoved his ass impatiently, and I heard him breathing hard. Surely this wasn't tiring him out?

A door opened onto the roof. I grabbed Patrick by the seat of his pants and pulled him back. He had been about to walk right out on the roof. Something that had been building up inside me for some hours now finally gave way. I was disgusted with him. I'd had to lead, cajole, and now even shove him every step of the way. It was like having a ball and chain around my ankle. A part of me considered just leaving him there on the roof, but we were in this together, we were family. I'd get him out of here.

I looked around the doorjamb and saw a rope with a grappling hook come over the side of the building . . . and then slide off. There wasn't a lot for the hook to hook up to, but there were a few places it would probably catch, and if they kept trying, they'd be up here soon. Time to move.

I pulled a pistol and grabbed Patrick's hand, slapped the gun into it. He stared at it like it was a rotten, dead fish.

"Here's what you're going to do, Patrick, and I don't want to hear any backtalk about it. If you see anyone coming over the edge, aim the gun down at the roof, at an angle, like this. Not close enough to blow off your toe, but not far enough away to hit anything but the roof. Then fire. I want them to hear it and see the muzzle flash. Keep your head down. Here's the trigger. To fire it, wrap your finger over it and pull." I noticed his hand was trembling, but he gripped the gun.

I hurried over to the last resort.

It was a little shacklike structure right in the middle of the roof. The door wasn't locked; there really wasn't any need to up here, accessible only through the apartment below. Inside were ordinary things like folding lawn chairs and lounges and tables, enough for a party. There was a barrel-shaped barbecue. There was a badminton set, a croquet set, other outdoor games. All of it looked dusty. And in one corner, flycycles.

They were folded up, small enough to fit several into a golf bag. I stripped them out of their coverings and took a quick look.

Junk. Good enough for dilettante night flyers, but way too heavy for serious tournament play. You could buy twenty of these for what I paid for mine . . . which was now junk, too. But that wasn't a problem just then. In fact, it might be better, in that these old clunkers were sturdier.

Even better, the first one I unfolded was a tandem. Designed for Marlee and Mike, I figured. It would do just fine for me and Patrick. I used the strap of a carrying case to put another cycle over my shoulder. Back in the shack, I brought out the two JATO units, hoping they were still charged. I fastened them in place on the cycle frame.

There was a gunshot behind me. I turned quickly, aiming my pistol in front of me, but no one was coming over the top.

"It was a grappling hook," Patrick admitted. "It didn't catch."

"That's fine. Come over here, we're about to go."

"Polly, I don't want to go."

"You'd rather stay here and get captured?"

"No . . . I . . . maybe I could . . ."

"We've got to go now, Patrick."

He swallowed hard and nodded.

"Get on," I said. I was holding the cycle a few feet off the ground. He stepped over it uncertainly, and I realized he had never been on one.

"It's easy," I told him. "You'll be in back, I'll be up front steering. Put that strap around your waist. I'll control the wings and the tail. We will be upright when we launch, but as soon as we get in the air we will stretch out almost prone. You grab this bar and hold on. Put your feet on these pedals back here, and when I tell you, pump like the dickens. Got that?"

I swung my leg over and was strapping in when I heard a clanking sound over to my left. I watched as another hook hit the roof, dragged . . . and hooked. I could see the rope grow taut. Someone was coming up.

"You stick your head over, and I'll blow it off," I yelled. "I'm not kidding. I haven't hurt anyone yet, but I'll kill you."

There was no response. I aimed at the hook and fired. The bullet hit the hook, which rang like a bell. I'd like to brag, but it was a lucky shot. Annie Oakley would have cut the rope, I'm sure. But the rope went slack, as whoever was on his way up changed his mind.

"You ready?" I called over my shoulder.

"Y-y-y-y . . . yes."

"Hang on to my waist. The first step is a killer." I hit the button, and the JATO units thrust us up into the air at a forty-five-degree angle.

JATO is Jet-Assisted Takeoff. The idea has been around since the midtwentieth century, and it's real simple. In this case, the bottles contain two chemicals that, when they mix, produce a great deal of gas very quickly. There is a nozzle, pointing down and back. Those suckers get you into the air quite smartly and are almost essential for a ground takeoff even under our relatively modest gravity. With Patrick behind me, clinging for dear life, getting up would have been completely impossible, and it would have been a heck of a strain for me alone, even with my competition cycle.

The units make a heck of a noise but don't leave a trail of smoke. This was the dicey part. That laser could cut us in half if they intended to kill us, and I still wasn't convinced they didn't. But it would be dicey for them, too, unless they just didn't care about collateral damage. A laser that powerful would reach clear across the interior, and do a lot of damage where it hit. It's crowded enough on the far side that there would be an excellent chance of starting a fire or even killing someone.

I itched like crazy between my shoulder blades, anticipating the searing heat of the laser, which would cut right through Patrick, but no shot came.

In about thirty seconds we were a third of a mile in the air and the JATOs cut off. I adjusted the wings to get as much of a glide as I could, because I had a fair-sized pedal ahead of me. I jettisoned the JATOs. They had parachutes and radio beepers so they could be recovered. I didn't want them to beep my location.

I very quickly began to wish I could jettison Patrick.

He was clinging to me like a barnacle, both arms wrapped around my waist, his face pressed to my back. I could feel his rapid breathing.

"Patrick, you're squeezing me to death. Can't you hold on to the handlebars?"

"I'm sorry, Polly. I can't."

I started pedaling, and knew instantly that his feet weren't on his pedals. "I need you to help, darn it. Find the pedals with your feet. Press down on them, and a latch will wrap around your feet so you can get power out of the up and the down stroke."

"I can't find them."

"Move your feet around. Look behind you, or down. You'll see them."

"I'm afraid I can't look down, Polly. I just can't."

"Are your eyes open?"

"No. It's the only way I can ride this thing. I think I may throw up."

"You'd better turn your head to the side if you do. I swear, if you vomit on my back, I'll ditch you." There was a short pause.

"I'm better. But I can't look."

After a few more heated exchanges, he did manage to get his feet in the proper position. And instantly some of the burden was taken off me. I heard the prop in back change pitch as it bit more powerfully into the air.

And, finally, I was able to devote a little time to navigation. I was headed away from Fantasyland, but in the wrong direction. In a few minutes I'd be over Duckburg, not where I wanted to go. I eased up through a ninety-degree turn—Patrick made loud, gasping sounds—and headed south.

"What is it called?" I asked. I thought maybe by getting him talking it would calm him down some.

"What is what called?"

"Your condition. I know there's a word for it, but I can't remember."

"Acrophobia. I've had it all my life."

"That sucks. I wouldn't think . . . I mean, here in the ship . . . there aren't many . . ."

"Tall buildings. I know. I don't even like to look out second-floor windows. I do, but it makes me queasy. Anything above four stories, forget about it. I'll have a panic attack. Like I'm having now."

I had heard the phrase, but it didn't mean much to me because I'd never had one. I guess they're pretty debilitating. I hoped he could continue to function because I couldn't do this all on my own. Maybe if I could keep him talking, it would help.

"So . . . you ever told anyone about it?"

"Mother and Father know. And now you."

"Well, your secret's safe with me. But hell, Patrick, it's not anything to be ashamed of. It's just something you have."

"I'm fucking exhausted, Polly."

"I'm beat, too. I could sure use a rest, and maybe a nap. But we can't do that up here, can we? We'd fall out—"

Okay, a damn stupid thing to say, but I was still getting used to this fear-of-heights business, I really didn't realize that could set him off. There's not an acrophobic bone in my body. It would be like being afraid of . . . I don't know, shoes or something.

He moaned, and clamped on to my waist so hard I was sure I'd have bruises. He stopped pedaling entirely.

"Ease up! Ease up, darn it! Get your feet on the pedals." I felt his grip loosen again and could feel the motion through my own pedals and the chain as his feet groped around. Finally, he was pushing again.

There wasn't much I could do about our other problem. I wasn't kidding when I said I was exhausted. I'd been running around for a long time now, much of yesterday and all night. It wasn't long until sun-on. I was thirsty, hungry, sleepy, and all the muscles in my legs were screaming at me. I was getting about half the power I needed from Patrick, and I knew he didn't have any more in the gas tank, either. I was about two-thirds of the way to the central axis and the sun, which helped a lot, but I didn't dare dip much lower. And I could feel that happening even though the heavy cycle had no positioning system. I kept working the wings to stay in a straight line, but my own positional sense, honed by years of skypool, told me I was slowly losing the battle.

Most of the low-grav "mountain" communities (of which there are about a dozen at each pole) are named for high places, places associated with real mountains back at Old Sun. There is a Geneva, a Nepal Town, a Machu Picchu, an Olympus. The place I was looking for was called Timberline, and was pretty high up, where the greenery and terraced farms gave way to barren rock, painted white. Any higher, and it would be too steep and too close to the sun. Most of the buildings were built out on stilts, hanging over the land below. The views were spectacular, and the living was easy, with the low grav. A lot of elderly and disabled lived up in that area. Timberline had two nursing homes that I knew of.

To my surprise, I spotted Timberline easily enough. Even better, it was almost straight ahead and a little down—that is, toward the interior surface—from my present position. Say, a quarter mile from where we were.

"Keep it up, Patrick, we're almost there." He made no reply.

Soon I could see individual buildings. The village was taller than it was wide, with the homes and other buildings stacked up above one another. The homes were pretty fancy. Most of them were dark, but a few had the lights of early risers. I didn't remember the place that well, but the main feature was the funicular railway, Angel's Flight, that climbed the increasingly steep slope from the train station down below. This was the last stop on the line, and a string of faint lights marked its path. I knew the place I was headed was near the station, in the middle of town.

With my last gasp of energy, and without much help from Patrick that I could detect, I reached a small plaza next to the funicular station.

"We're here," I said, as I set down in a landing I normally wouldn't have been proud of. This time I was happy to have landed at all. I was never so grateful for low gravity in my life. I don't know just what it was, but it couldn't have been more than a fifth of a gee. Made me very light on my toes, even as exhausted as I was.

"Really? We're on firm ground?"

"Put your feet down and feel it. Then get off and kiss it if you want."

He got off but didn't kiss the ground. I busied myself inspecting the cycle to see if it had sustained any damage. It looked good to me. I quickly folded it up and slid it into the carrying case. I hefted it and my backpack of other goodies and looked around.

"Any chance of getting something to eat?" Patrick asked. "I'm feeling a little faint."

I was starving, too. Also very thirsty. I looked around, and saw a small automated convenience store a block away. We went over there, both of us stumbling a little as we got our low-grav sea legs under us. It was just a little kiosk with a screen.

"Got any cash?" I asked.

It turned out that between us we had just enough to buy two cheeseburgers and one bottle of water. I punched in the order and fed our meager coins and bills into the slot.

The machine printed our burgers in a minute. The worst kind of food you can get, I know, right out of the injectors, but they were hot, and thick, and greasy, and had melted cheese dripping out of the sides. They looked very realistic, just like real food. I'd seldom tasted anything so delicious. We wolfed down the burgers, passing the bottle of water between us, until it was all gone. While we ate, the machine printed a nice little complimentary miniature of the Timberline Lodge, multicolored, very detailed. Those things are made of marzipan, which is mostly sugar. I wanted all the calories I could take aboard, so we broke it in two and ate it.

We were just wadding up the trash and dumping it in the container when my phone rang.

"Phone," I said to Patrick. Then I answered it, not sure I really wanted to. Someone was whispering on the other end. I couldn't make out a word.

"You'll have to speak up, whoever you are. And I'm hanging up in ten seconds if you don't identify yourself."

"I can't talk much louder," the voice said. "Cassie, is that you?"

"It's Polly," I said, my heart in my throat. I was pretty sure I recognized the voice.

"It's Aunt Elizabeth," she said, confirming my hunch.

"Aunt Elizabeth!" I breathed, nodding to Patrick. "What's—"

"I may not be able to talk long," she said. "I may have to hang up. If I do, I'll call you back. Now listen . . ."

I listened.

CHAPTER 16

Cassie:

Well, shit.

I'll admit to a bad moment there when Sheila informed me we couldn't get back in the way we'd come out. But surely Travis had made provision for a thing like that. Like, what if the hangars were damaged?

Sheila confirmed that.

"At the North Pole, there are docking facilities. In fact, most of the biggest ships for ferrying things down to a planet at our destination are located up there in the north."

"Yeah, but that'll be where the mutineers are most likely to be, isn't it? Near the control room, or in it?"

"I believe they are. Information is still sketchy, the war is still going on, but certain orders emanating from the control room lead me to suspect it is already occupied."

"Then . . . are we stuck out here?"

"Not necessarily. There is a third way in. I believe it may still be accessible."

"Where is it?"

"Where would you put it?"

Sometimes an AI can be too human for its own good. What was she doing, playing games?

Maybe she sensed this because she spoke again.

"The third way in is right where you would expect it to be. At the South Pole."

Oh, what wonderful news. Let's plunge right into the dragon's mouth.

———————

It didn't take long to get there, as I told her to do it as quickly as possible. I strapped in, and she burned the engines, hard, for almost a minute, then almost at once flipped around and burned them again. I was tossed around in my chair like a beanbag, but it was sufficiently well padded that I didn't break any bones or bruise anything. I didn't ask her how many gees we had pulled, but I knew it was a bunch.

I watched the scene change quickly outside. We came roaring around the curved, irregular, pockmarked stern of the ship, and the engines came into view.

The engines.

I had seen videos of them, of course, and illustrations of them compared to a man, a skyscraper back at Old Sun, the Egyptian pyramids, and so forth, but there was just no way to grasp the size of the things without seeing them with your own eyes. And other than the engineering crews who went out regularly to inspect them for signs of strain, very few people had done that. The stern of *Rolling Thunder* was a place that just felt all wrong for a human being to be. The engines made me feel very small in a way the infinite blackness of space couldn't quite achieve. And the power pouring out of them seemed to make space itself vibrate.

What they resembled was radio telescopes from the twentieth century. They were dishes supported on massive struts that allowed them to turn in any direction to listen to different parts of the sky. Those instruments had to be massively braced with steel girders to support the weight.

There were six engines, spaced evenly in a hexagon around the flat plane that was the stern of the ship. They were massive, a third of a mile high, with the struts spreading out to distribute the stresses, the bottoms of the legs plunging into the bare rock and anchored there. At the very tops of these structures were giant baskets, open at the top, woven around the silvery balls of squeezer bubbles a thousand feet in diameter.

"You're not going to get too high, are you?" I asked Sheila.

"Don't worry, I'll hug the ground. All the energy is going straight up, away from us. They've been running for twenty years, and the danger zones are well-known. You see that there is no heat damage to the rock beneath us."

She was right, of course, but sometimes logic doesn't offer a lot of reassurance. I looked at the six parallel columns of furious energy leaping into space behind the ship and thought about how we would be instantly vaporized if we even got too close.

As we got nearer and nearer, I began to realize how *really* huge the things were. Each girder was much wider than my little ship, but the spaces between them were also much wider than they had appeared from a distance. With nothing to give me a sense of scale, they went from being big objects in the distance, to being massive structures in the middle distance, to being gigantic, gargantuan, colossal, enormous. Brobdingnagian. Put that one in your thesaurus and think even bigger.

In a short time, we were at the axis, the actual South Pole of the rotating rock. There was a structure there, a domed building.

"How about it, Sheila? Can we get in?"

"I've just sent the signal, and there it is. The lock is opening."

I didn't realize how hard I'd been gripping the armrests until I let go.

Before I left the ship, Sheila told me where to find a small device I could use to get in touch with her at any time. It was the size of a wristwatch, designed to fit Travis, so I had to tighten it quite a bit. I armed myself with everything I could carry without slowing myself down: pistols, a few grenades, night-vision glasses, gas mask. Some I attached to a webbing belt, the rest I stuffed into a backpack designed to carry lethal stuff. None of it weighed anything there at the pole, but it would get heavier for every foot I descended.

I wasn't happy with the clothes I was wearing. If we were going to get into a fight, the casual stuff wasn't a great idea. I needed something more serious.

Travis had prepared for that, too. There was a unit that had liquid fabric in black, dark green, or brown. Sheila took my measurements and fed cloth into the printer, and in two minutes I had a snug, supple set of coveralls in basic black. I printed a pair of black boots. Just putting the things on made me feel somehow stronger and more sure of myself. We're coming for you, assholes!

I opened the lock cautiously, pistol in hand, looking all around. No one was in the hangar, which was almost empty. Just a few small ships like Sheila, and one larger freighter. All quiet as a tomb. I floated out, twisted, got my feet down to lock onto the metal floor.

Sheila guided me to the right air lock to enter the interior. I stepped inside and was about to cycle the lock when I was struck, hard, by the feeling that I was leaving something important behind. I stopped myself, ran a check in my mind of all the things I had put into the bag and attached to my belt, and all the things I had left behind. There didn't seem to be anything back there that I could reasonably use, and that would be light enough to carry without impeding me. It was driving me nuts . . . and then I had it.

Papa. Damn! I just didn't feel right leaving him back there suspended in the timeless black bubble.

It was a problem. Leaving him behind began to seem less and less an option the more I thought about it. But talk about a bulky, intractable object to bring along! I'd rejected the long guns for that reason; Papa would be twice as inconvenient, like taking a baby into combat. Sorry, Papa, but you and I know your fear of weightlessness, your anbarophobia, would make you helpless here at the pole, and your other phobias would get in the way of any violent action I might encounter.

But there was nothing for it. I had to take him out, and I had to take him along.

Papa looked around, saw he was in the same place, and that I was there. He gasped as he felt the weightlessness, but he managed not to get sick. I had a bag in my hand just in case.

I remembered the last time he came out of a bubble and promptly uttered the words that had led to all this mess. He didn't have anything so dramatic this time, but there was something unusual. After his initial re-action and a quick smile at me, he frowned and looked thoughtful.

"Something just popped into my head," he said. "I might have an idea, me. I might have me an idea."

Uh-oh. Not another one. Or, hooray, another one! I didn't need my world shaken up again, but on the other hand, his new brainstorm might be the best thing that ever happened to us. One never knew.

"Papa, we have to leave the ship—"

"What time is it? I mean, what year? You don't look no older."

"I'm just like I was. It's only been a few hours."

"'Kay."

"We need to leave here and get you to a safe place where you can think about your new idea."

"'Kay." He frowned. "I'd like you to take me home, *cher*. I need to do some thinkin', and my lab be a good place for that."

"We can't do that right now, Papa. Can you just trust me on that?"

"'Kay."

He was off in some place of his own, some Papa-planet where his dam-aged mind wandered through byways not half a dozen humans had ever entered. And some places where *no one* but him had ever entered. It was a stroke of luck, really. Whatever had happened to him in the bubble this time was apparently so profound that he was hardly aware of his sur-roundings. It made him a lot easier to manage.

I found another satchel and stuffed it with bottles of water and some food Sheila produced. He might have to hide away for a few days. Best not to order out unless he had to.

I couldn't think of anything else. I strapped the satchel tightly to him so it wouldn't float away, and tugged him like a big balloon toward the door of the air lock. Once more I cautiously stuck my head out. Nobody was there. Just a bare corridor, like so many underground spaces. I pulled him through and down the hall.

———

Papa was still amazingly passive and uninvolved as I stuffed him into an elevator and got his feet firmly on the floor. He gulped and looked sick for a moment as we started down and got a dose of Coriolis force pulling us sideways, but the weight gradually began to build up, and we settled firmly with a local "down," and he seemed okay with it.

"Papa, are you all right?"

"I been better, *cher*, but I'm improvin'."

"That's good. Listen, I'm going to get you to a safe place, then I've got some things I need to explain to you."

"I figgered. First, you tell me I can't go home right now. Then you say you takin' me to a safe place. I guess somethin' bad goin' on. Right?"

"Yes. Something bad."

He sighed. "Somebody comin' after me again?"

"I don't want to tell you all of it right now, okay?"

"You do what you think best, Cassandra Ann."

———

Sheila called me when we got off the elevator.

"I've been in contact with your sister."

"Polly! Is she okay?"

"She's safe for the moment."

"Can I call her?"

"Phone service is erratic at the moment. People have noticed it by now, and are starting to disbelieve the official explanations coming from the mutineers. Unrest is growing."

Where would that lead? I wondered. We had been a peaceful society for my lifetime aboard the ship. But we hadn't been stressed much. Everything had functioned well up to now. The sun had turned on and off without fail. Social squabbles were never much of a problem, limited to fistfights, hardly ever to murder. There were no groups that I'd ever heard of so dissatisfied as to resort to violence. What would happen if people had to choose up sides?

"Where is she?"

"Not far away. I'll guide you to her."

The elevator soon deposited us in a long, long corridor that was dimly lit in the distance. Eventually, we came to a lock and got in. The lock cycled and opened onto a short dirt pathway that led to a paved cycling and walking track. It was only ten yards or so to the little path, which would be a circular one, running around the smaller diameter of the interior at this elevation. We came out onto the path, and Papa stopped.

"Oh, my, ain't that lovely?" He was looking out over the interior, which was still dark, sparkled with a million lights, and stretched six miles to the North Pole. It was just minutes to sun-on, and it sure was lovely, but we didn't have time for this.

"We'll look at it later, Papa."

We hadn't gone far around the curve when the sun came on. We made our way along the trail and soon were approaching the hillside hamlet of Timberline.

This is a place my sister and I had visited during summer vacation a few years before with Mama and Papa. We swam in the low-grav pool though Polly and I preferred stretching out on a lounge at poolside in our skimpiest bikinis and waiting for the boys to drop by and try their luck. Also, you can really get some height on the three-meter springboard, and you have a lot of hang time to do flips and such.

There were also three covered ski slopes, which we all tried out. It wasn't very satisfying to me. You get a real slow start, even if the slope is almost vertical. But you gain weight quickly as you get lower, and by the time you reach the bottom, you're going fairly fast. We quickly graduated from the bunny slope to the medium, but after that I gave it up and never went back. It just wasn't as exciting as skypool.

Even Papa went down the bunny slope, falling a lot and having a great time. He's not afraid of *every*thing, and he's quite strong.

This was where Mama tried out skycycling for the first and last time. Polly and I rode on each side of her, trying to act as training wheels, sort of, but she got away from us and took a fall, and broke her arm. Not a bad one—I've had worse twice—but enough to put her off flying.

I didn't want to just walk in with Papa. If possible, I'd have liked to keep his presence a secret. So I found a little picnic table in a small park near the lodge and sat him down there. The park was enclosed in mesh, an aviary. Aside from ducks, we don't allow many birds to roam free in the ship. Many of them would destroy crops, and some would overpopulate and take over. So we keep exotics—songbirds and tropical birds with splendid colors—in small enclosures like that one. Papa was happy there. He loved birds. There was a dispenser that sold cups of apple juice to feed the lorikeets, which would perch on your shoulder or head or hand. I bought him a cup with a few coins, not wanting to use credit.

Timberline Lodge, like so many buildings in the ship, was inspired by a building back on Old Earth. It wasn't nearly as big as the original, on the slopes of Mount Hood in Oregon, not having nearly as many rooms, but the cavernous lobby made of wood and stone was the same. It was a lovely space, looking out over the interior of the ship. There was a huge fireplace, with a faux fire burning, and a balcony encircling the main floor, leading to the rooms. I entered and looked around, didn't see Polly, and started for the front desk.

Something hit me in the back of the head. It didn't hurt, much, but it clattered on the floor, and I jumped and almost drew my pistol. I looked around and saw Polly up on the balcony. She was squatting, just her head over the balcony rail. I looked down and saw she had thrown a bullet at me. I was impressed with her accuracy.

I picked up the bullet and put it in my pocket, then signaled to her that I'd just be a minute. I ran into the automated gift shop and spotted a wide-brimmed straw hat with TIMBERLINE sewn into the crown, more fitting for a tropical resort than a ski lodge, but I wasn't complaining. I put a couple bucks in the cashier and hurried out with the hat.

I found Papa just where I'd left him. There were several birds sitting quietly on his shoulders and on the table, but he wasn't feeding them anymore or even looking at them. He was still, with a thoughtful look on his face. I knew that look. He was thinking about something, thinking hard, and when Papa thinks hard, there's no telling what the result will be. But you can be sure it will be interesting.

I put the hat on his head and pulled it down so it partially hid his face. It was the best I could do to hide him from the security cameras. He didn't resist when I pulled his arm. He was almost in a trance state, just glancing up at me, then following along. We went back into the lodge and up the stairs, where Polly was waiting for us. I handed her the bullet.

"You have a good arm," I told her, "but I think you're supposed to put these things in a gun. They get there faster."

"Yeah, and it would have hurt your hard head less. Hi, Papa." She put her arms around him and hugged tight. Papa's face lit up, and he murmured something in her ear. When they broke the embrace, I saw Polly wipe away a tear, which choked me up a little, too.

"Let's go," she said. "No time to waste."

We followed her down the pine-paneled hallway with the rustic light fixtures and the paintings of the Oregon Cascades and coast on the walls, and entered a room.

It was a suite, actually, two bedrooms with a large sitting room that could have come through a time machine from 1938. No data screen on the wall, no computer station, an old-fashioned telephone with a dial on it. There were bulky, overstuffed chairs and a sofa, and a stuffed elk head on the wall. I thought that was sort of creepy. There was a simple, polished-pine table that would seat eight by the windows overlooking the interior.

Patrick was sitting in one of the chairs, his arms folded and his head resting on them. He looked exhausted, and for that matter, so did Polly. I knew they must have been through a lot to get there. My own trip had been easy. All the comforts of home. Good food, good companionship until Papa got sick, a new friend . . .

I looked over at Patrick, barely able to keep his eyes open. There was the remains of a room-service meal on the table. He looked so gorgeous, and so tired, like a puppy who's played too hard. I wanted to go over there and cradle his head in my lap.

I had to figure that Polly had made some time with him. I was jealous as hell, but I had to put all that behind me. For now. But just wait, sis.

"I need a pencil and paper, me," Papa said.

"You need . . ." Polly was clueless.

"I think he had another brainstorm," I told her. "I had to put him in a bubble because I didn't want to upset him with all this."

"What's all this?" Papa said.

"I'll get into that in a minute," I told him. "Meantime, let's get you a pencil and paper." I pulled open a desk drawer and found what I suspected would be there. It was a clear, roll-up, twelve-inch pad. I broke the latch and carried it over to the table, unrolled it. The screen came to life, and a little chime sounded to let us know it was ready. Papa frowned at it.

"I work better with a pencil, me," he said.

I wondered if they even had paper in the room, or if I'd have to go buy something in the gift shop. But we were in luck. In keeping with the historical theme, there was a sheaf of heavy letterhead stationery in a desk drawer, and several ballpoint pens also inscribed with the name of the lodge. Even a paper room-service menu. Polly brought them to Papa. He frowned at the pen but shrugged and started scrawling diagrams and equations on the paper.

We left him and went to sit on the couch.

"So tell me what you know first," Polly said.

It didn't take long. Then I asked her what had been going on with her. Oh, my.

———

I had had no idea. The fight at our house, the abduction of our entire family. The swim and the chase. The parade . . . unbelievable, and my respect for my sister soared. That was pretty ingenious. And I really wished I'd seen it. Patrick as a clown, Polly as a showgirl? The mind boggled.

The horror over the casino. She began to cry at that point, and I put my arm around her and let her sob for a moment. But we couldn't waste too much time, and we both knew it. No time for tears, anyway.

Finally, the skycycle trip, with Patrick basically a deadweight. No wonder she was tired. No wonder he was.

I glanced over at Patrick. He was sound asleep.

"You say he's afraid of heights?" I whispered.

"Sad to say, yes. Not his fault."

"Of course not." But to someone like me, who loved nothing more than being on a flimsy cycle with a mile of empty space below me, it seemed like quite a disability indeed.

"He managed. You gotta respect someone able to make it through a phobia like that. It wasn't easy for him."

"Of course not." I wanted to go over and comfort him, poor baby. But that might be Polly's prerogative now. I wouldn't poach on her guy—if he *was* her guy—until I knew for sure where we all stood.

"Anyway, that's all behind us now," she said. "What do you figure our chances are of staying undetected here?"

"Did you pay cash?"

"Patrick did. We thought he was a little more anonymous than me since we're direct Broussard family."

"That makes sense. But I wonder, if everything was working right with the computers, would we stand a chance?"

"I doubt it. That's probably all that's keeping us free now. The mess that's going on in the security systems as Max tries to take them over."

"You think he will?"

"Who knows? But I'm optimistic because I haven't given you the best news yet. I talked to Travis and Aunt Elizabeth."

"Tell me more."

———

Polly said that the way Elizabeth put it, the mutiny didn't seem to be going very well, at least from what they could gather. The number of conspirators seemed to be small. The computer war was either not going their way or was a standoff.

"How do they—"

"Let me tell it, okay?" Okay.

The captives, hostages, internees, however you wanted to put it, were being held somewhere near the control room, at the North Pole. Elizabeth didn't think the control room itself had been breached yet.

They had been taken, unconscious, from our house and didn't wake up until they were all in some sort of underground reception room. There was no prison in this ship big enough for them all. They had been searched, stripped of everything that could be used as a weapon or a tool, and all communication devices had been deactivated. They were watched constantly, the lights were never turned off, there were no chairs, only a stack of mattresses to sit or sleep on. Every once in a while, one of them was taken out for questioning, but so far it hadn't been rough. Travis, of course, was questioned most of all. He was the only one they were sure had the codes to unlock places they needed to be to complete their takeover, the only one they knew could shut down the cyber war. All of them were still a bit woozy and sick from the knockout gas, which was no fun at all to breathe. But no one was badly hurt.

So how had Elizabeth managed to get through to Polly? They had forgotten, or didn't know about, her hand.

Elizabeth has had a dozen hands over the years, each an improvement over the old one. I've seen pictures of her first one, which looked real from a distance but was obviously plastic when you got close, and I heard it felt nothing like a real hand. But it was as supple as a real one, and when she had learned to use it, the same nerve impulses that were read by the hand could be used to operate remote ones, big or small, or *extremely* small. She pioneered the field of nanosurgery, and for years was the one everyone went to when they wanted to learn how to do it. She was also the one the very rich sought out when they wanted the best . . . and she usually turned them down. Her sole criterion for taking a patient was how critical the need was. She would refer a billionaire to another surgeon and operate on a pauper if she felt the poor person needed it worse. I've always admired her for that even if she does still treat us like bratty little children.

The current one is almost indistinguishable from a living hand. In fact, the skin that covers it is real skin. You even have to look closely to see where it joins the stump of her arm. She usually wears long sleeves to cover it, but she doesn't really need to. So I'm not surprised that whoever searched her either missed it or didn't think it needed to be removed. That would probably have made even a mutineer feel small.

"They missed it," Polly assured me. Okay, but so what?

Well, Aunt Elizabeth has a few tricks up her sleeve, so to speak.

The same electronics that allow her to remotely use a surgical device can be used for communication, just like a phone. She records notes on it as she's working. The stuff in her hand is better than any phone she could buy.

"It has a positioning device, too," Polly said. "She knows her location to within a few feet. I've used that information to locate her on a map of the spaces near the control room."

"So . . . we know where they are. How do we get them out?"

"I don't know yet. She didn't try to call out to anyone earlier because she didn't know that Patrick and I had escaped. She thought we were being held somewhere else. And she knew you were out there gallivanting with Papa. When she tried to call, she dialed both of us, and I guess mine was the only call that went through." She paused for a moment. "What does Papa know?"

"Not much," I admitted. "I didn't want to upset him, that's why I put him in the bubble for a while. I've been wondering if we should tell him."

"I think he deserves to know."

"Yeah, I guess so. But how can we put it so it doesn't drive him off the rails? If he thought someone would hurt Mama . . ."

"Not so good." She looked over at Papa, who was utterly absorbed in his paper and pen. "What's the deal with that?"

"I don't know. He got a brainstorm. I don't know what it's about, and I don't know if it's a good idea to interrupt him. You never know what he might come up with. But I guess we better tell him."

"Okay. But listen, Aunt Elizabeth said she would try to call in . . . twenty minutes. So I hope we can avoid a meltdown."

We went over to where Papa was scribbling things that might have been Mayan hieroglyphs or Japanese haiku or odds on a horse race. We sat on either side of him. In a few moments, he noticed us. Patrick lifted his head, yawned, and rubbed his eyes. Papa gave me a sheepish look that melted my heart.

"You girls got somethin' to tell me, don't you," he said, putting down his pen. "I'm sorry, I shoulda been payin' more close attention, me. We got some troubles, am I right?"

"You're right, Papa," Polly said. She took a deep breath. "There's been a sort of . . . a sort of uprising. They're not happy with what they see as a plan to stop the ship and turn it around."

"I figgered they wouldn't be. I ain't happy about it, neither. But I never said we had to . . . well, wait a minute, I guess I did, didn't I? But I didn't know enough then. What I did know scared me, is all."

"What do you know now, Papa?" I asked.

"We found out the dark lightning is just the same whether we be behind of the big bubble out front, or if it ain't even there. Which been botherin' me somethin' awful, oh yes. It shouldn't be that way, *cher*, no. Nothin' should be able to get through the bubble. But this stuff is. Now I gotta figger out why, and how."

"Do you know anything yet?"

"Mostly I know what I don't know. I mean, I don't know some stuff, but I know I don't know it. Oh, girls, my tongue done tangled again."

"We understand," I said. "What do you know?"

"I couldn't 'splain it to y'all. But I'm chipping away at what I don't know, and figgerin' out things." That was as good as we were going to get. He sighed, and looked at us one at a time. "So tell me what I need to know," he said. "Some people are tryin' to take over the ship? 'Cause they don't want to turn it around?"

"That's about it."

"But we may not have to. I could talk to 'em. Maybe 'splain?"

"The leader seems to be Max Karpinski," I told him. He was about as shocked as I expected him to be. "He and some others . . . well, they've put most of our family in jail."

"Max? Not Max, how could he did that?" He grabbed my arm, unaware that he was squeezing a bit hard. "Podkayne, she cain't be in jail, too, is she?"

"I'm afraid so, Papa," I said, loosening his grip. "Now, don't worry. Nobody's going to hurt them." I hoped.

"Who else?"

"Well, Travis, Mike, Marlee." I mentioned a lot of others, and his frown deepened.

"You wouldn't lie to your old Papa, would you, Cassie? They're not bein' hurt or anything?"

"You know we don't like to upset you, Papa, but no, we're not lying."

Papa said, "Well, I been in jail a time or two, long time ago. It wasn't no fun, but as long as they feedin' you . . ."

"They're being fed and cared for, don't worry."

"Then I won't. Are you girls doin' somethin' about it?"

"We're planning to get them all out and take the ship back."

He grinned at us.

"Okay, then. Everythin' gonna be all right then."

———————

I was glad he felt that way. We left him to his calculations, and Patrick joined us to wait for the phone call.

"Did she say anything about my parents?" he asked.

"You asked me that before, Patrick," Polly said. "No, not specifically, she just said everyone was okay."

After that, there wasn't much to say. In a few more minutes the call came in. Not only for Polly, but me and Patrick as well.

"Where are you?" Aunt Elizabeth wanted to know.

"At the South Pole," Polly told her, unwilling to be more specific.

"Is Jubal there?" That was Travis, sounding more worried than I'd ever heard him.

"Yes, Travis. He's fine. He had another brainstorm while he was in the bubble. He's working on it."

Our words were only going to Elizabeth's ears, through her clandestine phone. I heard her say yes.

"Okay. Okay. That sounds good. Keep his mind off all this other stuff. How much does he know?"

"We told him you were all in jail," Polly said. I heard Elizabeth repeating her words, quietly.

"We're going to orient you now," Elizabeth said. "Just a minute . . . okay, here we go."

A picture appeared in my peripheral vision. I blinked it to the center.

It was fairly steady, but a bit lopsided. Part of it near the top was obscured by something out of focus. I realized it was a couple of Aunt Elizabeth's fingers. The almost microscopic lens must have been located in the palm of her hand, concealed in a wrinkle when she didn't want it to be seen. I could see the top of one of her knees near the bottom of the picture. Beyond that, Travis was sitting, his back against a wall off to my right, looking away at nothing I could see. He almost filled the scene, though I could see vague shapes beyond him that looked like more people sitting against the same wall.

Putting the spatial relationships together in my head, I figured Elizabeth was sitting with her elbow on her knee and her head resting on her open fist. You could pretend you were dozing off in that position and still be able to speak into the microphone.

"Can you see?" Elizabeth asked.

"I can see fine," I said, and Polly and Patrick echoed me.

"I'm going to do a slow pan," she said. "At some point you'll see the guards. And the rest of the room, and the people here. I have to be careful. They watch us all the time. You ready?"

"Ready." And ready, and ready, from sis and Patrick.

The camera moved away from Travis's profile and slowly took in the wall beyond him. I saw a door. The wall was an ugly green, and it looked like some screens had been mounted on it not too long ago. Naked wires protruded here and there, and what looked like holes for bolts.

There was one man standing with his back to that wall, close to the door. He wore black clothing. There was a yellow armband around one biceps, and a riot helmet on his head.

He was holding a long, bulky stick that I knew was a stun rifle, the most potent weapon our police forces had. Guaranteed to put down a charging rhino if you set it high enough. They could be lethal at that setting.

Past the corner and on to an identical wall that had no features that I could see. A couple of dozen people were sitting, leaning against the wall. Mike and Marlee were sitting together. I heard Patrick's sharp intake of breath but didn't look at him. I was trying to take it all in at once, not miss anything. But I didn't see anything useful.

Past the next corner there was another bare wall with some wires sticking out, and two more guys and one girl dressed in black with the yellow armbands, also cradling stun rifles. That made four guards.

At last, Elizabeth had panned 180 degrees, and I saw more of my family sitting against the wall. Closest to the camera, almost filling the screen when the pan stopped, was Mama, also in profile. Suddenly, there was a burning sensation in the back of my throat. I coughed to get rid of it and hastily wiped my eyes, which had started to water.

Mama looked disheveled, like all the others. Her hair was a mess, and her eyes were dark circles, and not from makeup.

"Girls," she whispered. "Are you all right?"

"Yes, Mama," we both whispered back. The camera moved slightly, which I interpreted as Elizabeth's nodding.

"And Jubal . . ." Her lips were barely moving, in what I think they call a jailhouse whisper. Which was exactly what it was.

"Yes, Mama. We've got him safe."

"I love you more than I've ever been able to tell you, Cassandra Ann, Pollyanna Sue."

"We know, Mama," Polly said. Her eyes were red, and she sounded like her nose was stuffy. Well, mine was, too. I put my arm over her shoulders and squeezed.

"They know, Podkayne," Elizabeth whispered.

"I love you, and I'm so proud of you two my heart could just explode. You realize you're our only hope?"

"Yes, ma'am."

"You're too young to have this burden fall on you. But there it is."

"We're not much younger than you were when you had all that trouble on Europa," I said. "I only hope we can do as well as you did."

"You'll have to do better," she said. "I didn't save everybody. We can't lose any of these people."

"We won't, Mama."

"Okay then. I have to shut up. I think one of those guards is looking at me." As she said it, she raised her hand. "I have to pee, you guys."

She must have gotten an okay, because she got up and walked away. The picture jerked around, and we got a view of Elizabeth's lap, then her hair as she brushed it back behind one ear. Then she resumed the position.

"I'm sorry you couldn't talk to her directly," she said. "But I passed on everything you said, word for word."

"That's okay," Polly said. "We appreciate it."

"Patrick, we aren't allowed to move around much, but if I can, I'll get next to your parents and see if you can talk to them. I've already signaled them that you're okay. Not hurt."

"I appreciate that, Elizabeth, but don't take any unnecessary chances."

"Let me add that I'm just as proud of you all as Podkayne is, and Travis, too. Now I'm going to turn it over to Travis, and he's going to tell you what he has in mind."

"He has a plan?" That was Polly, who sounded as relieved as I felt.

"Travis always has a plan. There's more up his sleeve than Max ever imagined. You'll have to be smart, and quick, and strong, but I know all three of you are. So listen carefully. Take notes. Girls, I want you to study it like it was the game plan for the biggest skypool game in your lives."

"That we can do," I said, with a laugh.

Then Travis came on the line. And it was a hell of a plan. Impossible, but a hell of a plan.

———————

First, we had to figure out what to do with Papa. The trouble was, none of the options we had made me happy.

One, put him in the ship, in or out of the bubble. If someone came looking, Sheila would defend herself and him and, if it came to it, leave *Rolling*

Thunder and stand off at a safe distance until this thing was decided, one way or another.

Two, take him with us. I list that one only because it was barely possible to do so. But it was by far the worst alternative.

Three, leave him here, at the lodge.

"It's too chancy," I said. "They could get on our trail somehow and track him right to this room."

"How would they do that?" Patrick asked.

"How the dickens should I know? That's all happening in the cyber war we're not even able to eavesdrop on. My point, we have no idea how many of them there are or how close they might be."

"I don't like leaving Papa behind at all," Polly said. "I think we ought to take him with us."

"Into a possible battle?" I asked, incredulously. I lightly tapped the side of her forehead. "Hello? Hello? Anybody home up there, sister? Can you imagine Papa in a firefight like you just went through?"

She didn't reply, but her lower lip stuck out stubbornly. I've always hoped I don't do that, but maybe I do. We can both be mighty determined to get our own way.

"I don't think it's such a bad idea to stay right here," Patrick said. "I can watch over him. Or if I see anyone coming, we can run."

That got him a laserlike glare from *both* of us.

"What do you mean, take care of him? We're going to need you."

He looked very uncomfortable and wouldn't meet our eyes. "It was just a thought," he said. "He obviously needs somebody to stay with him."

"Sheila can do that," I said, firmly.

It took a little longer, but Polly finally gave in, and Patrick didn't seem like he even wanted to vote on the matter.

"I think we need to hear from one more person," Polly said. *After* we had decided, I thought. She nodded toward the bedroom door.

I sighed. She was right. In the end, it was really up to him to decide what he was up to and what he wasn't.

"I want to stay right here, me," he said, shocking us all.

"But, Papa . . ."

"I can't think on that ship, where it be weightless. And I need to think. I need it worse than I ever have, I think. So, unless y'all can bring the ship down here where there's gravity . . . I'm stayin' right here."

Okay. None of us liked it, but what can you do? Papa is so gentle and makes so few demands that it's possible to forget that, like someone he sometimes refers to, a comic book character called Pappy Yokum, when he has spoke, he has *spoke*!

We showed Patrick a variety of weapons and tried to convince him to take the simplest to use, which was a shotgun with a big magazine. Just point and shoot, another shell would be in the chamber before the noise had even died down. But he wouldn't take it.

"I'm sure I'd only blow my own foot off," he said. Okay, if you say so, Patrick. We finally got him to take a small handgun. We fitted him with a shoulder holster, as he was clearly horrified at putting it in his waistband. It was also clear what parts he was afraid of blowing off if he had it there.

Boys. What are you gonna do?

With final hugs for Papa, we headed out.

There were three ways for us to get from the South Pole to the North Pole. The first way was underground. Sheila was dubious about that but had no evidence that it was impossible, and it had a lot of advantages over the other alternatives.

The second way was out in the open, on the interior. We would have to sneak six miles through densely populated land, dressed like everybody's worst nightmare escaped from a virtual game, armed to the teeth, with an unknown number of people looking for us. If we traveled by day, even regular, uninvolved citizens would notice us and cause a ruckus and be alarmed. Also, various cameras up around the curve could spot us easily. Even at night we wouldn't be able to hide from the infrared cams.

Third was to fly it. We had the skycycles for it, and we also had a pas-

senger who would be in full panic mode all the way. Even without Patrick—
something I was thinking more and more about—it would be damn near
impossible at night. We would be the only ones in the air, and once more
our infrared signatures would give us away.

So underground seemed the best way.

Using the maps embedded in our phones we located a concealed entrance to an elevator that would take us below the interior level. To say we
were edgy would be an understatement. I was not shaking, so much as
shivering, like a racehorse at the gate. I was eager to get started because I
was equally eager to get it over, one way or another.

We took positions at the sides of the elevator when it came time for the
doors to open. Outside was . . . nothing. Or the next thing to it. A small,
bare room, a long, long tunnel lit only in the parts near us. And along a
magtrack, a little car big enough for six people.

"That looks like a death trap to me," I said. "We going to just get on the
little toy train there and go zipping along? And how many ambush points
do you think there might be along the way?"

"They don't seem to have projectile weapons," Polly said. "That gives
us an advantage."

"Yeah, but not if we're in the middle of epileptic seizures from their
stun guns. Besides, I don't want to kill anybody."

"Me either," Patrick said.

"And that makes three," Polly said, angrily. "But we found out these
guns are real good at making people keep their heads down."

We looked down that long tunnel. Here was a place easy to choke off
with just one or two or three soldiers or police or whatever they were calling themselves. Even if we scared them with a few bullets, they could instantly alert people down the line to block the tunnel, then block it behind
us. We'd be trapped like rats in a maze. And how many stations were there
ahead? I counted eight. There could be people at any or all of them.

"I say we at least give it a try," Polly said.

I gave in, and we all took seats. Polly spoke to the car. And nothing
happened. It just sat there, no lights, no action.

"They've turned it off," Patrick said.

"Which means they're aware of it," I said. "We were hoping this was Travis's secret underground railway, remember?"

"All right. We'll walk it," Polly said.

I was about to ask who appointed her squad leader . . . then realized I was okay with it. She had recently been through a real-life fight, as opposed to a survival course, so maybe her skills were a bit sharper than mine. And damn it, we did have to get to the North Pole some way.

But I really didn't want to shoot at anybody, much less kill them.

We were all wearing boots with soft soles, but in a tunnel like that it's almost impossible to move in complete silence. To do so, you have to move so slowly we wouldn't make it to the North Pole in a week. So we compromised, careful not to stomp our feet but managing a moderate walking pace.

Among the things we had picked up at the armory were three sets of goggles. They had lenses that flipped up or down, could give you starlight vision or infrared. You got a sick green picture with one, a sullen red with the other. There was also a directional mike in the goggles, and an earbud. The goggles were made for sneaky work, seeing and hearing someone before they see or hear you. That's always a big advantage.

It was pitch-dark in there without the glasses. I was glad we didn't have to resort to our flashlights.

We had come about halfway to the first station, Polly slightly in the lead, when she stopped and held up a hand. We had agreed, no talking, not even whispering. They were just as likely to have listening equipment as we were.

It became quiet. Very quiet. If I faced Polly, I could hear her heartbeat thundering, her breath roaring in and out. But facing straight ahead, there was nothing . . . until I heard the faintest of sounds. I strained to make it out, and I was soon convinced of what it was. I faced Polly, and so did Patrick.

She put her hand beside her mouth, opening it and closing it while she moved her mouth, then jerked her thumb ahead of us. Translation: *I hear someone talking down there.* I nodded.

She pointed back down the tunnel, lifting her eyebrows inquisitively, then pointed ahead, again asking. *Forward or retreat?* I hesitated, then pointed ahead, and cupped my hand around my ear. *Maybe if we get closer, we can hear what they're saying.* Patrick nodded, and so did Polly. I'll admit I wouldn't have minded if I'd been outvoted.

So we continued, even slower, and very gradually the sounds got louder. I couldn't make out words, but it was definitely people talking. How many? I couldn't tell. Someone coughed, and it was like they were standing right beside me. We all stopped, and I heard what was surely laughter.

We all looked at each other again. Go on? Go back? And if we go back, what then?

Polly turned toward the sounds again, and as she did a buckle on her belt clanked against the pistol in its holster. Anywhere else, it would have vanished in the background noise, but here there was no background, just hard steel surfaces to bounce it all the way to the next station.

The talking stopped. Once more it was silent as a tomb. Then, for the first time, we understood words.

"Is somebody down there?"

Yeah, the bogeyman, and he's coming to get you. It was a woman's voice, and it sounded pretty tentative to me.

"I didn't hear anything."

"I didn't, either."

"I did. I think we ought to go down there and take a look."

"You see anything in the infrared?"

"Nothing we haven't seen before. They could be down there in the vanishing point, and I don't think we'd see them."

"We would if we got closer."

I picked out four voices for sure, maybe five. One of them sounded like a man on a macho kick, sounding tough, or at least trying to. Another didn't sound happy at all.

Polly held up five fingers. Patrick nodded and did the same. I held up four, then five, with a shrug. There were at least that many up there. Polly once again shrugged, then pointed forward, and back. I pointed back. So did Patrick. Polly nodded, and we headed back the way we came.

The next hours were some of the most frustrating I've ever experienced. We didn't have to go so slowly on the way back, as we figured they weren't coming after us. But once back at the elevator, we had another choice to make.

"Looks like we have to do it on the surface," Patrick said.

"What, are you nuts?" That was Polly. "The only way I can see us doing that is to just go straight ahead to the north, on foot or in a vehicle, and kill anybody who gets in our way."

"Which we may have to do," I pointed out.

"You think I don't know that? And I'll do it, and you two will, too, if it comes to that. But, one, unless they are only a handful—and I don't believe that, if they've posted five people on that one underground line—I don't even know if we have enough *ammunition* for that."

I didn't think we did, either, but I didn't say anything.

"And two, is that where we want to start? I mean, shouldn't that be our last option if everything else fails?"

"I'm on board with that," Patrick said.

"Me, too." But she wasn't finished. She was really worked up, about as much as I've ever seen her.

"Add to that, we'll be like bugs in a jar out there. They'll spot us as soon as we start north. Cameras, and spies, and . . ." She tapered off. I patted her on the shoulder.

"It's okay, sis. We'll explore every option."

So we agreed that meant the other tunnels.

———

And that's where the frustration came in. According to the map Travis had unlocked for us, there were two more North–South private trains. They were spaced evenly around the poles. One of them was the one we had recently traveled on to get from our house to the bridge. It was 120 degrees away from this one, reachable through a door off to our right as we had exited the elevator.

The door opened onto another plain corridor. This one was not as wide, as no train cars would ever run through it. And whereas the train-tunnel lights only came on when a car was passing, this one was lit. Very dim, with a small light every twenty yards or so, but lit. And the floor curved upward ahead of us. If we walked a little over six miles, we would end up right back there.

We reached the next door in about twenty minutes. Patrick was breathing a little hard and looked tired. The guy wasn't in as good shape as me and the twin.

So we repeated the whole process, down the train tunnel. We knew this time about when we might be able to hear something, so we slowed down and listened, still maintaining silence.

There wasn't much, at first. But it turned out these people just weren't as talkative as the first group. Eventually, we heard them, and just a little later they heard something from us, because we could hear them asking each other if they heard anything. There was some difference of opinion on that, but then we heard something distinct.

"Elton, Roger, you come with me. The rest of you, stay here."

That was enough for us.

———————

The last tunnel was more of the same, the only difference being that shortly after we heard them, one of them fired a stun gun at us. The rifles fired small projectiles that would sting like the devil if they hit you. They trailed two fine wires that uncoiled out of the gun, and when they hit something, they discharged the stunning electricity. The wires had a range of about a hundred yards.

We heard the bang, and at the same time saw a flash of light from the propellant charge, but the stinger fell well short of us.

We fell back and regrouped.

"What do you think?" I asked. "Do we fight our way through one of these tunnels? Or go back and try the surface route?"

"They must know we're trying to get through," Patrick pointed out. "They would be talking to each other and know that each group heard something about half an hour apart. What would you do if you knew that?"

"Bring in reinforcements," I said, glumly.

"No question," Polly agreed.

"So maybe our best chance is a lightning run along the interior," I said. "I don't fancy fighting down here, trapped in these damn tubes. There's nowhere to go but forward or back. It's gotta be easier to defend than attack, right? Hell, they could just barricade the tunnel."

"You're right," Polly said. "That's hopeless. I guess we've wasted our time. I think it's because we don't want to face the alternatives."

"The surface," Patrick, said.

"No," she said. She looked at us, and she wasn't happy. "There's another way. I've had an idea."

It was a hell of an idea. I would soon be wishing she had kept her goddam ideas to herself.

CHAPTER 17

Polly:

I never said it was a great plan. I just said it was the one I thought had the best chance of success, which was looking like slim or zero.

We were a pretty bedraggled and exhausted bunch by the time we got back to the hotel. Papa was happy to see us, but pretty soon he was back in his "thinkin'" zone. We all immediately scrambled for something cold to drink and ordered food from room service.

Cassie had her back up, and she hadn't even heard the worst part of my plan. I wondered if it was going to be hard to sell her on it. Heck, I wasn't even sure I was sold on it myself.

"Fly?" she said for what seemed like the twentieth time. "You talk about being bugs in a jar if we try to fight our way through on the surface. How easy do you think we would be to spot with heat scopes at night, being the only thing in the air?"

"That's the thing," I said. "Infrared sensors. Like you say, flying at night we would be ridiculously easy to spot." I paused. "That's why we'll do it during the day."

Her jaw dropped open, then closed again. I don't know if I'd ever seen her speechless, but she was then. But not forever.

"You must be out of your f—. . . your cockamamie mind! In the daytime?

If we fly low, we'll still be sitting ducks, and I don't think we could make six miles in that kind of gravity. And if we fly high, we'll burn up. Remember Icarus?"

"Icarus disregarded his father, remember? What was his name . . . ?"

"Daedalus," Patrick supplied.

"Right. But he flew too high. The other part of the story is that Daedalus made it. He took his own advice and kept to the right altitude."

Cassie was mulling it over. I glanced at Papa, off in his own world, but I was about to say things it was best he didn't hear if he happened to come up for air. I gestured toward the door, and the three of us went into the other room.

"So what we'd be looking for is the Goldilocks zone," Cassie said, thoughtfully. "Too low, and we'd be spotted. Too high, and we fry. We have to find a distance that's just right. And where would that be?"

"It's wherever it is," I said. Not helpful, I guess, but true. We would have to find the right spot by experimenting.

"I don't get it," Patrick said. "Why wouldn't they spot you?"

"The sun would dazzle any device they used to look for us," Cassie said, absently. "We'd be invisible in the glare, in visible light or infrared."

"That's part of it," I agreed. "There's also the fact that no one would think we would be stupid enough to fly close enough to the sun to hide."

"What I'm wondering about," Cassie said, "is if anyone *is* stupid enough to do it."

"Well, there's one of us who's stupid enough to try."

She glared at me. Putting it in the form of a dare was my best chance of getting her with me. Cassie has seldom turned down a dare, short of certain death.

"Let's see those flycycles," she finally said.

We got them out and unfolded them. I had wondered if Cassie's sour face could get any sourer. It could.

"So, we're going to undertake the most dangerous flycycle trip ever attempted, and we're going to do it on junk?"

"C'mon, twin, where's your team spirit?"

"I think I left it in that hog pen after I saved your worthless butt."

I'd never seen her so negative. That's usually my role in our mirror-image relationship. Truth be told, I was probably even more dubious about the whole thing than she was, but since fate or whatever had granted me the idea, it fell to me to be the optimist. Like my name. Switched at birth, we were, if that means anything with twins.

"They're sturdy," I pointed out.

"So is a steam locomotive. You want to fly one? You got these from Mike and Marlee? And Patrick?"

Patrick was standing off to the side a bit. Now he cleared his throat.

"I hope you know I won't be going with you."

Cassie looked at him.

"Acrophobia," he said, with a shrug.

"It's true, Cass. He barely made it here."

"If we're voting here, if I have a vote, I want to fight in the tunnels."

"You have a vote," I told him. "Cassie, that doesn't really matter. He couldn't fly a cycle that far, anyway. He's a novice."

"With acrophobia." Cassie sighed. "I didn't feel good about leaving Papa behind, alone, no matter what we decided. I guess he could take care of Papa."

"So what's your vote, Cassie?"

Another deep, deep sigh.

"I guess we do our Icarus thing," she said.

"Daedalus."

"Whatever."

———

Preparations didn't take long. Most of it was being sure we would bring everything we needed, and the rest was finding ways to keep as cool as possible.

We had never needed suntan lotion, but we had never been that close to the sun. We sent Patrick to the Timberline gift shop to get some to put on our faces, the only parts of us that would be exposed.

Water would be essential. I expected to sweat off five pounds or more. I usually lost two or three pounds just in a regular skypool game. We couldn't risk dehydration. But water is heavy, and we couldn't take too much of it along with all the other stuff we had to carry.

Then we turned our attention to the tandem cycle itself. Cassie was far from convinced the ultrathin membranes of the wings wouldn't melt from the heat. I wasn't, either, but I pretended I was. There was nothing we could do about it, anyway.

And, finally, there was nothing to do but wait.

When we were done with our preparations, the sun was just about to go out, according to my watch. We intended to start off as soon as it had reached its full intensity in the morning, to be sure it was bright enough to conceal us in the dazzle.

Papa was already asleep at the table. He had simply drifted off and toppled over, as he often did when he was working on something. Cassie and I carried him to the bedroom and took off his shoes, put a blanket over him, and listened for a moment to his soft snoring.

Patrick bunked on the couch in the living room, and Cassie and I went to the bedroom. I was so tired I thought I'd be asleep instantly, but that was not the case.

"Cassie, you asleep?" I whispered.

"Yes," she whispered back.

"I thought so. Are we crazy to do this?"

"Yes."

"I think you're right."

Somehow, at some point, I drifted off.

———————

We made our way up the increasingly steep slope from the Timberline access door, getting lighter with every step. Toward the end, we were in skypool air, almost weightless. Games are never played near either of the poles, I don't really know why, so we were seeing something we had never seen up close before: the junction of the sun with the rock of the ship.

There wasn't really much to see. I had always imagined some sort of huge socket, like a fluorescent light tube. Guide the ends into the socket and twist it.

I suddenly wondered what would happen if this monster bulb ever burned out. I was sure the engineers had planned for that, would have some way to repair it, but I had no idea what it was.

There was no socket, though. The tube just entered a big hole in the rock, with a gap just about wide enough to put your fist in. It needed that space because when it got hot, it expanded a little in girth. It expanded a *lot* in length, over its six-mile length, so that was allowed for somewhere beneath the rock where it was plugged in. Right then, cold, it was as short as it would ever get.

I couldn't resist touching it. At the same time, I was a little spooked by it. It felt a little like a clay pot. Some sort of ceramic.

We had tried to calculate where we were going to fly. It wasn't easy. The specs mentioned a distance of a hundred yards as the point where it would surely kill you from heat prostration. Any closer than that, and you would eventually get hot enough to ignite, burn to a crisp. But what was the inner limit of being able to function and make a six-mile trip?

We found a figure for how much heat an unprotected human could stand over a period of an hour or so. We found another figure for how much heat the sun put out, per square yard, at various distances. It was enough that, on the surface, you could feel uncomfortable after an hour, but sunstroke would never be a problem.

"We've spent half an hour in a sauna," Cassie pointed out. "We were probably hotter in there than we'll be here."

"But we weren't working in the sauna."

"There you go again, spoilsport." We seemed to have shifted roles again, back to my normal negativity and her sunny disposition.

Papa could have done the calculation in his head in about a second, but we couldn't ask him to without revealing our plan, which he would forbid. So we struggled with it. Or rather, Cassie did, as I really suck at math. Patrick helped out, and we finally settled on a figure and put it into our positioning apps. It seemed way too close, to me.

But we paced it out with ten minutes left until sun-on. It still seemed far too close, but that was the whole idea. We opened the cycle and did one last check. I found a loose connection and tightened it up to specs. Cassie watched me until I straightened out, and I gave her a thumbs-up.

"No parachutes," she pointed out.

"Then we just have to do it right all the way."

"I'd kick the tires," she said, "but I'm afraid it would fall apart. I wonder where that expression came from? Kick the tires?"

"I have no idea and couldn't care less. You want to match for the front seat?"

"Two out of three."

She covered my rock with paper, I smashed her scissors with my rock. Then she cut my paper. Damn the bitch. How does she always do that?

MILE ONE

It started out well enough. The sun warmed up for about a minute, flickering a little, and then blasted us with heat. I hastily lowered my dark glasses, slipped my feet into the stirrups. I assumed the position, almost prone, and started pedaling. Behind me the prop began to whirl and chatter as it cut through the air. We pulled away from the solid rock of the pole and were airborne. Cassie had the altitude control, being in the front.

"Going up a little," she said. "About twenty feet gets us where we planned to be. Feeling hot?"

"Actually, not too bad at the moment."

"It'll get hotter."

It did, but not a lot. I began to feel a little better. Maybe our main problem would be having enough strength to power our way through, and not the heat itself. I felt refreshed from a night's sleep and a good breakfast. I felt strong. Six miles? Do it standing on my head.

MILE TWO

I was getting tired already of staring at Cassie's ass. Other than my recent trip with Patrick back in steerage, it had been a long time since I'd been on a tandem cycle, all the way back to my learning days, when I was in front, and my teaching and student-coaching days, when I was in back. The joy of cycling is in the freedom, the flexibility, of swooping through the air like a bird . . . well, not quite, but a lot more agile than any aircraft. Of course, that was the least of my worries. It's just that it was better to think about what was annoying me than about what was torturing me. Which was the heat.

It was pounding right through the back of my helmet. It was sitting on my back like a ton of hot bricks. It was raking along the backs of my legs, on my shoulders, my arms. And we weren't even a third of the way there.

"How are you doing?" Cassie called back.

"Just fine," I said.

"Me, too. Piece of cake."

MILE THREE

You think it can't get any worse, and then it gets worse. And worse again.

I was pretty sure the heat wouldn't kill me, but I had begun to wish it would. This wasn't an all-enveloping heat, like in a sauna. It was all coming from one side, the back, and maybe the contrast had something to do with the pain I was feeling. Being on a rotisserie would have been better. At least one side would have a little time to cool off from the air flowing over us. I felt like I was on a barbecue grill, and it was about time to turn me over because I was sure done on the one side.

We were over Grand Fenwick, crossing the border with Lake Wobegon. Something was wrong down there. I saw three places where thin columns of smoke were rising, all of them from the middle of villages. From almost a mile up, people were antlike, but I could still make them out, and I didn't like what I saw there, either. I could see groups hurrying around or assembled in one place.

"Looks like the rebellion has finally reached the level of the common people," Cassie said.

"I wonder what they know."

"I'm not getting anything now. Are you?"

I tried a few phone calls and got nothing. Ditto connecting to any information source. For a moment, I got a staticky picture of a newsreader sitting at her desk and mouthing something, with no sound, but that soon broke up, too. The only things I was getting on my visual display were internal programs like time and orientation. Which was depressing, as we weren't even halfway there yet. I wished I had had the temperature sensor installed when I got my most recent phone . . . and then I was glad I hadn't. I didn't want to know.

MILE FOUR

I turned to the side and threw up. That breakfast had been a mistake.

"That's going to be a nice surprise for someone on the ground," Cassie said.

"Shut the heck up."

"You'd better take on some water."

We had both been drinking. My primary water bottle was about two-thirds empty now. I only had one spare.

I got the bottle and put my lips around it and sucked in a mouthful. It had had ice in it when we started, but now it was tepid. I had another mouthful, and then squeezed a little into my hand. My face was covered in sweat already, but it was hot sweat. And in the near-weightless zone we were in, it didn't drip. Water didn't flow here, it beaded in the air. I splashed my handful of water on my face and rubbed it around. It cooled me slightly.

My whole body was bathed in sweat. My thirst was almost overpowering, but I forced myself to clip the water bottle back to the cycle frame.

"We're over halfway there, Poll," Cassie said. "How are your legs holding out?"

"Not too bad," I managed to say. In truth, that hadn't been a problem until the last few minutes, when I had started to feel tired, then nauseous.

"It's a hell of a workout," she said. "I'll tell you, I'll admit it, I'm more tired than I ever remember being."

"Me, too. But we'll make it."

"Sure we will."

MILE FIVE

I really, really didn't want to be the first. We have been competitive all our lives, trying to make hard things look easy, not acknowledging pain or weariness. But I had to give in. I thought I might be dying, and I didn't want to die in fire.

"Cassie, can we maybe go down a little? Just a little bit?"

She didn't say anything for a while, and I felt my face burning with shame, on top of all the other burns. My body was a mass of pain. The heat had cranked up to a point that I was seriously thinking we might both die from this. My first water bottle was empty and there wasn't a lot left in the second one. Drinking it was like pouring it down the drain. As soon as it went down my throat—almost too hot to drink, but welcome all the same— an equal amount squirted out my pores. It must be sloshing around in my clothes, but I was too hot to feel it. I was roasted, parboiled, fried, and baked. I thought my hair might catch fire right through my helmet, which was too hot to touch. I wanted to wrench it off, it was like wearing an oven, but I knew that if I did, my brains would be sizzling even more than they were already.

My whole body was wearing out. It took a conscious effort to keep my legs moving, and each stroke was harder than the last. My hands were numb from gripping the handlebars, my lungs burned with every breath. The muscles of my abdomen felt like I had been punched in the stomach over and over, and my back had been worked over with a baseball bat. Everything hurt from my toes to my nose. I wasn't even sure my mind was working well. A couple of times, I thought I almost drifted off into unconsciousness.

When Cassie did reply, I realized the delay had been because she was trying to gather the strength to talk.

"I've never wanted anything so much in my life," she said. "But can we go on just a little longer before we do that? I'd hate to come all this way for nothing. Just get bagged up like a couple of roast turkeys because somebody saw us before we got there."

"How much longer?"

"I don't know. I'm not seeing very clearly. Things have been swimming around in my vision. How about you?"

"My vision is still okay. It's about the only thing that's okay. My legs are about to give out on me."

"Me, too. You want to alternate? One minute on, and one minute off?"

I desperately wanted that, one of us pushing and one freewheeling. I thought I might be able to catch my breath, get a second wind, *something*. But I also knew that if we did that, we would be longer in the oven.

"I guess I'd rather get there sooner."

"You're right. You're right. You have any water left?"

"Just a little."

"I dropped my bottle. Just slipped out of my hand. It was half-full."

"I'd share if I could get mine to you." There was no way my hand could meet hers, I was too far behind her.

"I know you would. Well, maybe I can lick some off my arm, or wipe some from my face and into my mouth."

Not likely, but I didn't say anything.

"Mile six," I said, "When we start into that last mile, maybe we can fall a little lower then. We wouldn't be exposed for so long."

"Sounds like a plan."

My last plan had put us up here in the heat. I hoped this one would work out a little better.

MILE SIX

I felt the increased resistance in the pedals as the cycle started to roll to the right. It was a very slow roll, but up to that point we had been perfectly level with respect to the sun, and now I started to feel blazing heat on my left side, which hadn't been in intense light before.

For a moment I thought I was hallucinating. I hadn't noticed what was right in front of me, which was Cassie laid out prone over the handlebars. I hadn't even noticed the increased resistance of the pedals, as she began freewheeling. The only thing holding her feet to the pedals were the clips.

"Hey!" I shouted. "Hey, wake up, Cassie."

Nothing happened. I shouted again, and exerted what limited control I had from the backseat on the attitude controls, trying to stop the roll. I think I slowed it a little, but I couldn't be sure. We had rotated almost forty-five degrees by then.

I shook the handlebars, and the skeletal frame of the bike lurched up and down. I didn't like the creaking sounds the wings were making.

Nothing seemed to rouse her. Even worse, she seemed to have frozen, with her hand pulling one of the stabilizing levers. We were rising. Slowly, but definitely rising. At this point, I didn't think we could possibly survive getting any closer to the sun.

"Wings gonna melt, wings gonna melt." I found myself chanting that with a tongue that would hardly move through lips cracked and peeling. I tried to work up spit, and nothing came. And we continued to rise, and turn. The blazing light fell on my left ear for the first time, and I actually cried out.

I needed a drink. I needed to think. I needed a drink to think or we were gonna sink. I thought that was funny. I reached for the water bottle. I shook it. It was empty. That was the saddest thing I'd ever heard of, an empty water bottle. I cried. I sobbed aloud, but no tears came. I'd never have enough water to make tears again. Then I got angry.

"Damn you, Cassie! Wake up!"

Asleep at the wheel. I'd never have gone to sleep at the wheel. I'd never have passed out, gone into a coma . . . died? Could she be dead?

"You can't die on me, you bitch!" I threw the water bottle at her and it clanked off her helmet.

She jerked like a fish on a hook, shook her head, looked around.

"What? What? I'm not asleep, Coach."

"Coach my sunburned ass, damn you! This is your sister, dummy, and you almost fell off."

"No, I didn't. I was awake."

"Then why are we drifting? Why aren't you pedaling?"

"I was just resting for a minute. Sorry. Sorry. I . . . Where are we?"

"About a quarter mile away."

"I can't see much, Polly. My eyes have been swelling shut. Do you have any water? I'm real thirsty."

"That was my last empty water bottle that woke you up. What do you mean, you can't see?"

"It's not all black, but it's all blurry. Something must have got in my eyes."

I couldn't imagine what that might be. Sweat? Could sweat blind you? I was sweating, too, and I could still see well enough.

"We need to roll to the left," I said.

"Right." And we began to roll even more to the right.

"Other left, dummy."

"Oh, right. Polly, I can't remember which side is left."

Oh, man. She was more delirious than I was.

"The side that's getting hotter, that's your left."

"I feel just as hot all over. *Polly, I'm burning alive!*"

I was crying again, great tearless sobs. Every breath burned down my throat and all the way into my lungs.

"We're almost there. Think of signing your name. Holding a pen in your hand. That's your right. Roll the *other way*."

"Oh, right. No, I mean left."

We finally started to roll the right way. But that was causing the whole cycle frame to creak and groan in protest. I realized the damn thing was on its last legs. Or wings, or something. I was the one on my last legs.

"Where are we going to land this thing?"

I couldn't remember. It was a small village. There was nothing else up there at the poles. Were we going to the North Pole or the South Pole? Let's go to the west pole! Anything to get out of this red hot pole.

"Just keep going straight. I'll know it when I see it." Would I? Did it matter? I tried to remember why we were doing this.

"What? What?" That sounded like my sister. Or else it was me, because we were the only ones up here. The only ones stupid enough to be up here, going somewhere. I started sobbing again. I didn't want to go there. I didn't want to be here. I wanted a bath and a drink of something and a bed with cool sheets. Why did everything hurt?

Did I smell smoke coming from my hair? My hair was on fire! It was on fire, and something was sitting on my head. It was a helmet. I was going to yank it off, but my arms wouldn't move for some reason. My hands were glued to the handlebars. I had to let go, I had to let go. I tried opening my hands, and the fingers moved slowly. A little at a time, slowly, slowly, they opened. And then I didn't know what to do with them.

"Are we on course?"

Course for what? Of course we were on course. A course is a course, of course, unless it's coarse. I laughed, and started to share that with Cassie. Then I noticed we were almost upside down. That is, the sun was coming from . . . where? I couldn't remember, but it was in my eyes.

"It feels like . . . we're falling?" she said.

"Can't fall in free fall. We're too tall, that's all." I laughed again.

"I can see a little, damn you. But I can't tell how close we are."

"Just keep pedaling," I said. "It's under control. Goal. We have a goal. It's the goal pole. There's the eight ball!"

"Polly, you sound drunk."

"Skunk drunk, punk!" I laughed again. Oh, I was on a roll. Goal. Goal pole . . . we were going somewhere. We had a goal. The goal was the pole. Somebody was there at the pole. Mama?

"Mama," I sobbed. "Mama, where are you? I want my mama."

"She's up ahead," Cassie shouted. "But how far ahead?"

For the first time in a while, I lifted my head. I was surprised to realize that my hair was not on fire. But my hands weren't on the handlebars, either. And ahead was . . .

Some shred of sanity came back to me, and for a lucid moment the view in front of me crystallized. We were close, mighty close, too close.

"*Reverse, reverse!*" I shouted, and groped for the gearshift. I realized I didn't have one. Cassie had it, that bitch. Why didn't I have one?

I heard an unpleasant grinding sound, the pop of a strut coming loose from its mount. Above me, one of the wings was crumpling. It was happening in slow motion, and it was beautiful. The material is so thin that it makes swirly rainbows, like oil on water. The central strut snapped, and just like that, we were tumbling head over heels, held together only by the wiry tangles of the remains of the skycycle.

I don't know how fast we were going. It had to be a lot slower than when we started out. But it was fast enough that, when the impact came, it knocked the breath out of me. I didn't have any breath to spare. I was woozily aware that I was lying on my back in the direct sunlight.

Have to get out of the sun. Have to get into the shade somehow. We'll burn up. My hair is on fire. My legs are on fire.

That was my last thought as I plunged down into a welcoming blackness.

When I next opened my eyes, I was looking up into the face of my old enemy, Cheryl Chang.

I screamed.

CHAPTER 18

―――――――

Cassie:

I was as surprised as Polly was to see Chang.

We crashed . . . well, we weren't going all that fast, but the impact was a big jar for me because I hadn't been able to see where we were going. And the crash was enough to destroy the cycle, which had already been falling apart. I banged my head on something, and even protected by the helmet, I was a little dazed by it. I sprawled out there on a ledge of some kind, still far too close to the sun, and tried to get my breath back through a throat so parched it was like burning sandpaper. There was no saliva to swallow. I knew that if we didn't get down the slope and get some water soon, we might die. We were still far from out of the woods.

"We made it, Polly," I croaked. There was no response. I groped around through the tangle of wreckage, still all but blind. I could just see a little out of one eye, but nothing would focus.

"Hey, no more slacking off. We have to move. Where are you?"

Still no answer. I began to get real worried. Finally, I felt what seemed to be a boot and worked my way up her leg and body until I had her face. I slapped her a few times. I felt around her neck, not sure exactly where to look, but I soon found a pulse. It seemed steady and regular to me. I felt a huge relief that she was alive. But we had to get down.

At this altitude, of course, "down" was not a concept that made itself immediately obvious. I couldn't orient myself visually. So I held still for a moment and slowly sank in the right direction. I felt it on my butt, so I was sitting in an "upright" position. Polly was off to my right. I got my arms around her and moved us both in the direction I was pretty sure was parallel to the sun. As soon as we were floating in the air, it was just about impossible for me to know which way I was going. I held still, and in a moment I felt a slight pressure on my shoulder. I had twisted in the air. But that was okay. I pointed my head down, and let the gradually increasing gravity pull me in the direction we had to go.

We bounced several times. I figured we would soon be in the regions where people lived, and that could be dangerous, but I couldn't think of what else to do. We didn't dare go all the way to the bottom, but there was no possibility of lingering near the sun until night came. I was going to have to trust to luck, hope that we would not come crashing down into one of the pole villages and into the hands of our enemies. From there, I'd have to find a way to wake Polly up. Blind as I was, I wasn't going to be much use until I could find a way to get the swelling down around my eyes.

What the hell had caused that? I wondered. Polly hadn't gone blind. Aunt Elizabeth could probably explain it.

Before long, we were falling faster than I wanted to, so I turned us around and put my back to the surface. I was able to slow our fall with my hands, boots, and butt against it. Finally, my feet hit what felt like a pathway, and I tumbled forward into some bushes. It was much, much cooler but still too damn hot.

"Goddam you, Polly," I said to her. "Wake up! I can't do this alone."

"What the hell happened here?" It wasn't Polly. I looked all around, feeling panicked, expecting to be handcuffed and trotted off to prison. But no one touched me. By squinting, I could make out a figure standing over us. That's all I could tell for sure.

"We need some water," I choked out.

"Where the hell did you come from?" The voice was a girl's voice. "I saw you way up there, just before you crashed. Why did you idiots fly so close to the sun? Don't you know that can kill you?"

"Water. Please."

She opened my face shield. I heard a gurgling sound, and saw a tubular shape floating in front of my eyes. Some water splashed on my face and I gasped. It was cool! It was cold! My savior held the water bottle to my lips and poured. My mouth flooded with cold water, and I gulped it.

"Easy, I don't think you should drink it all. That other girl needs some, too. What's wrong with her?"

"Passed out. Please, give her some." She did, I could hear it. "Is she drinking?"

"Well, her throat's working . . . Ohmigod! You!"

"What? Who are you?"

"Which one are you, anyway? Your face looks like you've been worked over by an expert boxer."

"I'm Cassie Broussard."

"I knew you're one of the twins. I'm Cheryl Chang."

"Ohmigod!"

I didn't know at first if she was going to help me or kick my ass all the way back to the South Pole. But it never became an issue. Generally, skypoolers are friendly out of the playing sphere, but I had always thought of Cheryl as an exception. She was so intimidating, so mean, and so focused on doing damage that it was hard not to take it personally. And, specifically, I thought she had a grudge against me and Polly. We had been offensive stars, and she was pure defense; that is, if defense can be viewed as an aggressive act, and the way she played, it sure could. She wasn't a skilled rider, and seldom scored, but she was powerful on the pedals and could display real stealth in sneaking up on your blind side and letting you have it. Add to that the fact that she was big, not fat, outweighing most of us by 50 percent or more. She had to have a specially strengthened cycle, or she would have torn it apart just by pedaling.

Skypool is not a contact sport. Yeah, right, and neither is basketball, but watch that scrum under the net sometime. No blood, no foul.

But I had never met her socially. I had heard her screaming abuse at our team, and I'd shouted right back. But when she spoke now, it was softly, almost timidly.

"We've got to get you some help." She picked Polly up like she weighed nothing—well, she was light up here, but we were still big girls—and took my hand and led me, stumbling, down a path I could barely see.

Cheryl took us to her home in Hilltown. I couldn't see it at the time, but when the swelling around my eyes went down, I thought it was a neat and tidy dwelling though a bit small. She lived there with her mother and father, who were both at work, and a younger brother, Woody, about twelve and as large as his sister. She immediately sent Woody off to fetch a neighbor who was a nurse, or EMT, or something like that. Meantime, she stretched Polly out on a couch and got cool water and some washcloths.

She came to all at once, took one look at Cheryl, and screamed. Well, it must have been a rude awakening, to be looking up into the face of the girl who, last time she saw her, wrecked her cycle and sent her tumbling to the ground. But I got her calmed down, telling her Cheryl was on our side.

I hoped.

I still hadn't explained the situation to her and was saved having to do that for a little bit by the arrival of the nurse. He examined Polly first—temperature, blood pressure, vital signs—and pronounced her exhausted, dehydrated, but otherwise not in too bad shape. He told her to keep taking sips of the cold water, not to gulp it. Then he turned to me and took my vital signs and peered into my eyes.

"Looks like an allergic reaction to the sunblock on your face," he said.

"That doesn't make sense. Why didn't Polly get it? We're twins."

"I suspect she didn't get any in her eyes."

He gave me a pill, and in a surprisingly short time, the swelling went down almost to normal. I could tell that he was full of questions, but I caught Cheryl shaking her head at him. He shrugged and apparently decided to stick to medical confidentiality.

"So." Big Cheryl, the Punisher, looked me in the eye, and was clearly not happy. "You think it's about time you tell me what's happening?"

I figured that in the next few minutes she would either kick us out of her house and tell us to get lost, best case, or turn us over to the mutineers, worst case. And there was precious little I could do about it, short of shooting her. And even that option was unlikely, as I realized that sometime during the chaotic trip to her house, our backpacks with all our lethal equipment had been left behind, and I didn't even know where to look for them.

"Okay," I said, cautiously. "First off, did you know that there's a mutiny under way, right here in the ship?"

———————

We told our story, beginning to end, as quickly as we could. I was very aware that time was passing, and we had no idea what the condition of the prisoners was. When my throat became too raw to go on, Polly took over, and we passed the story back and forth between blessed swallows of water, then hot coffee. I had thought I'd never want a hot drink again, but it was amazing how much the bitter black brew perked me up.

Cheryl listened without comment. At one point she sent Woody into the kitchen and he came back with BLT sandwiches, which we fell on like a couple of starving monkeys. Cheryl chewed hers more thoughtfully. Woody was sitting cross-legged on the floor, staring wide-eyed at us.

We came to the part about the flycycle trip and the reasons we had no other good options, and she sat up straighter. I got the feeling that Cheryl wasn't the sharpest knife in the block, and probably wasn't good at much but skypool, but she was very good at that. She understood flycycling and knew just how difficult and dangerous our trip had been.

Then we stopped. And waited.

"How long did it take you?" she asked. "Pole to pole?"

I really hadn't known, but my trip meter had been quietly keeping all the stats, and I took a look at it. A little less than one hour.

"Six miles per hour," she said, and whistled. "And on a piece of junk like that. That's pretty good, considering you were cooking all the way."

Hell, even I was impressed, now that I thought about it.

"Okay," she said, getting to her feet. "I'm with you. There are some things I need to do. It'll take a while, and I figure you two need to rest up for a little bit, get your strength back. Then you can tell me your plan."

"Just like that?" Polly said.

"Just like that. Oh, I know, you guys don't like me, but I got nothing against you. I'm the Punisher because I'm so big. It's what Coach tells me to do. But I'm not bad. Not really. Ask Woody."

"Well . . ." Woody started. She laughed and aimed a kick at him, but he was too agile.

"Come on, my room's upstairs. I'll get you bedded down."

She insisted on taking all our clothes, which were still sopping with sweat. She gave us nightgowns, and told us to sack out. Her bed was a double.

I wasn't sure I trusted her completely, and I felt vulnerable without my combat outfit and gear, but I didn't know what else to do. If she wanted to turn us in, she could have held us down with one hand while Woody went for the authorities.

"She would have tried for the backpacks if she was pulling something cute, wouldn't she?" Polly asked me, showing she was having the same thoughts I was. "Unless she's way more stupid than I take her for."

"I don't think there's anything stupid about her. Not swift, maybe, but smart where it counts."

"Me, too. Still, it wasn't all that long ago she nearly killed me." She was unconsciously rubbing her butt where the broken spar had gone in, and where she would have a dime-sized scar for the rest of her life. You want to tell us apart? Ask us to turn around and drop our knickers.

"You know what?" I said. "If she's fooling with us, there's not a damn thing I can think of we could do about it. So how about let's stack some Zs."

"Sounds good to me."

Stress is one of those things that can keep you awake, and we had plenty of that. But exhaustion is the best sleeping powder I know of. I had thought it might take a while, but I was asleep within a minute, and the last sound I heard was Polly's soft snoring.

There was a loud party going on downstairs. I thought about going down there and telling them to keep it quiet, for goodness' sake, didn't they know we were in trouble, didn't they know people were looking for us? I knew all that to be true, but for a while I couldn't seem to remember just why people were after us.

And I didn't want to deal with it. I was so tired. I rolled over and pulled a pillow over my head, but it didn't do any good. Then somebody started poking me roughly. I opened my eyes, and saw it was Polly. She was half-dressed in her black battle outfit, and it all come rushing back to me.

"Get your ass out of bed," she whispered. "I don't know what's going on downstairs, but it's got me worried."

I saw my own clothes carefully laid out on a wooden chair, not only cleaned, but starched and pressed. What the well-dressed freedom fighter was wearing today. Our weapons-filled backpacks were there, too. I yawned, stretched, then hit the floor and hurried into Cheryl's bathroom and relieved myself of a lot of the water I had guzzled a few hours before.

As I dressed, I took stock of my body to see just how bad off I was, and it was nowhere near as bad as I feared. My face was still a little swollen, and my hands hurt from gripping the handlebars. There was a pain in my back when I turned a certain way, but nothing I couldn't tolerate.

When we were dressed, with helmets and backpacks and boots and all, we looked at each other and silently decided to each put a pistol in a belt holster, but not to carry one in our hands. If the ruckus downstairs was trouble, we could get to them in seconds.

What we encountered downstairs was basically the Hilltown Hillbillies girls' skypool team, with a few additions.

I almost didn't recognize them without their helmets and uniforms. You don't spend a lot of game time looking at faces; it's arms and legs and wings you watch. But then I recognized Mazzie Niven, and Violet Silversteen and Suki Kurosawa, and the other faces fell into place. But I didn't spend a lot of time looking at them, because I was astonished to see some of my own teammates. There was Pippa Mendez and Jynx Molloy and PJ

Leaping Deer. And there was Milton Kaslov from the boys' team. There were a few other boys. I didn't recognize any of them. Either the boys' team of the Hillbillies or boyfriends of the girls, I figured.

Most exciting of all was Coach Peggy, dwarfed by most of the other players, smiling up at us. I was so moved I could hardly speak at first.

"We've got a call out for the rest of the team," Coach Peggy told us.

"Communications are completely gone now," Cheryl said. "No phone service, no news."

"It's all word of mouth," Coach confirmed. "Things are pretty chaotic down there. There's been fighting. Fires have broken out, and the firefighters have had trouble getting to them. They can't coordinate."

"Yeah, but who's fighting who?" Polly asked.

"It's kind of a free-for-all," PJ said. "Some of them look like cops, but there's some of them on both sides."

"There were rumors of a mutiny." That was Milton. "And now you say that's what's happening."

"That your parents and the captain are prisoners," someone said. "That's what Cheryl told us, anyway."

"We'd like to hear what happened," Coach said.

I looked out over the group. I noticed now that most of them were armed with something. There were axes and hand hatchets, and a lot of knives in sheaths. I saw a baseball bat, and a couple of other club-type things. One girl carried a deadly-looking field javelin. There were no firearms, of course. Now I wished we could have brought more from Sheila's arsenal. But would they know how to use them or be more dangerous to themselves and the rest of us if we had more?

It was a motley army, but it was all we had. I liked our chances in a more or less even match on open ground. Our guns would make a big difference even if we were outnumbered. But if we ended up fighting in the corridors, it could get messy.

I sighed. No matter what, having all these people with us would be a lot better than what I had been envisioning, which was me and Polly going up against the guards all by ourselves.

"Pour us some of that coffee I smell brewing," I said, "and we'll tell you what we know."

———————

All we needed was a campfire. The girls huddled around us on the floor as we sat and told our stories one more time. You get better at anything with practice, so it didn't take as long this time. When we were done, no one spoke for a while. Then someone piped up.

"So what's the cause of all the confusion? Nobody seems to know what's going on. Nobody's announced anything."

"I have some ideas," Coach Peggy said. Everyone turned to her eagerly, as the only adult in the room. She stood up.

"It seems to me that if this was going well for them, they would be talking to people, reassuring them that everything's going to be all right. But the exact opposite has happened. No information is coming out. All the regular sources of information are shut down. Which means, to me, that their war in cyberspace is not going well for them. Cassie, Polly, you said that Captain Broussard expects the systems in place to fight back."

"Count on it," Polly said. "Travis is the world's greatest paranoid. He wouldn't make it easy for someone to get control of the ship's systems."

Coach said, "I can't imagine what might be going on in those machines. But if it's gone on this long, and the issue is still in doubt, that must be demoralizing."

"I can't imagine it, either," I chipped in. "But I figure that Max Karpinski didn't count on things being this hard. He must have thought he could take over quickly, but so far, it doesn't look like he has."

"He's a mathematician, right?" Suki asked. "Numbers are nice and neat. You'd think computers would be nice and neat, too, but they're not."

Polly said, "I think he's out of his depth. He obviously thinks Papa was wrong in the calculations he did. I've never known Papa to be wrong about numbers."

"There's always a first time," someone said, from the back.

An uneasy murmur went through the crowd.

"Papa doesn't *want* to stop the ship or turn it around—"

"Nobody does." I saw the objecting person this time. It was one of the boys from Hilltown. I shifted in my seat to make my weapon handier.

"Whatever the answer to that question is," Cheryl said, raising her voice over the growing whispers, "stop the ship, don't stop the ship, we're in danger, we're not in danger . . . whatever. Taking over the ship by force is wrong. Just flat wrong."

To my great relief, the reaction to that was much stronger than the tentative disquiet over the dark lightning issue.

Polly spoke up.

"I can tell you one thing. The engines aren't going to stop, the ship is not going to be turned around, until there's been a full discussion and a vote. Travis will be open to hearing anyone, just as he has been so far in this thing. But if he's a prisoner, he can't do anything."

I did my best to show no reaction. Then I nodded with what I hoped was a show of great enthusiasm. But the plain fact was that she had no right to say that. If I was betting, I would say that Travis's reaction to massive opposition about his decisions would be the exact opposite. He would hunker down and exercise his rights as captain to do what he felt best for the ship, and popular opinion be damned.

But these people didn't need to hear that. When I realized that, I wondered if I might make a good politician someday. Or better yet, Polly. She seemed to have no qualms about telling a lie to these folks. Well, hell, neither did I, when it came right down to it. What made it easier was knowing that Papa was right. If we had to lie to do what we had to do to save everyone's life, then so be it.

There was a little more talk, but it looked like Polly and Cheryl, between them, had won over any doubters. What we needed next was to tell them our plan.

———

This was a bunch of girls—and a few boys, as several more stragglers from both teams arrived—who didn't shy from action. But, of course, they had never faced a situation where their lives might be in danger.

It didn't seem to make much difference. They say teenagers feel they are immortal, they can't imagine that any real harm could come to them. Maybe that's true for some, but I question it. For myself, I was quite aware that I was mortal.

The bottom line, everyone was raring to go.

A little more time was spent with Polly and me adapting our plan to the new circumstances of having more than just ourselves to rely on. Not exactly Alexandra the Great laying out marching orders for the army, you understand, but we knew we would have to react on the fly and understood that no battle plan survives first contact with the enemy. Then we explained it all to the irregular troops. Then flycycles were found for all, and we made our way back to a spot near where we had crash-landed our tandem.

———————

We took off like bats leaving a belfry. Or at least that's how I envisioned bats, though I've never seen any. *Big* bats.

It was the middle of the night, but lights were still burning all over the surface, and the air was thick enough with smoke that we couldn't see the South Pole. There were no huge conflagrations, but here and there we could see the small orange flares of structure fires.

We were in the air over Frostbite Falls. The largest fire I could see was in the center of town, and seemed to involve several buildings. Tiny figures were directing streams of water toward the fire. I could hear their shouts. I even thought I could feel the heat, though that might have been my imagination. They were far too busy down there to look up and see the bat squadron flying over, and we were high enough they were unlikely to see us anyway. But we would be visible to infrared cameras, to anyone who was watching for us. So we had resolved to make the trip as quickly as we could.

Starting up in the low-gee regions, we were able to build up some pretty good speed simply by losing altitude and letting the air around us accelerate us. That way we could save our strength for what was ahead.

I looked back, past Polly flying just off my left wing, and my heart leaped at the sight. Twenty-four of us, flying like geese in a V formation for the same reason geese did it, to profit from the draft. Every few minutes Polly would spell me in the lead. Behind us, flying almost wing tip to wing tip, were all our old friends and new friends. I didn't even know all their names, but I was so proud of them.

I knew Polly and I had to step up to this job, provide leadership, and that was bit of a burden. Before, when it was just me and the sibling, I hadn't felt so much pressure. I mean, my family was relying on us, and that was tough, but now there were all these other people. We had to keep them safe and healthy. I didn't know if we could do it.

We weren't in the air more than six or seven minutes. We swooped over Frostbite and angled into Dogpatch, where the entrance we were seeking was located. As we descended, our speed increased, and the cycles became harder to control. We were heavier, and powering a cycle at the lower altitudes took a lot more muscle than it did up at the gaming level near the nighttime sun. I was really straining as we neared the ground, but I felt I could handle it. I hoped everyone else could.

Then the ground was there, hard to see in the dark. It was a strawberry field, producing fruit as big as your fist. The rows were elevated to provide easier picking, and coincidentally to present a real landing hazard. But there had been nowhere else that looked better for landing.

Polly and I flared up as we reached about ten feet of altitude, to kill our speed, and stalled out. But the spread wings slowed our fall, and we both landed on our feet. We quickly started collapsing the cycles as the others landed in different places around us. Some landed with a *thump* I could hear. Even experienced fliers were not used to getting down to ground level.

In a few moments we had gathered and moved into the copse of pine trees where the subway station was. One girl I didn't know was limping. We quickly diagnosed a twisted ankle and told her she couldn't come with us. She was about thirteen years old, and bitterly disappointed. I couldn't help thinking she might be the luckiest of us all.

Polly and I had to cast around a bit to find the entrance. Our positioning system told us to within ten feet or so, but with all the pine needles and such underfoot, it wasn't as simple as it sounded. We all got on our hands and knees and brushed debris away until Jynx found a patch of concrete. In short order, we had it cleared and pulled up the hatch that covered it. Dim lights showed a narrow staircase leading into the depths.

We checked our weapons, and Polly and I led the troops down the steps. We were as quiet as we could be, but there's no way we could do it silently. As it turned out, there was no one down there at the subway station.

A lot of the girls were looking around, pretty impressed. They hadn't even known about the captain's private transportation system. Not that it was anything fancy. Just the long, long narrow tube, and the little subway car sitting there.

I noticed that one of the Hilltown girls was trembling. She looked sick, and wild-eyed.

"What's the problem, spacegirl?" I asked her.

"I . . . I can't stand small spaces. I feel like I can't breathe."

"Claustrophobia," I diagnosed, and she nodded. "Nothing shameful about that. Go on back up and tend to that other girl."

She nodded, glumly, and didn't waste any time going back up the stairs. Now our army numbered twenty-two, and we hadn't even seen the enemy. But it's best to get your wounded out of the area so you don't have to spend a lot of time tending to them.

Polly had already taken a place in the car and put her thumb to the ID plate. It should have accepted her as an authorized user, but when she looked at me, she shook her head. Either no power, or someone had reset the codes.

"Well, we couldn't have all fit in it, anyway," Cheryl said.

"No, but we could have sent six or seven high-speed scouts and maybe take them by surprise."

Polly was still fiddling with the car. I couldn't see what good that would do, but I watched her. She found a little lever and clicked it up and down. Nothing seemed to happen. Then I noticed that it had moved a little, edging away from a boy who was leaning against it.

"I think it might be the parking brake," I said.

Sure enough, when the lever was up, we could move the car. Which meant the power was still on in the rail, making the car float a half an inch over the ground. Polly got out and we shoved the thing back and forth. It moved slick as a hockey puck on ice. Polly and I talked it over with Cheryl and a few others, then turned to the troops.

"Here's the plan," I said. "We want two of you with the shields to sit up front. Polly and I will be right behind you with our guns. The rest will be on the ground. We'll need three or four of you to push, and get us up to trotting speed. We hope we can come at them fast and overwhelm them, wherever we find them. It's not a battle tank, but it will have to do."

Polly took over. "We don't know what kind of arms they might have. They've had time to build guns. What we do know they have is gas and stun guns. We don't have but the two masks, so if we encounter that, we'll give the signal and you all run like hell in the other direction. You won't do anyone any good if you're passed out.

"As for the stun guns, they have a long range. Up to about a hundred yards. They shoot small hooks that pierce your clothes and skin, and very fine wires that deliver the charge. They are fast, but not impossible to deflect. That's what we're hoping we can do with the shield girls up front. Deflect them, and hide behind the shields. If you all string out behind us, your chances of getting through will be a lot better."

She handed it over to me. "If you're hit, we will leave you behind. You'll feel a hell of a jolt, and you'll collapse and shake a lot. In ten or fifteen minutes you'll recover, and then you do whatever you want to do. Follow us, try to catch up, or go home. If Polly and I both get zapped . . . well, you're on your own. We would appreciate it if you could drag us back somewhere until we can recover, and we'll continue, alone or with whoever still wants to go. You're all volunteers, and we really love you for it. But if you're having second thoughts, this would be the place to turn back. We won't hold it against you."

I paused for a moment. No one turned back. I hadn't expected them to. Put like that, you'd feel like a coward to leave. That didn't mean they would stick with us when the stun guns started to bang, though.

So we started off, our motley little task force.

Mazzie and Suki of the Hillbilly team were in front with their shields.

Suki was the one who had found them. She broke into an empty police station while all the cops were busy elsewhere with other matters, either on our side or not. Who knew? But they had been in a long-unused storage locker that had been opened only hours before. One of the functions of police was crowd control, riot control. So far as I knew, there had never been a riot in the ship, but on a voyage this long, there was no telling what social tensions might evolve, so the man Travis had appointed as police chief twenty years ago had asked for them, and now they were being used.

But not all of them. The cops had left a few, and Suki had scooped them up. It was good thinking, and we had congratulated her on it. They were clear plexi with a slight curve, about three feet tall and two wide. Straps on the concave side held them to your arm. It was a simple design developed over many decades on Earth, where violent confrontations were common. When the girls sat in the front seats and held them up, the shields provided what we hoped would be protection against the stun guns. Bullets was another matter. They were described as "bullet-resistant," and I hoped that wasn't wishful thinking.

Two boys and a girl got behind the car and started pushing. Once it started rolling, there was almost no resistance. What there was, was the one-twentieth gee from the engines, which made the tunnel appear to be uphill, when it was really parallel to the inner surface and a few hundred yards beneath it. But even with that, one boy could keep it going easily. Everyone else strung out behind us.

We went down the tunnel at a trot. Well, everybody but me and Polly and Suki and Mazzie did, anyway. I got a free ride. I wished it was on the roller coaster in Fantasyland instead of where we were.

Not all the overhead lights were working. Some were flickering. We figured it was just more of the screwed-up systems from the fighting going on in the computers.

We were watching the positioning system, and when we got a quarter mile from the last station, we slowed down and advanced as quietly as we could. Flashlights were off, there was no talking. Suddenly, there were bright lights in our eyes, and two big explosions. I was deafened for a moment.

"Mask on!" Polly shouted to me. "Everybody, fall back!"

"I'm staying," Suki shouted, and Mazzie chimed in that she was, too. Smoke approached us, then enveloped us. I saw the two girls trying to hold their breath, and finally inhaling. They looked at each other. They were coughing a bit, but not collapsing.

"Flashbangs," I said. "Everybody, cover your ears!"

We were all wearing our skypool helmets, which had holes over the ears and padding inside that pressed in a circle around the ears. Polly and I had stuffed cloths in the ear holes. We hoped we could still hear each other but that the cloth would deaden any shock waves. Still, my ears were ringing, and it was hard to hear anything softer than a shout. However, in a situation like that, *everyone* is shouting, and it's hard to hear anything at all.

There were two more explosions, much smaller, and two bolts of electricity came sizzling out of the smoke. Well, no, that wasn't the sequence. Two small projectiles caromed off the shields in front of us, *then* the lightning bolts hit. What was happening was a visual effect of those stun rifles. They trailed very fine, almost monofilament wires behind them, and when they hit something, the charge came down the line and burned the wires up, shooting fire like holiday sparklers. It was dazzling.

"Anybody hit?" Polly shouted. I couldn't tell what the answer was, but it didn't look to me like the charges had hit anyone. Suki and Mazzie were still holding up the shields, looking frightened.

"Fuck this," I said. "They want to play rough? Let's give it right back to them." I dug in my pack and got out a grenade. Polly watched me as I set the timer to ten seconds and held my thumb on the release.

"That will tear them up," she said.

"Right now, I don't really care." I ducked as two more shots were fired at us, followed very closely by two more projectiles, and two more sizzling sets of wires. "But I don't think so. We're at the far range of those stun guns, and I can't throw a grenade more than half that distance."

"Okay. But it might roll back at us."

She was talking about the twentieth gee, and she was right. It would be slow, but still . . .

I reset the timer for five seconds, and saw Polly doing the same.

"Get down and cover your ears!" I called to the ones in back of us.

We threw as hard as we could, then all four of us hunkered down in the car and I counted.

The explosions were almost simultaneous, and much louder than the flashbangs they had fired at us. I could feel the pressure all over my body. Damn. Using grenades in a tunnel was maybe not such a good idea. But we only had one alternative, and that one was lethal.

I took my hands away from the ear holes and thought I heard a scream. Impossible to be sure what it was.

Well, they started it.

"I think we need to get moving," Polly said.

"Right. Right." I was still a little stunned from the explosions. Suki looked that way, too, but Mazzie was raring to go.

"Let's move!" I called to the troops in back, and at once two determined-looking girls and one boy ran up and started to push. Polly and I stood up and braced ourselves, pistols in hand, aiming forward.

It seemed the fans were still working. In fact, they were working overtime, loud enough to hear them. If things were working right—and there was no way of telling   somewhere a fire alarm would be going off, alerting the fire brigades who were, most likely, too busy with other fires to bother about this unknown subway.

But the smoke was clearing rapidly. There was no need for stealth now, and behind us two girls were aiming flashlights ahead of us. And behind us a strange sound began to build. It was a combination of the warbling war cry of my team, the Gators, borrowed from celebrating Arab women, and the harsh *"Hua! Hua! Hua!"* of the Hillbillies, borrowed from the United States Marines.

Almost at once, we came on a body, dressed in black and wearing body armor and a black helmet. It was a man, lying on his back. His face was a bloody mess, blood streaming from his forehead. It looked like one of his legs might be broken, from the way his foot lay twisted too far. I fought an urge to throw up.

But he was moving, feebly, like a turtle on its back. Trying to raise his head. We slowed as we neared him, and I kept my pistol pointed at him.

"Medic," I called back. Coach Peggy had turned out to be a conscientious objector, some religious thing. But she had wanted to go along to treat any injuries. She hurried to the front.

"Check him and see if he's bleeding bad," I said. "Someone, tie his hands behind his back. Someone take that stun rifle and move up to the front with us." All that was done quickly, and we headed forward again.

We passed two other people lying on the floor. The first was another man, unconscious, but not looking too badly injured. We paused while someone tied his hands behind him. The second was a woman sitting with her back to the wall. She was dressed like the others, in riot gear. She had shoved her stun rifle away from herself with her foot, and held one hand high in the air. Her other hand was trying to staunch the bleeding from a piece of shrapnel in her left leg. She looked terrified.

"Please don't kill me," she pleaded. "I have a three-year-old son."

"You shouldn't have shot at us," Cheryl said, picking up the rifle.

I looked at Polly. "What do you think? Should we question her? We might learn something."

"I think we ought to press on. I feel like we'd lose our momentum if we hung around here too long. Plus, I feel so damned exposed here in this tunnel. It channels anything they fire right at us."

Just at that moment, there were two more of the bangs we now knew were stun rifles firing. I didn't even have time to shout for everyone to take cover, and sadly, the troops had bunched up around the car to see the injured woman.

One round ricocheted off one of the shields ahead, hit the ceiling over my head, and then bounced back down into the crowd. Two girls fell down and started jerking. I guess the charge hit one and passed to the other by contact. I didn't see where the second round went for a minute, then realized it had hit the injured woman. She was jerking, too.

I saw red. I mean, I literally saw a red haze in front of my eyes. I pushed the shields aside and fired three bursts of three shots directly down the tunnel. I could hear them clattering back and forth from wall to wall, a weird sort of siren wail as the slugs tumbled and shattered.

Polly fired a single group of three, and pulled at my hand. I had meant to keep squeezing the trigger, but I calmed down.

"You," I said, pointing to one of the younger girls, "see if you can stop the bleeding on that woman. And tie her up. And if she comes to, see what you can learn about what's ahead of us."

"I want to go with you all," she said. I knew I had no way to force her to do anything, no real authority except what Polly and I had seized, and that could stop at any time.

"Look," Polly told her. "We really need to know what she knows. Try to wake her up. And please, stay with these girls who got stunned."

One of those girls was sitting up, looking a little dazed but game to go on. She must not have experienced the full charge.

That all got sorted out quickly. Our blood was up, all of us, and we hurried down the last yards of the tunnel.

———————

It didn't take long to pass the first body.

It was another man, and there was no point taking a closer look at him. The bullet, or fragment, had hit him in the neck, and he had bled out. It had done a lot of damage. I looked away, then forced myself to look back. Then I looked at Polly. She was pale. At that moment, I was very glad that she had fired, too. We would never know who had fired the fatal bullet. I looked down at the gun, which had suddenly grown to look very ugly.

I looked back and saw that the troops had bunched up again, getting closer to see what had happened.

"Spread out!" I yelled, louder than I needed to. "They can still fire at us, dammit." I paused to get myself under control as they obediently moved into a ragged double line behind us.

"Here's another chance for all of y'all to turn back," Polly said. "Take a look at this guy as we pass him. Take a good look. This isn't a game. This is a real mutiny, and if we lose, you could all be in big trouble. Think about it, please. Cassie and I did the shooting; we'll take the fall if it comes to that. This might be your last chance."

I signaled to the pushers, and we started up again. I looked back. Two girls and a boy had remained just short of the body. One of the girls turned back and started running. I didn't know her name. The other two walked past the body and followed us.

We didn't pick up the man's stun rifle though we could have used it. It felt too much like robbery, and not the spoils of war.

———————

There was another body, a man, and a third person, also male, badly wounded. Coach Peggy had caught up with us. We paused only a moment to see her begin work to stop the bleeding, which was from the thigh. It wasn't spurting; she gave us the thumbs-up, which I took to mean she thought he would be all right. We didn't talk about the second dead man.

The station, when we arrived there, was chaotic. Nothing was moving, there were no dead bodies, but there was a lot of equipment and some blood. Some of it was the remains of medical supplies, sterile gauze packs ripped open, a few empty syringes, stuff like that. There was some torn black clothing. There were spatters of blood here and there, but no deep pools.

"They've carried their wounded away," Polly said.

From the station, which was a circular room about thirty feet in diameter, a single corridor led to a pressure door. It was closed and locked, and we knew our people were only about a hundred yards beyond that door.

We put our heads together. All the others gathered around us.

"First thing, I guess we try thumbprints," I said. Polly walked over to the door and put her thumb to the plate. Nothing happened.

"Plan B?" she said.

"Blow the door."

So we got out grenades. We peeled off the paper patch on one side of each, exposing the sticky stuff underneath, and arranged three of them where we thought they would do the most good, pressing them in place.

We set the fuses for twenty seconds, which was the maximum. We told everyone to go back in the tunnel and keep their heads down.

"And cover your ears! This will be noisy."

We pressed the start buttons, and sprinted back along the tunnel and got down on the floor.

Twenty seconds never took so long.

The explosions, when they came, fractions of a second apart, seemed to lift me right up off the floor and blow me backwards, but that might have been my imagination. Seconds after the bang, we were all on our feet and racing toward the cloud of smoke.

Coughing, we slowed down a little as the fans worked at clearing the smoke. The door was a few feet down the newly revealed corridor, slightly distorted, blackened in three places.

"Let's go!" I shouted, and stepped over the door and into the smoke on the other side.

That's when the stun bolt came out of the smoke and hit me right in the gut. The next thing I knew, I was flopping like a fish, unable to control any of my muscles.

It didn't seem fair.

CHAPTER 19

Polly:

I probably should have shot when Cassie went down, but I held my fire. I guess I was still shaken by the idea that we had killed people. I guess all soldiers in a war are shook up the first time they kill someone. I guess the still-vivid images, which I knew would stay with me all my life, stayed my hand.

It didn't stay anyone else's.

The troops with the stun rifles were in the breach almost before my sister hit the floor, three of them, two girls and one boy, firing bolts rapidly and moving forward at the same time.

They were also being fired at. Bolts came out of the smoke, and one of the girls went down, jerking like an epileptic. A bolt sailed over my head as I crouched there, and I heard a thud as someone else went down.

Then something different. It was the sound of a shotgun going off, and a terrible pain ripped through my left shoulder. My whole left arm went numb. Though my gun was in my right hand, the shock made me drop it. I heard people crying out, and a scream. The smoke was still thick, and I couldn't see much, but it looked like all the people in the front, crammed together there in the corridor, had gone down. I saw blood.

The shotgun fired again, and something hit my helmet so hard it was jerked off my head, which rang like a bell. I was groping around for my pistol.

"Everyone get back!" I shouted. "These aren't stun guns!"

Cassie was still flopping, but feebly now. I couldn't find my own gun, so I rolled over on top of her and found hers in her hand. I pried it from her stiff fist and aimed it down the corridor. I fired three-round bursts until the clip was empty. Then I ejected the magazine and managed to get another from my backpack, which had been torn open. I jammed it in and fired more until that clip was empty.

No fire was being returned. I sat up, cautiously, and looked down at my left upper arm. I wished I hadn't. A flap of skin about three inches wide was hanging out there where it shouldn't be. It wasn't bleeding a lot, and I guess that was the good news. And it didn't hurt much.

Not just then.

I must have been sort of stunned there for a while. I don't know how long. There were soft moans from some of the people around me. I looked around, found my helmet, picked it up. I saw that a round metal object, a ball bearing, was embedded in the thick plastic. It would have taken the top of my head off if the helmet hadn't been there.

I gradually became aware of activity around me. The uninjured people who had been behind us had moved up and were tending to the wounded. There were several who were just stunned and were pulled out of the way to recover on their own. Four girls and one boy had been hit by pellets from the shotgun. Three of the wounds were not any more serious than mine. The boy had been hit in the stomach and was groaning pitifully.

"We've got to get this one to a hospital," Peggy said. She moved over to one of the shapes that wasn't moving.

It was Cheryl. Coach Peggy took a look at her head, which had a deep hole in one side. She straightened up, looked at me, and shook her head.

Suddenly, I felt a lot better about all that shooting I had done.

And a lot worse about leading these girls and boys into the line of fire.

We were almost there, but far from out of the woods. Peggy put a compress around my wound, which was beginning to make itself known, and I was able to stand up and try to get things under control.

This was always going to be the tricky part.

Two girls had gone down the corridor where the firing had come from. They reported five corpses and two badly injured. They brought back an ugly piece of metal, a tube bolted to a piece of plastic. I realized it was a homemade shotgun, probably turned on a metal lathe, bored from a steel rod. It was a muzzleloader, because building anything more complex would take a lot of designing and time. A big zip gun, and they didn't even have shotgun shells. You jammed in some powder and some shot, plugged it with something, and fired. Then you had to do it all over again. Just like in the eighteenth century, the American Civil War. It was the cumbersome nature of the weapon that had kept the carnage down and probably saved mine and Cassie's lives.

Yeah, tell it to Cheryl Chang.

The stragglers from down the subway tunnel all arrived. They brought with them one of the wounded mutineers. He objected to that term when I called him that.

"They told us that Captain Broussard had gone crazy, and they were taking control of the ship under . . . some regulation. They read it to us."

"What are you, anyway?"

"I'm a cop, from the Castle Rock police force. I've never done anything like this before. You killed some cops!"

"They were shooting at us, and we represent the legal authorities under the law. They fooled you. And by the way, who *are* they?"

He seemed to be debating whether or not to talk to me anymore, but he was also struggling with the idea that he might be in big trouble if his side lost, and it didn't look good for his side at the moment.

"Some big fat guy. I don't know him. Max . . ."

"Max Karpinski."

"That's him. Some others. They showed us what looked like legal authority. It was verified by the computer protocols."

"I'll bet it was. Come here."

Two others and myself frog-marched him down the hall until we were facing the door where everyone important to me except Papa was being held. There was a little Judas window in the door, closed tight just then. I grabbed the prisoner's collar and shook him.

"We have to get in there. Can you communicate with the guards? Is there a password? A secret knock-knock signal?"

This was the part that had worried Cassie and me from the start, when Travis gave us the broad outline of the plan . . .

Well, we were also a bit nervous about what he planned to do after we got them all out, but he had refused to discuss that. Get us out, and I'll deal with the rest, he had said. I presumed it had to do with getting to one of his concealed and protected arsenals and using those weapons.

But first things first. We needed to get into that room, and the only way we had figured out to do that was to blow the door.

But who might be sitting against that door? Who might be sitting a few yards way? We desperately needed a way either to get through the door without violence or give those inside some warning so they could move away, even if they had to risk being stunned.

Speaking of stunned, Cassie was awake and alert, and almost ready to stand on her feet again. All this had taken about fifteen minutes. She was following our conversation intently.

"We haven't had much communication with our people inside for half a day," the prisoner said. "All the phones are down. What we've been doing is knocking on the door."

"And they take a look at you, right?"

"That's it. They know me."

"What's your name?" I put my gun under his chin and pushed so hard his head was forced back. "And if you lie to me, it's the last lie you'll ever tell."

"My name's Vince. I got ID in my pocket."

Cassie reached into his pocket and pulled out a badge. Vince, all right, and a lieutenant in the Castle Rock force, just like he said.

I looked at Cassie. We were clearly on the same page.

"Here's how it's going to be, Vince," she said. "We're going over to that door. You will knock on it, and stand with your face close to the glass.

When they ask you, you'll identify yourself. When the little door opens, you will tell them that you need help out here, and you need it fast. Tell them there's been a firefight, and you've got some of the . . . the . . ."

"How about rebels?" I suggested.

"That's good. Some of the rebels are cornered, and you need some help rooting them out. And, Vince, are you an actor?"

"An actor? No."

"Well, you're going to give the performance of your life, anyway." She pulled the waistband of his pants away from his belly and shoved the muzzle of her gun down the front. "If you say anything else to them, I'll shoot your cock off. If you don't convince them to open the door, I'll shoot your cock off. If you try to take this gun from me, I'll shoot your cock off. Are we clear, Vince?"

I nudged under his chin with my gun again in case he needed any more prodding. He didn't. He nodded, carefully, swallowed hard, and we took him to the door.

He stood for a moment.

"Take your time, Vince. Rehearse your lines. Get it right, because you won't have a second chance."

He nodded again and started breathing hard, hyperventilating. I liked that. It meant he was thinking carefully. A method actor. Getting into the part.

At last he knocked on the door. Cassie was off to one side, to the left, and all the other uninjured were close up behind us. The plan was to hit it hard as soon as the door opened, do our best to surprise them.

Vince knocked. Someone not far from the other side of the door called out, asking who it was.

"It's me, Vince! Hurry up, we need some help out here." Maybe overacting a little, but on the whole, not bad. I kept my eyes on his face, my gun down out of sight, as the little door opened. I couldn't see any sort of facial signal, and I really didn't think these people were well enough organized to have set up something like that, but you never know.

He read his lines perfectly, with just the right mixture of fear (which was probably easy enough, with Cassie threatening Little Vincie and the family jewels) and excitement. The guard inside shut the little door and almost at once yanked open the big one and started outside—

—when Cassie grabbed her by the shirtfront and yanked her out of the room to go sprawling under a pileup of very angry skypool players. Cassie and I leaped inside—

—scanned the room quickly—

—spotted the two other guards, who had already started toward us—

—and we yelled for them to drop their weapons—

—and one of them stutter-stepped and dropped his—

—and the other started to bring his stun rifle up—

—and Cassie and I both shot him, my round into his leg, and hers knocking the rifle out of his hands. He went down and started to yell.

"Lucky shot," I told Cassie. And suddenly I was feeling faint. I sat down, and in an instant Mama was at my side, crying, hugging me, reaching out for Cassie, and she was crying, too. I don't know when two girls have ever needed their mama so badly.

And just like that, it was over.

Well, not *over* over, you know. But we had done what we set out to do, and it was like the weight, all the gigatons of the whole ship, was lifted off my shoulders. I just wanted to sit there and cry for a long time. But we didn't have time for that. Because it wasn't truly all over, and we knew it.

Aunt Elizabeth was a whirlwind. We had brought along basic first-aid supplies, and she pounced on them as soon as the others entered the room carrying them. First, she went to the injured guard, stopped the bleeding. She was issuing orders just about as fast as she could talk, with Dorothy acting as her nurse. When she heard there were more casualties outside she started in that direction, but Mama grabbed her arm and put her roughly down beside me. She zeroed in on my wound like a heat-seeking missile.

"Sorry, Podkayne, girls," she said. "I didn't realize." She got a good look at it and shouted for more bandages. She clucked her tongue. Don't you just hate it when a doctor does that? And don't you just hate it even more when taking off the bloody bandage feels like skin being stripped right down to the bone? Well, I sure did, and I let everyone know about it, too. I'm not one to suffer in silence. That's highly overrated, that's a macho thing, a boy thing. I *howled*.

I howled even louder when I got a better look down into the wound, where I was pretty sure I could see a little bit of bone. It looked like the ball bearing had gone right on through, and Elizabeth confirmed it.

"That's good news," she said. "Means all we need to do it clean you out and patch you up. Girls! Have any of those stretchers arrived yet? We need to get Polly to a hospital."

"No way," I said. "Where's Travis? I'm going with him."

"You're out of your mind, Polly," Mama said.

"Totally crazy," Dorothy confirmed.

"Elizabeth, I want you to patch me up. I'm okay, I'm not bleeding much. After all this I'm not going to miss the end." I struggled to my feet. I was only a little bit dizzy.

"You sit right back down there, Pollyanna Sue," Mama said, in that steely voice that brooked no argument. Well, the heck with that, too.

"I'm going, Mama. Where's Travis?"

She looked startled and, for the first time in my life, backed down. She pointed mutely to the far wall.

Travis was a wreck. I gasped when I saw him and quickly knelt beside Cassie. His face was swollen so badly that his eyes were closed. There was blood all over his clothes, and one of his front teeth was knocked out. Part of one ear was missing, one arm was cradled in a makeshift sling, and that hand looked like it had been burned, and three fingers were swollen, like they had been broken. He heard my gasp, or Cassie's, as she had reacted the same way, and he managed to open one eye. One side of his battered mouth twisted up in a grin.

"What took you so long?" he said. Typical Travis. A line right out of a bad action-hero movie, only this blood was real.

"We had to kill some of them, Travis," Cassie said. Instantly, his grin collapsed, and he reached out to her with his good arm.

"Oh, girls, I am so sorry. But there was no other way."

It didn't seem like the time to tell him about Cheryl and our wounded. I was amazed that he was conscious.

Mike and Marlee had been waiting anxiously while I was being patched up. I spotted them and waved them over.

"Patrick was okay when we left him," I told them. "He's with Papa, either at the Timberline Lodge or aboard Travis's private ship. She's a terrific AI, and she will take care of them."

Marlee hugged me carefully, and Mike was wiping tears away. Then Travis spoke from down on the floor.

"Help me up, Polly." He reached out to me, and I took his undamaged hand. Cassie scooted around in back of him, gingerly got her hands under his armpits, and lifted. He winced but didn't complain.

"Who did this to you, Travis?" I asked him.

"I don't know. I never saw them, just heard their voices. They had a hood over me, so I couldn't see it coming when they hit me."

"Was it Max?" I was so steamed I wanted to go out and kill him, just blow the bastard away.

"I never heard his voice. He might have been there. But I think he found a couple of repressed sadists to do what he didn't have the stomach for. You can't find them all, you know. We did psychological testing on all the passengers, but some will get through."

"Why did they do it, Travis?" Cassie asked. "Why so brutal?"

"Information. They need the codes that exist only in my head to finish their takeover." He stopped, raised a bloody cloth to his mouth, and tried to be as quiet as possible as he spit bloody stuff into it. He grinned again, but it was horribly lopsided.

"I'll be all right. I've had worse than this outside a bar in Miami, drunk on my ass." He paused, then shook his head. "That's a lie. I had broken bones then, but this was worse because I wasn't drunk, and they took their time. It's the waiting for the next punch to land that's the worst."

I looked at his mangled hand and didn't say anything.

"I always wondered how I'd stand up to it. Torture, I mean. I understand everybody breaks sooner or later. They only had the one long session with me, then they tossed me back in here to think it over."

It was still mayhem all around us, with many angry people itching to do something about this outrage that had been done to them and no really good outlet for it. No one else I saw seemed to have been harmed, physically, but I saw several people crying, clinging to each other. In a way, I guess they'd had it harder than Cassie and I had, locked up and unable to do a thing about it, completely in the dark as to what was happening outside that small room. At least we were able to move around. I stopped thinking about that and focused on Travis again as we helped him out into the hallway. He looked at the casualties being treated, at the body of Cheryl, who he hadn't even known, her face covered with someone's shirt. He looked away quickly.

"I thought I held up pretty well," he went on. "I don't know how much longer I could have. I have to tell you, my darling girls, the thought of you two out there coming to get us helped a lot. Every time they hit me I just pictured you two, coming to the rescue . . . and how the *hell* did you make it all that way?"

"Well," Cassie began, "we—"

"No, sorry, I'm babbling, no time for that. We'll sit around the fire with Jubal and your mother one day . . . How is Jubal? Is he safe?"

"He should be. We left him with Patrick. If there was trouble, they were supposed to go to Sheila. We figured she could handle it."

"Damn right she would. Good thinking." He paused, and pulled himself as erect as he could. I thought he might have some broken ribs.

"Okay, we've got some things to do. We need to get out of here."

"I'm coming, too." I looked behind me, and saw that Mama had been following us, listening to everything.

"Sure, Podkayne," Travis said. "You can help prop me up if these girls get tired of it."

I was as tired as I'd ever been in my life, I guess, but there was no way I was going to be too tired to hold him up.

We hadn't gotten very far when he stopped, shook his head, and made a rude sound.

"The old bean ain't working as well as it should, girls. They tell me the security systems have screwed up a lot of things. I thought I heard some explosions, louder than gunshots. Do the doors work? With thumbprints?"

"A lot of them don't," I said.

"I guess that's good news. It has to be making things tough for them, too. Where did you get those guns?"

"Mike and Marlee's apartment."

"You went there? I can tell this is going to be one interesting story."

"And some from your arsenal under the bed in the ship."

"So you maybe brought along some grenades?"

"Several. We have a few left."

"We need to get them. We might have to blow some doors."

"I'll do it," Cassie said, and hurried back to our backpacks. Travis was still looking groggy. His eyes fell on my bandaged shoulder. He frowned.

"What happened to you, honey?"

"Aw, they made a shotgun or two. Stuffed them with ball bearings and made some black powder, I guess. I got a little nick." Aw shucks, t'warn't nothin', Cap'n Travis. But what was I going to do, with him looking like that? I guess his emotions were pretty close to the surface because he looked devastated. Tears were leaking from his eyes.

"When this is over, Polly, this ship belongs to you and your sister. You've saved it. We owe you *everything*." Mama was crying, too, and took my hand and squeezed it.

"It ain't over till the fat lady sings," I told them. I don't know what that means, but Travis used to say it sometimes.

"She's taking a deep breath, baby. Don't you worry. Your uncle Travis still has a few tricks up his sleeve."

Cassie returned with the backpacks. She gave Mama and Travis a handgun each, and we counted the grenades. Six left.

We continued around the circumferential corridor. We passed dozens of other doors, and Travis tried a few with his thumb, and so did I, but none of them opened. He stopped a couple of times, thinking hard.

"I've got a pretty good map in my head," he explained. "Trouble is, I don't have a very good head at the moment." There were numbers over the doors, with no explanation of what might be inside. After a while, he stopped in front of a door and patted it with his free hand.

"This is the one . . . I'm pretty sure. But in case it isn't, let's see if we can blow it off with just one grenade."

Cassie took one from her pack and stuck it to the lock mechanism. We all moved back about a hundred yards. I was wishing for something to crouch behind, but the corridor was completely bare.

"Fifteen seconds," Cassie shouted, then, "Fire in the hole!"

She raced back to us and we all crouched, facing away from the explosive, and covered our ears.

When the smoke cleared, we could see the door hanging open. It was a garage for electric maintenance vehicles. There were a dozen in there, and a door on the far end of the garage that I assumed led eventually to the surface. Some had mower attachments and showed a lot of use. Some had stake beds in back, for carrying gardening supplies.

"We have a ways to go, and I'm not up to walking it," Travis said. "And I don't think any of you lovely broads are up to carrying me."

I didn't know what a broad was, but if it was lovely, I'd accept it.

He picked out one of the smaller vehicles, and we dumped the stuff in the back and all piled in. It was just narrow enough to make it through the door we'd blown open, make a turn, and go racing quietly down the corridor.

I estimate that we went about a third of the way around the ship. Then another corridor branched off, to the left. It was wide, and descending, and we raced along that for a while. Cassie was driving, and I was sitting beside her. We both had our weapons handy, as did Mama and Travis. But we encountered no one. Not surprising. No one but maintenance workers usually came down there, and I presumed most of them were busy dealing with the crisis above, protecting their families, keeping their heads down. Maybe joining in the riots, fighting, protests, whatever was happening.

All my life I had been used to instant news, to being able to find out what was going on, anywhere, with the blink of an eye. One of the most frightening things about this whole situation was to be so in the dark. To have no idea at all what was going on a hundred feet over my head. No idea what was happening to my friends, my home. At least I knew most of my family was safe. For now.

We soon came into one of the huge warehouses where everything was stored in black time-stasis bubbles. Racks of cantaloupe-sized ones, all the way up to some as big as three-story houses. We weaved around, left, right, left, right again, following some arcane notations on the floor that only Travis could read. He directed Cassie down long rows in almost total silence except for the quiet whirring of our motor. It was very spooky down there. Some of those bubbles held people. Some of them held cornflakes. Some of them held water or kerosene or boxes of crayons or salamanders lying in mud or huge tents or . . . you name it. Literally. No way at all to tell what was what by looking at them. Each was a black, featureless, reflectionless hole in space, and hole in time. Not really a part of our reality at all until they were turned off and revealed their contents.

We came to a massive door in a far wall. I had no idea where we were; my positioning system had stopped working sometime during the trip. I'm sure that wasn't an accident. This place was on no map.

Travis got out and limped over to the door. We started to follow, but he stopped and turned to us.

"I'm sorry, my darlings, but I'll have to ask y'all to stay back, out of earshot, and where you can't see this screen. This is the most secure place in the ship. No one knows the codes here except me. A thumbprint won't work. I have to answer a series of questions that only I would know the answers to, plus a lot of other stuff to be sure I'm not under duress. The only way anyone else could get in here would be if I was dead, in which case the codes would be delivered to Podkayne. I won't get into that."

"You think it will still work, Travis?" Mama asked. "With all the computer problems?"

"It damn well ought to. It's not networked. It has its own power source, and a lot of ways of defending itself if someone tries to get it. This is my last refuge, the final trick up my sleeve."

He turned from us and limped over to a wall panel. He opened it, and the door screened us from seeing what was in there. The three of us moved away and stood against the wall.

For a while, he punched buttons.

"We have to wait a little," he said. "The AI has to solve some pretty complex algorithms. Jubal designed them." He looked at us, and smiled. "I had a lot of time to plan this trip. It took quite a while to build the ship, and even longer to get it all running.

"So have you ever thought about your neighbors? Not family, they were all invited. Other people. The ones you went to school with, the friends you know from here and there in the townships. Can you tell me anything about them?"

Mama looked puzzled. She shrugged.

"Normal people. Friendly. All in all, I'd say they were a nicer bunch than the people I knew back on Mars. But only a little. They're not saints."

"No, I have little interest in saints," Travis agreed. "Nor fanatics, nor people with huge anger issues, nor wimps. I had a team of the best, most realistic, down-to-earth psychologists I could find make up tests that all potential passengers had to pass. And we selected . . . Hang on a minute."

He turned back to the security panel and did some more things for a bit. Then he faced us again.

"We selected people with what I'd call . . . an even keel. People who could work with others. People of all races and nationalities, and religions, so long as they weren't holy-rolling Bible thumpers or jihadists or anything like that. And we selected for skills. If you think about it, a very large number of our citizens are farmers or experts in animal husbandry. We will need that where we're going. Also people with mechanical skills. Some people who are good at running things, and some people who are good at taking orders. Artistic people here and there, though it's hard to pick for artistic talent. I never set out to make a utopia because I don't be-lieve in them, and I want a certain amount of orneriness in the colonists, too. Shrinking violets have no place on a frontier.

"But because I *don't* believe in utopias, I planned for the worst as well as the best. I knew something could happen on a trip this long. Now it's happened. I hoped the *real* troubles wouldn't happen until we got to New Sun. All we know about it is that it has enough water and oxygen to support

life . . . and that life is *already there*. But we don't know what it is. Dinosaurs? Huge sea monsters? No land animals at all, yet, and nothing but
jellyfish in the sea? We don't know. But look at Earth's history. Four and a
half billion years, and land life didn't appear for the first several billion
years. Where is this planet on the evolutionary scale?

"There's a tiny chance we might encounter intelligent life, already
there. We view that possibility as a small one. Humans have only been
around for a hundred thousand years or so. 'Civilization' is even younger.
A blip on the timeline of Earth's history. How long does a civilization last?
A million years? Or only a few thousand, until it destroys itself with eco-
logical disasters and nuclear wars? We don't know. But the likelihood that
two stars as close as Old Sun and New Sun would have intelligent life at
the same time is pretty small.

"But if there are . . . people or something like people there, I would
hope to bargain with them for some living space. I . . . Wait a sec."

Once more he communed with the very touchy AI.

"One more step, and we're in," he said. "Where was I? Oh, yeah. It's
looking like we *can't* go to another star. I never wanted to be a colonialist,
I don't want to fight or subjugate or in any way have bad dealings with any
inhabitants . . . but what if they don't want us? We would have no other
choice but to fight for some living space."

"I don't like the sound of that, Travis," Mama said.

"You think I do? And as I said, I don't think it's likely. We'll cross that
bridge if we come to it, but our bridges to home, or to another star, are
burned, Poddy my darling. And anyway, the most likely thing I expected
we could face is a hostile wilderness. Big, scary animals. How would you
like to fight a *T. rex*? Not me."

The panel made a contented sound, and the big doors began to roll
open. Travis was still looking at us.

"So I knew I had to take some people who were up to that sort of thing
and up to dealing with any human problem we might have along the way."

The doors clanged into their recessed sockets, and Travis gestured us
to follow him inside. It was a huge room. It had to be, to contain everything

Travis had stored there. I had thought of the weapons beneath the bunk in Sheila as his arsenal. That was just a gun safe. This was the arsenal. This was a pocket army, navy, and air force.

There were dozens of battle tanks and other assault vehicles I couldn't identify. There were amphibious vehicles. There were pilotless drones, and manned fighter and small bomber aircraft. There were other things I had no idea what they were, and wasn't eager to find out. Some *big* guns, with bores big enough to fit my fist into.

"Army surplus," Travis said. "Most of these are obsolete things, not much use since the Europan invasion, where everyone's been too busy staying alive to fight each other. I got most of it real cheap. But it's all refurbished and ready to go if we have to."

"Let's hope we don't have to," I said.

"Amen to that. And we won't need much of this stuff today. Just a few vehicles."

"Travis," Mom said, "are we going into battle with this stuff?"

"Not you, Pod. And not your wonderful daughters. And not me, for that matter. The war is over for us."

He had reached a long, long row of black bubbles arrayed on racks and held in place with light cargo netting. He went to another keypad and fed it some numbers. He pressed a button.

"It's going to be her war now," he said.

The netting in front of the nearest bubble rolled up, and the bubble was shoved out of the rack. It hung there in midair, weightless, a spot of emptiness about five feet off the ground. Then it was gone, and a woman tumbled out.

No, tumbled was the wrong word. She was stretched out more or less prone when she appeared—you never know how the contents will be oriented when the bubble goes away—but she twisted in the air like a cat and landed on her feet, crouched, sweeping the area with her goggled eyes and the barrel of a huge gun. All this happened in the first second. By the next second she had relaxed and straightened. I could see her taking in Travis's ravaged face. She frowned, then dismissed it. I realized that some sign of trouble like that was something she had been expecting.

"Podkayne, Cassie, Polly, meet Colonel Jane Litchfield. Jane, meet Podkayne. Polly's the one with the bandage. Cassie's the one with her jaw hanging open."

She flipped up the goggles and zeroed in on Mama, and a big grin split her face. She took a few strides forward, right hand held out. Mama, looking a bit stunned, shook her hand.

"Podkayne, I'm a big fan of your music."

"Um . . . thank you."

She was a big woman, a few inches taller than me and Cass, but built heftier. She was dressed in full black battle gear, a bit like us only a lot more serious. It fit tightly, and showed off her lithe muscularity. She had strong, high, Nordic cheekbones, but was far too brown for a pure Swede unless she had a hell of a suntan. She fell like a cat, and she moved like a cat. Quick, no wasted motion, an air of assurance and powerful control. It was hard to guess her age, but I'd say somewhere around forty.

She shouldered her weapon and swept off her helmet in what seemed like one smooth motion, and faced Travis, all business again. She had obviously scoped out the situation and knew there was no immediate threat, but she also knew she wouldn't be there if there wasn't some kind of problem.

"What's the situation, Travis? You look terrible."

He put one arm over her shoulder and they moved off a bit. I could hear some of it, but didn't really listen, as I knew what he was telling her as well as he did.

"Did you know anything about this, Mama?" Cassie asked.

"Not a clue, darling."

Cassie was looking kind of funny, keeping her eyes on Travis and Jane. They had moved off a ways, and now were coming back. Jane was nodding thoughtfully.

"I think three platoons could do it," she was saying. "I'm going to uncork four, just to be on the safe side."

"You're the boss."

She leaned over and a little down and kissed him on the least injured corner of his mouth. I saw him glance at us, a little nervously. Travis? I had never figured him for a monk, but he had always been discreet about his romantic affairs. Interesting.

She hurried over to the panel and frowned at it. Then she punched in some numbers and a whole lot of nets rolled up away from a whole lot of black bubbles. They started coming out of their cubbyholes.

"She was the head of my security detail," Travis was telling us. I knew he had maintained a pretty large force to protect Jubal and himself. There had been a lot of angry, or greedy, or crazy people who would have liked to get their hands on the two richest men in the Old Sun system and try to get something out of them, or kill them.

"She trained with the American SEALS, and some spook agency, then was with the Secret Service for a while, until she couldn't stomach being around presidents anymore. I hired her and gave her a free hand. And Jubal and I are alive and well."

I know very little about military organization, but I thought a platoon was about twenty-five soldiers. There were around a hundred bubbles, so four platoons. And they started opening. Each one contained one soldier, and each one arrived as alert and ready for anything as Jane Litchfield had.

"Except for Jane, who has popped out now and then, all these people went into the bubbles before we launched, twenty years ago. They understood they wouldn't come out except in case of bad trouble, or arrival at New Sun. They trained here for six months, as we were building. They know every nook and cranny, and they have practiced tactics for every situation we could think of."

"They look sort of scary, Travis," Mama said.

"I hope so. They *are* scary. But we've done the same testing on them as everyone else. They are soldiers, but I don't think we have any psychopaths among them. Jane wouldn't have recruited them, for one thing. This is the A-Team, girls, the toughest, meanest bitches and sons of bitches you ever saw. This is going to be easy for them."

I could believe it. They were all dressed in full body armor and were fully armed. Helmets, rifles, grenades, grenade launchers. They were about 30 percent female and 70 percent male. None of them were what you'd call small.

In ten minutes, Jane had them formed into combat teams, and they rolled out on little vehicles they called jeeps and a few larger personnel carriers, all bristling with guns.

And Travis was right. It was easy. Within twenty-four hours, the mutiny was over, all the leaders were in jail, all the followers taken in for questioning.

CHAPTER 20

Cassie:

It was love at first sight. The first time I saw Jane Litchfield, I fell madly in love with her.

Not sexually. I'm not even what they call bicurious. No, the love affair was because I wanted to *be* her.

For the last few years, Mama had been after both of us to decide what to *do* with our lives. Now here we were, a few months away from college, and neither of us had selected a career. At least, if Polly had, she hadn't mentioned it to me.

As for me, I had been drifting, no question. I was never a whiz-kid student. I brought home decent grades, not quite as good as Polly's, but I'd never failed a course. And I'd seldom aced a test even though I had often thought I could if I studied more. The reason was that I just didn't *care*. The only thing I had found so far in life that I loved was skypool.

There's an old song Mama played for us once that said don't know much about history, biology, science, don't know what something called . . . a slip rule? What it's for. I don't know, either. If I were writing a song—something else I don't know much about—it would more accurately say I've got a *smattering* of history, biology, science, etc. I am reasonably literate, I can express myself in the lingua franca of *Rolling Thunder*, which is English. I learned enough of those other subjects to be able to hold my own except among experts in the field. I studied them enough to know I didn't want to build my life around them.

I've looked at the jobs other people have, and none of them have ever leaped out at me and said, "*This* is what you want to do."

I'm not artistic. I don't want to sell anything.

What I figured, I'd take general courses, all over the map, for the first year or two at good old Rolling Thunder College, get on one of the skypool intramural teams (there's no varsity here, as the only teams we could play would be from Rolling Thunder University), and see what interested me.

But now I thought I had it. What I want to be when I grow up. An explorer. An adventurer. A soldier? Not unless we had to fight intelligent species that were our equal.

I had just finished the only adventure of my life, and it had been a dilly. Stopping now, resting, watching Travis and Jane organize the counterattack, I felt a terrific buzz, and nothing to do with it, nowhere to put it.

Yes, it was horrible. We suffered. A good girl died. Some other people, good or bad, died as well. People were injured, including Polly. But other than in a hard-fought game, I had never felt so alive. Was I an action junkie? Maybe. If so, what's wrong with that?

I had finally put my finger on something I'd never considered before but now realized had been bugging me most of my life. Life in the ship was . . . boring. Tame. Every blade of grass was carefully planned. Every structure and farm and animal and every human was there for a reason. The mutiny was basically the first time anything unexpected had happened in my lifetime. I'd have been happier if it had never happened . . . but it did, and I learned something about myself.

I wanted to hack my way through unexplored, virgin jungle.

I wanted to swashbuckle my way over the high seas, maybe harpoon a New Sun version of a whale. Or lasso one, put it in a black bubble, and bring it back alive to Earth, where they were all extinct now from the invasion.

I wanted to be the first to plumb the depths of the ancient underground city, abandoned by the inhabitants of our new planet a million years ago when they left for another galaxy. Well, could happen.

I wanted to discover new animal and plant species and, if necessary, fight off an attack of giant carnivorous rhododendrons.

We were going to have a whole planet to explore, and it wasn't going to be barren and dead, like Mars. Of course, it might harbor nothing more ominous than little ferns and tiny lizards and frogs, but who knew? *We* would know, eventually.

So for the next few weeks, as things sorted themselves out for a return to something approximating normal, I hung out with Jane. Actually, at first I tagged along wherever she went, and she paid little attention to me. I'm sure she saw me as a bumbling little puppy, eager to play adult games.

But eventually we talked some, and someone else told her what Polly and I had done (we modest adventurer types never brag about our exploits ourselves), and she started showing me considerable respect.

As well she should! I don't want to toot my own horn (well, not too loud), but looking back, it was pretty amazing that we did it all.

I told her of my newfound desire to become a part of her team, to be one of the first ones down to the planet, to . . . well, to be like her. I wanted to hear some of her adventures, but she wouldn't talk about them. I figured that someday I could pry some information out of Travis.

In short, I was a happy girl, a girl with a purpose.

I could hardly wait until we got there.

How could I know it would all change so quickly?

Polly:

I said it was all over, but, of course, it was not. There was the aftermath of it all to deal with. And we still had the problem that Papa had found that started it all.

Papa was fine. He had spent the time with Patrick, hardly aware of where he was. When we came to get him, he greeted us lovingly, as always, but he was very excited about something and couldn't wait to get back to his lab/workshop. I don't think he has more than vague memories of there being any trouble. And that was fine. That was Papa. The story of how Cassie and I made our way to the North Pole and what we did there is something he would never hear. He pays zero attention to the news, and none of us in the family would ever tell him.

There were around eight hundred people involved in the mutiny. There was a core group of Max and about a dozen others who planned it all. There were about a hundred who knew the real story. The rest were dupes who were roped in by a tall tale of Travis and others about to declare martial law, or something silly like that. Those people were given a stern talking-to, but what else could we do? Max exploited a weakness in the security systems or he would never have been able to sell that idea. In the end, aside from the mild social stigma of having been fooled, they mostly went back to their regular jobs.

It was different for the hard-core plotters. I expected that Travis's wrath would be enormous. Hang 'em high, draw and quarter the bastards, build an electric chair. Something like that. So I was a little surprised at what he did to them.

Nothing.

Okay, not quite nothing. But there was no trial, not even a hearing. Each of them was allowed to make a statement. Contrition, defiance, pleas for mercy, apologies. Whatever. And then they were popped into black bubbles.

"Let the elected civil authorities on New Sun take care of it," he said. "I wash my hands of it." He felt betrayed by an old friend and guilty that his elaborate safety measures had had just enough holes in them to allow that stinking son of a bitch to get away with as much as he did.

They would be let out of the bubbles sometime after we got there. And that was the scary part, for them. That *sometime* could be a long way off. Remember, the bulk of the colonists were already in bubbles, and they would not all be coming out at once. They would come out as their particular skills were needed. As Cassie pointed out to me a few days after the hearings, the need for mutineers would be quite small. I hadn't thought of that. It was possible they would never come out.

Max made an angry statement before vanishing into an unknown future. He said we were all crazy to accept Papa's calculations about the dark matter and dark energy. He called us all quitters, cowards, without the nerve to continue on to our new life. He cursed us if we decided to stop the ship, or turn it around. He singled out Cassie and me in the crowd and had a few nasty words to call us, which I won't repeat here.

I smiled, and waved at him. Bye-bye, Max!

Cassie had a hand gesture for him that Papa would have frowned at. But of course, Papa wasn't there. He was working on something.

My arm healed up nicely, with only a little scar. Why is it that I get all the scars? And why does Cassie keep winning that silly scissors-rock-paper game?

Cassie:

Life returned to normal fairly quickly. The damage from fires and such was not apocalyptic. If people had had guns, it would certainly have been much worse, like the pictures of bullet-riddled and bomb-blasted buildings I've seen from fighting on Earth. There were a lot of injuries from the hand-to-hand fighting with knives and clubs, broken bones and concussions and cuts and a few burns, but only seventeen people died. For people who aren't used to close combat, closing in with a knife or even a sledge-hammer is a scary thing to do. Most of them ran away as fast as they could, and I don't blame them.

One of the dead, of course, was Cheryl Chang. Polly and I and all the skypool teams in the ship, boys and girls, attended her memorial service, in our uniforms. Mama was there, and Travis gave a moving speech. Her parents were brokenhearted but stoic. They were Buddhists. They believed she had moved on to a better life, or something like that. I don't know much about religions. I hoped it helped.

Polly and I cried our eyes out. I still choke up when I think about it.

But we still had to decide what to do about the threat Papa had discovered and that he and I had left the ship to learn more about.

So one day, Travis summoned all the mayors of all the townships—except the one currently serving an indefinite sentence in stasis, awaiting trial many years from now—and had them assemble on the bridge. When Polly and I asked to be there, he said we had a right to be, no question. So we sat off to one side as the big shots took their seats on folding chairs and regarded Travis and Papa and something Papa had brought with him.

It was typical of one of Papa's gizmos, though a little large. He had had time to work on it for a few weeks, so it didn't have as much of the slapdash look of some of his creations.

How to describe it. It's hard, because it didn't have many parts you could call square, or spherical, or much of anything else. It slightly resembled some of those shapes I looked at once in a book on topology. Theoretical constructs that were twisted through some other dimensions, like a Möbius strip that had had a nervous breakdown.

It was mostly metal and glass, or plastic, with a few other things. It was about ten feet tall and four feet wide, bigger at the base, smaller here and there, with no rhyme or reason that I could see.

It didn't do anything. It just sat there. No blinking lights, no emissions of steam, no sizzling Jacob's ladders. Maybe it wasn't turned on. Maybe it would put on a better show later. Right then, it looked like it would be more at home in a museum of "modernist" sculpture than on the bridge.

Polly and I whispered to each other, and our consensus was that it might be something that would shield us from the deadly sleet of dark lightning. That would be good. The thought of turning back gave me an ache deep in my heart. The thought of an extra fifty or sixty years getting there was almost as heartbreaking. I *had* to get to New Sun. There wasn't much left back at Old Sun for an intrepid girl explorer.

We had talked to Papa, asking him what he was working on. He had let us get glimpses of it in various stages of construction. We asked him what the gizmo would do.

"Maybe nothing," was all he would say.

It was taking a while to get going, so the sibling and I continued to whisper. What I was most concerned about at the moment was Patrick. I had asked the lovely boy out on a date, and he had said yes. Which was a big surprise. I had been sure that, with the intense time Polly and Patrick had spent together, they would have formed some sort of bond.

"You knew I took Patrick to a dance?" I asked her, cautiously.

"Somebody mentioned it. How did it go?"

"Okay. He's a good dancer."

"Yeah, I figured he would be."

I knew her well enough to sense there was something she wasn't telling me. If it had been me, even in the midst of the crisis, I would have made some sort of attempt to get closer to him. I mean, life goes on, right?

Could it be his acrophobia? I'll admit I was a little surprised when I heard about that, him looking so strong and all, but none of us are responsible for our phobias. If you dropped a tarantula in my lap, I'd pee my pants. Papa's got more phobias than I can count, and yet he's the kindest, best person I know.

So I'll continue to take a hack at Patrick.

Travis's calling the meeting to order put an end to my speculation. I'm going to leave out all the niceties and formalities he engaged in and get right to the meat of the matter.

"So once more, let me go through our options at this point," he said.

"One, we continue as we have been, accelerating to the midpoint, where we will be moving at well over 98 percent of the speed of light, turn the ship around, and decelerate until we get there. In other words, our original plan. Jubal, do you have a better fix on when you think that would kill us all?"

"Nothin' exack," he said, looking very troubled. He was medicated to the eyeballs, doing better than usual in the low gravity, and still able to function. "But it be soon. Another couple a months at the most."

"Okay. Option two. We shut down the engines, drift at this speed, which Jubal thinks might be safe. *Might* be. When we get to the right point in space, we decelerate until we arrive.

"Option two A, decelerate some right now, to be on the safe side. That adds about seventy years to our trip. More years with option two A.

"Option three. We start decelerating right now, do that for twenty years until we are motionless relative to the sun, accelerate another twenty years to this speed, turn around again and decelerate another twenty years until we arrive back home, tails between our legs. Total, sixty years wasted, in addition to the twenty years we've already wasted."

So, tell us which option you *really* hate, Travis, why don't you? Duh. But Travis still had a trick or two up his sleeve.

"I rule out option one. I have never known Jubal to be wrong about something like this. I believe him completely. If we just keep going, we will all be dead, and soon. Just for my information, can I have a show of hands of anyone who also believes as I do?"

Just for his information, huh? A little clue that this was not going to be a consensus decision. This was going to be a captain's decision. The final word aboard an ocean ship, an airplane, and a spaceship.

I was relieved to see most of the hands go up. At least a three-quarters majority. Not that it was going to change Travis's decision; that much was obvious to anyone who knew him.

"Thanks," he said. "I hate option three so much I can hardly express it. Starting something like this, spending so much time on it already, then turning around and going home . . . the whole idea of it makes me sick. Is there anyone here who thinks that's what we should do? Don't be shy, I won't be mad at you."

No one raised a hand.

"Thanks for that, too. I would be surprised if any of you had wanted to go back. None of you were selected because you are quitters.

"That would seem to leave some variation on option two. It's not one I or any of you like, taking that long to get there, and I worry a bit about the ship. So far there have been no major technical problems, nothing unexpected except this 'dark lightning' flux that no one could have known about, I guess. But as the best of bad options, it's what I had intended to do."

He paused, then smiled.

"Until Jubal provided me with a fourth option."

There was considerable murmuring about that. Polly and I looked at each other, and I'm sure my eyebrows were raised as high as hers were.

Travis walked to the gizmo in the middle of the round room. He gave it a little time for our curiosity to build up. For a moment I glanced up at the huge screen that simulated what we would see outside if we weren't under a quarter mile of rock. The view forward. New Sun in the center, no brighter than any other star in the scrunched-up universe. If it hadn't been in the exact center, it would have been impossible to pick it out from any of the others. Our destination, still many long years away, even at our present speed. My new home, someday.

"Jubal, I know you have trouble explaining things like this, but I'd like you to lay it out for them, just as you told it to me. I think they need to hear it from you."

Papa looked intensely uncomfortable, but he started to speak, looking down at his folded hands the whole time.

"It be all about space-time," he said. "It ain't solid, like a piece of wood. It be stretchable, like a sheet of rubber. What we could do, we could stretch that stuff. Behind the ship, we stretch the space-time out. In the front, we scrunch it up, like a wadded-up piece of paper. With the space-time spread out behind us, or sort of piled up, like a wave . . . sorry, I ain't good at this . . . we could ride that wave. There wouldn't be no acceleration. You might even say we ain't really movin', not like we're used to movin'. We just *go*, and when we get there, we just *stop*. People knowed about this for a long time, but there ain't been nothing we could do about it."

I looked at some of the other faces in the room. No one looked any more enlightened than I felt.

"Tell them why, Jubal," Travis said, gently.

"Oh, yeah, because it take a lot of power. A *lot* of power. If you took the planet Jupiter and converted it to energy, about that much power."

That got a rise. Even the power in any of the silver bubbles we carried for fuel and power wouldn't give that much power. I guess, theoretically, Papa could squeeze the actual planet Jupiter down to the size of a Ping-Pong ball, but then what would happen to Jupiter's moons, where plenty of people were living? And how would you apply all that power without blowing up the whole solar system? And what would you do when you wanted to do it again? Squeeze Saturn? You could use up a lot of solar systems that way.

"But you think you found a way, Jubal?" Travis prompted.

"A way? Oh, yeah. It be all that dark lightning."

Travis could see that many of them were lost. I would have been, too, if Papa hadn't talked about it some while we were away from the ship. So he explained about the dark matter and dark energy that makes up 95 percent of the stuff in the universe.

If it is actually *in* the universe, in the way we understand that. Because the way Travis put it, trying to clarify the things Papa said, Papa thought it wasn't, exactly.

It all had to do with superstring theory. My knowledge of strings is limited to yo-yos and Mama's guitars, and of superstrings I know nothing. It seems they are incredibly, *incredibly* tiny things. Compared to them, a proton would be as big as the Earth. Maybe bigger. They are folded through about eleven dimensions. Seriously, eleven, I'm not just picking a number out of the air! If you can unfold them a little, you can have access to a lot of power. Me, I got stuck trying to imagine five dimensions, and I wasn't sure I really had the fourth one down pat.

Papa thought all that dark energy was hiding in one of those dimensions. He thought the way to get at it involved the same kind of things he had discovered when he invented the squeezer bubbles and the black bubbles. He thought he could unlock it, and we would have virtually unlimited energy at our disposal. All around us, in interstellar space, it was just hanging around out there, around a corner of space-time where we couldn't see it and it didn't affect us much. Except for exerting gravity on regular matter, which is how we discovered dark matter, and for speeding up the expansion of the universe, which is how we discovered dark energy.

Until we got up around 70 percent of the speed of light, and the rules changed. Tapping into all that energy would be enough to squeeze and stretch space-time in front of us and behind us without having to destroy Jupiter in order to do it.

That's what he thought, anyway.

We could all see where this was going. All eyes turned to the gizmo sitting there like an eight-hundred-pound gorilla. This must be the space warper.

Somebody asked, "So you're telling us that this thing can get us to New Sun faster, and without exceeding your speed limit?"

"That's right," Papa said, pleased to have been understood. "Real quick-like."

"How quick?" someone else asked. Papa frowned.

"Very quick. A few hours? Even a few minutes? I'll have to try it out first, see just how it works."

"It might be even quicker than that, right Jubal?" Travis prompted him. "Isn't that what you told me?"

"I don't wanna say that, me. It's one way it might work out."

"This sounds crazy to me," said a third person. There were some murmurs of agreement.

"It does, doesn't it," Travis agreed. "Jubal, turn the machine on."

Papa got up and went to the machine. The murmurs got louder. There was a switch on the side, and Papa threw it.

Now that's more like it! The thing began to glow here and there, and a screen came alive with complex geometrical shapes. I smelled ozone, and felt a low vibration in the floor. There was a sense of suppressed energy pulsing though the room. I think we all felt it.

"Now, my friends," Travis said. "There's really no other way to see if this thing works than by testing it right now. Jubal, what happens if you throw that other switch?"

"Either we get where we goin' real quick, or nothin' happens at all if I ain't built it right."

"No other possibility? It won't blow us all up?"

"Cain't," he said with total assurance. "It ain't built that way. It'll either channel all that energy around us, or it won't work at all. No."

"Now wait," one of the doubters said. (I'm not using anyone's names here, to avoid embarrassment. Their concerns were real.) "Shouldn't we discuss this? Maybe put it to a vote?"

"The people should hear about this," someone agreed. "I think we should put it to a referendum."

Travis sighed.

"In a lot of situations, I'm all for democracy. When we get there, we can have all the democracy you want. I'll be pleasantly retired, and you folks can fight it all out among yourselves. But this is going to be an executive decision. As far as I'll go is to ask for another show of hands. Those who trust Jubal's judgment, let's see them."

There was a long, pregnant pause, and slowly the hands began to go up. Two, three, then five. A few more. It wasn't as ringing an endorsement as the first vote had been, but it was a slim majority. I was surprised, frankly. I would have voted yes if I had a vote, but in some ways it seemed to be moving all too quickly.

"Throw the switch, Jubal," Travis said. I found myself on my feet, alongside Polly, and we weren't the only ones.

Without even a pause, Papa threw the switch.

And the lights went out on the overhead screen. All of them. All the stars, just gone.

It's just a screen, I told myself. Maybe we're in some sort of limbo, and after a few weeks or a few months we would come out of it. Meanwhile, life seemed to be going on as normal. I was breathing. We weren't heating up or cooling down, at least not that we could sense.

All eyes were on the overhead screen. I think it was dark for around half a minute. Then it lit up again, with a simple message that stretched from one side to the other:

RECALCULATING

I guess that's how long it took the ship's navigating computer to assess all the new data and figure out where we were. That message was up there for maybe ten seconds, then all the stars came out again. Only right in the center of the screen was a blazing yellow star, brighter than any star I had ever seen, even Old Sun, looking back when I was young.

It was New Sun, and it was *close*.

But even that wasn't the star of the show. Off to one side, big as a beach ball tossed in the air, was a half-moon shape, vividly striped on the side facing New Sun. There was a faint system of rings around it, and I could see some smaller half moons here and there. It looked like pictures of Jupiter.

Travis was communing with his navigation console. He looked up, grinning.

"That would be New Sun Zeta, the sixth planet from New Sun. We've known about it and a lot of the others for decades. It's about 50 percent larger than Jupiter and has six moons that we know of . . ." He looked up, and smiled again. "And I can see a seventh, just from here."

There was a lot of cheering, a lot of backslapping. It felt like an occasion for champagne, but no one had brought any.

But after a few minutes, Polly noticed something.

"Look, Cassie. It's moving."

And it sure was. In only a few minutes, we had passed behind it and were leaving it behind. And New Sun had moved visibly. Travis turned to Jubal with a frown.

"What's happening, my friend?"

"What do you mean, Travis?"

"We seem to be moving right on through the system. What's the deal?"

"Well, sure," Papa said. "We be traveling at .78 of the speed of light. Sure, we gonna go through it right fast."

"But . . ."

"You said get us to New Sun, Travis. I figgered you knew we gonna be goin' through it real fast."

Polly:

Even if we had been stuck with the situation, it wouldn't have been as bad as the other choices we had faced. But it looked bad at first.

Our speed, our momentum, had been tunneled through space right along with our mass. There was no way for the warp drive to cancel out our speed, or our direction. We would have to do it the old-fashioned way.

Twenty years of deceleration, then a long time of accelerating to the halfway point, and the same amount decelerating until we arrived, more or less motionless to the New Sun system. But we would never be traveling at .78c again. We wouldn't reach nearly that speed on the way back.

So there were a lot of upset people, and Travis had to calm them down. He huddled with Papa for a while, then he started laughing. Papa looked indignant.

"You just ast me to get us to New Sun. And that's what I done."

"It's okay, Jubal. You did it, and no one else could have. Friends, listen up here. It turns out there's a simple solution. It's not a perfect one, but it's better than what we have now, and I think you'll all be happy with it. Remember, this warp drive got us out of hot water. We will never have to test out Jubal's warning about going any faster."

And he explained it to them, and soon we were all laughing in relief.

"I guess we would have seen it for ourselves, eventually," Travis told us all later, at a gathering of much of the family back at our house. We were still working on fixing the damage that had happened when we were forced out, but it wasn't extensive.

The solution really was simple, and obvious once you got your mind around the idea that we could now be anywhere, virtually instantaneously. I say virtually, because Papa's still working out just how long it took us. It was less than a second, he knew that for sure. "I think it was no time, but clocks don't figger real good when you get to messin' with space-time," was the best explanation I could get out of him.

So what we did was use the warp drive again, and move ourselves back to a point where twenty years of deceleration would bring us to rest in a comfortable orbit around New Sun, right near New Earth. And *bam*, there we were. Not even that dramatic, actually. Papa just threw the switch, and there we were.

We had to turn the ship, which was a messy project that took almost a week. The engines had to be shut down, which meant that everything was suddenly at a slight slant. We had to drain a lot of water from the lakes, shut down the rivers. And everything had to be tied down. We were given a week, but still, when the engines shut down, a lot of crockery spilled from cupboards, a lot of furniture slid slowly to a wall. Nothing catastrophic, but a lot of little messes.

So now we're decelerating. We will be getting to New Sun in only twenty years. We shaved many years off the trip.

But as usual with Papa, there was a kicker I hadn't even thought of.

One day not long ago Travis was sitting around with Cassie and me, talking about all the excitement, now that it was wrapped up and back to more or less normal. I mentioned what an impressive device the warp drive was. He laughed and looked me in the eye.

"So you bought it too, huh?" he said.

Which made no sense at all. And then something horrible hit me. Could he have . . . would it be possible for him to . . . but if so, why?

What I was thinking was, that big display we had all been looking at overhead on the bridge was a screen. Nothing but a screen. Now that he had the computers back under control, it could show anything Travis wanted it to show. Who had been outside since then, to take a look at the actual stars, like Cassie and Papa did?

I looked at her, and it was clear she still didn't get it. How many people would it take? The astronomers, who were also the navigators, I guess. A dozen of them? But did they actually look at the stars, themselves? I mean with an eye to a telescope? I know that for many years now, just about all astronomy was done with CCDs, charge-coupled devices, that enhanced the light or adjusted it for atmospheric distortion. They were nothing more than little screens themselves. Could those images be phonied up, too? I was pretty sure they could be.

I saw it dawn on Cassie, and we both looked back to Travis, and I expect we looked like little girls who had just been told there was no Santa Claus.

He let it play out a little longer, then he laughed again.

"You kids have tricky minds, just like me. And I'm proud of you for it. But no, it's not a hoax. Not that part of it, anyway. We really are where I said we are, twenty years from New Sun, slowing down. No, I'm talking about that lousy machine. The one that did everything but send up a starshell with the American flag. The real machine, the one that did the miracle, is not very far from where we're sitting, in your father's lab. It's considerably less impressive. People want a show, so I gave them one. But the real one is small enough to fit into a ship like Sheila."

I was so relieved that for a moment I didn't get it. Then Cassie got it before me.

"You mean . . . we could go . . . just about anywhere?"

"No 'just about' about it," he said. "When we get slowed down, twenty years from now, you girls can pop back to Old Sun for lunch on Ganymede, and get back in time for dinner with your mother." He frowned. "Well, that may be an exaggeration, but I don't think it's much of one. Your father just gave us the stars, honey childs. Not the stars after an eighty-year voyage, but the stars like driving across town, like running a circumference of *Rolling Thunder*. Once more, this changes *everything*."

Boy, did it ever. It put all the stars just a hop, skip, and a warp away. We couldn't use it yet, except for exploratory missions, because wherever we went, we would arrive at .78c. But that's enough for a quick look to see if it's worth coming back. We didn't have much time at New Sun when we went whizzing by, but we got a better idea of what New Earth looked like. (And isn't it about time we settled on a name for New Sun Delta, the fourth planet, instead of just New Earth? A contest or something? I guess there's still plenty of time for that.) New Earth looks to be about half ocean and half land. There are plate-tectonic mountains, and ice at both poles. Nothing we saw makes it seem any less than the perfect "Goldilocks" planet—not too hot, not too cold—which is the reason why Travis chose it in the first place. We didn't see any lights on the dark side, which is good, and we found two fair-sized moons, so there will be tides.

And if it sucks, for some reason, we'll just warp over to the next likely candidate. And pop back to Earth to give the warp drive to the folks back there and in, oh, I figure about twenty-one years, humans will be swarming this arm of the galaxy like termites.

Which is a sobering thought in itself.

In fact, we are already planning a quick reconnaissance trip back to New Sun in a newly outfitted Sheila. That's all it takes, just a little space yacht. We'll come out on one side and pass very close to New Earth, and really get a good look at it. Cassie and I are invited, and heck, now that we've graduated, we don't have a lot else to do on our summer vacation.

Cassie has been spending a lot of time with Jane Litchfield, hoping some of that broad's charisma will rub off on her, I guess. She wants to be Cassie B., girl explorer. And it doesn't sound all that bad. Sooner or later we're going to encounter some intelligent life, and I'd like to be there for that. My verbal skills are a lot better than hers, so maybe I could learn their language, explore their culture.

Or maybe we'll both have to fight them off. I'm still thinking about that.

She's been spending a lot of time with Patrick, too. I have to laugh. Wait until she has to drag him through the lake and hide with him in a giant Mardi Gras float, or get him moving during a shootout with mutineers. He's not a bad person, just sort of slow and uninteresting. Not a fit mate for the intrepid Cassie B., that's for sure. She'll find that out, and I'll give her a shoulder to cry on. It won't take long.

So she's been talking about going into the bubble. Her reasoning, such as it is, is that it's better to be an eighteen-year-old explorer than a thirty-eight-year-old one. And I can't say she's wrong about that. Twenty more years of this quiet, bland existence doesn't sound as good to me as it once did. And sticking it out, then encountering a young Cassie as we arrive, me being twice her age . . . that doesn't have much appeal.

It's something we'll have to talk over with Mama and Papa, who have their own agendas, trying to reach a point where they're approximately the same age. But it will just be talking it over. It's going to be my decision. I'm old enough now. And I feel even older than that, some days, seeing Cheryl and the people we killed in my nightmares.

Side by side into the future, inseparable twins? I don't know about that. In fact, I doubt it. But will we stay in touch? I don't doubt that. Something a little closer than exchanging Christmas cards, anyway.

If I know my sister, and I do, she will want the last word. So say goodbye, Cassie.

Cassie:

Good-bye, Polly.